"AIN'T NOTHIN' TO BE SCARED OF."

Dory's voice had an eerie ring to it, like something coming out of an echo chamber. "It's jus' me. Jus' little Dory, Sheriff."

Ainson swallowed hard. The room seemed colder. Those glowing eyes held him riveted in his tracks. He wanted out of this room, but he couldn't move. "The thing that got you an' Billy Ed," he said woodenly, "what'd it look like?"

"Ain't talkin' about that. Ask Raven."

"Ask who? Who's this Raven fella?"

Dory smiled. "You'll find out," she said, and turned those glowing, burning eyes on him once more ...

TOMBLEY'S WALK

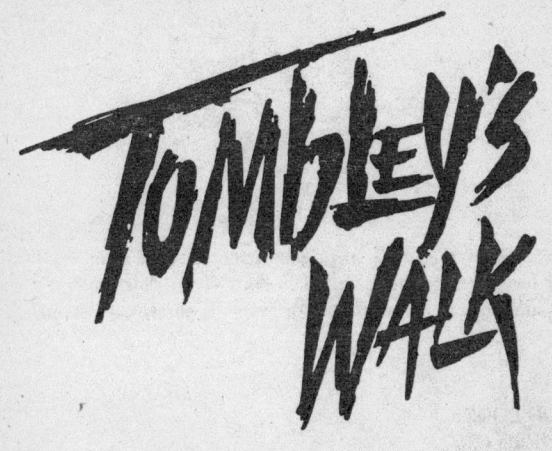

CROSLAND BROWN

AVON BOOKS NEW YORK

TOMBLEY'S WALK is an original publication of Avon Books. This work has never before appeared in book form. This work is a novel. Any similarity to actual persons or events is purely coincidental.

AVON BOOKS
A division of
The Hearst Corporation
105 Madison Avenue
New York, New York 10016

Cover art by Lee MacLeod
Published by arrangement with the author
Library of Congress Catalog Card Number: 90-93393
ISBN: 0-380-76097-5

First Avon Books Printing: February 1991

Printed in the U.S.A.

RA 10 9 8 7 6 5 4 3 2 1

For Virginia Crosland,
without whose name I might have been
Albert something.

PART I

Infection

"You jes think dat ole fox mean. You wait. You wait 'til de sun go down an' de roun' yellow moon get up high. Dat when ole Br'er Wolf come a-callin' wid his big sharp teef. Dat when you see somethin' really mean."

—Br'er Possum

1

ON the night that the slaughter began in the town of Tombley's Walk, Texas, no one had died of unnatural causes in Tombley's Walk for fifteen years. To the day. The last killings before then had been grisly enough.

A decade and a half earlier, at 9:30 P.M. on the night of July 8, 1971, two drifters—a black man and a white man, both parolees from Angola, Louisiana Penitentiary, and both on the street for less than a month—walked into the Kentucky Fried Chicken on Interstate 20 at the Tombley's Road overpass. They'd been traveling from Shreveport to Dallas, and both were brandishing shotguns. Business inside the Colonel Sanders was sparse—four late-night customers and two teenage, summer-help employees. After forcing the cooks and customers to lie facedown on the floor (and ignoring the pleas of one man whose pregnant wife couldn't lie comfortably on her stomach), the two ex-convicts ransacked the cash register. Then they escorted the victims one at a time into the kitchen and executed each with a shotgun blast to the head.

The murderers ran out of gas two miles down the road and set out on foot. A band of Texas Rangers, aided by three helicopters with searchlights, which hovered, droning, over the tall East Texas piney woods, surrounded the pair within hours. They killed one fugitive with a rifle bullet to the heart and beat the other senseless with clubs and pistols. The battered survivor, a hulking white cretin named John Ed Dearborn, eventually became the third man in Texas to die by lethal injection after the Supreme Court reinstated the death penalty in 1977. But not for the Tombley's Walk killings did John Ed die; the eight-year national moratorium on the death penalty, which began in 1969, granted him a life sentence. It was a later incident, the bare-handed strangling of a prison guard, which finally handed old John Ed his just reward.

Tombley's Walk survived, and folks passed away, and kids graduated and moved on to make room for more kids who graduated and moved on as well. The pine trees greened and grew, then shed their needles and shivered bare branches under cold gray skies, then greened and grew some more. By the summer of 1986 John Ed Dearborn was only a memory, a camp fire tale to make preteens huddle and quiver and giggle inside their bedrolls.

ON the night of July 8, 1986, everybody who was drinking and dancing and raising hell in Jasper's, a shitkicking honky-tonk on the I-20 access road outside of town, knew Dory Barnes was looking to get herself laid. Rog Hornby could tell easier than most what Dory was up to, but then he ought to've known. He'd spent enough nights waiting up for her, back when they'd been married.

Dory came off of the dance floor, flaming red hair wild, wide hips snug in women's boot-cut jeans, and wriggled onto a barstool beside the citified stranger. Raising her voice to be heard over the driving guitars of Waylon Jennings's band doing "I Don't Think Hank Done It This Way," she said across the wooden bar to Rog Hornby, "Dory's thirsty, darlin'. Come *on,* precious, put out little Dory's fire." She leaned sideways and pressed against the stranger's arm.

"You better slow down, woman, if you're plannin' to be on yore feet at midnight," Rog Hornby said. He opened the cooler, fished out a Pearl longneck, and put Dory's empty into the bottle rack. Then he gave her a fresh chilled glass and popped her beer's cap on the cooler opener with a tiny, quick hiss. He forced himself not to meet her gaze, forced her insolent, taunting grin out of his mind. For Rog to fly off the handle was just what she wanted, and damned if she was going to get the satisfaction. It wasn't easy, though. He picked up a spotless glass and pretended to wipe some water drops from its edge.

"Darlin', I've outlasted you before, I'll do it tonight. Always been more'n enough woman for you, I done proven that." She was wearing a red bandanna-patterned blouse tied underneath her breasts, her fleshy midriff bare. Beside her, the stranger shot an irritated glance in her direction and moved his arm away from her touch. He studied his bottle of Michelob. Dory's grin broadened and she snuggled closer to him.

Rog set the clean glass down and forced his jaw muscles to relax. Sure it hurt. Dory *meant* for it to hurt. He said, "Don't matter to me what you do. I jus' hate to see you make a big show of yourself." Rog was wearing a black Stetson tilted back and size 36 Wrangler jeans that were too small. But damned if he'd 'fess up to needing a larger size, Rog buttoned his pants low and let his belly overhang. He had a full dark beard that could have stood some trimming.

Dory put her lips close to the stranger's ear and adjusted her position so that her breasts were flattened against him. Still shouting over the music, she said, "Well, will you listen to the old fart? A *big show?* What do *you* think, darlin'? You think Dory's puttin' on a show?"

The stranger winced and moved farther from her. He looked to be in his thirties, wearing a blue knit shirt with a little red horseshoe stitched over its breast pocket. Uptown country-club clothes. He smiled. "I wouldn't exactly say that you were putting on a show, but he might have a point, you could be hitting the booze a little too heavy. Why don't you sit for a while, maybe have some coffee?" The stranger was clean-shaven with a full head of center-parted brown hair and wore pressed gray slacks. This was the fourth night in a row that he'd sat on this same stool—drinking Michelob, no less, and Rog had decided that if the newcomer was going to be a regular, Jasper's was going to have to stock up on his brand of beer. A few of the boys had even asked Rog to check the stranger out because a couple of nights a week some of the regulars liked to stay after-hours and shoot a little craps on the pool table.

As owner, barkeep, chief cook and bottle-washer, it was up to Rog to make certain that the stranger wasn't a federal man. The guy spoke with an accent that really wasn't an accent at all, and Rog had decided that the stranger must be from some melting-pot region like Southern California. Even before he figured that out, Rog had been satisfied that he wasn't dealing with a federal agent. The stranger stood out like a sore thumb among Jasper's regulars; cops as a rule dressed like shitkickers and yelled like hog-callers. And the way that the newcomer was handling Dory, putting her down without being nasty about it, was making Rog take a shine to the man. A cop would've patted Dory's behind and tried to talk her into selling him some pussy, so's he could bust her. Not that Miz Dory Hot-Pants Barnes was ever going to jail for being a prostitute. She was too busy *giving* it away.

''Coffee?'' Dory said, wriggling even closer to the stranger. ''Shee-it, darlin', coffee gets me out of a fun mood. It's a *downer,* darlin'. Why, you talk just like that old fart behind the bar. Don't you want Dory to have herself a little fun?''

SEATED at a table beside Jasper's dance floor, Linda Lacy peered toward the bar through a moving forest of men and women dressed in boots and jeans and dancing western swing. Turning to her friend Becky, Linda said, ''That man there's fixin' to get himself a dose of that rabies that's goin' around if Dory gets her teeth into him.''

''Gotcha claws out, girl,'' Becky Stoner said. She was a redhead the same as Dory, but her hair was a couple of shades darker and she didn't have near as many freckles. She was thirty, a good ten years younger than Dory Barnes, and she had small breasts and narrow hips. She shuddered. ''Ooo, an' don't go talkin' about that rabies thing, it gives me big ol' goose bumps. Didja hear about Deputy Beamer and the rats?''

Linda, a pert blond of twenty-five, who worked day shift at the Dairy Queen on Tombley County Road between town and the interstate, and who didn't cotton to men without manners—which really narrowed the field in a roadside honky-tonk like Jasper's—said, "Deputy Beamer *and* the rats? Why, Sonny Beamer *is* a rat, honey, don'tcha know?"

"There you go again, Linda," Becky said. "Takin' out after Sonny Beamer. Don'tcha know if you can't say something nice you ain't supposed to say nothing at all?" She had a tiny sip of Pearl beer. The two girls' glasses sat side by side, each one about a quarter full, with a single longneck bottle, practically empty, between them. They were splitting a beer because it was Monday night. Two-bit beer for unescorted ladies was on Friday, and had it been Friday night they would have been ordering the longnecks four at a time.

"I jus' said he was a rat. That's a pretty nice thing to say if you're talkin' about Sonny."

"Well, don't we change?" Becky said. "Wasn't two months ago you thought Sonny was the greatest, back when he was comin' around you. Seems like I recall."

Linda uncrossed her legs and shifted in her chair (being slow and careful about it, being certain to look cute while making the move) and didn't answer. In the far corner of the dimly lit club was the pool table. A shaded light hung over the green felt, and a squatty balding man, wearing a western shirt with its sleeves rolled up to his elbows, was surveying a combination shot from all angles. A floor waitress with a sprayed beehive hairdo, her big hips snug in brown corduroy Levi's, touched the pool shooter's elbow. He quit stalking the table long enough to look at the waitress and shake his head. She shrugged and moved on. The Waylon Jennings was over. The rack inside the Wurlitzer jukebox rotated, and Ronnie Milsap began to croon over the speakers: "Lost in the Fifties Tonight," a slow new tune that sounded like an old number. More couples moved onto the dance floor, where they snuggled close and did box steps together.

Becky said, "Well, you can say what you want about him. Sonny done a brave thing yesterday. Two rats—ooo, it makes me shudder to think about this—two rats grabbed ahold of a cocker spaniel over on Third Street and went to chewin' on its underbelly. Sonny grabbed a shovel from his pickup and bashed the rats to death right out in the middle of the street. Doc Petty says them rats was mad as loons. Ooo, them that saw it say that one of the rats was screamin' and wigglin' and tryin' to bite Sonny all the while he was beatin' its brains out." A tall skinny cowboy moved over close to the table and held out a beckoning hand. Becky shook her head. The cowhand looked disappointed and moved on.

"I heard they're havin' to put the cocker to sleep," Linda said. "Then I heard Miz Radner's chow Toby went plumb crazy and bit one of the Ellison kids, and then Doug Ellison went and shot Toby. They cut his head off"—she giggled and cupped a hand over her mouth—"the *chow's* head, not Doug Ellison's head, o' course. The head got shipped over to Tyler and guess what? Toby'd gone mad and the Ellison kid is havin' to take all those awful shots. It's an epidemic right enough, it's what folks say."

"Ooo, let's change the subject, girl," Becky said. "My god, all this talk about crazy mad dogs gets me to where I can't sleep at night." Becky leaned forward, hugged herself, and peered toward the bar. Dory Barnes now had an arm draped around the stranger's shoulders. Becky said, "That Dory's really makin' a show out of herself tonight. Kind of pitiful, I think, right there in front of poor ol' Rog and him bein' her ex. They say Rog still has a thing for her, but I don't see why. Who's *that* guy? The one Dory's hittin' on."

"*Now* who's gettin' their claws out, girl?" Linda tossed her permed curls. "I don't know the man personally, but they say his name's Bud Tanner and he's writin' a book or somethin'. He ain't been in Tombley's Walk but a week or two, and he ain't been out with nobody that anybody can find out about."

Becky tilted her head to one side. "For somebody that don't know somebody, you sure are tellin' a lot."

"He's the very talk of the town, girl. And he's a *hunk*, you can see that with one eye closed. Lots of girls have been sidling up to him, but they say he's stuck up. Real, real stuck up."

Becky said thoughtfully, "Maybe he's just shy."

"*That* hunk? He ain't got no reason to be. Why look, ol' Dory's 'bout ready to yank his pants down and him just a-sittin' there. You don't reckon he's a *homosectual,* do you? Be a shame." The dance floor lights shone through a filmy haze of cigarette smoke. Over behind the bar, Rog Hornby threw a switch. Exhaust fans chugged to life and the smoke began to disappear.

Becky stiffened. Her jaw slacked, her gaze toward the exit. She leaned forward and said to Linda, "Oh my god. Will you look, girl, at who jus' wandered in? I swear, Linda, if he comes over to this table I'll jus' *die.*"

Linda followed Becky's gaze, then said, "Well, you ain't dreaming, girl. Ooo, an' he looks *drunk.*"

The subject of their conversation stood just inside the doorway, weaving slightly on his feet. He was a young slim-waisted cowpoke who wore his western shirt unbuttoned to a point just above his navel. The shirt was white with blue quilted embroidering covering his shoulders and coming to twin points over his breast pockets. He wore a straw molded hat whose brim practically touched the tip of his slim nose, and black and white zebra boots. He was tan as a tamale; in the bluish light from the club he could be taken for an Indian or a Mexican. He lurched forward, bumped a couple of tables with his hip, and finally made his way over to stand before Becky and Linda.

Becky forced a smile. "Hi, Billy Ed. How you doin'?"

Billy Ed spoke in a thick-tongued, slurred tenor. "Want to dance with me?"

Linda folded her hands on the table and said primly, "We jus' ain't in a dancin' mood. Where's Brenda Jean?" She glanced quickly around the club.

"Home." Billy Ed's nose was slightly crooked, and it now twisted even more as he frowned. "Home. Mindin' her own business. My ol' lady don't tell *me* what to do an' what not to do. I ain't home, I'm wantin' to dance. Have me some fun." He grabbed Linda's arm and tried to hoist her to her feet.

"Billy *Eh*-yud. You be-*have.* Let me *go.*" Linda yanked free, sat back stiffly, and folded her arms. "Now we done told you we ain't here to dance. You go on, now."

He supported himself with one hand, leaning unsteadily on the table. He bent over, his thrusting jaw just inches from Linda's nose, and said loudly, "Well, *fuck you* then, woman. See'f I care." He turned and stalked—or *staggered*, rather—away, weaving across the dance floor in the direction of the bar, colliding with two different couples along the way.

"Well, can you be-*lieve* . . . ?" Linda said. "Man ain't got no call to act like that, drunk *or* sober."

"You gunna do it, or you want *me* to?" Becky said.

"Do what, girl?"

"Call Brenda Jean, o' course. Brenda Jean or Mr. Whitley one. I 'spect we better call *her.* His wife'll jus' come on down an' take him home, but his daddy'd beat the daylights out of him."

THE stranger, Bud Tanner, had about decided that there wasn't any graceful way out of this. The thought of going to bed with this drunken redhead who was slobbering all over him gave him the willies. He felt sorry for her—ten to one she had a drinking problem along with no telling what other hang-ups—but not sorry enough to let her go on rubbing her tits all over him and breathing beer-breath in his face. Besides, any fool could see that she was only doing it to get to Rog Hornby. Bud had enough problems without getting in a cross fire between a man and his woman. A newcomer in town couldn't afford to get mixed up in such a hassle. Besides, his longing for Beth was still too heavy in Bud's midsection for him to get heated up over *any* woman, much less this one. Dory had to be on the dark side of forty. And not an easy forty; though it wasn't hard to tell she'd been good-looking once upon a time. Too many bumpy miles down the road had ruined all that.

Bud assumed that what Dory was now showing him was her version of a sexy grin, but it was more of a dirty-old-lady leer. "I bet you'd like to play, darlin'. I jus' bet you would." Her hand on his neck was hot and clammy; her breasts against his arm like heated foam pillows.

Rog Hornby leaned across the bar. "You behave, Dory Hornby. This fella ain't wanting nothing to do with you."

"Dory who? Dory *who?*" she said. "I ain't married to you no more, you ol' fart, an' I sure ain't using your name. Now why don't you go sell somebody a beer or somethin' an' leave us be?"

Jesus Christ, thought Bud, she's his *ex*. Now that's about all I need. He untwined her arm from about his neck and stood, keeping the barstool between him and Dory. Bud said to Rog, "Hey, I'm sure not starting anything."

Rog turned a miserable stare in Bud's direction. "I know. Ain't your fault," Rog said.

"Well, to clear things up I think I'll be going," Bud said. "No use looking for trouble."

"You ain't going to have any trouble, not from me," Rog said. "Likely it ain't Dory's fault neither, jus' one of them things nobody can do anything about." He placed his hands on the bar, his elbows at angles.

Hornby's look was . . . wounded? trapped? A little of both, Tanner thought.

"Well, can't nobody stop me," Dory said, listing. "I do as I fuckin' well please." She reached over the stool for Tanner. He moved a foot or so farther away from her. She grabbed at air, lost her balance, leaned heavily on the bar.

A young man—Tanner's first thought was that the cowboy was a cheap imitation of Newman playing Hud—came off the dance floor, put his arms around Dory, and planted a full lover's kiss on her lips. At first she stiffened, then, relaxing, moved her head sensuously with the kiss and gyrated her hips against him. Bud averted his gaze from the smooching couple, came in contact with Rog Hornby's piteous stare, then concentrated on the Lone Star Beer clock over the cash register. Now Tanner *really* wanted to be gone.

They came up for air. "You lookin' to play, Miz Dory?" the cowboy said.

She laughed, glancing at Hornby, then said, "What's this? A *man?* A real man in Tombley's Walk?" She leaned against the young guy, and hugged his neck as she said to

Hornby, "How 'bout that, you ol' fart? Here's young Billy Ed Whitley, barely growed up and still more man than you ever were or you'll ever be."

"You come dance with me, I'll show you a man," Billy Ed said. He hugged Dory closer to him. Both of them were swaying on their feet.

The song now playing was "Twinkle, Twinkle, Lucky Star" by Merle Haggard. Dory showed Rog a final, spiteful, toss of her red mane, grabbed Billy Ed Whitley's hand and yanked the giddy youngster onto the dance floor. About ten feet from the floor's edge, she wriggled close to him. The two embraced and began to squirm in rhythm to the music.

Bud Tanner watched Rog Hornby, watched the wounded expression in Rog's eyes, the give-up lines at the corners of Rog's mouth. It was none of Bud's business, of course, and he told himself as much. Then instinct took over; Bud reached across the bar and touched Rog's arm. The arm was tense as twisted rope. "I don't want to butt in," Bud said, "but I've seen enough to know it's not worth what you're going through."

Rog expelled a long sigh and scratched his whiskers, his eyes watering. "Yeah, you're right. I know goddamn well you're right. Trouble is that it's easier to say than do." He tried to smile. "Tell you what, lemme buy you a beer. On the house." He reached into the cooler and opened a Michelob. "I know that damn woman ain't worth it. But she's under my hide, what's a man gonna do about it?"

Bud knew the answer, but didn't want to give it. What a man did, at least what Bud Tanner had done, was lie awake at night and picture Beth fixing dinner, Beth humming softly in the garden as she planted her roses; picture Jenny on the changing table with the chubby little legs that Beth had called Jenny's porkchops sticking up into the air; picture Beth and Jenny and pray that someday the terrible ache would go away. Beth *had* been worth loving and that had made losing her all the harder blow to take.

"Doesn't look as though there's much you *can* do about it," Bud said. "So talk to me. Ignore her. Tell me the local gossip. I hear tell there's a rabies scare in town. Anything to that?''

Rog looked directly at Bud, averting his gaze from the wriggling couple on the dance floor. Rog's expression said that he was going to try, though it was taking some effort. He said vacantly, ''Rabies? Well, there's talk of it. Hasn't been any rabid animals in Tombley's Walk, or in the whole county for that matter, in fifteen or twenty years. But Doc Petty thinks we got a real live epidemic on our hands.''

The floor waitress approached the bar, set her tip tray on the counter, and called out, ''Two Bud, six Pearl, gimme a Lone Star an' one Miller Light. Couple of fresh glasses, Rog, will you, hon?'' She was chewing gum. Rog slammed cooler doors open and filled her order.

When the waitress had gone, Bud Tanner said, ''Doc Petty the vet?''

''Doc's . . . well, he's everything around here,'' Rog said. ''He's the only man from Tombley's Walk ever to get a medical degree and not move off to Dallas or Houston or someplace. But no, he ain't a vet. Doctored a horse or cow or dog or two in his time, though. Long as we're asking questions, how 'bout you? New people come to Tombley's Walk about once a decade.''

It was just the kind of question that Tanner didn't want. But he'd set himself up for it, so he chose his words carefully and said, ''Oh, not much to me. I'm working on a book, but isn't everybody?''

Rog looked interested, really interested, for the first time. ''That's damn sure somethin' new. Ain't never been a writer around here, far as I can remember. Nothing to write about here unless you're wantin' to write about who's screwin' who.'' His gaze dropped. ''Or whose wife. What kind of book?''

What kind of book? God, but I'm stupid, Bud thought, one question leading to another, each answer more dangerous than the last. Maybe Tanner should call his old lit prof at Cal Poly and ask what kind of book he *ought* to write. Any contact with California would give Tanner about twenty-four hours before an interstate warrant showed up. Maybe longer than that in an isolated burg like Tombley's Walk. Tanner cleared his throat. "No place is as dull as all that. *Every* place has its story, you just have to dig it out. That's a writer's job." And, he thought, it's a *make-believe* writer's job to put out a lot of bullshit about what he's doing around here. He mentally crossed his fingers and hoped that Rog Hornby would let well enough alone.

"Doc Petty's a half-assed writer," Rog said. " 'Course he ain't had nothing published 'cept one article in *Farm Journal.* Maybe you and him should . . ." He trailed off, his gaze once again to the dance floor. His features sagged and he was suddenly older.

Tanner swiveled his stool around. Beyond the swaying couples on the dance floor, beyond the shadowy tables, beyond the pool table where two cowboys were now shaking clenched fists at each other, Dory Barnes and Billy Ed Whitley were headed for the exit. They were in a hurry. Their arms tight about each other's waists, they went through the swinging doors. The doors banged together once, recoiled, and closed more slowly.

Behind Tanner, Rog Hornby whimpered like a dog out in the rain.

Tanner spun back around. "Easy, Rog. I told you and you know yourself. It's just not worth it, take it from me. Hard as it seems, you've got to ignore it."

THE cooling summer night air cleared Dory Barnes's head some. For an instant she felt guilty. Just a mite guilty, then the feeling went away. Little Dory was going to have herself some fun.

Giggling, weaving, hugging, and touching one another, the couple went around the outside of the building to the asphalt parking lot. A quarter mile away on their left, twin headlight beams moved over the surface of the interstate, headed west toward Big D. The car's tires made a faraway whispering sound. The headlamps disappeared as the car passed, then the red taillights moved silently away down a corridor of tall dark pines on either side of the highway. There was a fifty-yard stretch of knee-high brush beyond Jasper's parking lot; on the other side of the brushy clearing was the dark, piney woods. In the clearing, what must have been a million crickets chirruped and whirred. The neon honky-tonk sign blinked on and off, on and off, and sent flashes of ghostly red dancing over the asphalt.

The parking lot held forty-odd Jeeps, older-model Chevvys and Buicks, and big shiny supercabs with white-lettered tires. Billy Ed took Dory over to his own pickup, a blue-and-white GMC with a gun rack behind the cab. He bent over the truck's bed, unfolded a green army blanket and laid it out, then took Dory's arm and started to boost her over the side.

She stopped and pulled back from him, stumbling slightly as she did. "Shit, Billy Ed. I ain't doing it in the back of no *pickup truck.* That's for high school kids."

He kept smiling, but his eyes in the moonlight were like lumps of coal. "Come on, Miz Dory. Ain't no high school girls can hold a candle to the way *you're* put together. We'll set this old truck to rockin' an' rollin' is what we'll do."

Through her beery haze, Dory was suddenly just a tad uneasy. Maybe a little scared as well. Also she felt just a little bit silly, thinking about climbing up and humping this boy right here in the wide open spaces of the parking lot. At least the older guys knew what a motel was for. A tiny shiver ran up her back. She shook her head firmly and didn't say anything.

"Well, if your head's set against the pickup," Billy Ed said, "then how 'bout right over there in them woods? Nobody over there to see us."

Dory was sobering up, and wasn't liking the vibes she was getting. Showing up Rog Hornby was one thing; making a plumb jackass out of herself was something entirely different. She said, "Look, maybe we done wrong coming out here. I ain't . . . well, this just ain't such a good idea is all. I think I better go back inside." She turned and retreated for the front of the honky-tonk.

She'd gone three steps when Billy Ed caught up to her, took her upper arm in a viselike grip and spun her around. The army blanket was folded under his arm. The whites of his eyes stood out like cue balls in the blinking red neon. "You don't, you don't run out on me, woman. You don't start nothing with me you ain't aiming to finish. Now we're going over to them woods." He led her away. He was moving in long firm strides, and staggering, Dory quickened her own pace to keep from falling down.

Now Dory was sober, and she was just plain afraid. Goddam, this boy was strong. Strong and more'n a little crazy himself, what with all the booze. Dory recalled some other stories that had been going around, stories about how Billy Ed Whitley had a mean streak. About how his wife Brenda Jean had showed up more than once with black eyes and red puffy welts on her arms and shoulders. She glanced fearfully behind her, at the cars and trucks in the parking lot, at the boards that formed the wall of the honky-tonk, at metal trash cans overflowing with popcorn bags, pork rind wrappers, empty throwaway beer bottles. She whimpered deep in her throat. "Billy. Ed. I ain't fooling now, you let me be."

They'd stepped off the asphalt now, were a good third of the way across the clearing. There was a trampled footpath leading through the knee-high brush. Billy Ed had known the path, had known just where to find it. Silently, his expression a mask, he forced Dory on toward the woods. Above the pointed treetops, the full moon rode high on a wisp of cloud.

Her boots rustling through pine needles on the ground and bumping pine cones aside, the pressure of Billy Ed's grip numbing her arm, Dory tried to get her head straight. Nothing she could do about it now. What the hell, girl, you brought it on yourself, runnin' around a honky-tonk with your tail raised. What is it mama used to say, before she got fed up with washin' and ironin' and screamin' kids and run off with the rug salesman over to Texarkana? You make your bed you got to sleep in it. Well, you done made yours, Dory Barnes, so jus' lie back and enjoy it. Go into them dark woods over there and give this boy a little quickie, that's what you got to do. All these kids do it like rabbits anyhow, it's over for 'em practically before they get good and mounted up. Jus' you get on with it, Dory.

Get on with it and get it over and go on home. Be over before you—

In front of her and slightly to the right, just inside the perimeter of the woods, something howled. A howl mixed with a mournful whine, a high-pitched scream that reached a crescendo and trailed off into an echo.

Dory froze in her tracks, her windpipe taut. Billy Ed let go of her arm and stared for an instant toward the sound. At that moment Dory could have turned and run back across the clearing. But she didn't; it was as though she'd been hypnotized, as though whatever had made that awful sound in the woods was telling her not to move.

The first line of towering pines was less than twenty yards away. Standing there in deep purple shadow, Dory squinted. Was it . . . ? Something, it was something, moving among clustered tree trunks. Something . . . or *was* it? Dory wasn't sure. A black shape moved among blacker shapes, blended in and disappeared.

Suddenly Billy Ed had her in his grasp once more, his breath whistling between his teeth. He dragged her, step by faltering step, toward the forest.

She put her hand against his breastbone. "Jesus God," she said. "Jesus God, ain't you *hearing?* Billy Ed, there's rabies going around. Jesus God, ain't you—?"

"You hush up, woman." His eyes were hidden in the shadow of his hat brim. "Bullshit, it ain't nothing but a coyote. Wolf, maybe, but ain't no wolf or coyote going to stop me, you hear? You was wanting to get fucked, Miz Dory, and you're going to. No wolf or coyote, not even no haint can do nothing about it, so hush your mouth." He dragged her on.

They entered the woods. It was black as pitch in there; Dory's boots slogged through a two-inch carpet of needles. She gasped as the rough bark of a limb brushed her arm. The sickly odor of pinesap filled her nostrils, and her ears rang with the sound of . . . silence. She was aware that the crickets had stopped singing.

Billy Ed stopped, his chin inches from her forehead. His grip still hurting her arm, he shook the blanket out with his free hand and dropped it softly onto the pine needles at their feet.

Sweet Mary, Dory thought. *Jesus God, he's really going to do it. Just flop me right down on that blanket and—*

"Now lessee what you got, woman," he said. Then he was on her, tearing at her clothes, yanking down the zipper on her jeans. He groped her through her panties. His breath stank. (Jesus God, back there on the dance floor she hadn't noticed his foul, stinking breath.) Nylon slid over her crotch under his probing fingers. Jesus God, this boy was rough. What was she going to—?

His voice was hoarse, close to a growl. "Jesus, woman, you got me hot. You get down on that blanket, you hear?"

Suddenly a strange calm came over her, as though she were standing aside watching this, as though it were happening to someone else. *Lie back and enjoy it, Dory girl, it ain't going to take long.* Moving as if in a dream—no, a nightmare, one she'd started herself—she knelt slowly, then scooted backward on her rump across the coarse blanket. Weaving unsteadily on his feet, Billy Ed took his shirt off. Visible over his shoulder through needle-covered branches, the Little Dipper twinkled.

Dory lifted her legs and, struggling, yanked one boot off, then the other. *Be over 'fore you know it, girl. Lie back an'—*Now, wriggling and twisting on the blanket, she pulled her jeans down to her knees. Before her, Billy Ed was hopping on one foot as he pulled one leg of his own pants off. Okay, little man, Dory thought. You got me here, now do your thing, you ain't getting no cherry in Dory Barnes. I been here before, you're just another sorry bastard that's going to—

Something was watching them.

Not ten feet behind where Billy Ed struggled out of his clothes, something leaned against the base of a pine. Something that stood like a man. No, not quite like a man, more like a hunchbacked gnome. Like a little hunchbacked man, only it was . . .

It ain't nothing, Dory, she told herself. Nothing but a shadow, like the things you think you see right there in your own house when you get up at night to use the bathroom. Nothing there. Nothing there but a—

The thing was *breathing*.

Not just breathing, it was *panting*. Its sides moved in and out. It wasn't hunched over as Dory had first thought, either, the thing was crouching, tensing itself, getting ready to—

Sitting upright on the blanket, panic in her gullet like bile, pine needles prickling her behind through nylon panties, Dory Barnes said, "Billy Ed, it's—"

The dark thing moved, silent, swift as flowing water. As Billy Ed half turned toward it, the shape slammed into him between his shoulder and elbow. He grunted and fell over. Dory bit her knuckles in fear as a twig (or was it a bone?) snapped in the darkness. A vicious snarling filled her ears. She covered them with her hands and squinched her eyes tightly closed.

Scant feet from where Dory huddled in terror, Billy Ed Whitley screamed.

As he sat on the barstool and practically shouted at Rog Hornby in order to be heard over the pulsing music, Bud was mentally kicking himself. It didn't seem that he was helping Rog any, and butting into someone else's problem when he had plenty to worry about himself was one of the stupidest things that Bud could do. For one thing, he didn't know any of these Tombley's Walk piney-woods billies and under the circumstances thought it advisable to keep it that way. Once he left this godforsaken town—Bud had moved from place to place so often of late that he just assumed that he'd be traveling again before long—he was never going to see any of them again, and sitting here sympathizing with Rog Hornby would just lead to questions. *Who's that fella we seen you talking to, Rog ole boy? I dunno, says his name's Bud Tanner. Reckon we need to check him out?* Coast to coast, small-town people were nosy.

But this fellow Rog *was* likable, and so . . . *pitiful* to boot. And Bud had been missing having a friend. Not near so much as he'd missed Beth and Jenny, of course, but he'd always had a lot of friends in the past. Had always seemed natural to him.

Rog had located a long chrome flashlight by the register and was checking it out by pointing it into the beer cooler and flipping the switch on and off. The beam that stabbed into the cooler appeared weak, as though the flashlight needed batteries.

Bud said to Rog, "I can't stop you. No way can I if your mind's made up. But charging out into the night after her isn't going to help anything. Ignoring her, and I mean acting like you don't even know she's alive, that's the only chance you've got. Why don't you try it that way?"

Rog turned off the flashlight and jammed it into his back pocket. Then he thrust his arm up to the shoulder inside the cooler. As he fished around in the cooler he said, "I ain't expecting you to understand, mister. And believe me, I 'preciate what you're trying to do. But things in Tombley's Walk are just . . . different than most places. There's a whole lot more to this than I got time to explain." His hand came out of the beer box holding a small-caliber revolver, probably a .22. He spun the cylinder, nodded in satisfaction, and stuffed the gun into his waistband. Behind him on the wall was a rectangular printed sign announcing that the carrying of a firearm in a place where alcoholic beverages were sold was a felony in Texas.

"Are you out of your mind?" Bud said. "For you to shoot somebody would be just what she wants. You think for a minute she'd care if you went to jail? Hell no, she'd—"

"I ain't *aimin'* to shoot nobody," Rog said. "That's part of what I'm tryin' to tell you about Tombley's Walk bein' different. I ain't off to shoot nobody, this pistol's for pertection. That boy Dory left with. He's wild as a March hare, and before he gets through with her he's apt to hurt her. Don't matter what she done to me, I ain't letting nobody knock her around. Go with me, mister? I want a witness, case something *does* happen." In the dimness of the club, standing there with the pistol's grip making an indentation in the roundness of his overhanging belly, Rog's eyes were pleading.

Now Bud had *really* stepped into it. Hell, he couldn't be a witness. No way could he. Rog was waiting for an answer. Bud nodded.

"Good," Rog said with a grateful nod. Then, raising his voice, "Katy Jane. Hey, c'm'ere." The waitress came over, her beehive hairdo stiff as papier-mâché. She set her tip tray on the bar and raised her eyebrows. Rog said, "Watch the bar for me, I might be awhile." She nodded, went around behind the bar, and stood with hands on hips, chewing her gum slowly as though the sight of Rog storming out into the night toting a pistol was as normal as room temperature.

Rog walked a few paces in the direction of the exit, then turned and beckoned. Reluctantly, certain that he was headed for trouble, Bud got up and followed.

Rog moved on. He walked with a slight limp, as though his pointed-toed western boots hurt his feet. Halfway to the door, just across the dance floor, he stopped before a table. Two girls were sitting there, a thin redhead and a short, peppy-looking blond. The looks on their faces said that they would've preferred for Rog to keep moving. Bud stood at Rog's side. On the jukebox, Tom T. Hall crooned, "I Love Little Baby Ducks."

Rog leaned over and said to the blond, "Where's Billy Ed take 'em to, Linda?"

The girl had a pretty porcelain face that reminded Bud of someone out of Tennessee Williams or Erskine Caldwell. She pursed her lips. "Whatcha talkin' about? Take what where?"

"I ain't got time to dawdle, girl. I'm talkin' about where Billy Ed takes his women when he leaves outta here with 'em."

She touched the point of her breastbone. "How'm *I* s'posed to know?"

Rog took his flashlight out of his back pocket and hefted it from one hand to the other. "You're wastin' time. You think I'm so busy over yonder"—he jerked his head toward the bar—"that I don't see what's goin' on? You left with Billy Ed two different times last week, 'fore that I don't know how many times. I ain't tryin' to embarrass you none. I'm jus' tryin' to find out where Dory might be.''

The redhead half stood, looking first to Rog, then at Linda. *''Lin*-da. You *didn'.''*

The blond got up and leaned close to Rog. Her face a dark shade that in daylight would have been crimson, she hissed, ''You hush, Rog Hornby. Now I ain't been noplace with Billy Ed, you hear? Now I *heard*—an' that's all it was, jus' hearin'—that he's too cheap to rent a room and that, 'course, he can't take nobody home with him because of Brenda Jean bein' there. So he likes it in his pickup or right over there in them woods. You know, that path across the clearin'? I heard. You get that? I *heard.* It's what everbody says. Now you hush your face 'bout me.'' She sat down and folded her arms, her head bowed.

''Well, I 'preciate hearin' what you heard, then.'' Rog tipped his hat to the redhead. ''Evenin', Becky,'' he said. Then he shuffled along on his way with Bud bringing up the rear, shaking his head. As they went outside through the swinging doors, a cowboy slapped a greenback down on the edge of the pool table and bent to position two quarters into the plunger slots.

Bud followed Rog across a cement porch and stepped down onto gravel. A mosquito whined near his ear. He slapped it away. Rog's boots crunched first on gravel, then on asphalt, as he led Bud around to the parking lot. A gust of wind sent a cluster of sunbaked leaves skittering over the asphalt like flushed tiny birds.

Rog stopped alongside a blue-and-white GMC Supercab and shone his flashlight in the driver's-side window. His free hand resting on the pistol grip, his round shoulders hunched, he said, ''Damn. Ain't here. They're over in them woods, I guess.'' He led the way toward the clearing, muttering, ''Damn. Damn, damn, Dory, you done sunk a long way, ain'tcha?''

Bud couldn't keep quiet any longer. He quickened his pace, stepped firmly in front of Rog and faced him. Bud held out his hand, palm up. ''I said I'd go along with you, and I'm not changing that. But give me the gun. And the flashlight. The state you're in, I'm going to feel a lot better if I'm leading the way. And if you'll think about what I'm saying, it'll make sense to you."

Rog fingered the pistol. For a crazy fleeting instant Bud fully expected Rog to draw and begin slinging hot lead, as though this were a western movie. Then Rog's shoulders sagged. He handed over the flashlight, then the gun, holding the barrel gingerly between a thumb and forefinger. "You're right," Rog said. "I might do something dumb on my lonesome."

Bud nodded. With the flashlight extended in front of him, and the pistol—it *was* a .22, the *Colt Woodsman* in the grip clearly visible in the moonlight—dangling by his hip, he led the way over to the path and across the clearing toward the woods. The wind came in tiny, whipping gusts. In the light of the moon the tall pines looked like ghost trees. The flashlight's beam revealed scrubby weeds that cast little shadows on the ground. The spray of fallen pine needles along the pathway thickened into a carpet as they neared the woods. Rog's breathing was loud and rapid.

They moved into the woods. A single blue-white star glittered fleetingly through the thatched roof formed by the treetops. Irregular patterns of moonlight and the beam from the flash illuminated gray bark on tree trunks, patches of damp earth in the carpet of pine needles, and a random littering of pine cones. Glowing eyes were suddenly low on the right. Bud gasped. The skunk or possum scuttled away among the trees. On Bud's left, an owl hooted.

"I reckon you think I'm pretty foolish," Rog said. "In fact I'm feelin' dumber with every step we take." He was whispering, but his voice in the silence was loud.

Bud said, "Now you're beginning to show some sense. We're—"

He kicked something. He stumbled slightly and the something—a branch?—rolled off to one side. He shone the flashlight on it. He froze.

His voice quavering, Bud said softly, "Jesus Christ."

Rog came alongside, huffing and puffing. "What is it?"

"See for yourself," Bud said.

He was looking at a severed arm. The cuff of a western shirt was still buttoned around the wrist; the sleeve was in blood-soaked tatters. The fingers on the hand were twitching.

2

SHERIFF Buck Ainson wondered if the devil had finally given the crowd of good-for-nothings who hung around Jasper's what they had coming to them. That had been the subject of Brother Leroy Abbey's sermon that past Sunday, how evil breeds evil and fire reaps fire. Brother Abbey's hellfire-and-damnation delivery had made a lasting impression on a brand-new born-again Christian like Sheriff Ainson. It wasn't the first time that Buck Ainson had been born again—it was the fourth or fifth—but this time Buck had his mind set that he was going to give up whiskey and tobacco and lying around naked with the likes of Tulip Patterson, the divorced schoolteacher who lived out south of town, and dedicate his life to the Lord on High. Hallelujah.

The beam of the sheriff's flashlight probed the creekbed. The finger of light showed him broken limbs, trampled bushes, and a trail of four-toed footprints that cut through the woods at an angle, then made a sharp descent down the muddy, weed-infested bank. The creek was a tributary of the Austin River, and at this point it wound to within fifty yards of the clearing that separated the piney woods from Jasper's. The creek's murky water was about six feet deep at the moment; later on in the summer it would recede to a bare trickle.

Sonny Beamer trudged up from the water's edge, arms akimbo, deputy's brimmed hat pulled low, his eyes hidden behind mirrored shades. He cocked his narrow head to one side. "He come this way right enough. Trail ends down there at the waterline, even a couple of deep holes in the mud where his feet sunk in."

"I can see that from here," the sheriff said, "though it's a miracle *you* can see anything, runnin' around in them sunglasses in the dark. Tell me somethin' I don't already know."

"*Buh*-uck. You told me to have a look-see. Jesus Christ, I was just followin' orders. If you could see already, whadja send me down there for?" Sonny spoke in a whiny nasal tenor.

Ainson wondered briefly which one he liked the least, Sonny Beamer or his gossipy mother. Eleanor Beamer sang soprano in the Church of Christ Ladies' Choir next to Buck Ainson's wife Margaret, and spent what seemed to Ainson like about three-quarters of the daylight hours sitting around the sheriff's living room with Margaret and going on and on about everybody else in town. Even so, Sonny Beamer was a dependable deputy, and every once in a while Eleanor dropped a bit of news that the sheriff needed to know. And Sonny and Eleanor both had immortal souls beholden to God Almighty. Buck Ainson, squatting on his haunches and pointing the flashlight down the embankment, said calmly, "Think nothin' of it, son. You done good."

Sonny peered through the trees in the direction of the tavern, where two white-coated paramedics were methodically loading what was left of Billy Ed Whitley into the rear of an ambulance. Twenty minutes ago another ambulance had left, red lights flashing and siren blaring, carrying Dory Barnes off to the hospital over in Canton. With the dead, the paramedics could afford to take their time about it.

"Whatcha make of it, Buck?" Sonny Beamer said.

Ainson rose to his feet and scratched his ample belly. He wore a lawman's Stetson identical to Sonny's except for the chrome star affixed to Ainson's hat's crown. Ainson figured that Dory Barnes was going to pull through; the evil somehow seemed to. "What's to make?" the sheriff said. "Nobody saw nothing except Dory, and it's gunna be awhile before she can tell us anything. We got somebody up there takin' statements?''

''Sure do. Terry. If you want to call *him* somebody.''

Ainson's chin moved slightly in disapproval. He didn't like one of his deputies talking about another, they were supposed to be one big happy family. He thought for a second about letting Sonny know how he felt, then changed his mind. Visible through the trees and beyond the clearing, Tombley's Walk's two firemen, dressed in yellow slickers, were rewinding the hose on the town's only fire truck. In any Tombley's Walk emergency, somebody always called the fire department. Given a chance to strut their stuff, the boys sometimes got a little out of hand. On this occasion they'd drenched the outer walls of Jasper's before the patrons inside could get across to them that there wasn't any fire.

Sonny went on. ''Jesus Christ, Buck, the fucker musta been unreal. You figure it's the rabies got something to do with this?''

''Now don't go to cussin' around me, Sonny. If you want to talk dirty do it someplace else. I got to hear it from them beer-guzzlers up there''—Ainson jerked a thumb in the direction of the tavern—''but I'll be hanged if I'll put up with it from my own depity.'' His graying shaggy eyebrows bunched together behind the top rim of his glasses.

Sonny's angular jaw slacked. ''Jus' last week you was swiggin' and cussin' yourself, Buck. You on the kick again?''

''This time it ain't a—never mind. You're right, though, the rabies is the first thing comes to mind that would make a wild animal act like that. Anybody got anything on the new man in town? Tanner?''

''Vanished smooth,'' Sonny said. ''Folks say they looked around right after what happened and he was gone, though didn't anybody remember seein' him leave. His vehicle ain't here. Drives one of them little foreign pickups, it's what they say.''

''Well, he's one to have a talk with. Any idea where he lives?''

"None, but it ain't no problem to find out," Sonny said. "Assumin' he's stayin' somewhere in town. Rog Hornby says"—the sheriff wrinkled his nose at the mention of Rog Hornby's name; at the moment he figured the owner of Jasper's for the Number One Blaspheming Heathen; Sonny noticed the sheriff's displeasure and took a shallow breath before continuing—"that Tanner's been out here drinkin' ever night for the last week or two. Says the fella keeps mostly to himself, but some of the ladies say he's been a-hittin' on 'em. 'Tween you and me, Buck, I'd put more stock in what Rog says than the women. A lot of 'em around here figure a man's tryin' to get in their pants just 'cause he says hidy to 'em. But don't worry none about findin' him, not if he's stayin' in Tombley's Walk. It ain't exactly like Dallas or Houston. 'Course if he's moved on there ain't much we can do about it."

Ainson hacked and spit. He hadn't had a cigarette since he'd been born again this time, three weeks ago, and right now he was wanting a smoke. More punishment for doing the devil's work for lo these many years. "Well, I don't know if the harlots are lyin' or not," Ainson said. "If the man's been hanging around out to this honky-tonk it's likely he's been a-sleepin' with one or more of 'em. Might be good police work if you can find out which one. Or which *ones.*"

The sheriff had a side-angle view of Sonny now, with Sonny facing the tavern. Sonny's lips twisted in a disapproving frown as he said, "They ain't really *harlots*, Buck, not in the true sense. Just 'cause they like to dance an' have a good time."

"Bull," Ainson said. "Anybody that calls hangin' out in a roadhouse an' drinkin' beer with men and women rubbin' all over one another havin' a good time . . . it ain't nothin' but the work o' Satan. Sonny, you been brought up to know." He clicked his flashlight off and jammed it into his back pocket, then headed slowly through the woods toward Jasper's. Sonny Beamer fell into step, his head down, kicking a pine cone into a soft pile of needles and not saying anything.

By the time they reached the tavern parking lot, the

ambulance was loaded and its rear doors closed. The firemen were gone; right now they'd be down at the reservoir reloading the water tanks. Ainson's other deputy, a chubby youngster with fat pouches sticking out over the back of his khaki pants, and who along with Sonny Beamer and the sheriff made up the whole on-duty county police force (there were two more deputies on the day watch) was talking to Linda Lacy. The deputy's name was Terry Hackney, and he was writing a mile a minute on a small spiral pad while Linda Lacy tossed her blond curls, her hands on her hips, her jaw working nonstop. Ainson didn't see Big Ed Whitley anywhere around, which meant that nobody'd gotten up the nerve to tell Big Ed what had happened as yet. That would be Ainson's job, and Ainson didn't like the idea.

Ainson went over to Linda Lacy and tipped his hat. "Howdy," he said. "Terrible goin's on. I hope we ain't troublin' you none with the questions, but it's good police work to get information while it's fresh on people's minds." Ainson thought that Linda Lacy was an exception to the rule, not a bad girl, just being influenced by the older harlots who hung around Jasper's. Besides, her rounded hips and swelling bosom were a pure pleasure to see up close.

"Don't worry none about me, Sheriff," Linda said. "I'm all right. I'm tellin' your man the best I can remember. Holy shit, ain't nothin' like this ever happened in Tombley's Walk."

Somehow Ainson didn't think that Linda Lacy's cussing was nearly so sinful as Sonny Beamer's. He felt Sonny's gaze boring a hole in the small of his back as he patted Linda gently on the arm and said, "Just do your best, child." Then he turned, was about to go into Jasper's to have another word with Rog Hornby about the missing newcomer, Bud Tanner, when a fire-engine red Dodge mini-van wheeled off of the I-20 access road into the parking lot and threw on its brakes.

Ainson blinked in surprise. The van was the mobile news unit from the ABC affiliate over in Tyler. Ainson had personally seen the news unit one other time that he could recall; two years ago when the Tombley's Walk 'Roos had played the Atlanta Rabbits in the State AA Football Quarterfinals in Tyler Junior College Stadium, the one and only time in history that the 'Roos had been on TV.

Now, both of the van's front doors opened at once. From the passenger side stepped a lanky young man with razored hair, coatless and wearing a white short-sleeved shirt with the collar open. He had a portable video camera slung over one shoulder. As Ainson stood there with his mouth agape, a tall willowy black girl with long straightened hair, wearing high heels along with a dark tight skirt and a checkered blouse, hopped down from the van's driver's seat and approached Ainson with a smooth and confident stride. The sheriff knew who she was. She was the noon and 6:00 P.M. anchor woman, the one whom Ainson had told Sonny Beamer—they'd been drinking that night; Ainson hadn't been born-again at the time—was one high-toned nigger-gal that he wouldn't mind changing his luck with.

She smiled a pretty smile and extended her hand. "Sheriff? Barbara Clinger, Channel 7. This tragedy you folks have had over here is on the wire services. Our New York director called and dispatched us, and, well, can you favor us with an on-camera interview, sir?"

Right there in the parking lot of Jasper's with this smiling, confident black girl shaking his hand, Buck Ainson's spit dried up. Just the thought of speaking at the Tombley County Rotary Club made Ainson back up to the rail like a hog in the slaughter pen. He cleared his throat and did his best to untie the knots in his tongue. "I sup—I reckon I could," he said. "But I'll need to see the questions first. I can't say nothing that's going to impede our investigation, ma'am."

THE next morning was Saturday, and Sheriff Buck Ainson woke up lying on his side. Margaret had her back to him, one fleshy arm atop the quilt, one pink nylon strap crossing the top of her shoulder, her graying brown hair spread out on the pillow. The quilt rose and fell with her even slow breathing. Visible beyond her, rays of morning sunlight slanted downward from the venetian blinds. The blinds covered the upper half of the window; underneath the blinds an ancient G.E. window unit hummed and blew frigid air. Ainson sneezed. If he'd had his druthers they'd be sleeping with the window open; it seemed to him he'd spent half his life with a cold. He wiped his nose on the back of his hand and rolled quietly out of bed.

He stood for a moment in boxer shorts, yawning and scratching his privates, then padded barefoot over the hardwood floor into the closet. His Timex Commander digital watch, which had buttons for changing the face into a lap timer or blackjack game, but which Ainson never used for anything except to tell the time, lay on the shelf. He checked the watch: 6:55. He fastened the strap around his wrist and changed into his uniform. Then, in his stockinged feet, he walked softly on the balls of his feet toward the bedroom door.

Bedclothes rustled as Margaret rolled over and raised up on her elbow. "Ernie? What is it?"

He sighed and relaxed. He hadn't made it. "I wanted to let you rest some. I got to work today."

She sat on the edge of the bed and jammed her feet into pink houseshoes. "But I'll need to fix you something." Her cheeks were colorless and drooping. Ainson pictured Tulip Patterson's firm chin and neck. And Tulip would tell him in a split second that if he wanted something to eat he could damn well fend for himself. Plus, Tulip called him "Buck," along with everybody else in the county except Margaret. Ainson's born-again determination wavered slightly.

"Don't bother, old girl," Ainson said. "I'm not too hungry."

Her gaze dropped. "I guess I *am* old."

Ainson's jaws clenched, then relaxed. "No, you ain't. Two years younger'n me, and I sure as . . . shootin' ain't old. Let's us drink some coffee. You get doughnuts yesterday?"

"In the pantry," Margaret said. She'd gone into the bathroom and was splashing water in her face. "I'll be a minute, sweet. Lordy, I'm a mess." As Ainson left the room she was dabbing the sides of her nose with a washcloth.

By the time Margaret came into the kitchen, Ainson had poured two steaming cups—there was a picture of a snorting bull on his own brown mug; Margaret's featured a cow with big round eyes and long lashes—and added powdered cream and sugar to hers. He was seated at the table eating a chocolate doughnut. The white table was yellowed with age in places. Margaret was wearing a shapeless blue terry robe and approached the table in halting steps. "This town's goin' crazy, Ernie."

He took a bite of doughnut and washed it down with coffee to keep from answering her. He gestured toward the open pasteboard box. On the side of the box was a cartoon of a grinning fat man in a chef's hat. Margaret sat down and nibbled on a cinnamon sugar doughnut. "Everybody's scared to death, Ernie. Missy Ellison says Doug's ready to start shootin' all strays on sight. And Ruthie Guthrie called while you was gone last night. She got awful cranky, demandin' to know what you was goin' to do about all the mad animals. Me an' Ruthie been friends for years, Ernie, she's got no call to talk to me that way. You'd have thunk I personally bit all them dogs an' give 'em the rabies myself. Now those horble killin's, no tellin' what they're goin' to say."

Ainson flicked a piece of chocolate frosting onto the linoleum. Margaret didn't comment, which told Ainson that she was really worried. Well, she wasn't all by her lonesome. "All they're goin' to do is talk," he said. "Me, I'm workin' on the answer, but Lord knows the county don't have any money to do anything if the answer's going to cost much."

"It'll help if I can jus' tell everbody you got things in hand," Margaret said. "That'll be a relief to people." She picked up her doughnut and took a full-sized bite.

Ainson took a hot sip of coffee. That was a big trouble with Tombley's Walk. What was being done didn't matter, only what everybody could *tell* everybody. Ainson should have gotten used to it over the years, but the townfolks' attitude still bugged him. "Now, I didn't say I got things in hand. But if it makes you feel better go on ahead and tell 'em that. Sure, dear. Let the word out that between Buck Ainson and the Lord everything's gonna work out. Tell folks that this mornin' me an' Doc Petty are goin' to work on it."

Her round face tilted. "You see Ed Whitley yet?"

"No. No, I ain't got the stomach for it. I thought about talkin' to Big Ed last night, but I didn't want to be the one to drop the news on him. He'll know by now. I don't want to talk to him or nobody else until I can give some answers. For now just say I'm workin' on a lead. Has to do with a man." Ainson was blowing smoke, but if he was going to blow any smoke he was pointing it in the right direction. Margaret would let the whole town know by nightfall that their sheriff was hot on the trail. Blowing smoke in his wife's direction was probably what had gotten him elected sheriff to begin with. Dance with who brung ya, Buck Ainson always said.

Margaret blinked. "A *man?* A man around here got the rabies now?" She looked almost hopeful.

"Not that," Ainson said. "Just a man may know somethin' about what went on out at the honky-tonk last night. Don't be lettin' that out, though, not while I'm investigatin'." Ainson paused to let that sink in. Telling Margaret to keep something a secret would make dead certain that she let the secret out. "I'm gonna run him through the N.C.I.C. computer this mornin'."

She sat up a little straighter, and it occurred to Ainson that the simple act of straightening made Margaret look a whole lot younger. It was a shame that she'd gotten to slouching so over the past few years. She said, "You mean that FBI crime information thing, Ernie? Just last week you was tellin' Sonny it wadn' worth the powder to blow it to kingdom come, and every time you *did* get ahold of a wanted suspect nobody wanted to expedite. Waste of time, is what you told him."

"*Extradite.* I mightta said that, but the computer's all I got right now. Moses and Joshua, I can't even buy two rear tires for my county car. What do folks think, I can call out the militia on the dollar forty-nine I got in the treasury?''

She reached across the table and patted his arm. ''I don't think folks're really blamin' you. You been sheriff too long.''

''It's too long in more ways than one,'' Ainson said. ''I'm fifty-six. I'm thinking serious about checkin' it to 'em next election and devotin' my life to the work o' the Lord.''

Margaret favored Ainson with a dull blink. ''That's real nice, dear,'' she said. ''But don't you think you ought to be born-again for a little while longer 'fore you go jumpin' off the deep end?''

Ainson let that one pass. He could have told her the same thing he'd told Sonny Beamer out at Jasper's, that this time his life was changed for good. But he decided to let well enough alone. Besides, this morning he wasn't too sure about his resolutions himself. ''How long I been sheriff?'' he said. ''Twenty-six years?''

''Twenty-four.''

''Missed it by a couple, I can't remember no more. Well, however long it's been I never seen nothing to match what happened out there last night. Or heard of it, either. Not even the Kentucky Fried Chicken thing, back in seventy-one.''

''Was it really a wild animal?'' she said. ''That's what they say.''

''Whatever it was, girl, it was wild. Probably a timber wolf, only them that talked to Dory 'fore she went completely into shock say she talked about somethin' that stood upright, like a man. No wild critter I ever heard of does that. A bear, maybe, but not no wolf. 'Less . . . well, maybe a trained one? Lots of circuses pass through around here, might be one got away.''

She sipped coffee thoughtfully, chewed her doughnut, interested now, giving Ainson a fleeting glimpse of the light that had once shined in her eyes all of the time. ''I never heard of no trained wolf in a circus, Ernie.''

He expelled air from his lungs. ''Me neither. I guess all of this has got me a little loco. There sure was *some-*

thin' out there, though. Somethin' that could bite an arm clean off and fix Billy Ed Whitley so's they're having a closed casket funeral for him. And this fella I told you about, the one I'm checking up on? He run off soon as him and Rog Hornby found Billy Ed's body. Left 'fore Rog could figure out that Dory was still breathin'. Durn perculiar way for a man to act. Might be he knowed the animal."

She looked confused. "I never knowed anybody knowed an *animal.* You're havin' me on, ain't you?" Visible beyond her, magnetized have-a-nice-day faces smiled from the white surface of the refrigerator door.

"I don't mean knowed the animal *personally,*" Ainson said. "That's another thing I'm wanting to talk to Doc Petty about, whether or not it's possible for a man to give signals to an animal. Telepathy or some such.

"Listen, I know all this sounds crazy. It sounds pretty wild-haired to me, too. But the only way I know to get the county governors off my back is to try anything and everything. And there's a connection between what happened out there and this rabies thing, there's got to be." He drained the last of his coffee and stood. "I got to stop by the office and get some things to show the doc. I'm goin' now."

"Sure, sweet," Margaret Ainson said. "You run on. I feel a whole heap better, knowin' what to tell people."

AINSON went out on the screened back porch and put on his boots. Then he picked up his hat, polished his sheriff's badge on his shirt sleeve, and jammed the hat onto his head. He went out and let the screen door slam behind him. He stopped in the backyard to turn on the square-patterned sprinkler, then pulled on the hose until the glistening droplets were falling on Margaret's rosebushes. The roses had won a prize over at the Tyler Festival that spring, and Ainson believed that early watering was the trick. In the afternoon the blistering sun would evaporate the water before it could seep down to the roots. Ainson went out through the gate onto the gravel drive.

The county vehicle, a light blue four-year-old Impala

sedan with its bubble-gum flashing lights hidden behind the grille, was parked nose-on to the garage. The wooden garage hadn't been painted in ten years, and bare wood showed through in places. Something else that Ainson needed to tend to. Besides the two rear tires that the sheriff had complained to Margaret about, the car needed a tune-up once the budget could stand it. Until then Ainson was going to have to make do with what he had. He took off his hat, mopped his brow (Moses, if it was this hot early in July, August was going to be a plumb scorcher), dropped the hat onto the seat, and started the engine. It coughed, rattled, and chugged to life. He clipped a few leaves on the grapevine that grew at the end of the driveway as he backed out into the street.

Ainson had made the ten-minute drive downtown to his office so many times that he could have driven it with his eyes closed. First the two-block straightaway on Willow Lane, Ainson's own street, lined with houses built before World War II. The houses were old but most of them sparkled with fresh white paint, and stood proudly behind clipped, emerald-green lawns. At the end of Willow Lane, Ainson made his only turn, a left on First Avenue, and followed First all the way to the square.

He drove mechanically, going over what he'd seen out at Jasper's. It was a lot for a country boy to swallow. But swallow it he must; the animal that had killed Billy Ed Whitley and bitten a chunk out of Dory Barnes's shoulder wasn't any ordinary wolf or coyote. And the gaping hole in Dory Barnes wasn't made by any regular-sized critter's jaws, either. The thing had torn Dory from her shoulder joint to just above her breast.

And the footprints among the trampled bushes down by the creekbed didn't fit in, either. First of all, the prints just weren't that big—not big enough to go with the size of the jaws that had bitten into Dory. But the main thing—and this was something that the sheriff hadn't let on to Sonny Beamer—was the *kind* of prints they were. They'd belonged to a wolf—or one good-sized monster of a dog—there couldn't be much doubt about that. But they'd all looked to Ainson like *rear* prints, which went right along with Dory's crazy description of something that walked like a man. Ainson glanced at the sky. Clear blue, only a faraway wisp of cloud. That was good, the sheriff didn't want it to rain before he could get the zoologist over from Tyler to have a look at those footprints.

The talk with the girl from Tyler Junior College had gone a long way toward making up Ainson's mind to check out the stranger, Bud Tanner. She was an eighteen-year-old, not really old enough to be drinking legal in Jasper's (but where the college crowd was concerned, East Texas lawmen tended to look the other way), a plain girl with long stringy brown hair and not much curve to her lanky body, and who'd probably been in the grown-up honky-tonk looking for what she wasn't getting from the college boys. Attention.

She'd been trembling. After she'd steadied her nerves with a straight shot of bourbon (Ainson had eyed Rog Hornby while the girl had been drinking the whiskey, but Rog had drummed his fingers on the bar top and kept his gaze on the ceiling), she'd said in a soft, scared voice, "Weirdest thing I ever saw. I was standin' out there catchin' a breath when he comes runnin' lickety-split like a haint was after him. I go, 'Somethin' wrong, mister?' And he goes, 'Down there, you need to tell somebody,' or somethin' like that, and then he gives me this wild look and jumps in his little red truck and burns rubber gettin' out of here. Right as he was leavin' I heard Rog a-hollerin' down in the woods. So I went to see what was wrong, and . . . you know, sheriff. You know."

Ainson snapped out of his trance and jammed on his brakes. He'd nearly overrun the county parking lot across from the courthouse, and he now wheeled in and parked in the head-in space marked OFFICIAL—COUNTY SHERIFF. Ainson was sweating. The county vehicle's air-conditioning hadn't worked in a couple of years. He mopped his brow again, got his hat, stepped down from the car, and crossed the street.

The Tombley County Courthouse and Office Building took up the entire center of the town square, bounded on the north and south by First and Second avenues and on the east and west by Sam Houston Street and Davy Crockett Boulevard. Three proud stories high it stood, redbrick with a gilt domed roof, and its first floor branched out into three separate wings. The county and district courts (seventy-year-old Ezra Porter was the county judge and had been ever since Harry Truman had been in office; the presiding district judge was a former prosecutor from the neighboring town of Caldonia named Jack Puckett, a thirty-year-old who Ainson thought was an arrogant upstart) were on the second floor with the eight-cell county lockup on the third. Ainson's own office was in one of the first-floor wings, down the corridor from the tax assessor and directly across from the water commissioner, but when the sheriff was in the building he spent most of his time sitting around on the third floor and shooting the bull with his old friend, E.J. Joseph, the jailer. E.J. and Buck had been wing and tailback respectively on the '49 'Roo state finalist team, and they had been taking care of each other for a lot of years.

Just as Sheriff Ainson did every day, he paused for a moment outside the courthouse to pay his respects to Matthew Tombley. Tombley's Walk's founder was enshrined forevermore on the corner of the square in the form of a statue that was originally painted bronze, but which was now chipped in places and the color of a gray dead tree. The statue stood in front of the southeast wing of the courthouse between two tall fir trees, and directly in back of a bubbling fountain that doubled as a bath for most of the sparrows in the county. In 1879, Matthew Tombley had walked all the way from Texarkana to stake claim to some land in the center of what was now Tombley County. Legend aside, old Matthew hadn't really been that much of a pioneer. He'd originally vowed to walk all the way to California to hunt for gold, but Tombley's Walk had been as far as he'd made it. At least he'd *told* folks that California was his goal; there was a rumor that Matthew really only wanted to escape the confines of Texarkana, where the sheriff had a burglary warrant for him.

Nonetheless, there he stood, a pack on his back and his rumpled western hat tilted jauntily to one side. He hadn't been a resident of Tombley's Walk for very long, and nobody had ever located any of Matthew Tombley's descendants anywhere (at least none that would claim him). In fact, he'd lost whatever land he'd owned to the original Justin Barker in a poker game. Barker's grandson, Justin Barker III, was the current chairman of the Tombley County National Bank a half block from the square, and currently under investigation by the F.D.I.C. (though the story hadn't broken in the papers as yet). Hero or outlaw, though, there was one thing nobody could take away from Matthew Tombley. He really had walked all the way from Texarkana, and Sheriff Buck Ainson had thought for years that the expression on the statue's face looked as though its feet hurt.

The morning paper from Tyler—it was the nearest daily to Tombley's Walk and was shipped over each morning in bundles—was in the rack at the bottom of the courthouse steps. Ainson bent to read the headline through the plastic *(One Dead, One Hospitalized in Tavern Animal Attack)*, flipped a quarter into the slot, took two copies of the paper out (one for him and one for E.J.), and folded them underneath his arm. Then he slowly climbed the steps (there were twenty-two in all, he counted them every day), entered the courthouse through the revolving door, and went down the hallway to his office. The inside of the building seemed a little darker than normal and the sound of his footsteps echoing from the walls and vaulted ceiling seemed to linger in the air.

ACCORDING to the N.C.I.C. computer (for what it was worth, which Ainson didn't personally think was very much; he could go on and on about the number of blameless people he'd jailed and held for other authorities who'd later told him he had the wrong party), seventeen of the thirty-two men named Tanner who were wanted in the southwest part of the United States were black. That surprised the sheriff. Usually where a fairly common last name was involved—excluding, of course, presidents' names like Washington, Lincoln, or Madison, where the rate was even higher—what Ainson called the nigger factor was closer to 80 percent. Ainson had even seen blacks in the crime printouts who had chili-choker names. One in particular that he remembered was Willie Gomez, who'd once broken into the F.W. Woolworth's across the street from the courthouse and made off with a case of glass beads. "Show me a nigger," Ainson used to say, "and I'll show you a sumbitch that's fixin' to steal somethin'." But now that he was born-again, the sheriff knew he needed to show more brotherly love.

Eight of the remaining fifteen Tanners were under thirty (according to the witnesses the man at Jasper's had been older), so he crossed them off the list. That left seven that needed checking on. He reached to his right, depressed the PF5 button on the keyboard, and in a few seconds the Epson printer began to chatter and jerkily spit out paper. Ainson tilted his swivel chair back and folded his arms to wait. As he did, the door outside his office in the reception area opened and closed with a click.

Ainson tilted his hat to one side. Probably it was E.J., bored with the two drunk drivers in the jail upstairs and down to pick up his newspaper and shoot the breeze awhile. Ainson squinted as he peered into the reception room, seeing one corner of the cloth divan, the print on the wall of a desert scene showing prickly pear cactus growing in clumps in the sand, a tall floor lamp covered by a green shade. There was a shadow on the carpet, swaying slightly, someone standing there not coming in.

Ainson raised his voice over the chattering printer. "I'm in here," he said. "The secretary's off on Saturday." It was a lie. Madelyn Couch had retired in April and the county budget just didn't have room for her replacement.

There were muffled footsteps on the outer office's carpet and the shadow lengthened. Melody Parker, the only practicing lady lawyer in Tombley's Walk and also one of its best-looking women, and who was one of the last people in Tombley's Walk that Ainson wanted to see right at the moment, came around the doorjamb into the office and said, "I saw your car across the street. Can I have a word?"

Since Ainson didn't see any way out of it, he said, "Sure thing. Mornin'."

She grasped her upper arm with her opposite hand and stood with one foot slightly in front of the other. "I almost thought the better of it and went straight to the county attorney, but maybe an informal talk would be better. Sort of cut through the red tape." Melody had been born in Tombley's Walk; college and law school had nearly done away with her East Texas twang, but not quite. "Officially I *should* be seeing the county attorney, though."

"Officially?" Ainson said. "Bull, Melody. Officially I've seen you runnin' through the schoolyard like a wild Indian. Paddled your behind one afternoon you was skippin' school, case you forgot. Anytime I need Rod Lindenhall as a message carrier 'tween you and me we're all goin' downhill."

Melody was small, on the verge of tiny, and she wasn't afraid of the Maker himself. Ainson had seen her in action, tiny clenched fists at her waist, raised up on tiptoes as she'd stood nose-to-chin with a prosecutor or opposing counsel in a lawsuit and by-gosh made 'em holler uncle. Now, standing in Ainson's office with her shoulders squared, she said, "You probably know by now that I'm representing a group of parents. At least you *should* know, I've left enough messages for you at the switchboard. My clients are wanting to file suit." Her coal-black hair, which she wore in a bun in the courtroom, flowed soft and loose to her shoulders. She wore a gloss on her lips which lent a faint pinkish shine, and a blue sleeveless see-through blouse along with white puffy pants. Her look said that she didn't particularly like Ainson's I-knew-you-when routine.

"Well, that don't tell me much," Ainson said. "A group of parents in Tombley's Walk could mean just about anybody. Everybody that ain't gotten to be a parent around here don't live here no more. And as for suin', well, that's what everbody wants to do these days. Keeps you lawyers' cash registers dingin', I'll say that for it. But personally I think folks ought to settle their differences in a peaceable manner and take more time to worship the Lord." He showed Melody his best Shall-We-Gather-At-The-River expression.

Melody covered her mouth as though she were stifling a giggle. Then she rolled her eyes. "My clients are *trying* to settle their differences outside the courthouse, but we don't seem to be getting anywhere. Did you know about the little girl that got bit over by the school Friday and nobody can find the dog that did it? That poor child is having to take all those painful shots in her stomach, and they don't even know whether she's exposed or not. Now we've got an absolute *carnage* out at that honky-tonk—"

"Hold it, Melody. You ain't ratin' what happened to them revelers out there right along with somebody's child gettin' hurt."

"My god, Sheriff, it's people getting *killed.* I've known Dory Barnes all my life, and whatever else she might be she's still my friend. She's had a hard life, who are we to judge? And no matter *who* they are, the people of this community are entitled to police protection. Now, I don't know what it's going to take, more deputies, vigilantes, or what, but if Tombley County doesn't start doing something, and fast, you and the rest of the country up-de-ups can get ready for a trip to the federal courthouse over in Tyler. We've got constitutional rights at stake here." She thrust her fine jaw forward. Ainson had lost track of time, but he was pretty sure that Melody was under thirty. Maybe twenty-seven or -eight.

"Now, hold your horses, Miss Parker." Ainson folded his hands and sat up straight behind his desk. "Sure these people are entitled to pertection. I don't need nobody's advice on how to run my office down here. This animal control stuff"—here he tapped a thick file folder on his desk—"is gettin' top priority. You just caught me on my way out the door to see Doc Petty about some of this, that's why I'm down here workin' on Saturday. But you gotta remember that the county population is down to sixteen thousand right now and we ain't raised the per capita taxes in ten or fifteen years. I'm operatin' on the shorts, only six lawmen right now, and there ain't no way to finance a full-time dog catcher without cuttin' down someplace else. Everbody wants their kids gettin' an education, you want us to cut out the schools?" Or maybe E.J. could double as dogcatcher, Ainson thought. Make them dogs drunk as hooty-owls, just smellin' his breath.

Melody spread her dainty feet a little farther apart. Her smooth cheeks were flushed. "The budget's no excuse, Sheriff. There's already one dead, what's next? My people happen to think there's a lot of fat in the budget right now, by the way. Beginning with the judges' and sheriff's salaries."

Ainson shrugged. He really ought to ask Melody to sit, but maybe she wouldn't stay as long if she had to stand. "I think people got the wrong idea about Billy Ed Whitley gettin' killed. We ain't so sure that has anything to do with this rabies business. I'm workin' on a lead. Has to do with a man." He looked at the computer printout, still in the printer.

"A man?" she said. "A *man?* Lord, Sheriff, Billy Ed got torn limb from limb and something like to have bit Dory's shoulder off. A *man* did that?"

"I know it sounds way off, girl. But it wouldn't be good police work not to follow up. How often's a new fella move to Tombley's Walk, 'specially one that ain't got a job or nothin'? Once ever hunnerd years or so. Where there's smoke there's fire, most o' the time." Ainson did his best to look as though he knew something that no one else did.

Melody's pointed chin moved in a doubtful tilt. "What new man? You mean the writer? Rangy guy that talks with some kind of out-of-state accent, sounds well educated? Has enough hair on his head for three men? He's the only new one I know of."

"Your description sounds like what I'm getting. He was out to the honky-tonk last night. Why? You know something about him?" He eyed her suspiciously. The thought that Melody Parker might know something about any killing was plumb ridiculous, but the thought of making her squirm gave Ainson a little surge of satisfaction.

She laughed out loud, a pretty sound like high notes on a xylophone. "Why, if that's not the silliest thing I ever heard. Sure I know who he is, what woman in Tombley's

Walk doesn't? A single man can't walk around this town without talk starting. He's a writer, and he's at the library a lot. Doin' research is what they say. But trying to throw a mad-animal killing off on somebody like that, why, that's grasping at straws."

"I ain't surprised that the womenfolk want to paint the fella with a rose-colored brush," Ainson said. "He may be at the library by day, girl, but there's a darker side to him. He's been hangin' out evenin's out to that honky-tonk. Drinkin' beer and sittin' around."

"Sheriff," Melody said. "If drinkin' beer makes a man a suspect in a killin', then every man in Tombley's Walk would be on the list. Including you, Sheriff, when you're not out bein' born again. I can't believe this. Is that going to be your official word to my clients? That what you're doing about the killing last night is running an investigation on a . . . *fiction writer?*"

Ainson put a hand in his pocket and studied the toes of his boots. The boots could stand some polishing. "Well, Rog Hornby says he ain't never written anything that *he* ever heard of."

"You . . . Jesus!" Melody tossed her head and looked at the ceiling. "Well, that makes him guilty I guess. Look, I'm sorry to bother you, Sheriff, I've wasted both of our times. I should have taken this up with the county attorney to begin with. Which is what my clients are going to instruct me to do if there isn't positive action, and I mean something besides you and the judge sitting around shooting the bull, within the next week. Nice talking to you, Sheriff." She left, her backside twitching and her sandals whispering testily on the carpet.

Ainson wondered whether Melody Parker could ever make a good Christian wife for a man. Doubtful. Too headstrong to go along with the flock. Sure had a fine-looking bottom, though.

MELODY was mentally kicking her own behind for losing her cool. Highly unprofessional. One lawyer she knew over in Tyler, a chauvinist pig named Woodrow Beedle, had told her last week that women didn't have any business being lawyers to begin with because they got too personally wrapped up in their cases. A lot of sexist bullshit, Melody had told the guy, but maybe she *was* getting too het-up over this rabies thing.

And that phony old fart Buck Ainson made her mad enough to spit BB's. The *nerve* of the old bastard. One week going around sanctimonious as all get-out, spouting the Bible at everybody, the next week drunk as a coot and out at Tulip Patterson's house knocking off a little strange. Who did the old goat think he was fooling? Melody was pretty sure that the sheriff's wife, Margaret, was the only somebody in Tombley's Walk who didn't know about Ainson's ongoing affair, and Margaret Ainson was so spacey and tuned out that if she were to catch old Tulip giving the sheriff a blowjob right in the Ainson living room, she'd probably clap her chubby hands together and say, "Oh. Company. I'll fix y'all somethin'."

And Ainson's cornpone, I-knowed-ya-when-you-was-little routine was enough to make Melody regurgitate. She remembered the paddling incident, all right, and she *had* been skipping school, but what she recalled was that Ainson had spent one hell of a lot more time *rubbing* her bottom than he had paddling it. She'd been thirteen at the time, and the old bastard's hands on her had made her skin absolutely *crawl*.

She reached the bottom courthouse step and, with a final irritated hop-skip, stepped down onto the sidewalk and slowed her walk. She went to the end of the block, passed Matthew Tombley's statue, and rounded the corner onto Davy Crockett Boulevard. Her restored MG convertible, shiny red and neat as a pin, stood across Davy Crockett next to a parking meter. The city had installed the meters about a decade earlier—her brow furrowed as she tried to remember exactly what year but couldn't—but nobody who knew anything about Tombley's Walk ever deposited a coin in one of the meters because there weren't enough cops to patrol downtown and give anybody a ticket, and in the unlikely event that anyone *did* happen to get a ticket they always knew somebody on the county's board of governors who'd fix it for them.

The MG was parked, top down, in front of the F.W. Woolworth's store. The store hadn't been a *real* Woolworth's in years. The nationwide chain had given up the ghost in Tombley's Walk when Melody had been a little girl, and ever since then the owner of the store had been a local man named Thomas Norton. The fact that the Woolworth's sign (which Mr. Norton painted himself every four or five years) was still over the awning was living proof that nobody from Woolworth's had visited Tombley's Walk in twenty years, or if they had, they felt too sorry for Mr. Norton to file suit over use of the name.

The deserted Rialto Theatre, its faded red spire still over the marquee, was on the corner beside the Woolworth's. There were two black letters on the marquee, a **J** on the upper left and a **T** on the lower right. There had been other letters up there in the past, but the high school kids had stolen them over the years. Tombley's Walk, just like about every other Texas town of its size, had had its last picture show—two of them in fact. The first had been in the fifties, before Melody had been born. The second had come in the early seventies when a group headed by Justin Barker II, the current bank president's father, had made a game effort to revive the movie house for a time. The second last picture show in Tombley's Walk had been *The Sting,* and Melody recalled sitting in the balcony beside her father, munching on popcorn and falling head-over-heels for Robert Redford. She'd sent Redford a crush letter. She'd gotten back a three-line form reply signed by Redford's assistant, along with a black-and-white publicity photo.

Melody felt her stomach muscles tighten and her thighs press against the fabric of her slacks as she slid behind the wheel. She had good legs and a narrow waist. A damn good body, in fact, though a little lacking in the boob department. Melody liked the way she stacked up against other women, right up there in the race without being smug about it (except in private), and she didn't kid herself that her looks, rather than her closing argument, hadn't won a few verdicts from all-male juries. And what the hell, she thought, looking good is a trip. The only trouble was that looking good in Tombley's Walk wasn't worth the effort at times because of the lack of eligible men around.

She started the engine, raced it in neutral, dropped the lever into gear and headed north out Davy Crockett Boulevard. There were no "sides of the tracks" in Tombley's Walk because the T&P Railroad had detoured around the town for a straighter shot into Tyler, so the portion of Davy Crockett Boulevard on the north side of the square was the dividing line. On Melody's right were one-story frame houses belonging mostly to blue-collar folk who drove daily to Mount Pleasant to work at the foundry; the west side of Davy Crockett was the black side of town. Melody wasn't a racist, her college years had changed all that, but she still spent most of her time east of Crockett. As she drove on north she pictured Buck Ainson again, and her upper lip involuntarily curled.

MELODY turned the wheel and felt her weight press against the MG's door as she pulled off the interstate's access road and entered the parking lot of Denny's Restaurant. The car-generated wind had whipped her hair into streamers in the open convertible, and perspiration had formed on her lip in the heat from the rising sun. On her left, the westbound morning traffic on I-20 consisted mostly of pickups and trailer rigs; the eastbound lanes were practically bumper-to-bumper Caddys, Lincolns, and Mercedes, as the Dallas richos zipped over to Louisiana Downs Race Track in Bossier City for the weekend, hell-bent-for-leather to drink whiskey, holler loud, and fatten the racetrack's cash drawers.

Twice she cruised the length of the parking lot—past the yellow oval sign with the red letters that was Denny's trademark, making her U-turns in the driveway of the La Quinta Motel that stood next door to the restaurant—before a Ford pickup with a camper-cover over its bed vacated a parking space close to the entrance. The pickup's driver, a sunburnt man wearing a John Deere Tractors cap, leered at her as he backed up. Normally she would've ignored the guy, but her meeting with the sheriff had her in a nasty mood. She showed the pickup's driver a smile and shot him the finger.

She fished in her glove compartment, located a ballpoint and a ruled steno pad, tucked them under her arm, and went into the restaurant. She was wearing round Gloria Vanderbilt sunglasses with red plastic frames, and she moved them from the bridge of her nose to perch on top of her head. A half-dozen people—one teenage couple holding hands, a man and his wife, both in their thirties, and four wiggly little girls—waited on padded couches for the seating hostess. Melody stood on her tiptoes and peered around the restaurant at people crowded into booths and around tables, at waitresses in tan uniforms hustling around, some carrying clear glass pots of coffee, others lugging trays of syrupy pancakes, bacon, and sunny-side-up eggs.

The seating hostess, wearing the same uniform as the waitresses except for her checkered apron, came over and said, "It's a thirty-minute wait, hon, 'less you want to sit at the counter. What's the name?" She licked the end of a pencil and got ready to write.

"Well, I'm meeting somebody," Melody said. "He's . . . oh. There he is. Thanks." She smiled at the hostess and took off down the aisle, then slid into one side of a two-seater booth by the window where a man was sitting. "Sorry to be late. And hey, I'm sorry we couldn't meet at my office this week. My appointment calendar is just *crammed.*" She was being just a tad extra-professional with this guy to keep it all arm's length.

"Don't give it a thought," he said. "I like this better. More informal. The Texas way of doing things."

"Laid back, that's us," she said. This was her first close-up look at Tanner, though she'd gotten a pretty good look at him one day at the library, when he'd been at the fiction shelves and she'd been sneaking a peek at *Vernon's Annotated Texas Statutes.* Mop of hair and deep-set brown eyes that showed just a little sadness around the edges. The kind of eyes that brought out the mother in women. Or the hooker, one of the two.

Tanner waved for the waitress. As she filled his coffee

cup he said to Melody, "Like I told you on the phone, what I'm wanting to do isn't any big deal. Just form a little corporation, but I guess I need a lawyer for that."

Melody decided to have coffee, too, and pushed her cup over for the waitress to fill. "It's something I can do, Mr. Tanner. But I don't—hey, I'm going to be straight-out. I almost didn't come out here. I'm hearing things about you."

His eyebrows lifted. "Oh?"

The waitress moved on, the glass pot swinging at her hip. When she'd gone, Melody said, "Couple of things. I'm not hard-up enough for business that I've got to touch anything illegal."

"Forming a corporation?" he said. "That's illegal? You folks' laws sure are sure different than anyplace else I've ever been."

"Of course it's not illegal. That's not what I'm talking about. Other things."

"Other things?" He looked thoughtful, then shrugged. "Well, if you can't, you can't. Thanks for coming by. My treat." He reached into his pocket and jingled some change around.

She clutched the tabletop. "Wait a minute."

"Wait for what?" he said. "If you can't, you can't. No big deal."

The back of her neck was getting warm. "Now look, you. I've just spent the last half hour covering for you, the least you could do is tell me a couple of things."

"Why should I? You've already told me you don't want to be my lawyer." His eyes narrowed. "Covering for me how?"

"With our by-god High Sheriff. That's one thing, and the other reason I'm not sure about representing you in anything is something I found out on my own."

"Now wait, wait a minute." He lifted his hand, palm outward. "You just said flat-out that you're not going to be my lawyer, now you're saying you're not sure."

Melody had to admit that the guy had a way about him. "I'm *not* sure," she said lamely.

"You said that," he said.

"Well I . . . you're not even going to answer my questions?"

"You haven't asked any. You've just said you're not going to be my lawyer."

"Let's start over." She picked up her pen and began to doodle, writing her initials, then drawing little circles around the letters. "You have to tell me something first: Why'd you run away last night? I didn't know it was you that found the bodies, out at Jasper's. How can you sit here talking about forming a corporation, after that? I'd be in shock."

"I *was* in shock," he said. "That's why I left. I didn't want to have to answer a lot of questions." Visible behind him, the couple with the little girls, the couple whom Melody had passed on the way into the restaurant, got tired of waiting. They stalked into the parking lot. The mother was clutching one little girl's hand. The little girl was holding back and crying.

"Well, you're going to have to answer a lot of questions anyway," Melody said. "One way or the other. By leaving the scene you've turned yourself from a witness into a suspect."

"Suspect of what? That wasn't any murder down there, it was some kind of animal. What kind of sheriff does this town have?"

"That's debatable," she said. She took a sip of coffee, watching the man, his set square jaw, his expression. She had a lot of doubts about the guy, but not because of the way he looked. He looked like somebody she'd trust. It was what she'd heard that had her bothered. "But good sheriff or bad sheriff, you're on his list. You're going to be hearing from him. Look, don't get me wrong. I'm not even an investigator, and I didn't see what went on. But I've been told enough to . . . well, anybody that thinks a *man* has anything to do with it is really sort of bananas. But the sheriff is under a lot of heat over the animal control thing, he'll do anything to convince the voters around here that he's doing his job."

There was just the faintest twitch at the corner of his

eye, some worry lines around his mouth. "What's he likely to do?"

"Oh, not that much. Blow a lot of smoke. He'll investigate you; if you've got any skeletons in your closet, there'll be some bones rattling around. If he can find them."

"Well, everybody's got . . . *some* skeletons," he said. "But if all I've got to worry about is whether I've got something to do with what happened out there, then I really don't have anything to worry about at all. And neither do you, about doing legal work for me."

"Hey," she said, "I'm not worried one bit about you and that attack, that wouldn't stop me from working for you." She studied her doodles on the pad. "If that's all there was."

His chin moved to one side. "Well, what else is there?"

"It's none of my business," she said. "Really."

"Come on. It's enough of your business that you're worried about a simple little thing like forming a corporation for my writing income. What do you mean, none of your business?"

She felt a little strange. She'd intended to come out here and let him have it with both barrels, but something about him made her not want to. She said, "Look, I don't know you. I've seen you, okay? You call me out of the blue, you say you're Jacob E. Tanner and you want me to incorporate you. Okay, I do that stuff. You're a stranger here, nobody can move to Tombley's Walk without the Indian drum messages starting around. So I already knew who you were. I thought having a writer for a client would be cool, okay? I checked up. *Books in Print*, Copyright Office, Library of Congress, you name it. So do you write under a pen name or something?"

His gaze shifted just a hair, so he wasn't looking directly at her. "No," he said.

"In fact, you've never written anything at all, have you?"

Now his mouth twisted, then relaxed. "No," he said again.

"And that's my problem, Mr. Tanner. I'm a lawyer, I

like fees as much as the next lawyer. But you don't have any writing income to incorporate, which means only one thing. You want this corporation for some other reason than you're telling. And that's the problem. Without all the facts I can't do anything for you. I could be in deep shit."

He toyed with his spoon, his features sagging. He picked up his cup. He set it down. He expelled a long breath. "Brother," he said. "Do I ever need a friend."

She should tell this guy to stuff it and walk out, just like that. Christ, here she was again, getting mixed up in somebody else's problems. She should walk out. Right fucking out and don't pass go.

Her face softened. She smiled. "Say, you want another cup?" she said. "You look like you could use one."

3

DORY Barnes was in the hospital over in Canton, half asleep and half awake. Drifting in and out, dozing off, waking up to find different people wandering in and out of her room. The doctors were half good and half bad. The young dark-haired doctor on the night shift was one good-looking shit—once when he'd been bending over to check the bandage on her shoulder, Dory had winked at him, reached around and pinched him on the bottom; Jesus, but he'd gotten a funny look on his face—but the daytime doctor was one crabby old fart, as far as Dory was concerned. But all three of the nurses she'd seen—the young, slightly pigeon-toed blond; the short peppy brunet who chewed gum a mile a minute; the fiftyish woman with blued gray hair whom Dory had run across a time or two when she'd been honky-tonking—were A-OK in little Dory's book. All three of them had orders to give Dory a shot in the hip every two hours for pain if she wanted it, and it had taken Dory about two spins around the clock to figure out that she could say yes to the shot whether she was hurting at the time or not. *You drink whiskey, I'll drink wine, but I'll take demorol any ol' time.*

Her sleep was restless, her dreams full of the beast: the bloodthirsty snarls, the snapping jaws, Billy Ed Whitley's severed arm flopping on the ground (boy hidy, ol' Billy Ed's left-handed jackin'-off days are damn sure over, wouldya believe?). She'd wake up from each dream in a cold sweat, the bedclothes soaked. Groggy, her mind in a fog, she'd raise up (Jesus Christ, that shoulder's on fire, ain't it time for little Dory's feel-good shot?) and peer around the room, then roll over and sleep some more. And each time the dream would be different. Sometimes Dory herself would be the beast, hurtling along on all fours across the pine-needle-covered ground, foot-high weeds (Jesus, if my hay fever acts up, I'm gonna sneeze like a mother-fucker) slapping at her flanks, glaring hatred at Billy Ed's back while he hopped on one foot and took off his pants, beyond him her own image (hey, little Dory, whatcha doin' over there?) huddled on the blanket with her jeans pulled down to her knees. Then she'd be standing over Billy Ed with warm, sticky, sweet-tasting blood flowing down her chin, howling at the moon until it seemed her lungs would burst.

In some of her dreams she would be alone in a clearing with bright moonlight painting soft purple shadows on the ground, naked, her red hair flowing to her waist, running, breath whistling between her lips and wind roaring in her ears, her bare feet landing in wet spongy grass. Then the beast would be behind her, the monster itself, lips peeled back from huge yellowed fangs, its panting in rhythm with her own fast breath. Fear a sour bile in her mouth, she'd stop and let it catch her. In the misty dreamworld, she'd lower her chin to her chest and wait for the claws and fangs to rip her apart. But they wouldn't. Instead, the monster's warm snout would nuzzle her behind, its nose would push in between her legs. Then, panting, the beast would come around in front of her and lick at her thighs. Her fear would leave her and her body would tingle. She would be suddenly wet between her legs, shivering in anticipation. Right there in the moonlight she'd get down on all fours, the beast grunting softly as it mounted her from behind, thrusting, grinding into her, its paws tight against her sides, hunching slowly at first, then panting faster as its tempo increased. Her teeth biting hard into her lower lip, her eyes in wanton slits, she'd dig her nails into the soft earth beneath her as the air about her would be filled with her lustful, bestial moans . . .

She woke with bright sunlight streaming in through the window. The hospital bed was jacked into a half-sitting position and there was a bouquet of white and red chrysanthemums on the dresser. Who'd be sendin' *me* flowers?

Her brows knitted in puzzlement. Somehow, some way, she was different. Different in . . . She ran her hand underneath her green hospital gown and felt her stomach. It was ol' Dory all right, only . . . *Jesus Christ!* Where her stomach had been slightly puffy with a few stretch marks left over from when her daughter had been born, it was now flat as a washboard. She pressed with her fingers and felt slatted muscles under a thin layer of skin. She wasn't imagining things, either, not Dory Barnes who damn sure knew what her own round little tummy felt like, and who always made excuses not to show up in a bikini and whose eyes narrowed in jealousy every time a young flat-bellied girl strolled by. Jesus, reckon these doctors could've made a mistake, rolled ol' Dory into the operating room in the middle of the night and given her somebody else's tummy-tuck? Her belly was damn sure flat, she wasn't dreaming.

Her shoulder itched. Absently, still thinking about her tummy, she reached up, tore one corner of the bandage from her skin and probed with her fingers underneath the gauze. *Now ain't that funny? How the fuck long I been in this hospital?* The shoulder wasn't even sore, not even a little bit. Felt a little warm and tingly under her fingers, matter of fact.

At nine o'clock on Saturday morning, less than twelve hours after a doctor had used two hundred stitches to sew her up, Dory Barnes's wounds had practically healed.

4

"I didn't say you were doing a *bad* job," Dr. Jack Petty said. "Not that most kids in sixth-grade speech class couldn't do better. You ever thought about Toastmasters? If you're gonna be in the public eye, that ought to be required."

Petty was sitting on the corner of his desk at Pine Tree Clinic, located on Farm-to-Market Road No. 61 outside Tombley's Walk. Doc Petty had built the clinic out in the country in hopes of drawing business from Canton and Van and other neighboring communities, but since the new hospital had opened over in Canton, and since a couple of goddam osteopaths had set up shop in Van, Doc Petty's patients were 90 percent from his hometown. Tombley's Walk folk were loyal. They'd known Doc Petty for most of their lives, and he wouldn't dun them very hard when they were slow about paying their bills. The clinic was a neat one-story redbrick building surrounded by a paved parking lot that would accommodate fourteen normal-sized vehicles, less if there were a few supercab GMC's sitting around. There were tall pine forests on three sides of the building. Today there were only four cars in the lot except for Petty's four-door Fleetwood. During the morning a couple of patients—Hobie Farnsworth, the bookmaker, and Bert Adams, the hard-liquor bootlegger (the county was officially wet only for beer and wine)—had motored into the lot, had gotten a load of the sheriff's car nose-on to the entryway, and had turned around and made tracks back into town.

"You call bein' Tombley County sheriff in the public eye?" Buck Ainson said. "Twenty-eight years, my name's been four or five times in the newspapers. And as for TV, well, you're lookin' at the total exposure." The sheriff was seated in a recliner, ankles crossed on the footrest, drinking Coke Classic from a red can. He and Doc Petty were watching the noon edition on Channel 7 from Tyler. The TV set, a Sony 21-inch color portable, was atop a file cabinet and angled so that the picture was visible to anyone in the room. On the screen, anchorwoman Barbara Clinger was polished and at ease and black and beautiful and tall as she asked the questions, then showed sparkling white teeth to the camera as she pointed the mike in Buck Ainson's direction. Ainson stood at attention like a Marine boot, arms stiff at his sides, hat square on his head, big belly sticking out over his belt, and answered Ms. Clinger's questions in a voice that was too loud and sounded as though he were reading from prompt cards that weren't printed very clearly.

Doc Petty rubbed the face of a nine-iron with a damp towel, then held the club up to the light and squinted at the grooves. "So you got your chance to be a star and blew it. We all need to be prepared, you never know when fame is gonna come a-callin'."

The sheriff's TV interview ended abruptly—it had lasted less than forty-five seconds according to the sweep hand on Doc Petty's wall clock—and a Tide commercial popped onto the screen. Doc Petty went over to the TV and pressed a button. Two housewives who were grinning at each other over the top of a loaded washer faded instantly into gray blankness. "But I'll say one thing for you, Buck. You sure don't put much information out." He dropped the nine-iron, shaft first, into a big maroon leather golf bag, where it came to rest alongside a cluster of two-irons, four-woods, and assorted wedges and putters. It was Doc Petty's grab bag. He kept the selection on hand for use while the clubs that he broke over his knee and wrapped around tree trunks were in the repair shop. Framed on the beige walls of Petty's office were his bachelor's degree (from Stephen F. Austin University over in Nacogdoches), his medical sheepskin (from the U. of Texas at Galveston), and his state license, along with various charts showing the muscle structure of the human body, the male and female sex organs, and color three-dimensional prints of the inner and middle ear. Petty went back over to his desk and perched on its corner. "Yep, if that old wolf or whatever it is was watching TV just now, it sure don't know what leads you got."

"It's 'cause I ain't got none," Ainson said. "None. If I hadn' seen what was left o' Billy Ed for myself I'd swear that them heathens out to Jasper's had too many longnecks and amphetamines last night."

"Heathens?"

"Heathens. Blasphemers. Sinners. What else can you call 'em?"

"You on the holier-than-thou kick again? Shit, Buck, I like you better the other way." Doc Petty had a full head of iron-gray hair. He was tall and slender, and right now was wearing a blue Lily Daché golf shirt along with gray knit slacks. He was two years older than Buck Ainson, though the doc's slim waistline and the energy with which he moved made their ages appear the other way around, and then some.

Ainson peered at Doc Petty through sleepy, thick-lidded eyes. "Ain't much point in you an' me talkin' religion, Doc. You see things your way an' I see 'em mine, an' that's the way it's always been. What I'm doin' out here is tryin' to get a feel for what it is that's goin' around among these critters. I'll tell you, if you'd a-seen the damage that thing done out to Jasper's . . . well it wadn' no regular sane animal is all I can say."

"I'm afraid I *got* to see the damage," Doc Petty said. "Dory Barnes is my patient since she was little. Always behind on her bill, but she pays. You know her uncle, J.B. Wigam? He's damn sure one of those drinkin' heathens you're talkin' about, and I doubt if J.B.'s ever been to the doctor in his life. But he did call about Dory. I'm s'posed to go over to the hospital in Canton and look in on her. Tomorrow." He shot a wistful glance at the row of golf clubs. "This stuff is sure as hell raisin' my handicap. Not that tending to sick folk idn't more important."

"This is ol' Buck, Doc. I ain't one o' your patients. An' you call my *religion* a scam. I ain't here to quibble, tell me somethin' about rabies. An' don't get too technical, I'm just an ol' country boy."

Doc Petty left his desk and moved over to a small refrigerator. "There ain't nothin' really technical about it. Truth is, I don't know no more about rabies than you can read in a buck forty-nine medical journal. It's rare, it's dangerous, and I guess it's the hardest damn thing to prevent or cure there is. 'Ceptin' AIDS, and I ain't sure but what rabies is more dangerous. AIDS just kills you. Rabies turns animals an' people into things that're worse off than dead. I tell you somethin' else, too. This strain we got here is different, and that idn't for publication, Buck." He opened the freezer on the icebox, filled two squatty glasses with ice. Then he opened a cabinet, reached between bottles of pills and vials of liquid drugs, and fished out a fifth of W.L. Weller's that had about an inch of the whiskey gone. "Water or on the rocks?" he said.

Ainson held up pudgy hands, palms out. "I done told you now, I'm off that stuff. What's different about it?"

"You aren't off of anything around me," Doc Petty said. "Man wants information from Jack Petty an' won't have a drink with him? That's bullshit. Go on, Buck, I won't snitch you off to the citizens an' I will vote for your rotten ass. I could pour some in that Coke can, that way if anybody comes in they won't know what you're drinkin'. Coke sure does fuck up good whiskey, though."

Ainson eyed the bottle and licked his lips. "You ain't wantin' to talk to me lessen I have a drink?"

"No way, Jose."

"I guess I could have one for the good o' the county." Ainson held out his Coke. Doc Petty poured a good-sized slug into the can through the ring-tab hole. Ainson said, "God and Master Jesus'll understand if it's in the line o' duty." He swigged and made a face.

"God and Jesus an' old Jack Petty," the doc said. "Don't count *me* out." He took his own whiskey on the rocks, four stiff fingers over ice. He recapped the bottle, went back over to sit on the corner of his desk. He sipped. He smacked his lips. "Rabies, hell, there's a long Latin name for it, but that dudn't matter. It's a virus. Just like the flu, cold, a zillion other ailments. In the long run rabies idn't too hard to kill, but it's the short run that gets you. Say a rat, a rabid one, bites you on the toe. Idn't shit to that, we can shoot you fulla vaccine an' you'll never be sick a day. But if you get infected here"—he touched the nape of his neck—"or anyplace else along the spinal cord, then you're on your way to bein' a murderin', ravin' madman and dyin' in short order with not a damn thing anybody can do about it."

"What's the spinal cord got to do with it?" Ainson lifted his Coke, held the can at arm's length, and squinted at it. "Weller's an' Coke ain't too bad, if a man's into drinkin'."

Doc Petty lifted a gray eyebrow and cocked his head to one side. "Nerves. Nervous system. Rabies is a lot like syphilis, believe it or not. All those wiggly little germs want is entry into a man's—or dog's, Jesus Christ, less hope we don't get any human cases—nervous system, and once the little fuckers get lodged in there they're home free. Up to the point that the virus enters the spinal cord it's pretty easy to get rid of. But afterward, good luck."

Ainson took a sip from his can and licked his lips. He eyed the whiskey bottle on the counter beside the refrigerator. "You wouldn' have a little more of that, wouldja, Doc? This here's a mite on the weak side."

Petty went over and got the bottle. He was smirking. He poured another stiff belt into the sheriff's Coca-Cola can, then said, "That do ya?" Ainson took a swallow, then nodded sheepishly. Doc Petty replaced the bottle on the counter, then sat down behind his desk and folded his hands behind his head.

Ainson leaned forward and rested his forearms on his thighs, the Coke can dangling loosely between his knees. "You're talkin' a lot o' doom, but you ain't sayin' just how serious the sitchyation is. We got us an epidemic in Tombley's Walk?"

"Hard to say," Petty said. "What's an epidemic? We got five reported cases, you could call it that. These goddam animals, they go around with their noses up each other's ass and smellin' each other's shit. Not to mention fights and bites and clawin's and tics. Hell, one tic might suck three or four animals' blood 'fore it dies. Spreadin' rabies is easy. We got Old Lady Ratner's chow, the rats that jumped the cocker spaniel plus the girl gettin' bit at school, and now this mornin' we got a nature lover sayin' he saw a squirrel out in the woods, kickin' and squealin' and foamin' at the mouth. Five cases. An epidemic? Not in my book, Sheriff, but call it what you want to."

"Six," Ainson said.

"Huh?"

"Six cases. You plumb forgot about the wolf."

"What wolf?" Petty said.

"The one out to Jasper's. That wolf." Ainson stood and looked out the window, toward the pine forest and F.M. 61 beyond. "Six cases."

Petty drank some whiskey and swallowed thoughtfully. "That's great stuff. I don't know how you stand that fuckin' Coke with it. How you know it's a wolf?"

"I'm figurin' it was. I seen tracks," Ainson said.

"Okay, say it's a wolf. I didn't forget it."

"Yeah, you did. You said five cases, but you wadn' countin' the wolf."

"Your wolf or whatever it is idn't rabid, Buck," Petty said. Outside, the wind had picked up. Pine needles were blowing across the parking lot.

Ainson lifted the can to his lips and swigged. "You're confusin' me, Doc. Or this fuckin' whiskey is."

Petty grinned. "That's more like it."

"What is?"

"You said, 'fuckin'.' Sounds more like a real East Texas peace officer."

Ainson rolled his eyes. "Fergive me, Jesus. How you know this wolf ain't got no rabies?" The sheriff's cheeks were reddening slightly and his glasses had slipped down to where they rested on the small hump in his nose.

" 'Cause o' the way it happened. A rabid animal dudn't

attack anybody 'less they fuck with it. It's sick. But that thing last night, they tell me it charged right up to Billy Ed and Dory and went to bitin' and slashin'. Idn't no way that's rabies. 'Course, I'd let folks think it was if I was you. They might *really* panic if you don't."

Ainson carried the Coke can over and set it on the counter. He put ice in a glass and fixed himself a Weller's on the rocks, like Petty's. As he poured, the sheriff said, "You said somethin' earlier about this rabies bein' different. Somethin' that ain't for publication."

"Offer a man a drink he takes the bottle," Petty said. "It's the strain. The Public Health man over in Tyler talked to me about it. Buck, all these germs have got certain characteristics, it's how they identify what disease they're dealin' with. But this here rabies virus is different. These little critters wiggle just a little different under the microscope than the normal rabies bug, and . . . well, there's somethin' else. A round little sporelike apparatus. We aren't for certain what it is."

"What's that mean?" Ainson said.

Petty shrugged. "Well, it could mean it's gonna be harder to cure, we just don't know. The little girl's gonna tell us a lot. The one got bit over at the school. How she reacts to the vaccine is gonna tell us where to go from there."

"So you ain't even sure you can cure it?"

"Not dead for sure," Petty said.

"Shee-it," the sheriff said. "That makes it more desperate that I talk to this Tanner fella."

"Who?"

"New man in town. Acts kinda strange. It was him found Billy Ed's arm floppin' around out in them woods, and then he hightailed it without sayin' shit to nobody. Like he didn't want nobody talkin' to him. I need to visit with the fella, but I don't know how to find him. Got any ideas?"

Petty cocked his head. "If I was lookin' for somebody I'd try information down at the phone company. 'Course, I'm not a detective. That's your department, Sheriff."

* * *

AMY Averitt was the operator, and had been for three decades. She told Buck Ainson that "Tanner, Bud" had a listing at 453 Spruce Street. The address was two blocks from the sheriff's own house on Willow Lane. In fact, Ainson knew the house. It belonged to Justin Barker III, the banker, and Ainson had noticed just a few weeks ago that they'd taken down the FOR RENT sign. Feeling foolish, conscious of Doc Petty watching him, the sheriff dialed Tanner's number. After two rings a youthful male voice said hello, that the voice belonged to Bud Tanner but that Bud Tanner wasn't home, and asked that when the tone sounded the caller leave a message. Ainson listened to the tone, stared tongue-tied at the receiver for a few seconds, and hung up.

"You look sorta funny, Buck," Doc Petty said. "He cuss you out or somethin'?" Petty was now seated in the recliner where Ainson had lounged a few minutes ago. The sheriff was behind Petty's desk, using the phone.

"Fuckin' answerin' machine. I ain't leavin' no message with no fuckin' apparatus." Sheriff Ainson had polished off his second Weller's on the rocks. His third was by his elbow. His tongue felt a little thick. The Lord wouldn't be pleased. Hell with it, Buck Ainson was having himself a pretty good time. " 'Sides, I ain't sure it's a good idea to let this man know I'm onto him. I need to hit him when he ain't had time to get ready for me."

"Onto what?" Petty said. "I thought you were just gonna question him about what went on last night."

"Never can tell. He could wind up a suspect. Do me a favor, Doc."

"I would say, 'Name it,' " Petty said. "But you might want me to kill somebody or somethin'."

"No, I jus' . . ." Ainson took a sip of whiskey. It was cold in his mouth and warm going down. "I'm gonna be out an' about. I want to keep an eye on Tanner's place 'til he shows up, then I'm gonna ring his doorbell. I need you to call Margaret for me. Tell her I'm workin' on a case."

Petty scratched his head. "Shit, Buck. What's wrong with your dialin' finger?"

"I jus' don't want to talk to her right now. I been drinkin' a little."

"I guess I could do that much," Petty said.

"Thanks. I'm beholden. Oh, an' Doc. Listen, you got a roadie? Paper cup or somethin'? I'm takin' what's left o' this fuckin' whiskey along."

BUCK Ainson drove downtown at twenty miles an hour, holding the steering wheel in a death grip with one hand in order to keep the car from weaving. A Styrofoam cup with Weller's and ice sloshing in its bottom rode on the seat between his legs. He was being extra careful; Buck Ainson didn't need anybody to tell *him* how to drink and drive. Shit, Buck Ainson wrote the fuckin' book on the subject.

He stopped at the intersection of First Avenue and Davy Crockett Boulevard, across from the courthouse. On his left, a gang of sparrows hopped and twittered on Matthew Tombley's hat, and Ainson stared numbly while the statue got itself a hatbrim full of bird shit. Helluva way to treat the founder of this here community, Ainson thought.

Bud Tanner's house was straight ahead of him, a couple of miles out First Avenue. But the sneaky bastard probably wasn't home as yet. No way would he be. The sheriff would have to wait for no telling how long, parked in the heat of the day by Tanner's house. Fuckin' bummer is what it would be.

Ainson lifted his cup in the statue's direction, threw Matthew Tombley a toast and took a swig. "Fuck you, Matthew," the sheriff said. "An' the horse you rode in on." Then he turned right and headed south out Davy Crockett Boulevard. Five miles down the road was where Tulip Patterson lived.

5

AT noon on Saturday, at the same time Sheriff Buck Ainson was turning right on Davy Crockett Boulevard, and at the same time that Bud Tanner was worrying whether or not to tell Melody Parker a dangerous secret, Deputy Sonny Beamer was in a second-floor garage apartment on the north side of Tombley's Walk. Deputy Beamer was in the process of banging Deputy Terry Hackney's old lady, June. June Hackney was one of the better pieces of ass in the county, and well worth the risk so long as her baby didn't wake up in its crib and go to bawling, and so long as Sonny could keep one corner of the pillow stuffed in her mouth so that her yelps of passion didn't bring the neighbors running.

Spent, Sonny lay on top of June and waited for his breathing to slow. Her flesh was damp and slippery with sweat. He raised his head and looked around the room, at the wooden rocker in the corner, at the dirty white knitted shawl draped over the side of the crib, at the black General Electric oscillating fan moving slowly from left to right as it blew warm air. "Jesus Christ, it's a hot bitch in here. Lemme up, darlin'."

June giggled. She scissored his body with her legs and locked her ankles on top of his buttocks. Her big soft breasts slithered against him. "Not 'til you say it, lover."

"Come on, now. I mean it. It's hot enough to suffocate somebody."

"I mean it, too, Sonny. You saidja would."

"It's too damn silly. We ain't little kids."

She scootched her bottom downward on the damp rumpled sheets and squeezed him tighter with her legs. "You didn' think it was so silly when you was runnin' around with a boner up, wantin' to screw. It's time to pay up."

He sighed and glanced through the parted window drapes—the drapes were beige with streaks of grime mixed in and a couple of rips in the seams—across the fifty feet or so that separated the garage from the main house. The shingles on the main house's roof were baking; rising heat made little ripples in the air. "Okay," Sonny said. "Sure, iffen it turns you on."

"Say it like you really mean it, now." She opened her green eyes wide and looked expectant. Thick waves of ebony hair were spread out on both sides of her face on the pillow. There were drops of perspiration on her nose.

Sonny showed her his version of a tender smile. "You're the *best*, baby. Just the thought of you sets my knees to shakin'."

"Tremblin'. *Tremblin'*, you dumbass! An' you don't sound nothin' like the guy on *Days of Our Lives*, neither." She pursed her lips into a pouty bow.

"Jesus Christ. Lemme up, huh?" Sonny said.

She gave him a final squeeze with her legs and released him. Her feet now flat on the mattress, her knees parted and bent, she said, "You ain't no fun."

Sonny wriggled over to the side of the bed and stood up on the dusty hardwood floor. He walked naked over to the window, the breeze from the fan cooling his sweaty shoulders. He glanced down at the crib as he passed. Little Terry Jr. was asleep on his tummy, wearing puffy plastic pants over cloth diapers. His doll-like thumb was inches from his mouth and there were little red heat-bumps on his back.

Sonny's mirrored sunglasses lay on the windowsill. He put them on, leaned both hands on the sill and crossed his ankles. His brown '78 Pinto was parked between the main house and the garage, out of sight from the street. A gray splintery wood fence enclosed the backyard. The yard was strewn with wadded paper bags, a couple of dusty worn-out tires, two or three broken bottles. "You need to clean up that shit down there, Junie,'' Sonny said. ''Yore kid's gonna be crawlin' around that yard 'fore you know it.''

The sheets rustled behind him. ''Tell Terry about it,'' June said. ''He don't clean up nothin'.''

Sonny's jaws clenched. June was one of the wonders of the world in bed; she was also one of the dumbest fucking women he'd ever seen. ''So what do you think?'' he said. ''I'll just go up an' say, 'Hey, Terry, I was up there screwin' Junie the other day, an' I seen a lotta junk in your yard.' Hell, what time is it, anyway? I got to be at work pretty soon.''

''That's a good thing about havin' you for a lover,'' June said. ''My hubby can't come home 'til you spell him on the job. 'Course I don't know what Terry'd *do* about it, even iffen he caughtcha up here. The dork.''

Sonny pressed his lips together. Jesus, what a cold bitch. He pictured Terry Hackney, short, chubby, can-I-hep-ya Terry, running around out at Jasper's with a pad and pen asking questions. Every time the sheriff had told Terry that he was doing a good job—it didn't matter how *dumb* Terry's job happened to be—then Sonny would have sworn that if Terry had been a pup his tail would've been wagging. All of a sudden, Sonny didn't feel so hot about himself. Felt about one inch high.

''Ain't neither,'' Sonny said. ''Terry ain't no dork.''

''Is too. Ain't so much not a dork that you're afraid to visit his woman, darlin'.''

Which reminded Sonny just how nervous he'd felt lately about coming over here at all. Terry was working, sure, but no telling when he might take a notion to goof off for an hour or so and come by his own house. Hell, Sonny himself fucked off for a while just about every day when he was on duty.

''I ain't *afraid* to visit his woman,'' Sonny said. ''But I won't be visitin' her no more, either.'' He went over to the rocker and picked up his Jockey undershorts, then hopped on one foot as he stepped into them. The baby stirred in his crib and made a little sleepy sound.

''Who you foolin'?'' June rolled onto her belly and blew two smacky kisses in Sonny's direction. ''You'll be back,'' she said. "Next time you're drivin' around with a boner up."

Sonny couldn't believe her. Only somebody he'd ever met who absolutely didn't give a shit for anybody but herself. Not her husband, not her mother and daddy. Not even her own youngun over there in the crib, though she did try to make a big show out of chucking Terry Jr. under the chin and trying to get him to say something. Hell, the kid wasn't but seven months old, what'd she expect him to say?

He put on his shirt and buttoned it. It was tan, summerweight, shortsleeve, with the Tombley County shield stitched in gold thread on one sleeve. "Ain't no point in arguin' with you, Junie," he said. "But I won't be back, you can count on that. I'm jus' hopin' nobody finds out how dumb I been or how I ain't been able to control myself. Not Terry, anyway. An' sure not Sheriff Ainson, he'd fire my ass in a minute."

She turned over and sat up, her belly flat, her waist tiny, her big pink nipples jutting out, her hands spread out behind her, flat on the mattress. "The *sheriff?* Why, Buck Ainson'd like to have some of it hisself. Who you tryin' to kid?"

He averted his gaze from her. Jesus, that body. He picked up one boot, then the other, sat down in the rocker to put them on. "Well, maybe he would," Sonny said. "An' he's damn sure welcome to *my* portion of it, from now on." He stood to press one foot into place inside his boot.

June crossed her ankles and jiggled one foot. "Go on, then. See'f I care. You know somethin', Sonny? I got awful tired o' you anyhow. You ain't no good lover. You ain't no conversation. You're a dork, too, jus' like my old man. Dork, dork, dork, you hear me?"

"Yeah, Junie, I hear you." Dressed in his uniform now, Sonny picked up his hat from the dresser. "I hear you, but I ain't listenin'. What you say don't matter. Nothin' that you *do* matters. I'm goin'." He went over to the door and opened it.

June rose up on her haunches. "You *dork*. Wimp. Faggot! Sonny No-balls!" She grabbed a pillow and heaved it.

Sonny stepped out on the landing and closed the door. The pillow thudded against the wood from inside. Sonny expelled a breath and started downstairs. Jesus, but he was glad to get away from that . . . He had to get away from there. *Had* to.

He descended, touching the rickety handrail every couple of feet and steadying himself with the other hand against the adjacent garage wall. The fresh hot air didn't do much to take the smell of Junie out of his nostrils. She was all over him, her heavy perfume, the musky scent of the sweat between her breasts. His stomach was churning. How was he *ever* going to get rid of this sick feeling? Hell, he had to see Terry every day and watch the pudgy deputy's eyes light up whenever he talked about his Junie-pie. Sonny felt as low as a cur right now, every bit as low as the mangy yellow mongrel stray who was squatting at the bottom of the steps taking a dump.

The dog was relieving itself all right, relieving itself of a big watery load and blocking Sonny's descent to the ground. It had a broad flat head and droopy ears, one of which had been chewed into a rolled-up piece of leather. Its eyes were bloodshot roadmaps and were oozing yellow matter, and the dog was looking—no, *glaring*—at Sonny with a dull stupid grin on its face. There were globs of foamy spittle falling from its lower jaw and plopping on the ground.

Sonny's breath caught. He moved over on the steps and flattened against the garage wall. He'd never in his life seen a mad dog, had only heard about them, but this crazy-looking mongrel stopping right here in the open to take itself a shit wasn't normal. Damn sure wasn't normal at all. The dog wasn't acting the way it should have: when Sonny had approached it the cur should have either tucked its tail between its legs and run or come forward and tried to lick his hand. But it had done neither. And— Shit, Sonny thought as a cold shudder ran through him—those stupid eyes weren't focusing.

The dog growled from deep within its chest and bared

its teeth. Sonny had seen the expression before, the dull, stupid glare, and it took a second for it to dawn on him where. The same expression had been on the goddam *rat's* face, the same murder-bent rat who'd kept on snapping at him even as the shovel had split its head open. The dog's growling was interspersed with whines. The dripping foam had dried the fur on its neck and chin into a matted tangle.

Mad dog. That's what it was, all right. Showed every sign that Sonny had ever heard of, and there was nothing for Sonny to do but shoot the poor fucker. If it turned out later that the dog wasn't rabid, well, Sonny could feel badly about that, but that was a damn sight better than standing here and letting it bite him. He *had* to shoot it. Just reach down at his side and pull out his gun.

Only his gun, his goddam .38 longnose Colt revolver, was locked up in his glove compartment. Right over there in the driveway, not thirty steps away, thirty steps that may as well have been thirty miles.

Slowly, carefully, his gaze never leaving the dog and those mad stupid eyes, Sonny backed upstairs.

The dog followed. Its growl became a vicious snarl as it left the pile of watery droppings at the foot of the stairs and began to climb, one hesitant step at a time.

One bite is all it takes, Sonny thought. Just one fucking bite.

The mongrel kept its head low, its tail drooping and brushing each step as it climbed. It moved with a side-canted, shuffling gait. Suddenly it gathered its hindquarters as if to spring; Sonny lurched and flailed his arms for balance. The dog's hind foot slipped off the step, and Sonny relaxed momentarily as it whined and scrabbled for purchase. Fall, Sonny thought. Roll down them steps and break your fucking neck. Go on, *fall.* Right down those fucking . . .

The mongrel regained its balance, whined, and began to come at him again.

Sonny's foot reached behind him for another ascending step. The step wasn't there; he stumbled and almost went over backwards as his foot came down on empty air. He was on the landing outside June's apartment. The dog was two steps below him, its snout still wrinkled into a hateful grin. The back of Sonny's neck was cool and clammy and his hands were trembling.

Flinching, expecting the dog to be at him any second, Sonny reached out and knocked. "Junie?" he said.

The dog snarled louder. It climbed up on the landing, its savage head on a level with Sonny's belt. It raised its stupid gaze to meet his, and it knew. Goddam it, it *knew.* This mad dog wasn't supposed to know anything, but this one knew that it had old Sonny trapped up here, trapped and helpless, and it knew that it could take its time about tearing his throat out. This crazy-as-a-loon monster of a junkyard dog *knew.*

"Junie? Junie. Open that door," Sonny said.

From inside, muffled by the door: "Go fuck yourself."

"I ain't kidding. Open it right now."

Its dripping snout less than a yard from Sonny's crotch, the cur gathered itself.

The door opened, and June said, "Goddam it, I *told* you to—"

Snarling, the dog plunged into Sonny's midsection. It twisted; its teeth dug into Sonny's arm *(Oh God fucking damn, it's bit me!)* as he stumbled backwards into the apartment. Still naked, June screamed, went down on the floor, and doubled up into a fetal ball.

Sonny fell. The dog raged over him, snarling and tearing. There was sudden pain in Sonny's shoulder as he landed on hardwood, but he hardly noticed. Big clawed paws planted themselves on his chest. Sonny's upper arm was clenched in the monster jaws; the dog shook its head from side to side as its teeth ripped flesh and tendon and muscle. Somewhere in the mongrel's ancestry a bulldog doubtless lurked, and it was the bulldog instinct within the beast that saved Sonny's life. Most breeds gone mad would have torn at Sonny's jugular, but this cur sunk its teeth into the arm and hung on. It was a lifesaving break, but one that Sonny didn't notice any more than he noticed the pain in his shoulder; he was terrified, and all that he knew was that he wanted the fuck out of there.

Visible in the periphery of Sonny's vision, June got up

and moved. Her lips parted in fear, she skirted fallen man and raging dog and made tracks for the safety of the bathroom. "God, Sonny, don't let it *get me,*" she said.

Through the pain and fear a third emotion built within Sonny Beamer. Anger. Anger at this dumb brute of a dog who had to pick the exact moment of Sonny's descent down the stairs to take a crap. Ten minutes earlier or ten later, he would have been all right. Hell of a title for a horror picture, Sonny thought with an ironic giggle. *Crap and Kill.*

Besides anger at the dog there was anger at June (goddam her rotten ass) for luring him over here to begin with. Luring him over here to catch a dose, not of anything so simple as the clap, but of fucking *rabies.* Rabid people died just like rabid dogs, snarling and snapping and foaming at the mouth. Well, by God Sonny might have rabies and by God he might be going to die, but this mangy brute was going right along with him. His adrenaline fueled, Sonny Beamer began to fight.

He reached across his body with his free hand, grabbed the dog by the throat and squeezed. The dog ground its teeth harder into Sonny's arm. The teeth found a nerve; a bolt of pain ran like fire from Sonny's upper arm to the nape of his neck. Sonny shut his eyes tightly and for a split second saw stars and thought he was going to faint. Then the mist cleared from his gaze. He squeezed the dog's neck harder. His thumb found gristly windpipe and jammed against it. Take *that,* you fucker. The dog's teeth loosened their grip and, encouraged, Sonny kicked and rolled. Suddenly the mongrel was beneath him, squirming, thrusting against him with its paws, choking, wheezing. Sonny's left arm was useless; torn and bleeding it flopped around at his side. The dog wriggled furiously, found its footing and scrambled away. Sonny climbed to his feet, panting, touched his own wounded arm, winced. Its sides heaving, its tongue lolling and dripping foam, the dog circled him. For long seconds man and beast stalked one another like middleweights.

Sonny glanced down at his arm and resisted a strong impulse to gag. The wound was jagged and deep. Through the rip in his shirt sleeve, gray fatty tissue and oozing drops of blood were visible. Some nerves were severed; instead of shooting pain there was a dull, throbbing numbness. Jesus, he was going to lose the arm. They might get rid of the rabies if he could get to the doctor in time, but that fucking arm was . . .

Terry Hackney Jr. picked that exact moment to raise up in his crib and begin to scream at the top of his seven-month-old lungs. Chubby hands clutching the crib's rail, his little eyes squinched tightly together and tears rolling down his fat red cheeks, he blubbered and wailed.

The dog cringed and shied away from the noise in the crib at first, then it paused and snarled anew. It turned. The baby's cries were deafening. The dog's bloodshot eyes narrowed. As though Sonny Beamer had ceased to exist, as though Sonny wasn't even standing there with his arm shredded to ribbons, the beast crouched low and stalked toward the crib. It was growling. Its head was lowered. Its teeth were bared.

From the open bathroom doorway, June screamed, "God, my baby. My *bayyy*-by. You stop him, Sonny. I swear I'll kill you if you don't." Her gaze was frozen on the slowly advancing cur.

At that moment Sonny could have run, could have made his getaway, and later was to wish that he had. But there was the wailing infant in the crib, the crouched, snarling dog, June Hackney naked in the doorway. Gritting his teeth against the ache in his arm, Sonny moved. He charged past the dog, not daring to look at the beast, snatched the baby from its crib and dived headlong into the bathroom. "Now will you close the fucking door?" he yelled.

June slammed the door a split second before the dog rammed it full force. Hinges creaked, but the door held. Outside the bathroom, the dog snarled and charged again. *Bam!* The door shuddered, but held once more. In a few seconds there was a whining sound from the crack underneath the door, and the noise of the dog's fast panting.

Conscious of the heat and the pain in his arm, Sonny stumbled over to the window while June scooped little

Terry up and hugged him to her bare body. The bathroom window was open. Sonny peered down toward the main house. There was an old woman standing in the backyard, a stooped old woman wearing a shapeless print dress, her arms folded in front of her and her face upturned to the window.

The old woman cupped her hands at her mouth. "You folks all right up there? I seen that dog. I done called the *po*-lice, they'll be here soon. Don't y'all fret none."

At that moment the tan county deputy's Plymouth rolled into the gravel driveway and parked nose-on to Sonny's Pinto. Terry Hackney climbed out. He walked to Sonny's Pinto and looked it over. Then he raised his gaze to the window. His lips parted; his jaws opened in shock.

Sonny leaned his forehead against the windowsill and shut his eyes. He'd forgotten the mad dog. He'd forgotten everything except Terry Hackney. Everything except that Terry Hackney's .45 revolver was holstered at his side, and that Sonny's own gun was still down there in the Pinto, resting in the glove compartment.

6

BUD Tanner arrived at his rented house at five in the afternoon, still nervous, not satisfied that he'd told Melody Parker what he should have. What he'd told her was closer to the truth than the nonsense about being a fiction writer (But my life has become a series of made-up stories, Bud thought, why *don't* I put a few of them down on paper?), but it still wasn't the *whole* truth, and telling the real story to someone was something that he was bursting inside to do. Someday soon he was going to spill it all. And when that happened, they would come and take him away. It was inevitable.

He let himself in by the side door. In the few weeks that he'd lived (stayed? existed?) in this house he'd been through the front entrance only once, on the day that the man from the bank had showed it to him. Ever since then, Bud had come and gone by the side entry as though its use would make him less visible to the neighbors. Fat chance. In a town like Tombley's Walk, nobody was invisible. In a small town no one could make a move without someone else recording it—Bud had learned that in his travels. In the future he was going to have to stick to the big cities, much as he hated city life. People who came to a small town, paid their rents in cash, and tried to keep to themselves were just asking for trouble.

He went through the kitchen, passed on through the living room. The man from the bank had been apologetic about the amount of furniture in the house, and had assured Bud that there were more tables and chairs, and maybe even a nightstand or two, available at a moment's notice. Bud couldn't have cared less about the furniture. There was an icebox in the kitchen and a table where he could sit and eat, and an old sofa and a couple of chairs in the living room. Bud wasn't going to have any company, and by himself he couldn't sit but one place at a time. In fact, the only thing in the house that had really caught Bud's interest was the locking trunk in the bedroom, at the foot of the creaky old bed. He'd been careful not to make over the trunk too much when the banker had shown the house. Too much interest would have raised the banker's curiosity, and that would have been something that Bud couldn't have afforded. He'd pretended that it was only in passing that he'd asked about the key to the trunk. By that time the banker had had Bud's money in his hand, in hundred-dollar bills, and had barely seemed to notice the question about the key. Yes, there'd been a key, and Bud had dropped by the banker's office the following morning and picked it up from the secretary.

It was to the trunk that Bud went now. As he entered the bedroom he glanced nervously around him, another habit he'd developed while on the run. He always felt as though someone was watching. The feeling never went away; it was even stronger when he was alone than when he was in a crowd.

The rumpled sheets on the bed needed washing. Bud felt guilty about that; in his former life he'd been such a stickler for cleanliness that Beth had once given him a feather duster as a gag birthday present. Now he knelt before the trunk, in an oblong of light formed by the sun's rays streaming in through the dusty windowpane, fumbled with keys, inserted one in the lock, turned the key. The rusty lock squealed in protest. The latch clicked, and Bud raised the lid.

He'd carried the cash with him for so long now that the sight of it no longer made him jumpy. Early on, in the first weeks after he'd left California, the very thought of the stack of money had dried his throat, had conjured up images of masked men with guns stalking him in the twilight. He was still *nervous* about the money—the trumped-up corporation that he'd asked Melody Parker to form was for the purposes of opening a bank account in some name, any name, other than his own—but at least now he could gaze upon the stacks of bundled hundred-dollar bills without breaking out in a cold sweat. Anyone seeing this pile of cash, and knowing that Bud was a man on the run, would naturally jump to the conclusion that he was a bank robber or embezzler. That it was his own money—his own, hard-earned, nose-to-the-grindstone wealth that he'd carefully taken out of the bank a chunk at the time in preparation for his flight—would come as a surprise to them.

How much of the money was left? He hadn't counted it in a couple of months; there'd been over six hundred thousand dollars there the last time he'd taken a tally. Doesn't matter, he thought, there's still plenty to live on for a long time. To live for a whole lot longer than I'm going to stay a free man.

He counted out five hundred dollars, folded the bills and put them in his pocket. Habit. Five hundred dollars was the figure that had lodged itself in his mind somewhere along the way, and each time he ran out of pocket money, five hundred dollars more came out of the trunk. Bud had always been a man of habit. In his office, back when his chain of taco stands had dotted the southern half of the California coast (Bud wondered briefly whether the stands were still in business; he didn't have the slightest idea), he'd kept exactly six pencils in a brown mug on his desk. If a stray pencil turned up in the mug, he'd throw it away. If one disappeared, then he'd stop whatever he was doing, go to the supply room, and get a replacement. Six pencils. Five hundred dollars. It would be a small thing like that which would trip him up someday. A small thing like the pile of receipts that now lay in one corner of the trunk, underneath the stack of money. He dug out the receipts and went through them.

His accountant had trained him, had actually bludgeoned the lesson home during a particularly nasty I.R.S. audit a few years back, to never throw a receipt away. Anytime that Bud paid out money he asked for a receipt, and the receipt went safely into his wallet. When he got home—or, more recently, to the place where he was laying his head down for the night—the receipts went into a neat stack. He still had them. If he'd had to, he could have accounted for almost every dime he'd spent since leaving California. He knew that keeping the receipts was dumb; he just couldn't seem to break the habit.

The ticket from the Ramada Inn in Phoenix was made out to Bud Carson. The American Airlines ticket from Phoenix to Denver was in the name of Bud Taylor. There were more receipts, at least a hundred in all, and as he leafed through them he counted fourteen different last names that he'd used. He had to get rid of the receipts. He thought about these damning little pieces of paper every day, and every day he reached the same decision: throw them away. Then the next time he paid out money he'd ask for another receipt. Habit. Habit. Habit was going to do him in. As he stood in the bedroom, receipts in hand, someone knocked heavily on the front door. Three loud knocks, then silence.

He froze, still as a statue for a moment. Then the sharp, heavy pounding on the door resumed, louder this time, more persistent. Bud dropped the stack of receipts back into its hiding place, slammed the trunk lid, closed the padlock. There was more knocking. His throat constricting, Bud went through the living room and peered out through the drapes.

He wasn't surprised that it was the police. He'd been expecting them, had known all along that someday they'd come. The lawman on the front porch was an older man, paunchy, wearing a tan uniform with a shield outlined in gold thread on the short sleeve of the shirt, just below the shoulder. He wasn't wearing a gun. Bud had expected a gun. Likely there was a backup out there somewhere, either hiding behind the old Chevvy or perched overhead on the roof. At least, that's the way they'd always done it in the movies or on TV. Bud sighed, took a deep breath, walked what he assumed to be his last five steps of freedom, and opened the front door. He said, "What can I do for you?"

The cop had been drinking. He was slightly unsteady

on his feet, and a whiff of bourbon-breath hit Bud's nostrils. The cop's hat was tilted at an unruly angle. He said, "Mr. Tanner?"

At least the cop didn't have Bud's real last name. Or maybe he did, and was just covering up. "Yes, sir, that's me." He did his best to appear nonchalant.

"Mr. Tanner, I'm Buck Ainson." Ainson's East Texas drawl was only slightly slurred, the speech of a man who had possibly been on a toot, hadn't had a drink for an hour or so, and was beginning to sober up. "Folks around here elected me sheriff, and I got a duty to sit and visit with you a spell. Mind if I come in?"

The tightness in Bud's throat was still there, but he was beginning to feel better. Bud held the door open wide and stepped back. "Sure, come in. I don't have much furniture in here, but there are a couple of chairs."

"Just a place for me to set my backside," Ainson said, coming into the living room, looking around, removing his hat. He was practically bald on top, just a few strands of hair combed straight back from his forehead. His pudgy face was tanned; his forehead and scalp were pasty white. He went over, sat down in a padded rocking chair. He wore scarred boots. "Had a bit of excitement last night, out to Jasper's." It was a statement and not a question. Ainson put his hat in his lap and tilted back in the rocker.

Bud moved over to the old sofa and sat facing the sheriff, hoping against hope that the business last night was all that the lawman wanted to talk about. "I was there," Tanner said.

"So they tell me. I got to say, Mr. Tanner, that what you done was peculiar. Least it *seems* peculiar, to folks around here." Ainson wasn't as drunk as he'd appeared when he'd been on the porch. His breath was enough to knock one over, but his gaze was steady enough.

"Oh?" Bud said. "How's that?"

"Well, durn. You found them folks down there in the woods, you an' Rog Hornby. 'Pears you would have wanted to stick around an' give your version of what happened out there. I been havin' to hunt all over town just to talk to you." His gaze swept Bud from head to toe. "You're a Californian, ain't you?"

The lump that had been receding from Bud's throat rose up suddenly. "California?" he said. "I've lived there. How did you know?"

"Doggone, I knew it," Ainson said. "That's somethin' I sorta pride myself on, bein' able to spot where a fella comes from. It's the way you talk, Mr. Tanner. California folks talk the King's English better'n anybody from anyplace. New Yorkers and Chicagoans we can't hardly understand down here. We get folks through here from time to time, an' I went to a school out in Los Angeles"—Ainson pronounced the city's name "Los Angle-ease"—"a few years back. A sheriff's seminar, the F.B.I. put it on. You talk just like the fella that was teachin' us out there. You figure on settlin' in Tombley's Walk?"

Bud gave the stock answer, the one he'd programmed himself to give. "No," he said. "I'm working on a book, just long enough for this research I'm doing. Probably the rest of the summer, maybe on into the fall. It depends."

"Now, that's interestin'," Ainson said. "What is it in our little city that anybody'd want to write a book about?"

"Well, it's not . . . " Bud paused, felt his own gaze wavering, then forced himself to look the sheriff straight in the eye. Bud said, "It's not anything that's *happened* here. It's the locale. I'm doing a novel set in East Texas. Tombley's Walk is a typical town, and for me to set the novel realistically I need a general feeling. What the people around here are like and whatnot."

Ainson chuckled, a short dry laugh. He said, "I ain't a man of books. The Good Book, I know a lot about that, but them books they sell down to the drugstore, the ones with them women in their underwear on the cover, I don't cotton to. That the kind of books you write?"

"I'm not a cover artist, Sheriff. I'm just a writer." Bud was glad that the lawman wasn't a reader, a reader would be harder to feed a line of bullshit. Bud said, "I made a mistake last night. You're right, I shouldn't have left the scene."

"That's puttin' it mildly, son. Yore memory ain't going

to be as fresh today, and runnin' off like that makes a body wonder if you got somethin' to hide. We got a statement from Rog Hornby. You want to give me one, too? So's we can account for any diffrences in what you an' Rog remember seein'?"

"I can tell you what I saw," Bud said. "Right now if you like."

Ainson picked up his hat and polished his badge on his sleeve. "It'll do for starters. 'Course, what you tell me now ain't gonna be official. I'll need to get you down to my office so's we can get a court reporter to write out a statement for you to sign. I think I can scare up a reporter on Monday mornin'. Any problem with that? I wouldn't want to put you out none." The sheriff's tone said that he didn't really care whether he was putting Bud out any or not.

Bud's mouth was suddenly dry. Signed official statements meant more checking into his background. More tightening of the noose. He swallowed. "Whatever you like. There's not that much to tell. I went into the woods with Mr. Hornby, I stumbled over what I first thought was a branch, and it turned out to be somebody's arm. Not a very pleasant experience."

The sheriff bent forward from the waist, holding his hat in both hands. "I 'magine it'd shake somebody up. Tell you the truth, Mr. Tanner, I 'spect it'd be better for you to take the weekend gettin' your thoughts in order. You can come to see me on Monday around nine in the mornin'. What you tell me here I might not remember myself." There was a round damp spot on the chair's cushion where the sheriff's head had been resting. Ainson said, almost casually, "Jus' where in California is it you hail from?"

Bud said quickly, "Santa Monica." It was the first town which had popped into his mind. "On the coast, just west of L.A."

"You got people out there?" Ainson said.

"None. None left. My folks are dead, I didn't have any brothers or sisters."

"What about friends? It ain't no big deal, Mr. Tanner,

jus' somebody that can vouch for you. Standard procedure, when we're doin' an investigation into a killin'."

"Well, why would you need that? You're not doing a murder investigation." Bud heard his own voice raise an octave. He tried to speak calmly, but couldn't quite manage it.

"Nope." The corners of Ainson's mouth turned skeptically upward. "Not at present, but it could lead to somethin' like that. One thing leads to another. You sayin' there ain't nobody in your hometown can vouch for you?"

"No, there's . . . yeah, a lot of people. Give me 'til Monday, I'll bring you a list."

Ainson licked his lips, started to say something. Suddenly there was a high-pitched beeping sound. Bud jumped in his seat on the sofa. In the stillness of the room the sound was shocking. Ainson reached around, took a small electronic beeper from his belt, pressed a button. The noise stopped immediately. "I got a call," the sheriff said. "There a phone here?"

Bud expelled air from between his lips. "In the bedroom."

Bud followed the sheriff's round, shuffling form into the bedroom. The lawman stopped by the bed and glanced around, his gaze lingering on the padlocked trunk. Bud held his breath. His mind raced. The lawman was about to ask about that damned trunk, the one with all the money and those damning receipts inside. The sheriff licked his lips, looked back over his shoulder. "You're travelin' light, Mr. Tanner," he said. He moved on around the bed toward the telephone.

The white princess phone was on the floor on one side of the bed, beside Bud's answering machine. Ainson picked up the phone, sat heavily on the edge of the bed and punched in a number. He held the receiver to his ear and watched Bud. Finally the sheriff said into the mouthpiece, "My beeper went off, Amy. Who's huntin' me?"

Bud leaned against the doorjamb, hooked his thumbs into his pants pockets. Now the sheriff said, "Moses. Where they takin' him to?" Then, after a pause, "I'm on my way. Yeah. Tell 'em I'm comin'." Ainson hung up, regarded Bud, then licked his lips. "As if I ain't got enough to do. One o' my deputies. He's got hisself shot, some way and they're sayin' one o' my other deputies done the shootin." He rose. "I got to be goin'. I ain't got enough staff as it is, and now I got this a-happ'nin'."

"Anything I can do?" Bud said.

"Yessir, there is," Ainson said. "You can get your think-tank to workin', so's I can get a good statement from you Monday. Don't matter what-all else I got to do, I'm gonna make time for you. You think real hard, Mr. Tanner."

THE visit from the sheriff had made up Bud's mind, once and for all. This country lawman wasn't going to stop at taking a statement, that was obvious. He was going to probe. That sheriff was going to find out all there was to know about a man called Bud Tanner; in fact, the sheriff's inquiries were probably already going out over the wires. Which left Bud only one choice, to disappear over the hill. Whatever horror was going on in Tombley's Walk was none of Bud's affair. Besides, the truth was that he didn't know anything the sheriff couldn't get from Rog Hornby. As soon as the sheriff's car had disappeared around the corner, Bud went back into the bedroom and began to pack.

His luggage consisted of two zip-up American Airlines tote bags, one for his wardrobe—four knit Polo shirts, two pair of jeans besides the slacks he was wearing, some white Reebok low-quarter sneakers—and the other for the money. His vehicle, the red Toyota pickup he'd bought for cash in Dallas and registered under the name of Bud DiAngelo, would have to go. That wouldn't be any problem. He'd found in his travels that used-car lots, cash in hand, would put whatever name on the title that he told them to and not even ask for identification. He'd opened one of the tote bags on the bed, folded and dropped two of his shirts inside, when the phone began to ring.

He paused, shirtless, his chest rising and falling. His Radio Shack answering machine—another thing which he considered a necessity; using the machine he could sort through messages and return only the calls he wanted to—

was programmed to cut in with his recorded message after the fourth ring. The problem was that he'd never been able to let the machine do what he'd intended it for; he was one of those people who simply couldn't ignore a ringing phone. Another habit that was likely to do him in. He sat down on the bed, picked up the receiver and hesitantly said, "Hello?"

A cultured female voice with just a hint of East Texas twang said over the line, "This is Melody Parker. I've been thinking about our talk. Look, I'm still not sure whether I should get involved in this, but I've done some research. Maybe we ought to kick around your corporation idea some more."

Bud shifted his weight. The bedsprings creaked. This girl was using the corporation business as an excuse to call. There wasn't anything he could tell her that they hadn't already gone over that afternoon at Denny's, and he hadn't mistaken the looks she'd given him as they'd sat across from one another in the booth. Or the stirrings he'd felt himself. It had been a long time. He pictured her. Small, almost tiny, firm of chin and set of purpose. Beth had been a much bigger woman. Into the phone, Bud said, "What did you have in mind?"

"Well, I . . ." She paused for a couple of heartbeats, then continued. "I've got a full schedule next week, so I thought maybe tonight."

Bud eyed the open tote bag. He was pretty sure that whatever the sheriff was going to do wouldn't begin until Monday. "On Saturday night?" Bud said.

Melody laughed. Bud liked the way she laughed, a pretty tinkling sound. She said, "You're in Tombley's Walk, sir, right next door to Monkeyjump, Egypt. Saturday night's a little livelier than, say, Tuesday night. On Saturday night sometimes the wild crowd down on the square doesn't break up 'til after dark." Her tone softened. "We could have dinner."

Bud leaned back on one elbow. He shouldn't do this. The sooner he could be gone from this town the better. He said, "At the Dairy Queen?"

"I'll have you know I cook a mean asparagus casserole,'' Melody said. ''At least nobody's ever choked on it, and it sure beats a greasy hamburger and a dipped cone.''

''At your house?'' he said.

''Well, I can't cook it in the middle of Davy Crockett Boulevard,'' she said.

Bud gazed out the window. The sun was setting, its rays highlighting the dust particles on the glass. He needed female company. Wherever she was right now, Beth would want him to know other women. Beth was like that.

''Where is it? And what time? I'm at your beck and call, Miss Parker.''

7

THE drive over to Canton sobered Buck Ainson up. Sobered him up and sent his spirits into a tailspin. The Lord moved in mysterious ways, and what had happened to Sonny Beamer was likely an omen. A warning to Buck Ainson that if he didn't mend his ways, something terrible was going to happen to him. The afternoon at Tulip Patterson's had been a giant step on the road to Hades, and if Buck Ainson didn't watch his step he'd plunge into hellfire right along with Sonny Beamer and the rest of his kind. Right down in the flames with Rog Hornby and Dory Barnes and the rest of them beer-guzzlers. And Doc Petty too, it was the doc who had steered Buck Ainson away from the straight and narrow. Heathen blasphemers, one and all.

He stopped in a 7-Eleven on the outskirts of Canton and bought a package of peppermint Certs. From the way that the Tanner fella had wrinkled his nose when he'd stood close to the sheriff, Ainson supposed that there was a spot of liquor on his breath. Wouldn't do for a servant of the Lord who was into upholding the law. By the time Ainson wheeled into the hospital parking lot, half of the mints were gone from the package.

The hospital was a tan brick one-story building—four connecting wings with a courtyard in the center—supporting a peaked roof of red Spanish tile. It was on the north side of Canton, the end of town nearest to Tombley's Walk, and had been built in that location, Doc Petty claimed, for the express purpose of luring Petty's business away. A circular drive led from the street to the hospital entrance. The drive enclosed an island of clipped and manicured Bermuda grass, which in turn surrounded a metal flagpole that waved Old Glory thirty feet high in the air. Paved tributaries led from both sides of the drive to adjoining parking lots. A big white sign at the front of one of the parking lots showed an arrow pointing to the emergency entrance at the back of the building. Ainson braked, studied the sign for a moment, then drove on ahead to the main hospital entryway. He parked, got out, and climbed the steps. Just before he went inside he blew into his cupped hands and sniffed his own breath. He smelled only peppermint.

Four steps inside the hospital he wished he'd used the emergency entrance. On a padded bench in the corridor just beyond the reception desk sat Eleanor Beamer and Margaret Ainson. Eleanor, a tall, thin, hatchet-faced woman with iron-gray hair done in old-timey, pinned-up braids, was crying. As Ainson approached the reception desk, she blew her nose into a tissue with a loud, irritating honk. Margaret Ainson had her arm around Eleanor's shoulders and was cooing sympathetically into Eleanor's ear. Neither woman had spotted the sheriff as yet, and he'd just as soon they didn't see him at all. The Certs would hide the smell of liquor from any normal person, but Margaret had a nose like a coon dog. Ainson turned on his heel and took one long stride back in the direction from which he'd come.

From behind him, the nurse at the reception desk said loudly, "Sheriff. Sheriff Ainson, we got one of your deputies in here."

Ainson stopped, his shoulders sagging. He turned. "Yes'm," he said. "That's what I'm a-checkin' on." At the sound of the nurse's voice, Margaret's head had turned. She was now looking directly at her husband, and recognition was spreading across her face. Ainson mentally crossed his fingers and popped another mint into his mouth.

The nurse was a round-faced blond in her twenties, wearing a starched white uniform. A white peaked nurse's hat was perched atop her sprayed hair. "It's Sonny Beamer," she said. "He's not in real good shape, I'm afraid to say."

"What's Deputy Beamer's sitchyation?" Buck Ainson said officially.

"A dog attack," the nurse said. "Plus a gunshot wound. I'm not s'posed to say too much about it. The doctor'll tell you—"

"Ernie." Margaret was now on her feet, circling the desk, approaching Ainson with her chubby calves pistoning. "*Er*-nie. It's terrible, honey."

Ainson hugged his wife. She smelled of laundry soap. As far as he could tell, she was wearing the same shapeless print dress that she'd worn the day before. "Take it slow," Buck Ainson said. "Tell me what happened." He was watching her closely. The look on her face told him that she hadn't smelled the whiskey. He breathed an inward sigh.

"Don't nobody seem to know for sure," Margaret said. "It was Terry Hackney called in. This big dog got into Terry's place somehow and chewed the daylights out of Sonny. Terry shot the dog an', I ain't for sure, 'pears Sonny got hit with a bullet, too. Terry's little wife, she's got that baby and all, but they're both okay. Don't take my word as the gospel, Ernie, I'm gettin' the story from Eleanor, and she ain't talked to Sonny herself. The ambulance driver told Eleanor what Terry Hackney had to say. Sonny, he ain't in any shape to be talkin' to nobody. They ain't even sure he's gonna live, Ernie."

Ainson didn't answer, just kept on patting Margaret's shoulder. He was thinking. Thinking that Sonny Beamer had had the afternoon off, and that Terry Hackney had had patrol duty, in the squad car. And Ainson was picturing Terry Hackney's young wife as well. Finally Buck said, " 'Spect I better talk to the doctor."

"You need to talk to Eleanor first," Margaret said reproachfully. "It's the most we can do in times like this, offer a comfort to folks."

Ainson glanced past the reception desk to where Eleanor Beamer still sat, weeping. As Buck watched, Eleanor blew her nose again. Her nostrils were red where she'd been wiping them with a Kleenex. With a small sigh of resignation, Buck Ainson said to his wife, "I'll do what I can, love." He left Margaret, went around and sat on the bench beside Eleanor Beamer.

Eleanor turned her red-rimmed gaze on him. "It's more'n I can take, Buck. First my Edgar, now my good boy. It's like I'm being punished, like one of the ten plagues of Egypt."

Ainson forced himself to look somber. Edgar Beamer had been dead for ten years; he'd been in Dallas, in a dive on Carroll Street, and the man who'd shot him had gotten off with a manslaughter charge. Seemed that Edgar's killer had been married to the woman who was sitting on Edgar's lap at the time of the shooting. And Eleanor calling Sonny Beamer her "good boy" was, well, sort of stretching the truth. Only in a Christian mother's eyes, Ainson thought. He said, "God ain't got no call to put a plague on you, Eleanor, not after all these years you been his servant. We'll all be prayin'. The Lord will do what's best for Sonny."

Eleanor Beamer cried even harder. She buried her face in Ainson's shoulder and threw her skinny arms around his neck. She blubbered, "I don't know what I'd do, Buck, without God's people to lean on in times of trial." Her tears were soaking Ainson's shirt. He sat helplessly for a moment and let her carry on, then signaled to Margaret Margaret came to take over for her husband, sitting on Eleanor's other side and hugging her. Eleanor switched support posts, burying her head in Margaret's neck and bawling even louder. Ainson got up and shuffled over to the nurse's desk.

" 'Spect I better see the doctor," Ainson said.

The nurse blinked professionally and indicated the hallway leading into the hospital's interior. "End of that corridor, take a right, Sheriff. Go through the intensive care doors, the doctor will be around there someplace. Dr. Cave. He's got salt-and-pepper hair, a young guy. He'll be the only doctor back there."

Ainson nodded and went down the hallway, averting his

gaze from Margaret's. He followed the nurse's directions and found the intensive care section, then entered it through double swinging doors. He was now in a big open area with a row of five hospital beds on either side. Only three of the beds were occupied, one by a woman with gray hair, pale as a ghost and hooked up to a pumping life-support machine. In a second bed lay a frail man in his eighties or older. His stringy white hair was long and uncut, and he was asleep. Beside the bed, glucose from a hanging bottle dripped into a tube. The tube was attached to a needle that was inserted into the old man's skinny arm, at the back of his wrist. Sonny Beamer was in the third occupied bed, lying on his stomach. His left arm was swathed in bandages. His butt, covered by a sheet, was sticking slightly upward. Sonny was asleep. He was snoring softly.

An athletic-looking man with razored salt-and-pepper hair was leaning against a counter just inside the swinging double doors, studying a chart on a clipboard. He wore an ankle-length white coat, had a narrow face and a protruding jawline. Citified-looking type. Ainson approached and said, "Dr. Cave? I'm Sheriff Ainson, from over to Tombley County."

The doctor finished writing something down, then favored Ainson with a pleasant, but impersonal, tilt of his head. "Evening, Sheriff." This doctor spoke with an educated, back-East accent, and Ainson understood in a flash why Doc Petty resented these big-city dudes. Every one of them acted as though he thought he was better than everybody else.

"That's my deputy over there," Ainson said. "He gonna make it?"

"Mr. Beamer? Oh, he's not in any danger of dying. He may lose that arm. The dog that mangled him, its head's over in Tyler for examination. We'll get those results tomorrow sometime, then we'll know whether to give the patient rabies shots. He's lost a lot of blood, it's not a good idea to be giving him injections 'til we're sure." Cave's tone was clinical, as though Sonny Beamer were a slab of frozen beef.

"What about the shootin'?" Ainson said. "They tell me Sonny's got a gunshot wound."

Cave smiled. "Strictly superficial. It's in his left cheek."

Ainson looked toward the bed where Sonny lay. "He got shot in the face?" Ainson said. "How'd that happen?"

"Not *that* cheek, Sheriff. In the posterior. Glutus maximus. Someone shot your deputy in the ass." Now Cave chuckled out loud.

"Hold on. My other man, Deputy Hackney. He was shootin' a mad dog and Deputy Beamer somehow stepped in the line of fire. Or so I'm told."

The doctor's lips twitched as though he was about to laugh some more. He bent his head and wrote something else on the chart. He looked up. "It didn't happen that way. It's two different bullets. Look, Sheriff, I'm not a witness to the shooting, but the dog was shot through the head, on a downward trajectory. The bullet that hit your deputy just clipped his buttock, like maybe Deputy Beamer was on all fours with his butt sticking up in the air." He grinned. "Or climbing out a window. Did you know there was a woman up there?"

Ainson was liking Dr. Cave less and less by the minute. At least Doc Petty didn't think folks getting shot was a joke. Ainson said, "That's touchy. Terry Hackney's little wife, I guess."

"Good guess, though the ambulance boys say there's nothing little about her knockers. I'm glad you came, Sheriff. I've got to report all gunshot wounds to the police, you can save me some trouble." Cave now regarded Ainson with a patronizing smirk.

"I ain't got no authority in this here county," Ainson said. "You should serve them papers on the Canton *police*."

"The shooting happened over in your territory, though," Cave said. "So I can make my report to you. We'll know whether we need to amputate that arm sometime tomorrow. I'd say it's fifty-fifty."

"Sonny's ma will have somethin' to say about that," Ainson said. "She'll want Doc Petty to look at the boy, you can count on it."

"Jack Petty can come over here and look all he wants to," Cave said. "But that's not going to change whether the arm's got to come off or not." The young doctor's smile tightened, a big smart city-guy trying to make the dumb country hick understand.

"You're dead wrong there," Ainson said. "It'll make a big difference. Doc Petty's hand was the first thing ever to touch Sonny, pullin' him out of the womb, and ain't nobody gonna be cuttin' the boy's arm off without Doc goes along with the idea. I ain't no doctor, but I got a heap of experience knowin' how us country folk think." Over on the bed, Sonny Beamer shifted under the sheet and drew one knee up near his chin.

"Well, of course," Cave said, bending once more to write on the chart, "we'll consult with him. And I will say that your deputy may have a better chance than most. The water over in Tombley's Walk must have a lot of healing power."

"Only the power give by God," Ainson said. "Power in the blood."

"Power of something, Sheriff. Everyone's religion is their own business. But I was referring to another patient from Tombley's Walk. A woman, victim of another animal attack."

"Dory Barnes?"

"That's the lady," Cave said. "She's quite a pistol. Came in here with wounds enough to kill most people, not twenty-four hours ago. She's already sitting up in her bed. I'm going to run some tests to find out how in the world she does it."

"Well, Dory's always been a strong girl," Ainson said, almost proudly.

"*Strong* isn't the word for it. She's . . . different. As long as you're here, why don't you look in on her?"

Doc Petty had said that he was coming over tomorrow to check on Dory himself. Ainson said, "You mean she can have visitors?"

"Have visitors? She can probably dance a jig if she wants. I'm not kidding, Sheriff, the lady's recovery rate beats anything I've ever seen."

Ainson stepped away from the counter and straightened his hat on his head. "Where's Dory at?"

Cave licked his lips and tapped one end of his ballpoint on the edge of the clipboard. "Room 128. That's one room everybody in the hospital knows by memory, she's about to drive the whole staff of nurses up the wall. Go back down the hallway, take a left at the first corridor and listen for the country-western music. That's her room."

"Obliged, Doctor," Ainson said. He took a couple of steps in the direction of the double doors, then stopped and turned. "And you won't go to cuttin' on Sonny Beamer without Doc Petty's okay, willya?"

Cave looked up from the chart on the clipboard and gave a small, exasperated sigh. "Wouldn't dream of it, Sheriff."

"I'm glad o' that. Just fix up the gunshot report, you can mail it to me." Ainson went out through the swinging doors, found the corridor, made a left turn. Just outside Room 128's partly open door, the sheriff paused.

He was suddenly uneasy. This hallway was cooler than the rest of the building, and there was a strange, sick-sweet odor in the air. Ainson had been around plenty of hospitals in his time, but this room didn't smell like a hospital room. It was a smell of rotting vegetation deep in the forest, an outdoor smell. And it wasn't constant; it seemed to come and go. There was a tingling sensation at the back of Ainson's neck. He muttered softly under his breath, squared his shoulders, started to go on in. Once more he stopped.

I'm going plumb crazy, Ainson thought. He peered beyond the open door.

There was no light on inside Room 128. There was music playing in there, the familiar sound, with the usual accompanying static, of KTVA in Tyler, the golden-oldie country station. The record now playing was Hank Williams's "Settin' the Woods on Fire," but the music wasn't quite like Ainson had ever heard it before. For no apparent reason, the man who had walked alone into the Kentucky Fried Chicken bloodbath and who had shot four men during his tenure as sheriff was suddenly so afraid that his knees were quivering.

He squinted. Through the entryway he could barely make out the shape of the bed. It seemed that there was someone in the bed, but Ainson couldn't be sure. Somewhere in his subconscious was a tiny voice, telling him to turn right around and go back to Tombley's Walk. He took a deep breath, gathered himself, and went inside. As he passed through the doorway, a shadow moved on his left. He flinched and raised a protective arm. It was nothing, nothing was there.

From the bed, Dory said, "S'matter, darlin' Sheriff? You look like you seen a ghost."

The bed was cranked into a sitting position. Dory's back was against the upright portion of the mattress and her arms were folded in front of her. Her hospital gown was bunched at her waist; one bare leg was bent with the opposite foot resting on its knee. Her white skin stood out pale in the dimness. Her eyes were glowing.

Moses, Ainson thought, they are. They're *glowing.* Dory's eyes were two points of light, like a possum's eyes in the woods at dusk. Ainson tried to speak, but his spit had dried up.

"Ain't nothin' to be scared of." Dory's voice had an eerie ring to it, the same quality as the voices over the radio. Almost as though the sheriff were hearing something coming out of an echo chamber. Or was he imagining it? Lordy, he had to be. Dory said, "It's jus' me. Jus' little Dory, Sheriff." She raised one leg and pointed her toes at the ceiling. "Dontcha think my legs are purtier? But you born-again Christians ain't into lookin' at women's legs, leastways where any o' the brethren would notice."

It was probably the light inside the room, but it did look to Ainson that Dory's shape was better than it had been. Firmer, better muscle tone. And he hadn't been on the straight and narrow the last time he'd seen her; he'd been about three sheets to the wind in fact, and had even thought about following her home from a tonk on the county line between Tyler and Kilgore. He hadn't seen Dory since then, how could she know he'd rediscovered the Master? Ainson managed to croak, "Evenin', Miz Dory."

" 'Course, now . . ." Dory moved, graceful as a cat, swung her legs around in the bed, and was suddenly on all fours, facing him. Ainson recoiled a half-step in the direction of the doorway at his back. Her eyes still glowing, Dory gave a low, throaty chuckle. " 'Course, now," she said, "you might make an exception when it comes to lookin' at Tulip Patterson's legs. You like Tulip's legs better'n Dory's?"

Ainson had known Dory Barnes for most of her life. She had been a real looker in her younger days, one of the choicest around Tombley's Walk as a matter of fact, but in recent years the booze had done her in. Her backside had widened, and in daylight (which Dory didn't see very often) her face had taken on a pasty, sagging look. But there had been nothing frowsy or slow in Dory's movements in changing from a sitting to a crouching position in the bed; she moved like a lithe young dancer. And in the dimness of the hospital room it seemed to Ainson that her chin and neck had firmed up overnight. The sheriff's hands were trembling. He steadied them by grabbing his own belt on both sides of his waist and said, "You 'pear to be feelin' better. You up to answerin' a few questions about what happened last night?" He was going to have to talk to Tulip; it appeared that Tulip had been spreading the word.

"You up to answerin' a few about you an' Tulip?" Dory said.

Ainson ignored her question. "I'm conductin' an investigation, Dory. Anything you can remember might help."

Dory moved sideways and leaned on her elbow. "Ain't much to it. Billy Ed Whitley tried to get himself a little piece o' tail an' wound up losin' a piece o' hisself. Jus' like your ol' deputy." Her eyes glowed even brighter.

Ainson swallowed hard. The room seemed even colder, and the static on the radio was practically drowning out the music. But nervous and fearful as he was, Ainson was strangely fascinated. The voice he was hearing was

Dory's, but it was a younger, more vibrant voice. Might have something to do with the weird echoing inside the room. And those eyes. Those glowing eyes. Their gaze held him, riveted him in his tracks. He wanted out of this room, but he couldn't move. He said woodenly, "The . . . Moses, girl, the . . . that thing that got you an' Billy Ed, what'd it look like?"

She stared at him for a second longer, then suddenly flipped over on her back. She was looking at the ceiling, and with those glowing eyes no longer staring at him, Ainson felt himself relax. Her eyes *couldn't* have glowed, there wasn't any light in this room. Had to have been his mind playing tricks. Dory folded her arms, raised her bare legs, crossed one over the other. She said peevishly, "Ain't talkin' about that. Ask Raven."

Ainson's eyes narrowed. "Ask who? Who's this Raven fella?"

"You'll find out," Dory said.

"You ain't makin' no sense, Miz Dory."

"I don't feel like talkin' no more. It's time for Dory's feel-good shot."

Ainson's fear had left him. It was just him and Dory Barnes in this room, nobody else. Just him and frowsy Dory Barnes. He said, "It ain't gonna help nobody for you not to talk to me. I got to make sure what happened to you an' Billy Ed don't happen to nobody else."

"I done said I don't want to talk, you ol' fart." Dory's voice was suddenly lower pitched, huskier. "But I bet I know what you'd like to do. You'd like to kiss little Dory." She raised up and turned her glowing eyes on him once more. "Would you, Sheriff?"

Riveted by her gaze, his throat constricting, Ainson said, "I ain't—"

Dory suddenly moved. Without warning, she rolled over and stood beside the bed. She took a step forward, reached out, put her arms around Ainson's neck and put her mouth against his. She moved her lips, gently at first, then firmer, more urgently. Her thighs ground against him.

Ainson was conscious of her body. Moses, that body, like a young girl's, firm, solid. There was the same dank odor in his nostrils that he'd smelled in the hallway, the odor of rotting earth, mixed with the scent of perfume. He returned her kiss and cupped his hand on her breast, squeezed her buttock, was just about to raise her gown up over her head, when suddenly, without warning, she bit fiercely into his lower lip.

His lust turned to panic in a flash. Dory's grip around his neck tightened, her arms like knotted wire. She moved her head and ground her lower jaw. Ainson felt his own flesh tear, felt pain shoot through his lip, felt thick sticky wetness on his chin. He screamed and flailed his arms. She held him tighter. He pushed against her. He was helpless.

Dory released him and stepped back. Nearly blinded by his own tears, Ainson groped in his back pocket for a handkerchief and held it against his lip. Dory grinned. Dark rivulets of blood ran from the corners of her mouth.

"Jus' a sample, darlin' Sheriff. Jus' a sample o' what Raven's got for you. You go on, now."

Ainson bolted. Out of the room and down the hall he ran, his boots thudding on tile, his breath rushing between his lips. He held the handkerchief as a compress against his mouth. All reason had left him; panic drove his chubby legs. He went out through the lobby, running, gasping for breath. Margaret and Eleanor stood and watched him go by, their jaws gaping. Ainson didn't even see them. He charged out the door and down the steps, stumbled into his county Plymouth, started the engine. He left the circular driveway with tires screeching and the Plymouth's rear end fishtailing.

Moses, he had to find Doc Petty. Had to get the doc to fix him, stitch him up. Had to get rid of the pain. Had to . . .

He licked his lower lip. The pain was gone. There was some dried blood, but . . . Moses, his lip was mending. His bleeding, torn lip was *mending.*

Ainson pulled to the side of the road and cut the engine. He was suddenly warm. Warm and comfortable and drowsy. What had that floozy done to him? What had she . . . ?

Buck Ainson lay down on the front seat and went to sleep. As his eyes closed, he was smiling.

8

"It's too big for me," Melody Parker said. "Upstairs and down we're talking twenty-five hundred square feet. Next year it'll be a hundred years old. There are things that can go wrong with this house that nobody left alive knows how to fix."

Bud liked her animated way of speaking, the way she gestured with her hands, this tiny girl seated beside him on a flower-patterned French Provincial sofa in her living room. She was wearing tasteful blue Bermuda shorts that showed six inches or so of tanned, smooth-muscled thigh. Bud sipped Drambuie from a tiny stemmed glass, then set the glass on the coffee table. "I wondered about that," he said. "What do you do when one of those old floor furnaces goes on the blink? I haven't seen a heating system like this since I was a kid."

"It's a bitch," she said. "There's one old guy around, Macko Breden. That's his given name, Macko, believe it or not, I notarized a car title for him one time. His father installed most of the old heating shit in this town, and Macko can fix anything in this house quicker than God can get a weather report. If you can get him to—that's the problem. Macko's drunk on his ass about half the time, and when he's sober there's people waiting in line to use him."

Bud's stomach was pleasantly full of home-cooked pot roast and a casserole of asparagus, cream of mushroom soup, and melted cheese, topped off by a slice of mince pie. Cursing women had always been more or less of a turnoff to him, but this feisty Melody Parker could make even four-letter words sound cute, the way she said them. He said, "Well, if you can keep things in running order that's a big part of the battle. I'm afraid I'd have to do some modernizing."

"It'd make more sense," she said. "But it would change the place. I think everybody'd like to live in their old growing-up house at one time or another. Right over there, those drapes on the front window. They're the same ones I used to poke my nose through to watch for the postman, when I was three or four. This house was the only thing my folks had to leave me. If I were to start installing central air and whatnot I'd feel like I was, well, fucking things up more than I was improving them." She raised a tiny hand from her lap and sipped her own Drambuie. "Plus the money. God, it would cost a fortune."

"I'd think a lawyer would do better in a big city," he said.

"No question about it, if you were a man. I looked around, up in Dallas. Girl lawyers can go with a big firm and be lost among the clones, or work for the government and spend their lives prosecuting dope dealers or kicking people out in the street when they can't pay their income taxes. Or take up a cause. You know, women's rights, black groups, a bunch of Mexicans." There was a table lamp beside her elbow, in the shape of an hourglass with flower patterns top and bottom.

He touched his shirt pocket. "Mind if I smoke?"

Her jaw set itself. "I'd rather you didn't, tell you the truth. I didn't notice you smoking out at Denny's."

He dropped his hand back into his lap. One thing about this Melody Parker, the girl wasn't afraid to speak her mind. A lot of people would have told him to go ahead, then sat there with smiles plastered on their faces while they nearly gagged from the smoke. "I've cut down a lot," he said. "And I know I've got to quit, one of these days. After meals is the hardest."

"So they tell me," she said. "You want something to chew on?"

"I'll suffer, thanks."

"Maybe you should try one of these support groups, though cold turkey's the only real way to lick it. You might be too nervous to stop." She narrowed her eyes and cocked her head slightly to one side. In addition to the Bermuda shorts she wore a white T-shirt with *I'm a Trekkie* written across the front in red. On the back of the shirt was a likeness of Mr. Spock, pointed ears and all.

"Do I look that nervous?" he said.

"Not the first time I saw you. And since I know now you've got something to be nervous about, maybe I'm not the one to ask. But yeah, you've got a few too many lines at the corners of your eyes, for a guy your age." She blinked. With most people, what Melody had just said would come across as a cheap shot intended to put him in his place, but Bud was convinced that this girl was just speaking her mind, with no malice about it.

He shrugged, crossed his legs, and draped one arm across the back of the sofa. "I'm forty-one," he said.

"You're kidding."

"No. Two, fourteen, forty-five, that's what's on my birth certificate."

She scootched around to face him and curled her legs up underneath her. "Well, maybe it's the hair," she said. "But most of the women in Tombley's Walk have you pegged to be much younger. Early thirties."

It was something he'd learned to live with. Looking younger than he was was an advantage in some ways, a hindrance in others. The banker who'd taken his loan application over the phone when Bud had started his first taco restaurant had almost balked at the deal when the two of them had met face-to-face. "I don't know how anybody around here would notice anyone being nervous," he said. "The whole town's got the heebie-jeebies."

"Not normally," Melody said. "It's pretty hard to be jittery when all you've got to do is sit around and watch grass grow. We don't have wild animals slaughtering people every day. That would scare the shit out of anybody."

The corners of his mouth tugged slightly upwards in a smile at her use of the four-letter word. "Well, at least you're one person who doesn't suspect *me*," he said.

"Nobody else does, either, except our goofy sheriff. And even he doesn't, really, he's just shooting his mouth off to make it look like he's doing something."

Bud leaned forward and adjusted his position on the couch. "Well, I think he's got more to worry about than me, now. One of his deputies got shot this afternoon."

Her eyes widened. "Sonny Beamer. How'd you know?"

"Who?"

"Sonny Beamer, he's the deputy that got shot. *And* mauled. I think it was another mad dog. Everybody in town's got the word, two women have already called to tell me about it," Melody said. "So how'd you know? Nobody's going to call *you,* you're a stranger in town."

"The sheriff told me. He was giving me the third degree when he got the call about the shooting. You say a dog attacked the guy?"

"That's what the jungle drums say. But it might be the sheriff's other deputy, Terry Hackney. Sonny's been screwing Terry's wife, maybe he got caught in the act."

"Christ, aren't there any secrets around here?"

"Not many," Melody said. "But you're right, that will keep Buck Ainson busy for a while." She lowered her lashes and lightly scratched her own thigh, just below the hem of her shorts. "And that still doesn't tell me what it is you've got to hide."

Bud sipped more Drambuie, sat forward and rested his forearms on his thighs. There was an old photo on the wall, of a gray-haired couple standing in front of the house with their arms around each other's waist. Melody had told him earlier that the picture was of her parents, though they appeared so much in love that Bud could've figured their identities out for himself. He steadied his gaze on the photo. "I thought you were going to talk to me about my corporation. That's what you said when you invited me to dinner."

Her lips twitched and she kept her gaze on her lap. "That's right. I did. And there's a way to do what you want. You're spooking me, Bud Tanner, or Murf the Surf, or whatever your name really is. I want to help you and for the life of me I can't understand why. Goddammit, look at us. We can't even look each other straight in the face. Me because I'm going to feel guilty about helping you, you because—Oh, hell, I don't know enough about you to even know why."

"Look, Melody. I want to tell you everything, but it's better for you not to know. Take it from me."

"Brother." She rolled her eyes. "What a lot of bullshit. Okay, Bud. You want to open a bank account, right? With a good-sized deposit."

"That's it," he said, "pure and simple. Six figures, and my name can't be on it. That's what the corporation's going to be for."

She raised her face to look at him, and the little lines of toughness bunched at the corners of her mouth. "And we're not talking drug money? Don't lie to me, I wouldn't get involved in something like that for my own mother."

"Not drug money. Not *stolen* money. It's just what I told you this afternoon, it's my own money, only if I open any accounts in my own name it's going to tell . . . certain people where I am. I can't afford that."

"Well, I'll take your word for it." She chuckled. "You don't know it, buster, but you got a lucky break in choosing Tombley's Walk over some other little burg. This town was founded on the proposition that money is money no matter where it comes from. The God Almighty *founder* of Tombley's Walk was running from the law. Justin Barker, if you make enough of a deposit with him, he could care less about the source."

"I've met him, incidentally," Bud said. "He owns the house I'm renting. I told him I'd pay him in cash every month, and that seems to be all he wanted to know."

"That's old Justin," Melody said. "So really, the corporation isn't any big deal. Anybody can be the incorporator on the papers with the state; who owns the stock isn't even a public record. I can be your front. I'll incorporate you under my name, but when we open the bank account I'll just authorize you to sign checks. Then you just open the account with cash. There's an IRS rule that any deposit in cash over ten thousand dollars has to be reported, so you just make your deposits in amounts smaller than that. Justin will look the other way—Lord knows he does that where his own money is concerned. He's got too many skeletons in his own closet to give you any shit."

"So let's do it," Bud said. "How long will it take?"

She shrugged small shoulders. "End of the week."

He thought about his belongings, already packed away and ready to move. And that maybe staying in Tombley's Walk wouldn't be so bad, as long as this girl was going to be around. "Fine," he said. "I've got to see your friend the sheriff on Monday. He wants a statement about what I found in the woods last night."

"Be careful what you say to that old fart. He's so nosy. If he gets the idea you're hiding something he won't rest until he finds out what it is."

"I got that impression," Bud said. "Also the impression that he drinks a bit. All I needed was my nose to tell me that."

She snickered. "So he's already gone off the wagon. I wondered how long that would take. He's probably been hitting the bottle and rolling around with Tulip Patterson."

"Who?"

"Tulip. She's his piece of ass on the side. Everybody in town knows it but his wife. Tulip's a good-looking woman, and a schoolteacher. Anyplace else she'd never give old Buck the time of day, but there's a real shortage of men in Tombley's Walk. Take it from me, I know."

He smiled. "Well, it looks like there's going to be one more addition to the male population, at least for a while. Me, though I'm not sure that adds much to the situation."

She touched her dark hair at the nape of her neck and met his gaze squarely. "I've thought about that," she said. "You staying around here. I think that will be nice."

He watched her for a moment, watched the light glisten on her full lower lip as something unspoken passed between them. It had been a long time since he'd had this feeling. Beth would like this girl. Finally he laughed nervously and looked over his shoulder, to where plates and glasses and leftover casserole sat on her linen-draped dining table. "You've got some cleaning up to do. Tell you what, Melody. You wash and I'll dry. I haven't done that in a while."

9

JEANNIE Breden was five years old, and like just about every five-year-old in this world, she understood a whole lot more than grown-ups gave her credit for. In fact, she was quite a bit smarter than most children her age, and in her own limited way she understood that, in dealing with five-year-olds, grown-ups were pretty dumb. She was really good at pretending to play with her torn Raggedy Ann and Andy dolls, or her broken Big Bird alarm clock, when all the while she was listening to what the grown-ups were saying. And the grown-ups, not paying her any mind, would talk on and on as though Jeannie wasn't even there. But she was. She was there and she was listening, and she understood just about everything that was going on.

She understood, for example, that her stepfather Macko hated all the rich people in Tombley's Walk who hired him to fix things around their houses, and that Melody Parker was apt to be in for a first-class humping from a by-God real man if she kept shaking her ass around in shorty-shorts while Macko Breden was fixing the plumbing underneath her sink. Jeannie also knew that the assholes at the 7-Eleven had gone up to three-and-a-half a six-pack on Lone Star Beer (three-and-a-half of *what,* Jeannie wasn't exactly sure), and that if the assholes at the 7-Eleven were going to be that way, then Macko Breden would just take his business out to Jasper's by the Interstate. And that while it was true that the Lone Star at Jasper's was a buck-and-a-half a pop (Pop goes the weasel? Jeannie wasn't sure), that at least out at Jasper's a man stood a chance of falling into a little pussy. Another thing that Jeannie understood was that Macko Breden did as he goddam well pleased, and that if Jeannie's mother or anybody else gave Macko any shit about it they'd be damn well sorry.

There were some other things that Jeannie Breden understood even though no one talked about them. She knew that her mother (like Jeannie, small and frail) was miserably unhappy and afraid of Jeannie's stepfather, and that the reason her mother drank herself into a stupor every day was to blot things out of her mind. Being only five, Jeannie couldn't drink in order to make the pain go away. So what Jeannie did when Macko smelled of booze, was loud, and looked at her with that gleam in his eyes, was to go to one of her secret hiding places. She had a lot of those. She'd learned that if she kept herself hid for long enough, Macko would pass out, and then she wouldn't have to go to his room and let him do the things to her that she didn't like. Sometimes, though, Macko would find her. And Jeannie also understood that what Macko did to her when he *did* find her was only a preview of what stuck-up rich bitches like Melody Parker were in for.

Aside from being a whole lot brighter than other five-year-olds, Jeannie had an active imagination. It was her gift for fantasy that probably saved her. When Macko would throw her tiny body across his bed and, grunting and breathing hard, yank her clothes off, Jeannie would merely close her eyes. Quick as a flash she could climb aboard Pegasus and soar high above the clouds, then dip back down to earth on whatever wonderful journey the great white flying horse chose to take her on. She'd been to Wonderland and had tea with the Mad Hatter, gone with Peter and John and the Lost Boys to battle Captain Hook, and had even landed on the yellow brick road to clippety-clop along atop her winged steed in the company of the Cowardly Lion, the Tin Woodsman, and the funny Scarecrow who sang songs and did a lot of happy, if disjointed, dances. So real was Jeannie's dreamworld to her that often at night, when Macko was through having his way with her, she believed with all her heart that the terrible pains in her pelvis and groin had come as a result of another happy day in Pegasus's saddle.

Jeannie's favorite fantasy character was the Cowardly Lion. In her fantasies the lion appeared fierce and savage, but would cower and whimper anytime that someone had the nerve to stand up to him.

Her fantasy lion was what caused her not to be afraid of her new friends, the first time she came into contact with them. Like the Cowardly Lion, Jeannie's new friends appeared fierce and savage—more fierce and savage, in fact, than the worst nightmares that the Cowardly Lion had ever dreamed. Their hairless bodies were gnarled and bent. They walked sometimes on all fours and sometimes upright. Their human ears were pointed like Spock's. Their foreheads were human, too, but their noses and jaws formed snouts and muzzles nearly twice the length of a wolf's or dog's. Their teeth were the size of curbstones, were pointed and sharp, and there were permanent grimaces of hate on their snarling faces. Two of them had short hairless tails, the other pair no tails at all.

There were four of them at first. They would gather after dusk at the old deserted dump site less than a quarter mile, through brush and piney forest, from the back stoop of Macko Breden's shack. There they'd huddle wolfpack-fashion for a while, growling and snapping at air, then scatter in all directions and disappear into the night. Just before dawn they'd return—some of them with dark red smears on their teeth and snouts—huddle together once more, then, just before daybreak, would go off in all directions once again.

The dump site hadn't been used in over twenty years, and only a few of the old-timers in Tombley's Walk even remembered that it was there.

The dump was a series of mounds, once trash and dirt from the excavation for what a group of Dallas developers had hoped would be a golf course, but now it was covered with wild grass and weeds. The forest had crept up around it and in another couple of decades would completely swallow the dumping ground once and for all. But for the present, the dumping ground was a natural clearing in the forest, and a perfect gathering place for Jeannie Breden's new friends. It was also Jeannie's favorite secret hiding place. Being the smart little five-year-old that she was, Jeannie understood that Macko Breden knew nothing of the dump's existence even though it was a stone's throw from his back door, and that even if he *had* known about it, Macko was likely to fall and break a leg if he were to go stumbling around in the woods after he'd been drinking.

The first time that Jeannie saw the creatures, she was quiet as a mouse. Any adult would have screamed and run. And, most likely, would have spent the last moments of their lives screaming. But not Jeannie Breden. Four different nights she watched, a tiny girl with stringy brown hair and scratches on her face where twigs had scraped her cheeks in her short run through the woods, and with smudgy feet stuffed into blue Kermit the Frog tennis shoes with the toes cut out because the shoes were too small for her; a pitiful waif crouched behind a mound, watching with not a hint of fear while the terrible beasts came and went.

Toward the end of the fourth night, almost at dawn, she grabbed the biggest monster by its short, flesh-colored tail. As she ran from her hiding place behind the mound, Jeannie was giggling. Her dirty hair trailing behind her, the mended hem of her smock whipping about her pumping legs, she crossed the hundred feet or so to where the pack was huddled. Suddenly she was in their midst, their bodies warm around her, the scent of their meaty breaths in her nostrils. For a half second, she panicked. Then her resolve came back to her (I'm not ascared of that Cowardly Lion, so who's afraid of *you* old poops?) and she grabbed the tail of the largest of the monsters and yanked with all the strength in her five-year-old arms. "I got you!" she shrieked.

There were a few seconds of silence, broken only by the shuffling of clawed feet on grass and dirt. Then the big beast turned on her with a vicious snarl of hatred, while the others shrank back to give him room. Still Jeannie wasn't afraid; she knew in her heart that if she were to be in real danger that Pegasus would come along to spirit her away to safety. Monstrous jaws opened inches from her face and stinking hot breath flowed on her cheeks. Jeannie closed her eyes and wished for Pegasus.

The beast paused. It snorted. It pawed the ground. Then it asked a question. Jeannie heard the question in her mind. It was a thought, a sudden presence in her brain, and the thought was as clear as though the monster had spoken to her.

Are you alone?

And her answer, also a thought: *Yes. I want to play.*

That was all that passed between them then, though they were to communicate many times in the days to come. The monster nuzzled her legs. Its nose was warm and dry, more like a man's nose than an animal's. It grunted softly, deep in its throat. The other creatures pressed eagerly around them.

And Jeannie Breden, five years old, without a human being in this world to comfort and protect her, stood in the clearing among the mounds and giggled while creatures of death nuzzled her and licked her face and neck and little bare legs.

ON Sunday morning, Macko Breden had a buddy over. The buddy was Becky Stoner's ex-husband, Bob Bill, who'd been out of work for four months since they'd laid him off at the foundry over to Mount Pleasant. The foreman at the foundry had *called* it a layoff, but Bob Bill Stoner allowed as how he knew better. He knew, in fact, that the foundry had done some hiring since they'd let him go, and he had it figured that the foreman had it in for him just because he drank a bit. The fact that Bob Bill liked to drink a little beer was nobody's business but his own, and E.J. Joseph down to the jail was a living witness that when Bob Bill had his head straight he made a damn good hand. So good, in fact, that the county held off having their vehicles serviced and their floors waxed and polished until such time as Bob Bill Stoner was down there working off a public intoxication charge. Bob Bill liked Macko Breden because Macko understood all the shit that came down. Also, Bob Bill knew that Macko was remodeling Miz Radner's kitchen, and as a result was likely to have a cooler full of Pearl or Lone Star. And finally, Macko was one of the only somebodies in Tombley's Walk on a Sunday morning who wouldn't be down to the church house getting their souls cleansed. The two of them were on Macko's back stoop, sitting in rockers with their feet propped against the railing. A washtub filled with ice and Lone Star longnecks sat on the wooden porch between them. They were tossing the empties out into the yard, in the direction of the woods. Macko's old lady Mae was in the kitchen, cleaning up, and Mae's little girl Jeannie was shirtless and wearing grimy underpants, sitting behind them on the porch and playing with two old torn rag dolls. Church bells were pealing faintly in the distance.

"Shee-it," Macko said, his upper lip curling, "what's that smell? Like a fuckin' cattle yard." He was wearing a cotton undershirt with a hole below his armpit, and he had a couple of days' growth of black beard.

Bob Bill had been noticing the odor, but hadn't said anything because the smell might've been something that Macko hadn't bothered to clean up around his place, and if Bob Bill were to say anything that Macko didn't cotton to, then Macko might run him off.

"Ain't that odor *loud?*" Macko said. "Almost make a man stay inside." He stood and leaned over the rail. Macko was gaunt, and in addition to the undershirt wore faded jeans and was barefoot.

Bob Bill wasn't sure just how old Macko Breden was, it was hard to tell a man's age. He knew that Macko had been growed when Bob Bill was still a boy, but Macko was too much of a man to be much older than fifty.

"Goddam, that wood's damp down there," Macko said, gazing at the foot of the stoop. "Shee-it, it's *drippin'.*"

Bob Bill didn't really want to get up from his seat and take a look, but knew he was going to have to. Though it was only ten in the morning, it was already muggy-hot on the porch. The morning sun had risen to the point that the roof overhanging the stoop offered shade, but if Bob Bill stood and looked down he was going to be in direct sunlight. The nearby forest was in deep shadow, and the bright sunlight shone on brown longneck bottles and rusty tin cans in the yard. The yard was thick Johnson grass that Macko mowed when he got around to it, and from the height of the grass Macko hadn't felt like mowing in a couple of weeks. Bob Bill scratched his belly and stood. He wasn't wearing a shirt, had a hairy chest and overhanging belly, and wore army fatigue pants and hard-toed Air Force brogans left over from his six-month stint in the federal prison camp in Texarkana for driving his pickup into the side of the post office. Destruction of government property. He leaned over the porch rail, squinted, and wrinkled his nose. The wood was wet down there, all right, and the stench was definitely rising from that direction. "You shore right, brother. Smells like acid or somethin'," Bob Bill said.

"Sure 'nuff does," Macko said, swigging beer, holding his index finger crooked around the bottle's neck, moonshine-jug fashion. He swiveled his head and yelled from the side of his mouth, "Mae. Edna Mae, you git yo ass out here." At the sound of his voice, the little girl Jeannie shrank back against the doorjamb and hugged her dolls to her scrawny bare chest.

Visible through the open doorway, Mae was in front of the sink. Her bare feet moved on cracked linoleum. She laid a dish towel aside and carefully set a plate on the drainboard, then moved in the direction of the porch. Macko said loudly, "Goddammit, woman, I call you, you move." The little girl's eyes widened and she chewed on a piece of red yarn that served as a strand of Raggedy Ann's hair. She looked fearfully toward her mother in the kitchen, then back to Macko.

Mae came onto the porch, wringing her hands. She was wearing jeans cut off at her knees and a black T-shirt with *Hard Rock Cafe—Dallas* written in gold on its front. The letters were fading. She was a slim girl whose hips were widening, and whose narrow shoulders were beginning to stoop. Her face was pretty, though gaunt, and her eyes pale blue without expression in them. "I didn' hear you at first, honey," she said.

"Well, dig the wax outta yore ears." Macko stepped aside and pointed downward. "Look here, you been throwin' somethin' offa this porch? I done told you about that."

Mae moved hesitantly to Macko's side, flinching as she stood near him, her lips quivering slightly. Another thing that Bob Bill liked about Macko, he sure knew how to keep his women in line. If Bob Bill had handled Becky the same way, he'd have been the better for it, and the next woman that came into Bob Bill's life was in for some taming. Mae looked down at the foot of the stoop. "Why, no, honey," she said. "I'd never throw nothin' down there nohow." Her nose wrinkled. "Lordy, Macko, what's that *smell?*"

Macko grabbed Mae's elbow and held it in a vise grip. "You wouldn' lie to me, wouldja?" he said. He studied his wife, looked at her eyes, her lashes down, docile, failing to meet his gaze. He released her. "Naw," he said. "You'd know better."

The second that Macko had grabbed Mae's elbow, Bob Bill had begun to look around the yard. He had the good sense not to keep his eyes on one of Macko's women when Macko was drinking; though he was a good twenty years younger, Bob Bill wasn't sure he could whip Macko's ass and wasn't interested in finding out. Bob Bill pointed out into the yard and said to Macko, "There's another wet spot on the side o' that outhouse."

The wooden outhouse was no longer functional since Macko had installed plumbing and dug a septic tank ten years earlier. But Macko had never done away with the shed, and it stood, swaying and rotting, thirty yards from the porch in the direction of the woods. The same liquid that clung to the bottom of the porch could be seen on the near side of the old wooden privy. In the glare from the sun it had a slight sheen, was sticky and thick like syrup, and it clung to the wood in a quivering mass, like Jell-O. And it *stunk.* Bob Bill Stoner figured he'd smelled just about every stink there was at one time or another, but this was a new one on him. Earlier in the day the smell had been faint, but as he and Macko had sat on the porch in the rising sun, the stench had grown stronger. At the moment it was all that Bob Bill could do to keep his nasal passages open.

Macko squinted, his jaw thrust forward, climbed down from the porch, and ambled toward the outhouse. He'd been drinking just enough so that he was listing some, but wasn't so drunk that he was stumbling. He picked his way carefully, putting his bare feet down so as not to step on one of the cans or bottles. He stopped a yard or so from the outhouse and squatted on his haunches, his forearms resting on his thighs and a Lone Star longneck dangling loosely from his fingers. "Goddam if it ain't," he said to nobody in particular. He looked behind him toward the porch and said, "It's that cat. Fuckin' cat, it's got to be."

From his position on the porch, Bob Bill automatically looked around the yard in search of the cat. The cat was a full-blood Persian and was as out of its element around Macko Breden's place as a rosebush would have been. Mae did some occasional housework in Tombley's Walk, when Macko didn't happen to have a repair job going, and Brother Leroy Abbey's cousin had given Mae a kitten from her own pampered cat's litter. The Persian had been around the place for about a year, and at first had been little Jeannie's pet. But as the cat had grown larger, and as Macko had kicked and mistreated it more and more, the Persian had become practically wild. It stayed hid most of the time, coming out to purr and brush against Jeannie's little calves only when Macko wasn't around. As he scanned the yard, it occurred to Bob Bill that thinking a *cat* had anything to do with the stinking mess plastered to the porch and outhouse was plumb ridiculous. But it was none of Bob Bill's knitting and, where Macko was concerned, Bob Bill had learned to stick to his own.

Now Macko's brow furrowed. He shifted his gaze from Mae to little Jeannie and back again. The beginning of a grin was on his face. "I told you 'at cat warn't no good," he said. "Fucker's gone and stunk my place up."

Mae's narrow shoulders hunched closer together. She wrung her hands and licked her lips. Bob Bill watched her, saw the fear in her eyes, knew deep in his insides what was coming. But Bob Bill Stoner had more sense than to give a shit what happened to a cat, so he kept his mouth shut. He thought for an instant that Mae might stand up to her husband, but before Mae could open her mouth to speak, the little girl ran forward and threw her arms around her mother's thighs. "Kitty-cat ain't done nothin', Mommy." Jeannie's voice was high and tearful.

Macko raised up out of his crouch and advanced toward the porch, swigging beer. In a high mimicking falsetto he said, "Ain't done nothin'. Ain't done nothin'." His voice lowered to its normal pitch. " 'At no-count critter done sprayed my house an' latrine an' I'm aimin' to see it learns better. Where's the bastard at?"

There was a moment of silence, during which man, wife, and stepdaughter stood motionless. Bob Bill nervously cleared his throat, but none of the three looked in his direction. It was as though Bob Bill wasn't even there, as though he were down at the old Rialto Theatre watching the picture show and Macko, Mae, and Jeannie were characters on screen. Finally Bob Bill said hesitantly, "Shee-it, Macko, ain't no cat done that. That stuff's thick as sorghum." The acidic stink was still in the air, growing stronger, but the scene in the yard had shoved the odor to the back of his mind.

"Ain't none o' yourn, Bob Bill Stoner," Macko said, never looking in Bob Bill's direction. "I want you to butt in, I'll ask. I said that fuckin' cat stunk up my place an' that's by-God the way it is." Macko's leer said that he knew damn well that the cat didn't have anything to do with it, but he was getting too much enjoyment out of making Mae and Jeannie squirm to let up.

Jeannie buried her face in her mother's skirts. Her little-girl voice muffled, she said, "He gonna hurt kitty-cat, Mommy."

Almost as if in a trance, Mae looked down at her daughter. Something within her seemed to take over, a protective instinct far older than a battered woman's fear of her abuser. She stood a little straighter and her shoulders squared. "You lay off, Macko," she said. "Ain't no cat sprayed nothin', a fool can see that."

Macko took a step forward. One hand tightened around the beer bottle's neck and his free hand balled into a fist. "You callin' me a fool, woman? You sure gettin' a smart mouth on you all of a sudden."

Bob Bill slowly lifted his beer to his lips and took a warm swallow. His adrenaline was beginning to flow. He sensed that old Macko wasn't about to let his wife get away with calling him down in front of anybody, and Bob Bill also sensed that he was about to get a lesson in how to handle a woman. In the yard, Macko's cocky grin was turning into a scowl.

Bob Bill caught movement in the lower left corner of his eye. It was the cat. The Persian had picked that exact instant to poke its head into view from underneath the stoop. A small plastic feeding bowl was on the ground about four feet from the end of the cat's nose, and Bob Bill supposed that the kitty was checking to see whether there was any food in the bowl. Whatever its reason, old pussy had picked one helluva time to show itself. Its round gray head was motionless, its eyes wide and green, its whiskers twitching. Bob Bill's breath caught in his throat.

"Well, I do de-*clare,*" Macko said, his hands relaxing. He began to advance slowly toward the porch. "I declare, I declare. Why here's that nasty ol' pussy now. You a nasty pussy? Are ya? C'm'ere, kitty. Here, kitty-kitty." He squatted and extended his hand to the cat, palm up. The nasty grin was returning to Macko's face.

The cat bared its teeth in a grimace that said that no way did it want any part of Macko Breden. Macko inched closer. The cat's head cocked to one side, and for just an instant its natural curiosity overcame its fear. The hesitation sealed the cat's fate. With an agility surprising for a man who'd been drinking beer all morning, Macko scrambled forward. His arm darted underneath the stoop. The cat's head disappeared. Macko crawled backward, his grin broadening. He stood triumphantly, holding the Persian by its long tail. The cat wriggled and twisted and spit and hissed. Helpless, it clawed at air.

Holding his prize at arm's length, Macko faced his wife. He sipped some beer. "Fucker made me spill some," he said. "Fucker pissed all over my place and stunk it up, then made me spill my beer. Whatcha think we ought to do about that?"

There was a lot to see in what was unfolding before him—the writhing, spitting Persian dangling upside down in Macko's grasp, the wicked grin on Macko's face, the helpless look on Mae as she realized what was going to happen—but Bob Bill was later to remember the child, Jeannie, most of all. She stopped crying, stood away from her mother, and watched Macko. Her underpants drooped around her bottom and legs. Her knees were dirty. Her scrawny chest rose and fell. She watched, expressionless, her eyes dead as coals.

Macko turned his beer up and drained it, then tossed the bottle aside. "Well, I tell you what we're gonna do," he said. He grabbed the tail in both hands and began to swing the trapped cat back and forth in ever-increasing arcs. "We're gonna give this nasty ol' pussy a ride." Bob Bill's insides turned to ice, and he grabbed the porch railing to steady himself.

Back and forth, back and forth the cat swung. It began to yowl, its pitiful cries rising, then decreasing in volume as Macko swung it higher and higher. On the porch, Mae sobbed and covered her eyes. Jeannie stood motionless, as though hypnotized. Still grinning, Macko swung the cat in a final arc high over his head and grunted as he bashed its head down on the porch railing.

The Persian stiffened, then went limp. Macko raised the animal once more and slammed it into the rail. There was a sound like a melon cracking as the cat's head split open. Blood and gray oozing matter gushed, splattering the rail and dripping thickly on the porch. Macko stood proudly back, the lifeless thing in his hand now twitching. He dropped the dead cat in the yard. More blood and brains dripped on the Johnson grass. Bob Bill Stoner's guts came up; the gagging rose in his throat and he leaned over and puked on the ground.

"That takes care o' one pussy," Macko said. "Now I got me two more to take care of." He looked at Bob Bill, seemed to see him for the first time. "You go on home, Bob Bill. Don't be talkin' this around, you hear?"

Bob Bill nodded dumbly. He wanted away from there. Christ, did he want away from there. He stumbled off the porch without another word. As Bob Bill left, Macko Breden climbed onto the stoop, glared at his wife, took his stepdaughter by the arm and led her inside.

THIS time, as Macko loomed over her and stripped off his clothes, Jeannie didn't call on Pegasus. She didn't call on anyone, no Mad Hatters, no Tin Men, no Cowardly Lions. She lay calmly and let it happen, didn't whimper, didn't make a sound. She was still as a stone, but her mind was working. In her mind, she was talking to her new friend.

And in Jeannie's mind, her new friend was talking back to her.

10

DR. Jack Petty had learned, years ago, that if he wanted to keep his oar in the water around the community, he had to go to church. The Tombley's Walk Rotary and Lions' clubs were also vehicles for drumming up customers, but most of the members of those organizations were excessively healthy young businessmen who sent their wives off to Dallas to get their babies born.

So the key to making money in the medical profession lay in the older folks. Senior citizens got sicker (or imagined they did), stayed in bed longer, and showed up for thirty-five dollar office visits more faithfully than younger persons, and bills sent out to Medicare were a certainty to collect on, even though the government generally rode the account for ninety days or so before spitting out the check. And Jack Petty's small-town Christian upbringing had taught him a very important, and very basic, common human trait: the older that people became, the more their dreams were filled with the rapidly opening pearly gates, and anyone who wanted to mix and mingle with the older set needed to drag himself down to the church house on Sunday mornings.

The fact that Jack Petty had never married created a problem—not a major hurdle, but one that needed dealing with. The important portion of Tombley's Walk's population was evenly divided between the Church of Christers and the Baptists. So what Petty did was attend the Baptist church part of the time and the Church of Christ the rest of the time, and tell the brethren at both places that he was confused as to which church held the true key to everlasting life. It was a pretty effective formula. Both the Baptist women and the Campbellite sisters had zeroed in on Doc Petty as one of the sheaves that needed bringing in, and members of both faiths used him as their doctor for fear that the opposition would get the upper hand in the saving of his soul.

On the same Sunday morning that Macko Breden and Bob Bill Stoner decided to drink a little beer, Doc Petty went to the Church of Christ. He sat toward the center of the auditorium, seventeen rows from the front, beside the widowed sister Rachel Matthews. Rachel Matthews was a slim, heavy-breasted girl in her early thirties with waist-length brown hair and big brown doe-eyes. She wasn't so beautiful that the women in Tombley's Walk hated her guts, but plenty attractive enough for Petty to sport around to the necessary local events. Rachel made a good church companion because she'd learned just when to nudge Petty to keep Brother Leroy Abbey's sermon from putting him to sleep, and to top it all off she liked to jump into bed and sin just as much as the good doctor did.

Brother Abbey's voice was reaching a crescendo that signaled that the sermon was drawing to a close.

"And I pray to God"—in good Bible Belt fashion, Brother Abbey pronounced it "*Gawd*—uh"—"that these trials will in a way become a blessing to us. That the stricken will in their hour of trouble be a lesson unto us all. That in death, young Billy Ed Whitley will show us life. That with her injuries, Dory Barnes will find a new faith. That like the leper at the gate of the temple, the Master will touch Dory and make her whole, physically and spiritually whole, brothers. That Dory will hear the invitation and heed. That same blessed invitation that is open to us all, the rich and the poor, the lame and the whole, while we all stand and sing."

Quickly, Abbey descended the two steps to the auditorium floor and stood waiting expectantly. There were a few seconds of silence, broken by the rustling of slips and pantyhose under gaily colored summer dresses and the papery rattling of songbook pages while the brethren searched hurriedly for the invitation hymn. Finally Mervin Wilson, the songleader, totally bald with a walrus mustache, wearing a light blue suit, spotless white shirt and gray tie, took the floor. He was blinking like a man who'd just been nudged into wakefulness.

Wilson made his living as the pharmacist at the new Piggly Wiggly that had opened up on the Interstate access road, but he'd been a music minor at East Texas State U. over in Commerce and his true love was in the making of a joyful noise unto the Lord. He lifted his right hand and began to direct, at the same time lifting his rich baritone voice in the opening stanza to "Whosoever Will."

The congregation joined in, and the rafters vibrated with sound. Light slanted in through the stained-glass windows on the east side of the building and made red and blue and green patterns on the beige carpet.

Rachel Matthews held her songbook so that Doc Petty could follow the music and lyrics by slightly inclining his head. Rachel sang in a pretty soprano voice that had had some training. Petty, who couldn't carry a tune in a gunnysack and damn well knew it, mouthed the words to the song but actually only sang every fourth or fifth word. A couple of women in the audience—a white-haired lady in her seventies wearing a navy-and-white polka-dot dress and a younger gal of sixty-five or so who was seated to the white-haired woman's right—looked over their shoulders at Doc Petty with gazes that said they were hoping against hope that this might be the glorious Sunday when the doctor would finally confess, be baptized, and enter the fold. Petty had *already* been baptized to his own way of thinking—he'd been sprinkled when he was six months old. But that didn't cut any ice with the Campbellites' dunked-or-damned philosophy. Petty kept his gaze trained on the songbook in Rachel's hand, and pretended not to notice the women. Finally someone *did* heed the invitation, a teary-eyed, puffy-jowled man who appeared slightly hung over. The man went down the aisle into Brother Leroy Abbey's open arms. The two women who'd been watching Petty were now smiling and whispering to one another. Petty breathed a sigh of relief.

Aside from pretending to sing, Doc Petty was thinking about Buck Ainson. Ainson was seated four rows toward the front and across the aisle, between his wife Margaret and Eleanor Beamer. Eleanor Beamer had left her son's bedside in the Canton hospital to attend the service, and would be hurrying back to sit with Sonny as soon as the benediction was said. Margaret had her head thrown back in enraptured, if off-key, song. Eleanor was blowing her nose. Buck Ainson stood like a wooden soldier, his arms at his sides, his shoulders tense. He wasn't singing.

Buck Ainson had been, for years, the closest thing that Doc Petty had to a buddy. The two understood each other. Each thought that the other's profession was one part for real and nine parts bullshit, and the mutual feeling had created a strange bond between them. When Ainson had left Petty's office the previous afternoon at a half-walk, half-stagger, Petty would have laid ten-to-one that the sheriff was headed for Tulip Patterson's place. When he'd run into Buck just outside the church that morning, Petty had said as much. He'd called Ainson aside, winked and said, "How was Miss Tulip feeling yesterday?"

Buck Ainson had favored Petty with an unblinking stare. His face expressionless, the sheriff had said, "Good morning, sir." His voice had been toneless and mechanical. His movements had been stiff and wooden as he turned and walked away without another word.

Now, as the congregation raised collective voices in the invitation hymn's finale ("Heeeëere the invitaaaaaa-tion, come whoooooo-soever will . . ."), Jack Petty let his gaze wander across the aisle to where Sheriff Buck Ainson stood. The corners of the doctor's mouth were bunched in worry.

LESS than a year ago, if someone had told Bud that he'd be spending the following July 10th Sunday morning in a Bible belt church service in the middle of the East Texas piney woods, Bud would have wondered whether the person speaking was "all there." Yet here he was, standing beside Melody Parker near the back of the auditorium in the Tombley's Walk Church of Christ while vibrations from the enthusiastic invitation hymn shook the one-story brick veneer building to its foundations.

Bud would have been uncomfortable standing there even if he hadn't been a man in hiding (most of the Bible-bangers he'd met in California had been members of some really far-out sects, and he tended to group all churchgoers in the same category with the California nuts), and the fact that Bud was in the church at all was more evidence of the feelings he was beginning to have where Melody Parker was concerned.

It had been her idea. Well, not really, it had been *his* idea to see her the following morning for breakfast, but it had been Melody who had nixed the breakfast idea and told him that she had to go to church. They'd been standing about three feet apart, him on her front porch and Melody just inside the house with the door partway open, with June bugs and other flying critters slamming into the yellow buglight overhead and electrocuting themselves with tiny sizzling hisses and little quick lightning flashes. He'd been dying to reach out and draw her to him, and was pretty sure that the same thing was passing through her mind, when the subject of breakfast over at Denny's had come up.

"Can't," she'd said.

"Oh?" He'd felt the disappointment creep into his own voice and knew she'd caught his disappointment as well.

She'd licked her lower lip. "Tomorrow's Sunday. Go-to-meetin' day. Can't miss it."

"You're kidding."

"No. No, I'm not. Bud, you . . . well, you'd just have to grow up in Tombley's Walk, or someplace like it. Listen, I went to school in Dallas. I used to do some snoozin' on Sunday morning, but my roommate always had to cover for me even then. Never knew when Mama was going to call to make sure her little girl was in church. And if I happened to answer the phone myself on Sunday morning and it was Mama callin', well, I was in deep shit. She used to call me from the minister's office just before she went into the service herself, up here in Tombley's Walk."

"But you're all grown-up now," Bud had said.

"Yeah. I'm grown and Mama's gone, and all that. But Tombley's Walk has a thousand mamas, and you can bet your ass if I didn't show up for mornin' worship, then somebody'd be calling me by noon. Somebody might even come over here, believe it or not, and you'd be surprised what it'd do to my law practice if word got around that I was a backslider."

"A what?"

"A backslider. It's . . . hell, you can figure it out." She leaned forward slightly, one hand on the edge of the door and the other on the doorjamb, and looked down at her own feet. "And there's more to it than that. Church makes me feel better. And I'm damn sure not Sister Sara or anything, but it does. Always has, I guess some of Mama's teachin' wore off on me."

"I wouldn't know about that," Bud had said. "Church wasn't in my diet as a kid."

Then Melody had said, rather quickly, "Of course, if it has to be breakfast for you, then it has to. But you could go to meetin' with me."

He'd laughed. "I thought you were worried about people talking. Now boom, you're wanting to show up with me in a public place."

"Church is different, city boy. And we won't be going together, we'll sort of, well, run into each other. And I'm single, and you're alone, and there won't be anything in the world wrong with us sittin' together in church. Then maybe after church we might happen to go eat together." One side of her face had squinched up in the cutest wink Bud could ever remember seeing. "There's nothing wrong, sir," she'd said, "with startin' local tongues to cluckin', as long as they're cluckin' and sayin' the right things. As long as everything *looks* on the up-and-up, then what people say around here won't hurt you any."

So here he was, wearing his only suit and tie (he'd bought the outfit on impulse in Phoenix; the suit was a proper conservative gray, the tie a modest blue), conscious of Melody at his side, the top of her head on a level with the tip of his shoulder, Melody smelling of face powder and everything nice, soft and bouncy in a tan filmy summer dress and singing the hymn in a pretty alto. Uncomfortable as he was, he realized that going to church (or anywhere, for that matter) with Melody Parker was something that could grow on him.

He'd seen the county sheriff outside the building before the service. He'd been walking along beside Melody, about to ascend the first step up to the church entrance, when suddenly he'd been face-to-face with Buck Ainson. Ainson had just turned away from a tall, slender gray-haired man with whom he'd been talking, and there hadn't been any way to avoid the confrontation. Bud hadn't seen the sheriff until it was too late and the two of them were practically nose-to-nose. "Morning," Bud had said, for want of anything better to say.

The sheriff had favored him with a dull, glazed-over look and had brushed by him without a word. Keep your cool, Bud had told himself, blowing your stack is almost sure to blow your cover as well. And now, standing in the midst of the congregation with the invitation hymn sounding in his ears, he shot a hurried glance eight rows forward and to his right. There was the sheriff between two women. Ainson was standing practically at attention during the song, his arms straight down and stiff as ramrods. It seemed to Bud that Ainson's bearing was different than it had been yesterday, but then yesterday the sheriff had been drinking. Maybe Sheriff Buck Ainson was just a man of many different moods. At that instant, Melody looked up from her songbook, turned her gaze on Bud and favored him with a smile. Bud forgot all about the sheriff and smiled back at her.

"HE delivered me," Melody said. "Plucked me right out of the womb and spanked my bottom."

All around the clipped lawn and on the sidewalk and the steps leading into the building, people dressed in Sunday clothes stood in clusters and chatted. Brother Leroy Abbey was in the parking lot, standing beside his tan Buick Park Avenue with the door open. An elderly white-haired woman was standing in front of Abbey and talking a mile a minute. The preacher appeared in a hurry to get away. It was hot as the blazes; though he'd only been outside for five minutes or so, Bud's collar was damp. Coming out of the cool church building had been like walking into a furnace. The noonday sun beat down on the two drive-in windows of the Tombley County National Bank catty-cornered from the church; seen in the distance over the bank's roof were tall green trees on the square and the domed roof of the Tombley County Courthouse and Office Building.

"It wasn't me, Melody," Dr. Jack Petty said. "Musta been some other doctor. How you doin', Mr. Tanner? Welcome to Tombley's Walk. You stayin' with us long?"

Bud hesitated, then said, "I'm not sure. Depends on how long it takes to do what I've come to do." He was really beginning to feel silly about the writer bit, and hoped that Petty wouldn't press the issue of what Bud was doing for a living.

Melody came to his rescue. "Bud's single, that's something you two have in common."

Petty said, "Us bachelors are a rare breed in this neck of the woods. You play any golf? I'm always lookin' for somebody that doesn't have to be home before dinner to play a round with. Most of the guys in town have to quit after nine."

Bud had carried a two handicap, once upon a time, at Mission Viejo Country Club in Orange County. Mission Viejo was one of the toughest courses up and down the West Coast; the pros had nicknamed the place "Mission Impossible." Bud said, "I like to play."

"Well, we'll have to get together. Melody, you give Mr. Tanner my—" Petty stopped midsentence, his gaze across the street in the direction of the Tombley County National Bank. "Christ," Petty said in a near-whisper.

Bud followed the doctor's gaze with his own. There was a dog over there, one monster of a German shepherd, trotting past one of the drive-in booths with its head hung low. It moved with a strange, side-canted gait. Its tongue was lolling. Flecks of foam dripped from its lower jaw and clung to its thick brown fur. There was a small sign on a two-foot pole that was set in the concrete island surrounding the drive-in booth. The sign was black plastic with white lettering, and Bud assumed from this distance that the small white letters spelled out the bank's business hours. As the dog went by the sign, its shoulder brushed against the plastic. It twisted its head and snapped viciously. Then it altered its course and moved in its odd canter into the street and headed directly toward the church.

Doc Petty moved a stride and cupped his hands over his mouth. He shouted, "Everybody back away."

All over the yard, steps, and parking lot, conversation ceased. Heads turned. Jaws dropped. One man, about twenty yards away on Bud's right, said in his best Christian demeanor, "Where's my fuckin' gun?"

From the steps, a young woman in a navy dress with a white sailor's collar yelled, "Jenny. My Lord, Jenny, you come here." She covered her mouth and screamed.

In the street about five feet from the curb, two children played. One was a boy of about three, wearing a Sunday suit with short pants that came to just above his chubby knees. The other child, a girl, around the same age as the boy, wore a flowered starched dress, spotless white socks, and white patent leather shoes with buckles on them. The children were tossing a blue Koosh-ball back and forth. They were directly in the German shepherd's path as it made its way across the street. As Bud shifted his gaze to the little boy and girl, the dog was about twenty feet from them and closing in.

Doc Petty touched Bud's elbow and said, "Come on." Then, with the coordinated pace of a man half his age, the doctor sprinted toward the children. Bud ran after him, legs pumping, leather shoes hitting pavement, his tie blowing around his neck. Petty reached the little girl and, without breaking stride, scooped her up in his arms and dashed onto the curb and toward the church. The child gave an indignant yelp. Bud, his chest heaving, was five strides behind Petty. Still running, he reached for the boy, realizing as he did that he wasn't going to make it.

The jaws of the German shepherd were scant inches from the child's shoulder, the jaws widening, foam dropping to the pavement with thick plopping noises. Bud flinched, the German shepherd's panting breath warm on his hands. The dog snapped its jaws closed on air, ducked its head, dodged around the little boy, and continued on in the direction of the church. Bud picked the child up and held him close. The little boy said, "Doggy bad. Doggy bad." And began to cry.

Bud stood in the middle of the road, cradling the child's head as tears further dampened Bud's collar. Bud was stunned. There'd been nothing, nothing at all, to stop the dog from tearing the child to shreds, but the brute of an animal had moved on as though it had a purpose in mind. Its drooping tail moved in rhythm from side to side as it trotted the final few feet up onto the curb and started up the sidewalk toward the church's front door.

There was a low ornate brick wall, perhaps three feet high, which curved partway along the front of the church property and extended along the sidewalk toward the building, with an identical brick wall on the opposite side of the walk. The wall on Bud's right supported a sign reading, in fancy stone, CHURCH OF CHRIST. Beneath the stone writing was a small marquee, which announced in changeable plastic letters that Brother Leroy Abbey was the current minister, and gave the times for the Sunday morning, Sunday evening, and Wednesday night services. About ten feet beyond the point where the walkway to the building led at right angles away from the sidewalk across the front of the property, the German shepherd paused. Its tongue lolling, foam dripping from its lower jaw, it sniffed the wall. Then it shifted its position and deliberately raised its leg, and looked around through red-rimmed eyes as it urinated on the bricks. Finished, it continued on its side-canted way.

Bud let the child slip from his grasp to stand on the ground. His dignity restored, the little boy ran around one end of the wall and into his mother's arms. She picked him up and hugged him. His fear of the animal slipping away, Bud went up the sidewalk about ten paces behind the dog. As he passed the curve in the brick wall a strange odor hit his nostrils. He wrinkled his nose and sniffed the air. The odor was an acidic stench, not the stink of urine, but something else. Bud had smelled it before, somewhere, sometime. He couldn't remember where.

The men, women, and children gathered in the churchyard and standing in little clusters on the steps were strangely quiet. The mother of the little boy whom Bud had rescued stood off to one side, still holding her child's head against her starched sailor's collar. She was watching the German shepherd as it continued on its way. Her lips were parted. She licked them. A gray-haired woman in her sixties or seventies stood beside the walk, wearing a blue high-necked dress and black orthopedic shoes. She was scant feet outside the dog's pathway, and as the shepherd went by her it brushed the hem of her skirt. It twisted its head around and snarled at her. She didn't move, her eyes glazed. The dog continued on its way.

At the foot of the church house steps stood Sheriff Buck Ainson. The sheriff was in uniform. He wore a black string tie and a tan waist-length jacket over his shirt. He'd put his hat on. The two women who'd sat by him in church—Bud assumed that one of the women was the sheriff's wife but didn't have the slightest idea which one—were on either side of him, and as the dog approached they shrank back and stood up on the steps. Ainson faced the animal, the sheriff's arms stiff at his sides, his face expressionless. The dog paused before him, and for an instant man and beast faced one another. As Bud watched, the German shepherd went forward and licked Sheriff Buck Ainson's hand.

There was movement in the crowd on Bud's right. A chubby man with a black pencil mustache, wearing a gray suit, came between two women and onto the sidewalk. He was brandishing a double-barreled shotgun, and he purposefully approached the German shepherd from the rear. Bud opened his mouth and started to say something, but before he could speak the man placed the barrels of the shotgun against the side of the dog's head and pulled the trigger.

There was an eardrum-shattering blast as both barrels spurted flame. The odor of burning gunpowder poisoned the air and singed Bud's nostrils as it mixed with the stench he'd noticed as he'd passed by the brick wall. The dog's body flew sideways as if kicked by a giant boot. The top half of its head disappeared. Bone fragments and soggy pieces of matter sprayed the ground, and the green grass was reddened by thick, dollar-sized drops. The shepherd landed in a tangle of furry legs close to the foot of the steps, twitched once, and was still. The man with the shotgun said gleefully, "Got the fucker, Buck."

Bud supposed that he was the only person there who'd watched the sheriff and not the dog, or the man with the gun, throughout the entire scene. He couldn't have explained it himself, but his gaze had been frozen on Buck Ainson's face from the moment the dog had stepped forward to lick the sheriff's hand until the shepherd's body had landed. When the dog had nuzzled his hand, Ainson had had a blissful look about him. At the sound of the shotgun blast, his eyes had widened, and his mouth had twisted as though . . . well, Bud thought, as though he'd been in pain. Almost as though the shotgun pellets had torn into Ainson himself and not the dog. Now, as the shepherd lay dead and the people around him began to chatter excitedly, Ainson regained his composure and stepped forward.

"Show's over, folks." Sheriff Ainson spoke with authority. "Show's over, now we'll be gettin' this critter outta here. C'mon, I'll be askin' you folks to go on home now."

The crowd backed off from the bloody carcass on the lawn. Ainson stood over the dog and looked—Bud searched once again for the word—well, protective. That was the only word to describe the way Buck Ainson hovered over the fallen shepherd, as though the dog's body was that of a fallen comrade. Bud's brows knitted as he turned away from the scene and scanned the area in search of Melody.

There she was, still tiny and cute as a well-dressed button. She was standing at the end of the sidewalk, near the street. Her arms were folded and one petite high-heeled shoe was slightly in front of the other.

Doc Petty stood beside Melody along with his girlfriend

(Ramona? No, Rachel, Bud remembered), and all three of them were looking at the brick wall where the shepherd had stopped and urinated on the way up the sidewalk to its death. Rachel appeared disgusted. Melody was wrinkling her nose. Doc Petty was scratching his thick gray hair. Bud went down the walk and joined them.

"Sump'n else, huh?" Melody said, her gaze still on the wall. "P.U."

Doc Petty said softly, "I tell you, been to fifteen county fairs and a pit bull fight. But this beats all."

Bud looked at the wall, the acidic stink growing stronger in his nostrils. There was a clear glob of something adhering to the brick—something which shined brightly in the sunlight and had a sheen about it. And it *stunk*. It was the same odor that Bud had smelled earlier, the one that was familiar to him, but that he couldn't quite place. Bud put his arm around Melody's shoulders. The clear glob was quivering like Jell-O.

11

IF Rog Hornby were to do away with customers like Bob Bill Stoner, Rog would be out of business. Out at Jasper's, Bob Bill was one of the boys. Young guy with a wild hair up his ass, liked to drink a little beer, didn't like anybody fooling around with his ex old lady. Had a good start on a beer gut that, in ten years or so, would be as big as Rog's belly. Bob Bill was the kind of customer that made Jasper's a right smart little gold mine, and when Bob Bill was working he'd been known to really lay his money down. No matter what the folks down to the church house or the collection agency had to say about him, Bob Bill Stoner was A-OK in Rog Hornby's book.

Bob Bill hadn't had a job in a while (Rog made it a point to know which ones of his steadies were working and which ones weren't), and Rog had to be careful how he handled the boy. He couldn't afford to let Bob Bill get to him for a credit tab, but at the same time Rog didn't want to piss Bob Bill off to where, when he *did* happen to come into something, he'd go to drinking his beer over to Tyler.

At one o'clock on Sunday afternoon, Rog Hornby was opening up. He had the exhaust fans going full blast in order to clear out some of last night's smoke, and had cases of warm longnecks sitting on the bar. He was restocking the coolers, setting the cold beers out on the counter, stacking the hot ones in at the bottom, then putting the cold ones back in at the top. There was sweat on Rog's forehead; he'd just turned the a/c on and it would be a half hour or so before the place cooled off. Aside from the glassy clink of the bottles and the papery slide of the cardboard boxes on the bar, the only sound was the hum of the coolers and the buzz of the Lone Star sign over the cash register.

The front doors opened and bright sunlight spilled into the dimness. Bob Bill Stoner came in. The double doors closed behind him. He blinked, staggered slightly as he came over to the bar, sat on a stool, and ordered a Pearl. Rog scratched his whiskers and reached for one of the cold ones on the bar. He hesitated with his hand on the neck of the bottle, smiled at Bob Bill, and said in a friendly tone, "You got money, aintcha?"

The boy dug in his pocket and came up with a crumpled bill. "Got fi' dollars," he said.

Rog opened the beer with a tiny hiss of air, set it on the bar along with a chilled glass. Bob Bill ignored the glass and swigged directly from the bottle. Rog took the bill, rang the beer up in the register, put three ones and jingly change on the bar. He tilted his hat back on his head and propped one foot up on the cooler. "You done been drinkin' this mornin', aintcha, boy?"

"Been out to Macko Breden's."

Rog's eyes narrowed slightly. Bob Bill appeared just a little pale, as though he was scared of something, but wasn't too drunk to be served alcohol. The undercover boys from the Texas Alcoholic Beverage Commission wouldn't come calling on a Sunday anyway. And Rog knew that Becky Stoner, Bob Bill's ex, had gone home last night with Randy Beard, the fertilizer salesman. Becky was likely to be shacked up at Randy's place over in Canton, at least for the rest of the day, and without Becky sitting around Jasper's on somebody's lap to egg Bob Bill on, the boy wouldn't start any shit. Rog said, "Well, how come you didn't bring Macko along? I need the business."

"Macko's takin' care of his old lady," Bob Bill said. "Goddam it stinks out there."

"Been noticin' it myself," Rog said, going back to work restocking the coolers. "Seems to be comin' from the woods."

Bob Bill paused with his longneck halfway to his lips. He was shirtless, his hairy chest showing, and had it been nighttime Rog would have made the boy either go outside and put on a shirt, or wear one of the T-shirts that Rog kept in the back just in case. Bob Bill said, "When you been out to Macko's place?"

"I ain't," Rog said. "Why?"

"You said you smelled that stink."

"I'm talkin' about out back. At the rear o' my parkin' lot. Crossed my mind that they left part o' Billy Ed out there to ripen, but what I been smellin' ain't no *dead* stink." Rog stopped his work and dried his hands on a bar towel.

" 'At smell over to Macko's ain't neither," Bob Bill said. "Macko played like he thought the cat done it, but that was just so's he could give his old lady shit about it. Least that's what I thought at first. Macko went and killed 'at cat. Give me the willies. Shit, gimme another'n." He turned up his longneck, drained it, set the bottle down. His face paled another shade.

"You mean he went and shot it?" Rog said.

"Shit no, he bashed it to death. With his bare hands, right out in the yard an' that little girl o' Mae's standin' right there a-lookin'."

Bob Bill's lips were trembling. Rog knew he was hearing the truth, Macko Breden could be one mean bastard when he wanted to. But Rog didn't want to talk Macko down; Bob Bill would go straight to Macko with whatever Rog had to say, and the next thing Rog knew Macko Breden would get it in for him. Rog said, "What's that stink over to Macko's smell like?"

"You ever smelled rotten eggs?" Bob Bill said.

"Yeah. Like batt'ry acid."

"A lot like that," Bob Bill said. "Only stronger. Sourer, too. An' there were these big globs o' somethin' clingin' to the porch an' shithouse."

"*Inside* the house?" Rog said.

"Naw, that ol' outhouse Macko's got out there. Stunk like I don't know what."

" 'S funny," Rog said. "That rotten-egg smell. That's

what's outside o' my place." He opened another beer and took the empty away. Bob Bill eyed the money on the bar hopefully. Rog took two dollars from the pile, rang up another beer in the register, dropped three quarters in change. Bob Bill looked disappointed.

"What you reckon that odor is?" Bob Bill said.

"Don't have no idee," Rog said.

Bob Bill split the soggy label on his beer bottle in half with his thumbnail, then eyed the bottle. "You seen my Becky?"

Rog pictured Becky the night before, her slim hips brushing Randy Beard's, Randy hugging her around the waist as the two of them had gone out of Jasper's around 1:00 A.M. "Not lately," Rog said, and mentally crossed his fingers in the hope that Bob Bill wouldn't push it. As Bob Bill licked his lips and opened his mouth to say more, the phone rang.

Rog had learned years ago that having a straight-in telephone line in a honky-tonk wasn't a good idea. The drunker that folks became, the more they thought about people they knew in Chicago and St. Louis, and the monthly phone bill in a honky-tonk would be enough to break anyone. The solution in Jasper's was a pay phone over by the pool tables, with a dialless extension in Rog's cubbyhole of an office. That eliminated the phone bill entirely and allowed the drunks to call anyone they wanted to so long as they had quarters to pump into the slot. Rog undid his apron, laid it on the cooler, then rubbed his ample belly as he crossed the room, skirted one pool table, and answered the pay phone. "Jasper's."

"I'm missin' you, darlin'," Dory Barnes said on the line. "How come you leave little Dory by her lonesome?"

A small painful lump rose in Rog's throat. He supposed that Bob Bill Stoner wasn't the only man who had a weak spot. Seemed that everybody did. He turned his back to the bar across the room and lowered his voice. "How you feelin'? I been meanin' to come by, once you're up to it."

"I'm up to it now, darlin'," Dory said. "Ain't nothin' wrong with me, it's these fuckin' doctors won't turn me loose."

"You ain't been there but *two nights,* Dory. I seen the shape you was in. You got to take it easy, girl." Rog glanced over his shoulder. Bob Bill had taken some of his change from off of the bar, and was now standing over beside the jukebox with his beer bottle held at chest level, looking over the music selections.

"You ought to *see* my shape, darlin'. Might do somethin' for you," Dory said.

"Always did, honey, you know that." And her shape really had been something, Rog thought, back before she went to drinking too much and hanging around the tonks all night. "Ain't no other girl can do what you can for me."

"I can do more now, darlin'. Come to see Dory, you got no idea what you're missin'." Dory's voice sounded strange and far away, as though she were calling from Ethiopia or someplace instead of just over to the Canton hospital. And her voice had a softer quality to it, a younger sound, like the Dory Barnes of fifteen, twenty years ago. Rog decided that he must have a bad connection.

"I'll be there, honey-bunch. Just soon as you get to where you can sit up an' visit," Rog said.

"Well, where you think I am right now?" Dory said. "I'm standin' here in the hall, talkin' on this here pay phone, same as you. Bet you're standin' over by them pool tables."

"That's where I am, all right." Rog pictured Dory's limp form as the paramedics had lifted her into the ambulance on a gurney. "But you oughtn't to be up. You get back in bed, Dory Hornby." There was a crackling noise from the speakers behind Rog, and the voice of George Jones began to sing "Third-Rate Romance, Low-Rent Rendevous." Rog pressed the phone tighter against his ear and cupped his hand over the mouthpiece.

"I'd like to be in bed with you, darlin'," Dory said. "You come on over tonight an' do somethin' to me."

"I can't do nothin' to you in no *hospital,* Dory."

"Don't bet on it, darlin'. I got me a ground-floor window ain't three feet off the ground. Ain't no nurses around at midnight."

"But you ain't well," Rog said. "I seen you, Dory, an' what that critter done to you made my heart stop."

Her voice had a sudden urgency to it. "Did you see the critter, too?"

"Didn' see no critter," Rog said. "But iffen I do it's one dead sumbitch, you can bet on that."

"What else you see in them woods?"

"Jus' Billy Ed's arm, an' then the rest o' Billy Ed, an' then you," Rog said. "It wadn' no fun."

Dory's tone softened once more. "If you come to the back o' this hospital buildin' I'm the third window from the east side. There's a crepe myrtle a-bloomin' right underneath, an' around midnight the shade'll be halfway up. You jus' knock on the sill, darlin'."

Rog studied the toes of his boots, the cue chalk on the carpet beside his feet. He nudged the chalk with his toe. It rolled over once. He said, "I'd like to."

"Like to never did nothin'," Dory said. "Stroke o' midnight, you come on, now." There was a soft click as she disconnected.

Rog stared at the receiver in his hand, replaced it in the cradle, went back to the bar. Bob Bill Stoner sat with his bare shoulders hunched. He'd poured his glass half full of beer and was watching the bubbles rise to the top. On the jukebox, George Jones's voice was a jumping, rhythmical moan.

"You sure you ain't seen Becky?" Bob Bill said.

Rog's eyes were misting. He wiped them with a bar towel. "I see her ever once in a while. She's always askin' for you, Bob Bill. You want some more beer, it's on the house. Man needs a friend sometimes."

ROG had been so darned excited about going over to see Dory at the hospital in Canton that he'd forgotten all about the front door key to the honky-tonk. There it was, dangling right there along with the other keys on the chain, swinging from the ignition on his Ford Bronco as he pulled into the outskirts of Canton. It was a cloudy night, might even rain before daylight. The Bronco's headlights showed cracks in the pavement and the gravel shoulder on the side of the road, and an occasional jackrabbit that would sit frozen in the beam, eyes wide, and then dart away into the underbrush. The moon shone through the cloud cover like a faraway searchlight in a fog.

Rog had left Katy Jane, the beehive-hairdooed floor waitress, in charge for the night. Sundays weren't too busy; most of Jasper's regular customers were either at the house nursing a hangover and trying to get some sleep so they could work on Monday, or explaining to their old ladies how come they hadn't been home all weekend. Katy Jane wouldn't have a whole lot to do. Rog wasn't paying her extra for being in charge because he knew she'd knock down enough from the cash register to make up the difference anyway. Stealing waitresses were one of the costs of doing business in a honky-tonk, and Katy Jane wouldn't take as much of the till money as some others Rog had had. But the fact that she didn't have a key to lock the front door at closing time was a problem. She'd shoot her mouth off to the Sunday-night hangers-on about how she didn't have any way to lock up, and Rog was likely to find a few cases of Pearl or Lone Star missing in the morning. He checked the digital clock on the Bronco's dashboard. Quarter 'til twelve. It was too late to do anything about the key; wasn't nothing going to keep Rog from calling on Dory.

In Canton, he kept to the side streets, bouncing along on gravel or rough asphalt between weatherbeaten houses with swings on their big wooden porches, and approached the hospital from the rear. He stopped for a moment and let the chugging motor idle, his gaze sweeping the low-slung brick building, the knee-high hedges along the walk, the curved drive at the emergency room entrance on the east end. A single bulb glowed over the emergency door; small bedlamps glowed through three windows along the building; the rest of the twenty-odd windows were dark. He counted three rooms down from the east end. No light there. The shade was halfway open. Rog squinted. There was a crepe myrtle there, barely visible in the darkness, its top branches extending just above the sill. With a final glance behind him, Rog cut the engine, shut off the lights, and climbed down on the pavement. His boots made scratchy dragging sounds. A slight warm breeze swept under his hat brim and tickled the hairs at the nape of his neck. He'd been chewing a wad of Beechnut tobacco, and he spat the soggy mess out on the street.

He crossed fifty feet of thick Bermuda lawn, mowed with blades raised to their highest level to protect the grass roots from the Texas summer heat, to stand before the window. The crepe myrtle bush stood in a tilled earthen flower bed two feet wide. A soaker hose was draped along the base of the building's outer wall; a damp hiss sounded as tiny drops of water sprayed the crepe myrtle and the flowers. Hornby's breath quickened in anticipation as he leaned over the flower bed, steadied himself with one hand against the brick, and rapped his knuckles on the windowsill. Moisture from the soaker hose wet his hand and arm and the short sleeve of his shirt. He didn't even notice.

A hand with painted nails appeared in the window, grabbed the shade, yanked it slightly downward, then held it taut as the spring-loaded roller raised the shade all the way to the top. The hand disappeared and a face came into view. It was Dory, but . . .

Rog squinched his eyes tightly closed, shook his head, and looked again. It was Dory, all right, no doubt about that, but the face was different somehow. The neck and chin were tight and firm. The flesh underneath the eyes was smooth. The cheeks were unwrinkled. No sag to the jowls. Rog glanced over his shoulder at the sky overhead. The cloud cover had thinned some but the outline of the moon still was faint, like that of a yellow ghost ship. Had to be the light that made Dory appear as she did. Had to be. As he turned back to the building, the window slid upward.

Dory smiled and said in a stage whisper, "You come in, darlin'. Dory's waitin'." Then she backed away and disappeared in the darkness inside the room.

Rog looked left and right. He was alone out here. There was no one on the lawn, no one in the street. A prickly sensation danced along both of Rog's collarbones. He took a deep breath and stepped around the crepe myrtle to the window. His boots sank into wet earth. He put one foot against the bricks and hoisted himself to a sitting position on the sill, then turned around and stepped into the room. The sweet scent of lilac entered his nostrils.

He couldn't see much at first. There was a dim slash of light on the floor, in the angled shape of the window, but aside from that it was pitch black. As his pupils began to dilate, Rog made out the bed with its white linen, and on the other side of the bed a few distorted outlines that he assumed to be chairs. Dory was seated on the bed, her legs outstretched and crossed at the ankles, her palms flat on the mattress behind her, and—here Rog's breath caught in his throat—she was naked. He wasn't sure at first, she could have been wearing *something,* but as his eyes grew accustomed to the dimness he saw the outline of her high bare breasts, the smooth unbroken sheen of her hipline, the gentle curve of her thigh. Visible beyond Dory, over her shoulder, was a vase of flowers standing alone; then another vase, identical to the first, and it took a few seconds for Hornby to realize that a single vase was on the bureau and he was seeing its reflection in the mirror. The bedsheets rustled as Dory uncrossed and recrossed her ankles.

"Whatcha waitin' on, darlin'?" she said. "Come see me." And it was Dory's voice, but at the same time it *wasn't* Dory's voice; the tone and inflection were the same, but the dry boozy crackle was gone.

He moved over to the bed and sat on its edge. Now he could see her clearly, but . . . well, it wasn't her. But it *was* Dory, of course, only . . . it wasn't the *same* Dory Barnes who had been at Jasper's only night before last. Her waist was sharply indented, the skin on her body taut. He was sitting on the bed with a woman who was—Rog had to think for a moment, hell, he *had* been married to her once upon a time—forty-six years old, and a rode-hard-and-put-up-wet forty-six at that, but the body he was seeing belonged to a girl half that age.

Rog cleared his throat and managed to whisper, "What happened to you, girl?"

"Well, *that's* a dumb question," she said. "You was down there in them woods, wasn't you?"

"Yeah, but I . . . Dory, I never seen . . ."

She moved, quick and supple as a cat, slid over and sat close to him. "Well, it's me, darlin'. Want to touch?"

Rog wanted to touch, all right, Lord God Almighty did he *ever* want to touch. His throat constricting, his fingers trembling, he reached out. His palm contacted firm vibrant flesh on her upper arm; he withdrew his hand as though he'd touched hot coals.

"That ain't *touchin'*, darlin', not in the way you want to touch," she said with a throaty chuckle. "Lord, you act *scared* o' Dory."

She moved even closer, drew up one leg, and rested her thigh on top of his. "Here," she said. She gripped his hand and moved it along her own thigh. "There," she said, then moved his hand upward and held it against her bare breast. "An' there," she said.

She felt real enough, her thigh warm, her breast slick, her nipple yielding. But there was something that *wasn't* real about her, too. If this wasn't Dory here with him, it was the *image* of Dory that Rog had dreamed about. Perspiration popping out on his forehead, he hugged her close and bent his head to kiss her breast.

She stopped him with a firm hand on his chest and said, "Not *here*, darlin'." Then slid catlike away from him to lie on her back in the center of the bed. "Over here," she said.

Rog Hornby forgot everything except that body on the bed. Thoughts of Jasper's, fear of being here in this hospital when he wasn't supposed to be, wonder at the changes in Dory . . . all of these flew from his mind as he scrambled feverishly across the mattress. He wanted his— by God he wanted his hands on this woman, apparition or not, he wanted to touch those . . . those *things* of hers and to put his mouth on her and to—

She stopped him once more and tugged at his belt buckle. "You can't do nothin' with your *clothes* on, darlin'," she said.

Can't? Rog thought. Can't do nothin'? By God, the woman was right. At least, he couldn't do what he wanted to do, which was throw this spooky heifer, this unbelievable prize of a cow, right down here on this hospital bed and once and for all fuck her ever-loving brains out. He tore at his clothes. A button popped. He had his pants down to his knees before he realized that his boots were in the way; he had to pull his pants back up, wriggle over to sit on the edge of the bed while he removed the boots with Dory's throaty chuckles reddening his ears. He stood, yanked his pants off one leg at a time, hurled the jeans into the corner of the room, stripped off his boxer shorts. Naked now himself, his belly jiggling, he crawled back into bed. He had her. By God, he had her, and he was going to—

She rolled and grasped his shoulders, her breath suddenly fierce, her eyes wild and piercing in the darkness. Suddenly she was on top of him, her nails raking his chest, her laughter now a low, almost manlike gurgle. She planted a shin on each of his upper arms and pinned him to the bed. There was pain in his biceps. He struggled, but couldn't move his arms. "We got him," she said.

Rog's eyes widened. "Got who, Dory?"

From behind her, from somewhere in the shadows, from some corner of the room that Hornby couldn't see because of Dory's lithe form towering over him, Deputy Sonny Beamer said, "Got *you,* you fat-gutted bastard. Raven's people got you."

Rog looked upward, past creamy-skinned, muscled thighs that held his arms pinned to the mattress, past the soft patch of down at her pelvis, past jutting breasts with quivering pink nipples, and his gaze was suddenly riveted on Dory's shoulder. On her right shoulder, the same shoulder that he'd seen torn and bleeding out in the woods behind Jasper's not forty-eight hours ago. On the shoulder that was now perfect, with smooth skin covering its rounded tip. And, finally, on a small white scar, not over an inch in length, on the front of Dory's shoulder just below her collarbone. A big pointed sliver of ice rammed its way up from Rog's belly and lodged itself firmly in his gullet. He tried once again to move his arms. He couldn't.

There was movement in the shadows and Sonny Beamer

was suddenly beside the bed. He leaned over and looked down at Hornby, and it *was* Sonny Beamer, was that same no-count deputy who came by Jasper's sometimes while he was supposed to be patrolling and drank a little beer and chased a little pussy. But like Dory, Sonny was different. He was dressed in a robe that was open down the front. He wasn't wearing his sunglasses (it occurred to Rog that he couldn't remember ever seeing Sonny, at least since Sonny had grown up and gone to work for the sheriff's department, without the silly mirrored shades) and his eyes seemed to glow red. And there was something different about his bearing, about the way he stood and cocked his head to look down at Hornby. Sonny had always been a skinny kid and had grown into a skinny man, but the Sonny Beamer who now stood beside the bed seemed larger. His chest was broader.

Dory shifted her position and ground Rog's biceps deeper into the mattress; tears of pain leaped into Hornby's eyes. Still smiling, her gaze never leaving Hornby's face, Dory said, "Do it."

Sonny Beamer backed away and vanished into the shadows. Rog's lips twitched. Do it, she'd said. Do what? God Almighty, do *what?* God Almighty, were they going to . . . ?

Sonny reappeared by the bed, glared red points of light at Hornby for an instant, then kneeled on the floor. He lifted Hornby's hand—the pressure of Dory's legs on Rog's biceps had cut the circulation off; Hornby's fingers were quickly numbing—and slid a sheet of paper underneath. Then Sonny fumbled inside his robe and, in a few seconds, placed a ballpoint pen in Rog's hand. "Sign your name, meat," Sonny Beamer said.

The words didn't register on Hornby at first. Sign your name? Sign *whose* name? What were these two critters . . . ?

Hornby shook his head. His own whiskers tickled him as they brushed his neck.

Keeping Rog's arms pinned with her legs, Dory arched her back and reached around behind her. First one long-nailed hand, then the other, closed deliberately around his scrotum. They were small hands, but their grip was like steel. "I can crush 'em, darlin'," Dory said. "I can crush 'em an' yank 'em out by the roots. I ain't foolin', I can. You sign your name."

She could do it. One look at the way she was staring down at him and Rog didn't have any doubt about it. She could do it and she would. He forced his numb fingers to move, pressed the pen down on the paper and scratched out his signature. Signed his name to what? He didn't know. He didn't care, either.

Dory took her hands from his scrotum and rested them on her thighs. "That's better, darlin'. That's a whole lot better." She turned her head. "He do it right?"

Sonny stood with the paper in his hand and bent his head to read. It dawned on Hornby that Sonny Beamer was reading in light by which Rog himself could barely see anything at all. He dropped the paper to his side and nodded to Dory.

"Well now," she said. "You been a good boy, Rog darlin'. You been so good that Dory ain't goin' to give you no pain. You won't feel nothin', darlin'. You'll see."

Now her hands went to Rog's throat. Her thumbs touched his windpipe. He closed his eyes, expected to gag, expected his lungs to shriek as they hungered for air. But none of that happened. There was no pain at all, no panic. Her hands were like gentle feathers. The image of Dory Barnes's gorgeous body floating in his mind, Rog Hornby eagerly gave up his life. He was smiling.

AT four in the morning, Nurse Billye Faye Adderly, twenty-nine years old, with bleached blond hair, a narrow waist and a swelling behind, and a slightly pigeon-toed walk, was finally able to make a round of the east wing of Canton Memorial Hospital. She'd missed the midnight and two o'clock circuits because of the excitement in the intensive-care unit.

At 11:50, Dr. Cave had swept into the hospital with coattails flying. He'd come storming in at that hour (Nurse Adderly couldn't ever recall seeing Dr. Cave at the hospital after eight o'clock before) because the night-duty nurse in intensive care had called him at home. Nurse Adderly had noted that the doctor's breath held a faint odor of bourbon, but that was none of her business. The doctor had come in because one of the patients in intensive care, Deputy Sonny Beamer from over in Tombley's Walk, was missing. According to the night nurse he'd been in his bed at eleven, but at eleven-thirty he hadn't been anywhere to be found. Apparently he had simply gotten up and wandered away.

So for the past three hours, Nurse Billye Faye Adderly had been with Dr. Cave in the doctor's office. Aside from her nurse's training at Baylor Medical Center in Dallas, Billye Faye had attended Draughn's Business College for a time, and she was the only one on duty who could take shorthand and run a typewriter. She'd been helping the doctor make sure that Sonny Beamer's medical records were up to snuff ("Be a bitch with the insurance assholes if anything comes of this," Dr. Cave had said), taking hurried dictation from Cave and typing up her notes. The fact that some of the treatments now listed in Sonny Beamer's medical record had never been performed at all was likewise none of her business; just like the alcohol on his breath, it was Dr. Cave's worry. Billye Faye Adderly didn't get paid for poking her nose where it wasn't wanted.

The fact that there had been no nurse on duty in the east wing all night really wasn't that much of a problem. None of the east wing patients were critical, and only took occasional medication that they didn't want to wake up for anyway. Nurse Adderly moved quickly, gently shaking sleeping people into grumpy wakefulness, smiling cheerfully as she offered capsules and pills and little paper cups of water with which to wash them down.

Outside the door to Room 128, she paused. There were noises inside, a few tiny shrieks, some muffled groans. Frightened, she pushed the door open a crack and peeped inside.

On the bed, Dory Barnes and Sonny Beamer were copulating. He was on top, humping for all he was worth. Her legs were wrapped tightly around his waist. Nurse Adderly gasped and quickly closed the door.

She stood in the hallway, her heart pounding. Then she heard a new sound from inside, a lower, more guttural noise. She wasn't about to look in there again, wasn't about to. She put her ear against the door. Her eyes widened.

The new sounds that she was hearing were growls.

12

On Monday afternoon, Bud went to Billy Ed Whitley's funeral. He couldn't think of anywhere in the world he'd less rather be (except perhaps the Los Angeles County Jail or the State of California Unit at Soledad, but it was a foregone conclusion as far as he was concerned that he would visit both of these establishments sooner or later), but he would have gone just about anywhere that Melody Parker wanted to go, so long as she was with him. She was having that much of an effect on him, and it occurred to him that that was strange. He'd assumed that if he ever did fall in love with someone, that someone would be a lot like Beth. But Melody was as different from Beth as daylight from dark, both physically and philosophically. He wasn't going to go into a deep analysis of his feelings, but the attraction might have been that she made him laugh. And laughter was something that he needed badly.

On Sunday night, sitting in her living room, she told him, "They're givin' the stiff a big send-off tomorrow. It ought to be as much fun as watching the guy shoot the dog."

"I don't follow," he said.

"Billy Ed Whitley. They're going to plant him before he gets to stinking too much. Couldn't happen to a nicer young man."

"I don't think I'll go," Bud said.

She was drinking Coca-Cola from one of the old-fashioned hourglass-shaped bottles, a six-ouncer. She turned up the Coke and drank. Two big bubbles of air glugged upward in the inverted bottle. "Don't be ridiculous," she said, setting the Coke on the end table. "The pallbearers can afford to miss it more than you can." She lowered her lashes. "Or me."

"Melody, don't joke about that. A funeral right now would just about do me in." He had his arm draped across the back of the sofa, and her shoulder was practically touching his side. He wanted to go to bed with her so badly he could taste it, and was wondering when it was finally going to happen. She gave him a quizzical glance as though she were reading his mind.

"Who's joking?" she said. "You have to go because our silly sheriff has got the rumor spread around that you might have something to do with Billy Ed dying. One thing about this town, nobody's going to talk about you while you're in earshot, but they'll all be looking to see whether you're at the funeral. Everybody in Tombley's Walk goes to everybody else's funeral whether they knew whoever is dead or not, unless they've got a reason *not* to go. Big Ed—that's Billy Ed's father—everyone that hates Big Ed's guts will be there right beside his friends. Nobody's going to call any official roll or anything, but by the time the burial is over Margaret Ainson and Eleanor Beamer will be able to recite the guest list from memory. If I didn't go, I'd lose clients over it."

"The Ainson family," Bud said, rolling his eyes. "Which reminds me. I've got to see the good sheriff in the morning."

"Nope," Melody said. "Not a chance."

"He even said he's going to have a court reporter to take down a statement from me."

"That was before the dog thing this morning. Buck Ainson had you lined up in the morning to show everybody what a peachy investigation he had going, but the mad dog at the church changed all that. Now you're on the back burner while good old Buck impresses everybody with how well he handled the dog thing. Not that he did anything, mind you, but he's going to have everybody convinced that he's the one that had Fred Gomer shoot the critter. Wait and see. Bet you a dollar that before morning you get a call that your interview's canceled. Or if you do show up, Buck and his court reporter won't be there."

"I don't think you like your sheriff," Bud said.

"Oh, I just love the old bastard. Ever since he tried to feel me up when I was thirteen years old." She laughed. "He pretended he was giving me a spanking, but he spent the whole time just squeezing my bottom. Never gave me a lick with his palm that I could feel."

"This town just slays me," Bud said.

"Don't it?" She was wearing jeans, not designer jeans but old-fashioned Levi's, not skintight but snug enough that the outline of her thigh stood out. She shifted her position and leaned against him. "Much as I can't stand him, I do hope old Buck stumbles around and does something about this mad-animal bit. It's really giving me the creeps."

"What happened at the church is the weirdest thing I've ever seen," Bud said. "I'm interested to see what the doctor finds out about that dog's . . . waste material. How about him? I guess he's more reliable than the sheriff."

Melody giggled. "Oh, Doc'll find out what's in the dog piss. He's all right. He's a letch and a money-grubber, but he doesn't let on that he's anything else. And he's a pretty good doctor, believe it or not. The older Jack Petty gets, the better-looking he gets, too." She looked directly at Bud, seemed to hesitate, licked her lower lip, and went on. "I had a thing with him for a while. A couple of years ago."

Bud wanted to think that the feeling that shot through him was only surprise, but he knew that it was mostly jealousy. "I don't want to pry," he said.

A smile touched her lips. "The hell you don't."

"No, really, I—"

"Look, Mr. Bud Whatever. Let's quit bullshitting. I wouldn't be telling you that if I wasn't interested, and if I didn't know you were interested. I don't go around saying, I screwed this guy and that guy just for the hell of it. It's Tombley's Walk, buster. You and I are probably going to get something going, and if I don't tell you about Jack Petty, then one of our well-meaning old biddies is going to. It was a fling, okay? That's all anything with Jack Petty is. It was fun for a while, and when the kick was gone the affair was over. That's it, no regrets.'' She got up and went over to the window. ''So Jack Petty's a damn good doctor and a pretty good lay. So what?''

Bud leaned forward from the waist, watched her look first to her left, then to the right, through the parted drapes. He said, ''I'm glad you told me. I guess I'd better level with you. About me.''

She turned back to face him and folded her arms. ''Not now. Sometime. I've got this strange feeling that whatever you're going to tell me is a little more involved than that you used to bang the head cheerleader or something. Not now. I want to let things settle first.'' She parted the drapes once again and began to peer around outside.

''What are you doing?'' he said.

''Casing the joint. Old Lady Merriman, she's on the right, she's gone to bed. The Normans are upstairs watching TV, I can see the light flickering.'' She went back to the sofa and sat close to him. ''The coast is clear.''

''Clear for what?'' Bud said.

''You dummy. Clear for you to put your car in the garage. Don't turn on your lights, Old Lady Merriman wakes up if a mosquito farts. And if you put one scratch on my MG, I'll strangle you.'' She winked. ''Get going, Budro. You're going to be out of here before daylight, and we've got a funeral to go to tomorrow.''

JUST like every other prediction she'd made about what was going to happen in Tombley's Walk, Melody had hit the nail on the head about the meeting with the sheriff. There was a message on Bud's answering machine when he arrived at his rented house at four in the morning. He almost didn't notice the blinking light. His thoughts were full of Melody, her frenzied thrusts when they had made love, the tenderness with which she'd kissed him when it was over, and he'd sat down on the edge of his bed to call her and tell her he'd made it home when the flashing yellow light caught his eye. When he'd pressed the playback button, a twangy female voice had told him, ''Sheriff Ainson don't have the time for your meetin' this mornin'. He'll call you later." Then had abruptly disconnected. Bud had called Melody and told her about the message. She'd giggled sleepily and said, "See there? I told you you'd get to catch up on the old sack time."

And now, refreshed by a morning of sleep, Bud stood in sunlight at two o'clock in the afternoon in the cemetery and watched the solemn-eyed funeral director turn the crank that slowly lowered Billy Ed Whitley's casket into its grave. The casket lurched slightly, scraped the dirt wall, then righted itself and continued smoothly downward. Melody was at Bud's side in a solemn navy business dress. There a canopy roof over the grave site with chairs in the shade for about three dozen. All of the seats were occupied by relatives (Melody had whispered, "Bet old Billy Ed's got cousins here he didn't even know about") and immediate family. Big Ed Whitley, a shambling bear of a man with thick brown hair, stood beside his wife and cried shamelessly into a handkerchief. Billy Ed's widow, Brenda Jean, a pretty girl in a straight black dress, wearing a hat with a thin veil that covered her face to just below her nose, wasn't crying. She appeared more relieved than grieved, and stood resolutely beside her father-in-law as though she were ready for it all to be over.

Melody had exaggerated somewhat when she'd said that *everybody* in Tombley's Walk would be at this funeral, but the funeral home auditorium had been jammed with four or five hundred people. Over half of the funeralgoers had joined the procession to the graveyard. Bud and Melody now stood in blistering heat two rows outside the canopy. Sheriff Buck Ainson and his wife were standing in the row nearest the seating area, and the sheriff had the same woodenness about his bearing that Bud had noticed in church on Sunday. Doc Petty was there, too, along with his girlfriend, and earlier Petty had thrown Bud a wink and nodded to Melody. Try as he might, Bud couldn't shake the pang of jealousy that had zipped through him when Melody had smiled and returned Petty's nod.

Just as the coffin was descending, someone gasped

loudly at the back of the crowd. There was a rustling of clothing as heads turned. Bud looked over his shoulder.

Past the fringes of the crowd, past rows of white and gray tombstones and flat grave markers, past asphalt pathways with clusters of roses and gladiolas growing alongside, past clipped patches of Bermuda lawn, a car stood at the curb with its passenger door was open. Walking confidently away from the parked car and toward Billy Ed Whitley's burial site was a woman in a tight white dress and matching spike-heeled shoes. She was walking like a model on a runway. She had a trim athletic figure and a red mane of hair, brushed to a sheen with its ends touching her shoulders. She was smiling. Behind her, a man was alighting from the Pinto's driver's seat. It was a uniformed county deputy, tall, broad-shouldered, with a narrow waist and slim hips. The brim of his hat was practically touching his nose, and he wore mirrored sunglasses. He moved in a half-strut, half-swagger, caught up with the redheaded woman and fell into step beside her.

Near Bud's shoulder, Melody Parker said in a whisper, "Christ."

Bud looked at Melody and cocked his head to one side.

"Christ," Melody repeated. "It's Dory Barnes. What health spa has *that* old broad been hanging out in?"

Bud looked—or stared, rather—at the approaching redhead as people throughout the graveside crowd whispered to one another. This couldn't be. Just *couldn't* be. The frowzy barfly who'd sat next to Bud out at Jasper's and blown smelly beer-breath in his ear had been a good fifteen years older than this creature. A good fifteen years older and a whole lot lumpier. This woman walked proudly erect, shoulders square, and her wealth of red hair made her appear from this distance like a reincarnation of Susan Hayward at her peak. As she approached the edge of the crowd, the whispers died away.

One man on Bud's right said, "It's Sonny, ain't it? Sonny Beamer?"

The woman with the man said, "He's growed, ain't he?"

Bud had never seen the injured deputy before, and

looked to Melody for confirmation. She gave an imperceptible nod and said again, "Christ."

Men, women, and children backed away to clear a path for the sashaying couple, and they strolled toward Billy Ed Whitley's grave like two nominees on Oscar night. Dory was obviously having the time of her life, her hips swinging in rhythm with her walk, her gaze moving from side to side as she nodded and smiled, first at one man in the crowd, then at another. When she passed Bud and Melody, she stopped for an instant. She locked gazes with Bud, then winked and said in a low voice, "Didn' know what you were missin', didja?"

Dory and Sonny approached Sheriff Buck Ainson and stood at his side. The sheriff's wife looked first confused, then distraught. Then Sheriff Ainson, Sonny Beamer, and Dory all three faced the grave site. Dory chuckled and said loudly, "Don't mind us. You go on an' give Billy Ed a nice send-off, now."

13

"MELODY saved my life," Rachel Matthews said to Bud Tanner. "I guess I'd be a-walkin' the street if it warnt for her."

"Oh, I didn't do that much," Melody said.

"Didn' do much? Changed my life completely is all you done. When my husband died, them insurance people wouldn't give me a penny. If she hadn't sued 'em for me they'd still be countin' money that's rightfully mine. Not to mention that a man like Jack Petty would never be takin' a shine to me."

Bud lowered his gaze and pretended to concentrate on the fried eggs on his plate. The eggs *did* require some attention; they were runny and kept sliding off his fork. He picked up a piece of toast to use as a scoop. The eggs tottered on his fork, then ran down between the blades when he tried to lift the mess from the plate to his mouth. Visible beyond Rachel Matthews, past rows of booths and scurrying waitresses dressed in Denny's uniforms, Jack Petty was using the pay phone. His shoulders were stooped slightly, his head bent, and he was talking a mile a minute into the mouthpiece.

Seated in the booth next to Bud, Melody said tightly, "Yeah, old Jack is a real shiner, okay."

Rachel was wearing a flowered dress with an open bodice that revealed her olive-complexioned chest (Melody had said, "Christ, that's *funeral garb?*"). The tops of her breasts quivered slightly as she lifted a glass of apple juice to her lips, sipped, and set the glass on the table. She smiled. "I got some learnin' to do, I suppose, if I'm goin' to keep up with an educated man."

"Well . . . maybe Jack likes you the way you are," Melody said. She nudged Bud's shin with her foot. He gulped coffee to keep from laughing out loud.

Jack Petty hung up the phone, sidestepped waitresses and one couple who were at the cash register paying their bill, and made his way back to the booth to sit beside Rachel. "Can't get a thing out of the bastards," he said. "Next to zero."

"But you're Dory's doctor," Melody said.

"Not where Cave's concerned. I'm not anybody's doctor according to the city slicks over in Canton."

"Oh, come *on,*" Bud said. "They must have told you *something.*" What was going on in this godforsaken East Texas town was taking his mind off his own troubles. It was the first time since he'd left California that Bud had thought of anything else, and he had to admit that he was feeling relieved.

"Well," Petty said, spooning grapefruit slices out of a bowl, "they told me something, but not any more than John Q. Citizen could find out. Dory and Sonny left the hospital together this morning at daybreak. Hell, Sonny's *mother* didn't even know he was going home. Eleanor Beamer showed up for her visit and they had to break the news to her. I've got to see some blood sample reports on those two, but when I asked for 'em all I got was the runaround. They told me I'd have to talk to Dr. Cave in person, and o' course Cave wasn't there and nobody knew when he was comin' in. I'll lay odds he was hiding in his office the whole time I was on the phone."

"What did Dory herself have to say?" Melody said. "I saw you talkin' to her after the burial."

"If you want to call it talkin'," Petty said, "then I was talkin' to her. All she wanted to know was how I liked her body. Over and over, it was all she'd say. And Christ Almighty, the changes in that woman. Maybe that's why Cave doesn't want to give up the blood samples, if he could bottle what's happened to Dory he'd make millions."

Rachel peevishly wriggled in her seat. "Don't nobody want to bottle what's *goin'* to happen to Miz Dory Barnes iffen she don't leave my man alone. I'll feed her to them howlin' critters out to Mae Breden's place."

Melody and Jack Petty looked at each other with raised eyebrows, then back at Rachel. Bud said, "*Who's* place?"

Melody said, "Mae Breden is Macko Breden's wife. I told you about him, he's the old guy who knows how to fix things around these houses in Tombley's Walk. Lives out at the edge of town, damn near in the woods. What howlin' critters, Rachel?"

"You know me an' Mae was friends before she married Macko. Poor thing, I call on her ever so often. She says there's been some real strange noises comin' from them woods late at night, like a pack o' werewolves howlin' or somethin'."

"Now, don't be gettin' that started, Rachel," Doc Petty said. "First thing you know folks'll be runnin' around shootin' silver bullets. But with everything else that's happening around here, any noises in the woods bear some investigatin'."

"Well, put Buck Ainson on it," Melody said. "That's what he needs, somethin' new to snoop around about."

Petty looked distant, then said, "Buck's one could stand some lookin' into himself, the way he's been actin'. You see him stand there like a wooden Indian when Sonny and Dory come strollin' up to him?"

Bud gave up on the runny eggs, buttered a triangle-shaped piece of toast. "He did look to be somewhere out in left field. Two days ago I was his number-one priority. I've seen him twice, yesterday at church and today at the funeral, both times he acted like he'd never seen me before. At first I thought he was playing some lawman mind games with me."

"No way," Melody said. "That takes a mind."

Doc Petty fished in his pocket, came up with a modest roll of bills, handed ten dollars over to Rachel with a patronizing smile. "Go settle our tab at the register, sweet. I'll join you in a minute and we'll take a drive over to

Canton. I want to visit with them hospital folks in person."

Rachel took the money, wriggled out of the booth, nodded first to Melody, then to Bud, and walked toward the front of the restaurant. Two men in a front booth, wearing straw western hats, watched her go by, caught Doc Petty looking at them, returned their attention to their cups of coffee. Doc Petty rose, then put both hands on the edge of the table and leaned slightly toward Bud and Melody. "I may need some help," Doc Petty said.

Bud glanced toward Melody, then said, "What kind of help?"

"I need a couple of level heads, an' you're right, from what I'm seein' of Buck Ainson the last couple of days he ain't goin' to be worth shootin'. We got problems in Tombley's Walk that ain't come to light yet, has to do with this rabies. I won't go into a lot of doctor talk with you, it ain't my style an' never has been. But this ain't no ordinary rabies, an' the people comin' into contact with it ain't actin' like no ordinary victims. That's not any news to anybody that saw Sonny an' Dory at that funeral."

"That's understatin' it," Melody said.

"Well, I don't know what we can do," Bud said, "but whatever we can, you just let me know."

"Well, for now," Petty said, "just keep your eyes an' ears open. It sounds crazy that I can't tell you exactly what to look for, but right now that's the sitchyation. I've got some of that, whatever it was, that I scraped off that wall over to the church yesterday, an' tomorrow I'm s'posed to visit with a guy over to Tyler that says he's an expert on funny goin's on. He's from way up in New England, Harvard or Yale or one of them fancy places, if you can believe that. He called me this mornin', long distance. I'm headed over to Canton right now after some blood samples from Dory an' Sonny. Any—an' I mean any—funny goin's-on around here that you see, I want to know about 'em. That's about it, for now, but after I see this fella over to Tyler I'll get back to you." He started to walk away, then paused. "You heard Rachel, talkin' about werewolves.

There's a lot of ignorant people around here, an' that's the kind of rumor that might cause I-don't-know-what to happen. So whatever you see, an' whatever we talk about, you keep it under your hat, you hear?''

14

FIRST Macko Breden allowed as how him and Bob Bill Stoner ought to bash in the front door to Jasper's right fuckin' now. Then Bob Bill showed him that there were two Pearl longnecks remaining in the six-pack that they'd bought at the 7-Eleven, so Macko agreed to hold off while the two of them polished off the beer. "Man wants my business he's got to keep reg'lar hours," Macko said.

Bob Bill reached underneath the front seat of his Dodge pickup, grasped the carton by its edge, and hauled it up into his lap. As he reached for the metal churchkey that hung suspended from his rearview mirror, he said, "Can't be long. 'At's Rog's car ov'ere, ain't it?" He opened a bottle and handed it over to Macko. " 'At Bronco?" Bob Bill Stoner said.

Macko propped a booted foot on the dash, swigged, rested his forearm on his thigh, and let the longneck dangle between loose fingers. His gaze swept the front of the building, came to rest on the rear end of the Ford Bronco that was parked around to the side. "Goddam if it ain't," Macko said. "Reckon Hornby's in there gettin' him some pussy?"

"Might be," Bob Bill said. "Or sleepin' one off. I seen him yesterday an' he wadn' in real good shape, moonin' over his ex old lady."

"Dory?" Macko said. "He's moonin' over *Dory?* Shee-it, she's too old an' broke-down to worry about."

"Ain't it the truth," Bob Bill said. "I says to him, I says, 'Shee-it, Rog, you don't see me a-carryin' on that way over Becky, do ya? You need to do like me an' getcha some real young gals.' "

"Or like me," Macko said. "Some real, *real* young-uns." He scratched his cheek. Macko had shaved that morning and put on some Old Spice Lime after-shave, along with a clean denim shirt and washed but faded jeans. "You need to getcha a fan in this truck, Bob Bill. I'm sweatin' like a hog."

"Is a mite on the hot side." Bob Bill propped his own beer against the steering wheel. The sun was beating down on the truck's roof. The roof, like the rest of the truck, was black, but rusty metal showed through the paint job in places. Beyond Jasper's parking lot in the clearing, grasshoppers whirred. A squirrel ran down the trunk of the nearest pine, paused for an instant in the clearing, and darted into the shadow of the woods. "Got some shade under that awnin' on the porch," Bob Bill said.

"Well, less take to it," Macko said. He opened the door, alighted on gravel, crunched his way over to the porch. Bob Bill got out on the driver's side and followed. Bob Bill hadn't shaved or bathed. He still wore his fatigue pants from yesterday and his Air Force brogans, and wasn't wearing a shirt. A rivulet of sweat trickled down his arm.

Macko walked into the shade on the porch and leaned on the doorjamb. "You don't reckon Rog is at Billy Ed's funeral, do ya?"

"Naw," Bob Bill said. "Shee-it, that door ain't locked." He indicated the dead bolt, pulled on the knob. The door creaked and came open a foot.

Macko stood spraddle-legged, put one hand on his hip and lifted the bottle to his lips. He swigged. He belched. He wiped his mouth with the back of his hand. "Well, less go in," he said. "We'll open this beer joint up our ownselves, if Rog ain't in there."

That sounded like a pretty good idea to Bob Bill, so he pushed the door all the way open and led the way. Sunlight slanted into the interior of the darkened club. It reflected from dust particles that whirled like confetti in the draft from the swinging door. Bob Bill stopped, squinted into the dimness. Macko collided with him from behind and uttered a soft grunt.

There was a hum from the beer boxes and a faint buzz from the lighted Lone Star sign over the cash register, but no other noise. The stools were upside down, in a row atop the bar. Bob Bill said, "Rog? Hey, Rog, you in here?"

Only the hum of the cooler and the buzz of the sign answered him.

"Shee-it," Macko said, stepping around Bob Bill and moving on. "We can have us a private party, maybe call some women an' get 'em out here. Get some beer outta them coolers, Bob Bill. I'll fire up this jukebox." Mumbling, cackling to himself, Macko ambled over to the Wurlitzer, dug into the pocket of his jeans and came up with jingly change.

Bob Bill walked softly around the bar, the cool metal edge of the counter brushing his bare belly. He stepped onto the wooden runway planks that ran along the floor behind the bar, beside the waist-high coolers, then stopped in his tracks. "Macko," Bob Bill said. "There's a pile o' clothin' back here."

And there was—boots and jeans and a shirt in an untidy heap on the back bar. "Reckon they're Hornby's?" Macko said. He pressed a button and the rack inside the jukebox began to turn. "I ain't heard no beer bein' opened," Macko said. "Whatcha waitin' on?"

A mournful guitar played over the speakers; an equally mournful male voice began to sing "There Stands the Glass." Bob Bill Stoner shrugged, slid the door to the beer cooler upward, bent, and reached down inside. His fingers closed around something and he pulled it up. He blinked. He was holding a bare human leg by its ankle. The flesh on the leg was chilly, but dry. The calf was swollen, and in the light cast by the Lone Star sign the skin was a soft purple color.

Bob Bill dropped the ankle like a hot poker. It fell back inside the cooler with a dull thud. "God Amighty," Bob Bill said. "God Amighty, it's a *laig.*"

With the moaning guitar twanging over the speakers,

Macko sauntered over and leaned on the bar. He was listing; they'd been drinking beer since ten in the morning and it was now nearly three in the afternoon. Bill Bob's own forehead was numb and there was a ringing in his ears. If he'd been stone sober when he'd grabbed the leg, he would have screamed like a banshee. Macko said, "A laig? Reckon it's Hornby's?"

"If it is he's one dead sumbitch," Bill Bob said.

Macko sniffed the air. "Smell that? You been steppin' in some o' that shit out to my place?"

Now the odor hit Bill Bob's nostrils, the foul, rotten-egg smell. "God Amighty, I smell it, too. We need to call the sheriff, Macko."

"Guess we ought to," Macko said. "Reach on in there an' fetch us a beer first. I gotta have somethin' to take my mind offen this shit."

15

BUD watched Melody roll onto her side with soft moonlight streaming through the window and illuminating her bare rounded hip, the faint tan line across her leg midway down her thigh, and casting little bluish twinkles through her raven hair. The sheets rustled as she brought her knee up and clasped her hands around her shin. "Whatcha lookin' at?" she said.

"You."

"Sure, me. Whatcha thinkin' about, then?"

He chuckled, shifted his position, reached down on the floor and picked up his glass of iced tea from beside his answering machine. He sipped. The ice cubes had melted to the size of poker chips, and a residue of sugar clung to the bottom of the glass. "I'm thinking about a cigarette. After meals, after lovemaking, that's the hardest times."

"You ought to think about your lungs," she said. "And your heart, and all the things that the studies show. That's really an enigma, all these educated people sitting around puffing on those things."

"You're pretty much of an enigma yourself, Miss Parker."

"How's that?" She scootched downward, moved onto her back and hooked her foot underneath his ankle. With her foot beneath his, the top of her head reached to a point just below his shoulder as they lay on his bed.

"That you use the word at all. About half the time you talk just like the rest of the quaint folks around here. Then suddenly you come across like a college prof. Are you conscious of it?''

''Of what?'' she said.

''Of the way you sort of get on whoever's level you happen to be having a conversation with.'' He sipped more tea, glanced through the parted drapes. There was a single light on in the house next door, in a back window. Bud pictured Melody, her quick little steps as she'd come around her garage after putting her car away and he'd sat in the alley with his own car's motor running. He tried to remember the last time he'd waited for a girl to sneak away from her house at night. It must have been when he was in high school.

''I'm not really *conscious* of it,'' she said. ''If I was I'd probably never talk East Texas, my diction's one thing I really worked on, all the way through college. My freshman year up at S.M.U., everybody laughed at me 'cause I talked like a hick. But, I don't know, around the hometown folks I guess I just revert. In the long run it's probably helped my business.''

His chin tilted slightly. ''What, to have a lawyer who talks like a corn pone?''

''You'd just have to be there. Or grow up there. There's a lot of jokes about the city slickers and the country bumpkins, but there's a lot of truth in it, too. Folks in Tombley's Walk just don't cotton to people who go around *acting* really well bred. They feel like they're being talked down to.''

He set his glass back on the floor. ''You and the doctor have got it down pat. The country-boy act.''

Melody sat up and hugged her knees to her bare chest, watched him over her shoulder. ''Jack Petty knows the territory,'' she said. ''And I don't have the foggiest what he's so worried about with the rabies and all, but with the funny goings-on around here he sure hit the nail on the head about us not talking about it. You get any kind of talk started in Tombley's Walk about something supernatural, and the first thing you know they'll have somebody down at the fountain in the square, trussed up to a ducking stool.''

"Christ, Melody. Nobody believes in that stuff anymore, do they?"

"In East Texas? Look, there's people out in these woods who go around sticking pins in dolls. This is one of the only places in the United States where an exorcist could still make a living. Better watch out, Budro. You might wake up some night with chicken blood all over you, and some people wearing masks rattling bones in your face."

He stood suddenly, went to the window. He put his hands on his hips, looked down past his slowly rising and falling chest, past his semi-erection, at the outline of his bare feet on the floor. In the darkness, he nodded. It was time. "I'm wanted," he said.

She laughed softly. "By somebody besides lusting women?"

He sat on the edge of the bed. "I'm afraid so. By the California police. Los Angeles. F.B.I. too, probably. I think they get in on interstate flight." He looked at her. "You want to hear this? Just tell me and I'll shut up."

"Well, I'm here in bed with you," she said. "I guess I'm committed. You've got that money you're wanting to launder, through a corporation. Some kind of robbery, I guess."

He gently held her chin between his thumb and forefinger. "I wish. It's murder."

She eased back slowly and sat leaning against the headboard. "Holy shit," she said. "Perfect. Let me guess, you screw all these girls and then strangle them, leave their mangled bodies stuffed into incinerators. What do I do now, say my prayers?"

He couldn't help chuckling. He wondered if there was any situation where Melody couldn't make him laugh. "Afraid not," he said. "If you want it all you're going to have to hear my life story. It's up to you."

"We've got 'til dawn," she said. "Please be Bud. I don't think I can stand it if your name is really Clarence or something else dorky."

"Bud." He rolled to face her, propped up on his elbow, and rested his cheek on his lightly clenched fist. "Yeah, I've been Bud since I was a kid, I've got two big sisters. James Ernest is my real name. James Ernest Rigler. My dad owned a restaurant in East L.A., called Rigler's, in fact. Pretty fancy cuisine, actually."

"Aha. Little arsenic in the chocolate mousse, hey? Right after you had 'em buy a life insurance policy with you as the beneficiary."

"We didn't serve chocolate mousse. Bananas Foster, only Dad called it Bananas Rigler. He flamed it with grenadine and used caramel-flavored ice cream instead of vanilla. We went on a high school band trip to New Orleans and marched at Mardi Gras. I was a— I'm wandering, Melody."

"That's the idea. I can let you lie on the couch if you want, by the time you get through I'll know all about why you turned to a life of crime." She looked at him passively, suddenly serious. "Tell it all, Budro. I want to know. Really."

He clasped his hands behind his head and crossed his ankles. "Right on. I was a pretty good tubist, how 'bout that? So we went to New Orleans, and all Dad wanted me to do was have Bananas Foster at Brennan's and give him a report. I took three other kids for breakfast at Brennan's, and you know what? The Bananas Foster was better, though I never had the heart to tell my old man that.

"I was always going in the restaurant business myself," Bud went on, "even through college. I went to Southern Cal and lugged my big old tuba through two Rose Bowl Parades, majored in accounting. Getting married in my junior year changed my career plans, though."

"The love interest," Melody said.

"Her name was Beth. Beth Taylor. She was a big girl, but she had it all in the right places. From Irvine, that's down in Orange County. So anyhow, we got married before we should have, and both of us wanted kids, so I decided I had to have a job. Bless her heart, she was great, and we did all the methods and contraceptives and whatnot because we weren't going to have any children until we could afford them."

"Couldn't your dad help?" Melody said.

"That's a big misconception. He had this big restaurant

with a lot of jacketed waiters and everybody thought he was rich. But it took every dime, every single month, just to pay the bills and for him and mother to live. He gave us what he could, but he couldn't help much. I went with a C.P.A. firm in Santa Monica and Beth went to work for some lawyers. We did okay, but the years went by and we never did seem to get to the point that we could afford any little ones.'' He brushed away a tear from the corner of his eye. ''God, I wish we'd gone ahead.''

''If *my* folks had waited until they could afford it,'' Melody said, ''I wouldn't be here.''

''That's true with most people. So I woke up at thirty-five and I belonged to the C.P.A. firm, and I wasn't happy and Beth wanted kids. That's about, well, six years ago when the fast-food business was booming and I had a client with some fried-chicken places. He was rich and I wasn't. I made him a proposition, and he said as long as I'd agree not to compete in the chicken business he'd loan me the money for some fast-food places on my own. I picked tacos.''

''That sounds okay,'' Melody said. ''Tacos Rigler. Caramel-flavored taco meat.''

''Nope. Plain vanilla tacos, and I admit I copied hell out of Taco Bueno. I was Taco Pronto—that's not even original but it worked. I paid the loan back in two years. By that time we had twenty-three places up and down the coast, and Beth quit work and got pregnant and we had a daughter.'' He breathed a long sigh. ''Jenny. I've got pictures, and someday when I can keep from bawling I'll show them to you.''

''I'd like to see them,'' Melody said softly.

''We bought this damn big house, down in Newport Beach. If I hadn't done that I'd still have Beth and Jenny. The kind of people, well, I'm going to tell you about. They prey on people living in Newport Beach and places like that.

''I came home one day, it was around dusk, this has been three years ago just about now. August. I'd taken the Pacific Southwest Airlines commuter flight up to San Francisco to check on a couple of our places, and I guess it was about seven o'clock. We had a big Spanish house with a red-tiled roof and big verandas and a pool—you can't live in Newport Beach without all that. I still remember how quiet it was. Jenny should have been playing in the front of the house and Beth should have been swimming or watching Jenny, but the house was like a big tomb. I got a funny feeling about it the second I walked in.

"They weren't there," Bud said. "Nowhere. Jenny's room was the worst, when I went in there the first thing I saw was her Care Bears. She had the whole collection, and they weren't in the right order, like someone had knocked them over and didn't know how to put them back. Jenny still slept in her baby bed, but we'd bought this brass bed with the bars you can put up on the sides, and Beth was just about to move her into it. Jenny was three. There was a note on her bed, right in the middle of the white bedspread." Bud sat up and hugged his knees to his chest and looked down. "It was a pretty brass bed," he said.

Bud was silent for a moment. Melody didn't move; the only sound was her soft breathing and a slight rustling of the drapes. Then Bud said, "It was the usual kidnap note, words cut from magazines and pasted onto notebook paper. They wanted a hundred thousand dollars." He laughed bitterly. "Hell, I would have paid a million if I had it, which at the time I think I did. The note said for me not to contact the police and to wait for a call. I did. God, Melody, I did just what the bastards told me to."

"Bud . . ." Melody put both small hands on his shoulders and began to massage them. "Hey, you asked me if I wanted to hear this and I said I did. But it's you that needs to decide. If it hurts too much, don't tell any more."

Bud rubbed his eyes with a thumb and forefinger. "I'll be okay. I've got to get it out, and mainly I want you to know. They'll come for me one day, I'm resigned to that, and I want you to know the whole story when they do."

He stretched out on his back, bent one leg, and rested his other ankle on its knee. "The call came the next morning. A real creep, talked like maybe a guy from Brooklyn. He told me to get the money in nothing larger than a twenty and to drive up Highway One along the coast and . . .

well, there was a place off the highway in some woods near Lompoc. I did all that, went to the bank, drove up, and put the money right where the guy said. He'd told me I'd get a call the next day and they'd tell me where to find Beth and Jenny. The second call never came, of course." He turned his head. Melody was watching him, her image slightly blurred by his own tears. "I waited and waited," he said.

"After four days of nothing, I finally called the police. They came out along with a gang of F.B.I. agents, and told me among other things how stupid I was for not bringing them in to begin with. I grabbed one F.B.I. agent by the collar, I guess I'm lucky they didn't lock me up right then.

"So the local cops and the feds began what they laughingly called an investigation. This went on four months. After thirty days I was resigned that they weren't going to find anything, but finally they came up with Beth and Jenny's bodies, on a hillside up in Coldwater Canyon. Then they gave me the pleasure of identifying them. They weren't pretty, but it wasn't as bad as I'd thought because I convinced myself that those two slabs of decayed meat weren't my wife and daughter at all. Beth and Jenny simply didn't live there anymore, they'd moved on somewhere else."

His voice was steady now, a matter-of-fact monotone. "Right after that was when I started getting ready for—I don't know what, but I knew I was going to be ready for it if the time ever came. You can stash a lot of money away, just a little cash at a time from twenty-three taco places. I started doing a lot of traveling around and I told my people I was just keeping an eye on the business, but what I was really doing was taking, maybe, a couple of hundred dollars at the time and stowing it away in a mini-warehouse I'd rented down close to San Diego. And I bugged the feds practically to death, I could see the looks on their faces every time I'd drop by—like, uh-oh, it's *this* guy again—but of course they were just keeping a file open in case anybody asked and they could say they were working on it.

"Finally, this was January now, two years ago, they got a break in the case. I'll tell you something, Melody, the F.B.I. did a lot of chest-pounding over it, but what really happened, what I've decided, was the only way that they ever solve anything. They had a guy down in Terminal Island Prison, this drug dealer, and I guess he'd been selling some drugs to the people that did that to Jenny and Beth, and they'd bragged to him all about it. So he said he'd tell if they'd make a deal with him about his own charges, and naturally they did. I got the call from an agent, and all the time he was telling how they'd arrested this guy and he was the one, but I didn't really feel anything at the time. I sat and listened and I wasn't happy or relieved or anything like that, all I could think about was my plan.

"I went down, I remember it was a Tuesday because that's the day we had soft tacos on for thirty-nine cents and that was the day I had to pay for the ad in the papers, but anyway I went down and got my money from the mini-warehouse and bought a used car and some old clothes. The guy, his name I'll never forget, Manuel Arriaga, a Cuban immigrant. They were bringing him up to the federal courthouse in L.A. for arraignment, so I just waited around on the steps like I was meeting somebody and these marshals brought him out of a van in leg irons and handcuffs, there were two marshals and he was between them and I just walked right up to them and shot the guy."

Melody laid the back of her hand softly against Bud's cheek. "God, you poor . . ." she said. "God, I read about that."

He shrugged. "Probably. Or saw it on TV, there was a lot of coverage. I'd never even fired that gun. It was a .38, one of those little snubnose revolvers like policemen carry, a Smith & Wesson I'd bought for Beth because she was home alone with Jenny so much. The whole thing couldn't have taken five seconds, but it seemed like a lot longer, I was standing there pointing the gun and the two marshals were staring at me like they couldn't believe it, but I barely saw them. I was eye-to-eye with this Manuel

Arriaga, and I'd never seen him before in my life, but now I know his face as well as I know my own. He had a Pancho Villa mustache and these sleepy-looking eyes, and he looked at me and I looked at him, and I'll tell you something. He knew who I was. He knew. Right at that last instant, and he could see what was coming, and he had this funny little smile on his face like he'd expected this to come just like I'd known someday it was going to. I shot him once, it wasn't like a wild man spraying bullets or anything, once right through the heart and it was over.

"Both of those marshals were armed, and I don't know to this day why they didn't kill me right there, but they just stood and looked. I guess they were wondering whether they could get their guns out before I could shoot them or something, I don't know. I said something to them like 'He killed my wife,' or something like that, and then I just walked away. The whole time I expected a bullet in my back, but I went right down those steps and down the street and around the corner. My car, it was an old Toyota and I must have had twenty different automobiles since then, but I was parallel-parked in the middle of the block and, believe it or not, I had a parking ticket. You never know why you do these things, but I took that ticket off the windshield, stopped right there and read it over before I drove away." Bud studied the shadows on the ceiling, the crack in the sheetrock that ran from the light fixture to one corner of the room. "And here I am. I've been a lot of places since then and I've been a lot of different people, and I'm not sure to this day why I didn't just turn myself in to those marshals. It's coming one day anyhow, I'm going to jail. I'm just putting off the inevitable."

He turned on his side and faced her, saw the tender tilt to her chin, watched her lick her upper lip. She didn't say anything. Finally he said, "I'll pack up my horse and ride off into the sunset if you want me to. It's up to you."

She scootched close to him, nudged her smooth bare leg in between his thighs, laid her head against his chest. "It's a lot to take in," she said. "Give me a couple of days, I'll be all right. Tell you what *I* did one time. I cheated on a final. Honest Injun, I'd been partying all night and I didn't have a chance to pass the damn thing. So now you've got something on me, Budro. I won't tell on you if you won't tell on me."

16

MORTON Pellington, senior partner in the Dallas firm of Atkins, Pellington, Brashear & Leeds, thought that all of these small-town bankers like Justin Barker III of Tombley's Walk were pretty much alike. Operated these podunk banks as though they were the banker's personal grocery store, then when the heat from the F.D.I.C. came down expected their lawyer to pull a rabbit out of the hat. Went around just-old-country-boying everybody, played a lot of high-stakes roulette with the depositors' money, then got these mournful woe-is-me expressions on their faces and pretended they couldn't imagine why in the world the feds were picking on them and their li'l ole country-boy banks. A lot of bullshit, all of it, but it was what kept firms like Atkins, Pellington, Brashear & Leeds in paralegals, and made the sixty-mile drive up from Big D well worth Morton Pellington's time.

Justin Barker III, Morton Pellington had to admit, had a bit more polish than the run-of-the-mill small-town banker; a slim athletic, fortyish man, relaxing in green boxer-type bathing trunks beside his pool while his attorney sweltered in full lawyer dress, a navy Brooks Brothers suit with a starched white collar. At two hundred and fifty bucks an hour, Morton Pellington was willing to do a lot of sweltering.

Barker, relaxed, leaning back in a treated-wood poolside chair, his legs outstretched and his ankles crossed, and sipping iced tea with a mint leaf floating on the surface, was saying, "They're way outta line, Morty. No way, not any way in this world are any of those loans in jeopardy. I been knowin' these boys.''

Pellington's jaws clenched slightly—nobody, but nobody, in the downtown Dallas canyons would ever have the nerve to address Morton Pellington as ''Morty''—but he didn't change expression. At two hundred and fifty bucks an hour, Morton Pellington could be Morty or anything else that this bumpkin banker wanted to call him. ''You know that, and because you're telling me, I know that,'' Pellington said. ''But the F.D.I.C. examiners don't happen to know it. They've got guidelines, every one of these federal agencies is run by a manual, and their guidelines say that these drilling rigs are financed for several times CMV.''

''Several times what?''

''Current market value. Which spells write-off if the loan isn't paid or additionally collateralized within thirty days, which also means that in thirty days your bank's balance sheet is going to get lopsided. Which means in all probability that the F.D.I.C. is going to take you over, unless you can come up with one helluva lot more capital.''

Barker adjusted the elastic band at his waist, showing pasty white flesh beneath the elastic in contrast with the nut-brown of his chest and upper belly. His sideburns were silver; the rest of his thick hair was salt-and-pepper. He lifted his free hand from the armrest, palm up. ''Why would I wanta do that? You ever know ol' Cal Briner?''

Pellington ran a finger underneath his collar. The collar was sopping wet. He eyed the frosty glass of iced tea that Barker was holding and licked his lips. Pellington said, ''Not personally. I know *of* him, we didn't represent him. Had the bank over in Hughes Springs, didn't he?''

''Had it. Yeah, had it for half a century, his pappy an' him. We useta play a lotta tennis, over to Van Zandt Country Club. That's the way them F.D.I.C. people done ol' Cal, told him to come up with, I can't remember, coupla million or so, and put it in his bank to keep it afloat. Cal run his ass all over the state, finally had to go to them cocksuckers up at MBank in Dallas to get the money, but he done it and put the money right into his ol' bank. Wadn' thirty days later them F.D.I.C.'s decided that the coupla million or whatever wadn' enough, an' give him forty-eight hours to come up with *another* big wad o' money. Ol' Cal couldn' do that, so the government swallered the bank *an'* the coupla million or whatever it was that Cal come up with. An' I guess I don't haveta tell you where ol' Cal's spendin' his nights these days.''

''He's in a prison camp, isn't he?'' Pellington said. His throat was so dry that his voice was a bare croak. ''I hate to trouble you, Justin, but could I maybe have a glass of what you're drinking?''

''You ain't shittin' he's— You thirsty, Morty? Hell, I guess it's hot for you city folk up here. Hon. *Hon.*'' Aqua water rolled and sloshed over the edge of the pool as the redhead who'd been floating on the inflated raft climbed onto the bank and approached them. Barker said, ''Ol' Cal's up there, all right. I seen his old lady over to the club an' you know what? They got Cal a-workin' in a fuckin' factory. Cuttin' cable, she said, at forty-four cents a fuckin' hour. That's what I got you for, Morty, to make sure ol' Justin Barker don't wind up cuttin' no cable.'' He rested a hand lightly on the redhead's waist as she stood beside his chair. ''Hon, go pour Morty here a glass o' this tea. It ain't got no sugar in it, Morty, we don't use that shit in this house. Go on now, get him one.'' He slapped the redhead's tight rump. She rested a steady green-eyed gaze on Pellington for an instant, then slid her feet into high-heeled sandals and went toward the veranda.

Pellington watched the redhead go. Jesus, but these country hicks kept some women around. The redhead had muscled calves and thighs, an ass like a gymnast, golden taut skin. Pellington's own wife had gone to flab, so much so that Morton Pellington had taken to spending a lot of time at his receptionist's place. He looked back at Barker, saw the amused twitch at the corners of Barker's mouth, which meant that Barker had seen his lawyer watching the redhead and thought his lawyer's reaction was funny. Pellington cleared his throat, then said, ''I'm glad you brought it up yourself, Justin. It's something we need to visit about."

"What, about them F.D.I.C.'s throwin' my ass in jail? What's to bring up, I know that's what they got on they minds."

"And talked about it," Pellington said solemnly, "right there in our last meeting. They say you're loaning money to . . . ventures that you've got a personal interest in. Anything to it? Remember, Justin, I'm your lawyer. You've got to level with me." The level-with-me speech was automatic; Morton Pellington used the speech on *all* of his clients, then expected the client to bullshit him anyway. Then, after the case was lost and the client was going down the tubes, Morton Pellington could point the finger, tell the client that he hadn't been honest with his lawyer, and raise his fee for the appeal.

"Shee-it," Justin Barker said, lifting the mint leaf from his tea, holding the leaf between a thumb and forefinger and looking it over. " 'Course there's somethin' to it, Morty. I got points in ever one o' them wells them boys are a-drillin'. Jus' like my daddy had points an' his daddy had points an' ever sumbitch ever owned a bank had points in deals. I ain't runnin' my bank no different from anybody else. How you think a banker makes his money on them two-bit service charges on *checkin' accounts?* Shee-it."

The sinking sun dipped below the edge of the umbrella that rose from the center of the metal table at Barker's elbow. Morton Pellington squinted, scooted his chair so that his face was once again in shade. "It may be a common practice," Pellington said, "but it's against the law. Loaning money to ventures you have a personal interest in is a crime."

"I know the fuckin' law, Morty. I don't need to pay you to tell me that. I'm wantin' to know what we're gonna do to keep them feds offa my ass. At least for a coupla three months, then it won't make no difference. Thanks, hon."

The redhead bent to set a frosty glass of tea, mint leaf floating, on the table close to Pellington. Her flowered bikini top fell slightly away from her breasts; Pellington pretended not to notice; the redhead chuckled deep in her throat. She said to Justin Barker, "Ain't nothin', darlin'." Then she sauntered back to the pool, sat languidly on the bank, boarded her inflated raft with a series of splashes, lay on her stomach, and closed her eyes. Visible beyond her was rippling aqua water, the treated concrete opposite bank of the pool, the stockade fence that surrounded the backyard and pool area.

Pellington sipped tea. The mint leaf tickled his lip. He set the glass down as he swallowed. "Can I speak frankly, Justin?"

"Sure," Barker said. "Long as you don't piss me off. I went to a funeral yesterday, Morty, I hope you ain't goin' to give me no send-off speech."

"You need to tone down your life-style," Pellington said. "If you get indicted, and we've got to assume that you will, and we have to go to trial, well, what you did and didn't do down at your bank is going to take a backseat. The jury's not going to know come-here-from-sic-'em about the law, so the feds are going to try to alienate them by putting on a lot of evidence about the way you live. You're living in the biggest house in Tombley's Walk, at least the biggest I've seen, there's two Caddys and a Mercedes in your driveway, your wife looks like she just stepped out of *Playboy—*"

"She ain't my wife," Barker said. "My wife's gone for a spell."

Pellington closed his mouth, took another sip of tea to give himself time to think. Jesus *Christ*, but these backwoods billies were dumb. Wasn't his wife? Wasn't his *wife?* Pellington forced himself to speak calmly as he said, "What you do is your own business, Justin. I'm only here to advise you, and you can take my advice or not take it, it's up to you. But these feds want to make a criminal case against you. They're chomping at the *bit* to make a criminal case against you. Your phone is more than likely bugged, not that we'll be able to prove it, and they're already snooping around everybody you've ever done any business with or anybody that knows you on a social basis, looking for potential witnesses against you. If you're like me, and most married men are, then nobody knows as much to tell about you as your wife does. That's a real gasser, but it's probably true. But the law protects you in that regard because a wife can't be forced to testify against her husband. The key word is *forced.* Now I don't know anything about''—Pellington lowered his voice—''that lady over there in the pool, but this is broad daylight and you've got neighbors and all . . . what's your wife going to say when she finds out you've been, well, entertaining while she was away? The feds would just love to find your wife in a mood that's less than, shall we say, amiable toward you.''

All the humor was gone from Barker's expression and for the first time he seemed uncomfortable. That had bugged Pellington up 'til now, this farm-boy banker sitting around two steps from the penitentiary and acting as though he was on some kind of holiday. Barker shifted in his wooden chair and sat forward, a little roll of flesh now sticking out slightly above the elastic in his swimming trunks. ''I don't—'' Barker stopped, cleared his throat, then said, ''Well, I don't know for sure if my old lady's comin' back or not. This gal here, she's just over a spell, I seen her yesterday at that funeral I was tellin' you. Shouldn' nobody think anything about her bein' over.''

''Christ, Justin,'' Pellington said. ''Bullshit.''

''Yeah, well . . .'' Barker straightened, once again the boss talking to his employee. ''Well, you jus' let me worry about this little lady over here. I ain't payin' you for that, Morty. How 'bout you doin' what I *am* payin' you for an' gettin' yore ass back up to Dallas an' figurin' out how to get me outta this shit?''

Morton Pellington came within an inch of telling off the first client of his career. But then he pictured his suite of offices, the posh reception area, his white Mercedes, his rambling Spanish-style home in Highland Park, complete with sunken pool and trophy room, and the fifteen thousand dollars a month required to keep the place up. Not to mention his receptionist's apartment rent. At two hundred and fifty dollars an hour, Morton Pellington was willing to take a lot of shit. Besides, in the long run he was going to have the satisfaction of seeing this podunk banker up at the federal prison camp.

Pellington sighed. "Sure, Justin. I'll go to work on it."

DORY stood on the front porch in her bikini, wearing a waist-length terrycloth robe, and watched the Dallas lawyer's Mercedes crunch its way down the gravel drive toward the street. She was drinking Scotch (don't *taste* as good as Pearl Beer, Dory girl, but you're sure as hell comin' up in the world). The lawyer's white Mercedes swung around Justin Barker's blue Mercedes, then turned right on the asphalt road and picked up speed. Beyond the blacktop road, the land sloped gently away toward the center of town; visible in the distance were fields of bluebonnets, clusters of majestic pines, the spire atop the Tombley's Walk Church of Christ, and, standing out like a palace, the faded gilt dome atop the Tombley County Courthouse and Office Building. Justin Barker put his hand on Dory's waist. His palm was dry. A little quiver of excitement ran through Dory, a feeling she couldn't remember having had in years. Barker sipped his own Scotch and hugged her close to him.

Dory licked her lips. "You're makin' me tingle, darlin' Raven. When you takin' Dory?"

"Tonight," Justin Barker said.

17

SHERIFF Buck Ainson was having his doubts. The Demon Whiskey he'd succumbed to on Saturday wasn't what was wrong with him. He'd had hundreds (thousands?) of battles with the Demon through the years, and though the whiskey might take charge of his soul for a time, Buck Ainson's beholden spirit had always triumphed in the long run. But this was different. Ever since he'd permitted the harlot Dory Barnes to kiss (bite? fuck? Ainson's memory wasn't clear) him in that darkened hospital room, Buck Ainson had been having evil spells. He could feel the evil coming over him, but try as he might he couldn't do anything about it. It was as though Beelzebub himself had invaded Buck Ainson's soul, was wrestling therein with the Angel Gabriel, and even on occasion was pinning Gabriel to the mat.

He couldn't remember anything that had happened between the time that Dory had moved close to him, her harlot's perfume in his nostrils, and that moment sometime after midnight when Margaret had gently shaken him awake in the front seat of his car. He'd been parked beside the road in the county vehicle, and apparently had drifted off to sleep. Margaret had told him that he'd charged out of the hospital as though he were on a mission assigned by the Master. Ainson had written the incident off in his own mind to the Demon Whiskey (of course he couldn't tell Margaret that, not without telling her about Tulip Patterson and the effect she had on him), and had almost forgotten it when the evil had come upon him for the first time.

It had been the dog. The folks outside the church house had seen a dog, but Buck Ainson had known better. The dog had been the evil (Raven? No, the *dog* wasn't Raven, but Raven had spoken to Ainson through the dog), and Buck Ainson had been a kindred to it. And when the shotgun pellets had ripped into the dog, Ainson had felt the buckshot tearing into his own brain. Just for an instant, searing pain in his head, then it had been over. The dog had toppled to one side and Ainson had been himself once more.

Since then Buck Ainson had been the same Rock-of-Gibraltar sheriff that Tombley County had known for lo these many years. At least on the outside. But on the inside the evil was lurking, he could feel it there. And when Sonny Beamer and the harlot Dory had stood with him at the funeral, the evil had taken over again. And Sonny had known it, and Sonny had been a part of it.

On Tuesday night at nine o'clock, just about four hours after Justin Barker had sent his lawyer packing off to Dallas, the evil took over Buck Ainson right smack in the middle of Ainson's favorite program "In the Heat of the Night."

Margaret was dozing there in her recliner when smack in the middle of a Miller Lite commercial, Buck Ainson felt the evil coming on. His hands on the armrests of his own recliner tightened into white-knuckled fists and he sat upright. He closed his eyes, shook his head, and fought the evil. It was no use. The evil coursed through him like blood. He stood, blinked, and looked around the room.

Margaret's head had drooped down, and the pasty folds of her chin lay on her breastbone. She was snoring. Ainson checked out the sofa, the red and blue knit shawl draped over its back, the straw Indian rug on the floor. The evil directed him. He went out through the kitchen, stopped on the screened back porch for his hat and boots, and went out through the backyard. Bright moonlight had turned the garage a spooky yellow shade. Margaret had left the square-patterned sprinkler running; Ainson knelt near the flower bed and turned off the faucet. He went through the gate into the drive. The county vehicle was nose-on to the garage. Buck Ainson got in and drove away.

He went down Willow Lane and turned left on First Avenue, and all during the trip to the square Ainson assumed that the evil was sending him to his office. But at the corner of First Avenue and Davy Crockett Boulevard, just across from Matthew Tombley's darkened statue, the evil told Buck Ainson to take a right turn. He was surprised, but he didn't question. He went north on Davy Crockett for a mile or so, then took another right on a dirt road and proceeded toward the tall piney woods. The headlight beams bounced up and down, showing scrubby weeds, a pile of grimy trash, the rotting carcass of a long-dead cow.

There was a fork in the road, maybe thirty yards in front of the Plymouth's nose. Ainson put on the brakes. One fork was a continuation of the road he was on; the other wasn't really a road, but two ruts, twin tracks, partly overgrown, angling off into the woods. Slowly, easing his foot onto the accelerator then hitting the brake and coming to bumpy stops, Ainson plowed deeper into the forest. Fifty yards down the rutty path, he pulled to one side, stopped alongside a brambly thicket, cut the engine, and got out. He sniffed the air, caught a whiff of dampness. He didn't recall ever being here in his life, but somehow he knew where he was. Off to his right, through maybe fifty yards of thicket and pine, was Macko Breden's shack. The mental image of Macko Breden brought out the born-again Christian in Ainson; he wrinkled his nose. Then, the evil taking over and directing him once more, he walked to the rear of the Plymouth and opened its trunk. His movements were mechanical, wooden. He dug into the trunk, came up with a Remington Pump 12-gauge shotgun, ejected an empty shell from the chamber, and rammed home a live one. He slammed the trunk lid. He crawled up, sat on the car's trunk, and propped his bootheels on the bumper. He laid the shotgun across his thighs. He stared unblinking into the darkness, oblivious to the moon above and the whirring of the crickets in the forest.

He was watching the road. Raven's people would be coming soon. If anyone, anyone at all, who didn't belong were to come down the path, the evil would let Buck Ainson know. And then, Buck Ainson would kill them.

THE tan Buick Park Avenue ground to a halt just short of the fork in the road. Its lights went out, its front door opened. A flashlight winked on and swept its fingerlike beam along the twin-rutted fork that led deeper into the woods. Brother Leroy Abbey alighted from the car, wearing his Tuesday night, visit-the-sick-and-wayfaring, light blue suit. He was humming "The Old Rugged Cross." Earlier in the evening he'd left some chicken soup for Sister Eleanor Beamer, and had dropped in on a man named Ralph Diedrick. Ralph Diedrick was a factory worker who hadn't been to worship since his wife had passed on in February, and the brethren were concerned about him. Brother Abbey had found Mr. Diedrick sitting on his couch drinking a highball. After a few minutes of pleasant one-sided conversation, with Brother Abbey doing all of the talking, Mr. Diedrick had invited Brother Abbey to leave Ralph Diedrick the hell alone. Brother Abbey had obliged. He could only lead the flock; he couldn't force them to follow him.

Still humming the melody deep in his throat, Abbey strode purposefully down the path toward the woods. Every ten steps or so, he'd click on the flashlight and then snap it quickly off. Finally the beam illuminated Sheriff Buck Ainson's knees, the shotgun lying across the sheriff's lap, the chrome bumper of the county Plymouth. Brother Abbey stopped. "Evening, brother," he said.

Ainson didn't answer. His gaze was past Abbey, back in the direction from which Abbey had come. Brother Leroy Abbey shrugged, resumed "The Old Rugged Cross," went around the Plymouth, and continued on his way.

THOMAS Norton, the owner of the Woolworth's, and Doug Ellison, the only full-time roofing contractor in Tombley's Walk, rode out to the woods together in Thomas Norton's station wagon. Norton, a thin man with an enormous Adam's apple, and with bony wrists poking out from shirt sleeves that were about an inch too short for his arms, had been the first of Raven's people. Doug Ellison, who lifted weights as a pastime, had a thick shock of blond hair, huge bulging arms and a massive neck. He was wearing a muscle shirt and tight jeans, and his wife thought that he was working late on a job. Ellison had been the second of Raven's people. He'd been standing on a stepladder, about to nail some siding up on Justin Barker's garage, when someone or something had come up behind him. He didn't remember anything else, nor did he want to. Miz Radner's chow had bitten Ellison's daughter, and Ellison had made a big show out of killing the dog. Actually, the fact that his little girl would join him soon made Doug Ellison feel warm inside.

The station wagon bumped to a halt behind the Buick Park Avenue, and the two men got out and went down the rutted pathway. They didn't carry a light; they'd been to Raven's meeting ground enough times that they could have found it with their eyes closed. They stopped side by side behind the county Plymouth and faced Buck Ainson. For a full half minute, no one spoke.

Finally, Thomas Norton said, "Has Raven come?"

"No," Buck Ainson said, shifting his position on the car's trunk and hefting the shotgun's barrel to rest on his shoulder. "But won't be long."

DORY Barnes had thought about coming alone, but now was glad that she'd let Sonny Beamer give her a ride. All of this supernatural bullshit aside, Dory was scared. Scared, of course, of stumbling around the woods at night on Justin Barker's (Raven's?) orders, but mostly Dory was afraid of what was happening to her. Afraid of her little memory losses (was that ol' Rog that come in my room the other night? What happened to the ol' fart?), and afraid of the physical changes in herself. Sure, looking in the mirror was a kick, but what in hell had happened to her?

Dory hesitantly followed Sonny Beamer down the rutted path, conscious of the four autos—the Buick Park Avenue, the station wagon, Sonny's own Ford Pinto, and the black four-door Cadillac Fleetwood—parked behind her in the darkness. She was wearing cutoff jeans, a bare-midriff halter top, and white sandals (just because her new physical proportions scared Dory didn't mean she didn't like to show them off), and she was wondering about Justin Barker. Why hadn't he brought her out here himself? Why had he sent her home and told her to make it out here on her own? All about her in the woods, crickets whirred. She hugged herself and shivered.

Sonny Beamer was carrying a kerosene lantern, swinging it gently by his hip and sending yellow flashes dancing through the underbrush. His narrow hips swayed cowboy-fashion as he walked. Suddenly he stopped and held the lantern aloft. The flickering light revealed Sheriff Buck Ainson, sitting on the trunk of a car with a shotgun held on his shoulder, military style. The dancing flame inside the lantern sent shadows moving across the sheriff's face and turned his skin a ghostly yellow shade. Dory gasped and touched the hollow of her throat.

Buck Ainson, with no expression on his face, turned his gaze on Sonny Beamer. "Raven's back yonder," the sheriff said. "You bringin' his woman?"

Sonny nodded, then went around the sheriff's car and on down the path. Her breath now quickening, a strange tingling beginning on the insides of her thighs, Dory followed. As she passed, Ainson returned his attention to the road.

Fifty yards beyond where the sheriff's car was parked, the path widened into a clearing. Dory hesitated at the clearing's edge and squinted. It was a big clearing, and in its center was a series of mounds. She said, "Sonny?"

Sonny Beamer didn't turn around. He said over his shoulder, "You wait." Then he continued on, the lantern swinging, climbed the nearest mound with long confident strides, and disappeared over its top. The lantern sank below the horizon and Dory was in darkness. From somewhere in front of her, something growled. She huddled against the trunk of a pine, her lips quivering.

Seconds later, Dory's chin lifted. Someone—or some

thing—was coming over the same hill over which Sonny Beamer had gone. Dory wanted to run. God, she wanted to run, but at the same time she wanted to . . . she wasn't sure. She huddled in the darkness and watched the shape come down the side of the mound and approach her.

The shape was nothing but a child. A little girl, a little girl whose white face seemed to glow in the darkness, seemed to reflect the light from the moon. The child came close, stopped, raised her face to look at Dory. The little girl had long stringy hair, wore a tattered dress and—as she looked down, Dory nearly *giggled*—little tennis shoes with the toes cut out. The little girl said, in a strange little-girl voice, "My father waits for you."

Dory wasn't sure she'd understood. She cocked her head to one side and didn't say anything.

The girl's voice was suddenly louder, more urgent: "Come with me, wench. My father waits. Undress and come."

Little Dory had had enough of this shit. Didn't nobody haul little Dory Barnes out in no forest and then send no little snip of a girl around barkin' orders. Dory was going to turn right around and go—

Feverishly, Dory kicked off her shoes, stripped off her shorts, pulled her halter top over her head and cast it aside. The child watched her, stood at attention with little arms at her sides, then said merely, "Come," and turned and began to lead the way over the hill.

Dory Barnes followed, first at a hesitant walk, then broke into a trot. A trot that . . . something was wrong, something was different. She was trotting, all right, but . . .

Dory realized as a shock ran through her that she was moving on all fours, her belly close to the ground. She looked down at her arms (forelegs?), and her hands were no longer hands. They were . . . feet? Claws? They were four-toed feet with claws. As she followed the child over the crest of the hill and started down over rough terrain, Dory's jaw thrust forward.

Or did it? Did it only move forward, or was it *growing?* Her face muscles tensing and straining, the cords in her neck standing out, Dory's eyes widened in fright as her jaw and nose elongated. She tried to scream, but only growled. The child turned and smiled at her. Visible beyond the child, standing proud in the clearing at the foot of the mound, Raven waited.

There were four of them down there, but she knew Raven. He was the biggest, the strongest, his teeth the largest and whitest. The others stood respectfully aside and worshiped Raven with their eyes. Her breath now coming out in gasps along with her own lustful snarls, Dory charged down the hillside to meet him.

First Raven, then the others, mounted her one at a time. She loved it, craved it, was one with them and them with her. She was conscious of the child, sitting atop a nearby mound and watching them. The child was smiling.

Then it was over. The pack, now five in number, huddled for a moment. Then Raven directed them, ordered them with his mind, and they heeded. One by one they loped toward the woods, toward the pathway and the town beyond.

Dory Barnes was the last to leave the clearing. She was hungry. She wanted meat.

PART II

Spread

"There's critters acomin', pa. Down by the windmill, them yella eyes are aglowin' real spooky-like."

"You fetch me my rifle, Josh. Then go in yonder an' sit with your ma. Sit beside her bed an' hold her hand an' tell her you love her, boy."

—*Comanche Winter Tales*

1

MELODY drove to the northwest side of town on Tuesday morning. There was a queasy feeling in the pit of her stomach, and she wasn't sure what was causing it. Might be a number of things.

It was probably thinking of Bud (Rigler? Well, that's not the worst name in the world, she thought) that was making her stomach do flip-flops. One thing about you, Melody Jane Parker, she thought, you sure can pick 'em. Christ almighty, a *fugitive* yet. The only thing missing was the one-armed man; the goddamned elusive one-armed man a step in front of David Janssen with Lieutenant Girard a step behind, snapping at Janssen's heels. What's wrong with you, anyway, Melody Jane? It's a wonder that somebody's not fitting you for a straightjacket. And it would serve you right if they did.

But it didn't *have* to be thoughts of Bud that were giving her the willies. It just might be the place where she was heading. In fact, as she went north from the square on Davy Crockett Boulevard and then turned east, the butterflies in her stomach seemed to beat their wings even harder. Going to the poor black neighborhood on the northeast side of town shouldn't have bothered her—*hadn't* bothered her, in fact, for a number of years, though when she'd been a girl she wouldn't have gone alone where she was going now on a bet—but maybe it did. Now *that* would be a trip, Melody Jane, she thought. Where in the everloving hell do you think your clients come from? She laughed, and her laughter quieted the butterflies. She stopped laughing and the butterflies rumbled even more strongly than before.

Niggertown really didn't look a whole lot different from the poor white trash neighborhood on the other side of Davy Crockett Boulevard; gray wooden firetrap houses, porch roofs sagging on rotten beams, old mongrel dogs, all of them yellow or black, one poor-man's color or the other, who lay in rock-strewn, weed-infested yards and raised their heads to cast moronic stares in the direction of the MG as it rattled on its way. Melody kept the speedometer's needle below twenty miles an hour. Potholes the size of craters dotted the unpaved streets, and the repair of a broken axle was something she'd just as soon not have to fit into the budget.

Her client, a construction worker who'd hurt his back in a fall a couple of weeks ago, lived three blocks ahead of her on an unnamed street that intersected Fishtrap Road, the rutted avenue down which she was now driving. Melody was on her way to take the man to the doctor—not Jack Petty, but a different sawbones. There was an orthopedist over in Tyler whom Melody used to treat all of her personal injury cases, and the fact that the plaintiff's doctor buddied around with the same doctor that the insurance companies employed—to try and prove that the plaintiff wasn't really injured—was something that neither side, by agreement, ever brought up when the respective doctors were testifying on the stand. Melody had just eased her way around a pothole and was about to speed up when something in the road in front of her caused her to jam on the brakes. Her jaw slackened. She moved her sunglasses from the bridge of her nose to the top of her head. She blinked.

Sheriff Buck Ainson's county vehicle was parked beside the road about twenty yards in front of the MG's bumper. In front of the lawman's car sat an ambulance, its rear doors open. It registered on Melody that the ambulance's lights weren't flashing, and that they should have been flashing if this were a medical emergency. As Melody watched, Buck Ainson, in full uniform, badge glinting on the crown of his hat, came out the front door of a house, crossed the rotting porch and stepped down into the yard. Two men who were lugging a stretcher followed the sheriff. There was something huddled on the stretcher, something covered in blankets. As the men stepped down from the porch and began to cross the yard with their burden, two more men came out of the house. They were also carrying something on a stretcher, something also swathed in blankets. Melody squinted for a clearer look at the stretcher-bearers, then rubbed her eyes in disbelief.

The lead man on the front stretcher was Deputy Sonny Beamer. There wasn't anything unusual about the sheriff's deputy being in the procession—other than the fact that Sonny was bigger and stronger than he'd been a week ago, but Melody had already seen that the previous afternoon at Billy Ed Whitley's funeral. It was the other members of the party who caused Melody's breath to catch.

Toting the rear end of the stretcher, his gaze straight ahead at the small of Sonny Beamer's back, was Brother Leroy Abbey. The small and wiry preacher-man was wearing a navy suit, a starched white collar, and navy tie. His black center-parted hair was perfectly in place, and were he not stooped slightly forward with his hands on the stretcher's handles, Melody would have sworn that Brother Abbey was about to step into the pulpit. He didn't even look as though he was working up a sweat. Christ, Melody thought (it was around nine in the morning and the temperature was close to ninety; Melody's bra and bikini briefs were clinging to her skin underneath her lightweight gray cotton pantsuit), he's cool as a cucumber.

Thomas Norton, the owner of the Woolworth's, and Doug Ellison, the roofer, were bringing up the rear with the second stretcher. Their movements appeared wooden. Thomas Norton, wearing a light tan business suit, his head forward and his Adam's apple protruding like an orange from his skinny neck, was in front. Doug Ellison's triceps muscles rippled as he ambled along, wearing a Tombley's Walk 'Roo football jersey with the sleeves cut out at the shoulders. His jaw muscles bunched as he chewed gum.

Melody squinched her eyes closed, reopened them, and took another look. No, she wasn't seeing things. The Tombley County sheriff was leading his deputy and three local businessmen from a house in niggertown at nine in the morning, and they were about to load two stretchers bearing God-knew-what into the rear of an ambulance. Where were the medics? What in the ever-loving name of Christ Almighty was going on?

She climbed down from the MG and approached the group. None of the four men seemed to notice her. They continued their procession, slowly but steadily, toward the parked ambulance. When she was about ten feet from Buck Ainson, Melody stopped and said, "Mornin', Sheriff. Funny meetin' youall down here."

The entire group skittered away from her like spooked horses. The stretcher that Sonny Beamer and Brother Abbey were carrying tilted dangerously to one side; whatever lay underneath the blankets rolled to the low edge of the stretcher and teetered precariously. Leroy Abbey regripped the handle, used his knee to help right the stretcher, staggered slightly to his right, then steadied himself. The preacher resumed his posture, eyes straight ahead.

Buck Ainson's head swiveled until he was looking at Melody. His eyes appeared glazed. His voice mechanical, he said, "Ain't nothin' to it, Miss Parker. Jus' some nigger problems, nothin' to worry over."

Melody's chin moved slightly. Something wrong here. Something *very* wrong; aside from the sheriff and the deputy there wasn't a man in the group who should be down in this section of town on a medical detail. And these men were acting . . . Melody wasn't sure just *how* they were acting, but they sure didn't appear normal. Like wooden soldiers suddenly brought to life. She licked her lips and started to ask just what *kind* of problems, but as she opened her mouth to speak, the screen door of the house opened and banged closed, and there were footsteps on the wooden porch. Melody turned toward the noise.

Dory Barnes was on the porch, her lips parted in surprise. She was wearing cutoff jeans, spike-heeled sandals, and a red-and-white polka-dot shirt whose tail was tied together in front, exposing her midriff. Dory was carrying—or dragging, rather—a lawn-size plastic garbage bag that was full of something weighty and bulging at the seams.

It was a lot to take in—first the sheriff followed by the stretcher bearers, now Dory Barnes trailing along like a one-woman cleanup detail—but through it all Melody was vaguely conscious of something she hadn't noticed before. A smell. A *stink,* really, the same acidic stench that had floated around the church on Sunday when the dog had urinated on the bricks. Melody closed her nasal passages, a small knot of fear growing in her chest. She said, "Well, I don't want to mess in police business, Sheriff, I'll just—"

The thing that had tottered on the edge of the stretcher now rolled off and flopped onto the ground. The blankets sagged and folded open. The inside cloth of the blankets was soaked in clotting blood. The thing now revealed on the ground might at first glance have been a slaughtered animal carcass, but it wasn't. It was a man's chest and upper torso. The portion of the skin on the torso that wasn't covered in blood was chocolate brown. The arms and head were missing. The torso was severed just above the hipbones.

Melody leaned forward, put her hand over her mouth, and gagged. She swallowed sour vomit. Buck Ainson and the four other men exchanged glances. Then, slowly, deliberately, Sonny Beamer and Leroy Abbey set down their stretcher. Thomas Norton and Doug Ellison followed suit. All four men stepped forward as one and walked toward Melody.

The sight of the mangled torso burned into her mind, the acidic stink in her nostrils, Melody turned and ran. Her breath came in short painful gasps as she reached the side of her MG, opened the door and dived behind the steering wheel. She looked fearfully through the windshield.

Neither the sheriff nor Dory Barnes had moved; he was still beside the ambulance and she was on the porch clutching the garbage bag. The four other men were still coming. Doug Ellison broke into a trot as he left the yard and entered the street.

Melody ground the starter. The engine coughed, fired,

and then died. Her eyes squinched tightly closed, she turned the key (*Start, you goddam piece of junk!*) and jammed the gas pedal to the floorboard. Doug Ellison's footsteps crunched on dirt as he reached the MG's nose.

The engine caught and raced. Not looking back, her gaze now riveted on Doug Ellison's thick chest, Melody jammed the shift lever in reverse. Tires burned rubber and the MG flew backward. Axles banged as it bounced over a pothole. Melody spun the wheel, jammed hard against the door as the car did a 180 reverse spin, then dropped the lever into first. She floored the accelerator. The MG responded, burning more rubber and fishtailing away with Melody holding on for dear life.

2

DR. Jack Petty hadn't expected to like any Yale or Harvard smart-ass, but this Winthrop Reed was a surprise. Pleasant-looking, down-to-earth guy of around forty, clean-shaven with clear gray eyes and dark brunet hair and brows. The hair was thinning on top, but Reed wasn't trying to hide it by combing the back forward or any of that nonsense. Reed was square-shouldered, with just the beginning of a belly poking against the front of his red Polo shirt with the horse and rider knitted in blue on the pocket. You'd never spot Reed for a Yalie or a Harvard smug, and as far as Jack Petty was concerned that was a mark in the man's favor.

"I confess it made me nervous to meet you out here at this junior college," Reed said in a clipped Massachusetts or Connecticut accent, one New England state or the other. Petty had done enough traveling in the East to spot an accent from Vermont or New Hampshire, but except for the easily identified Boston twang, Massachusetts and Connecticut threw him.

"Why's that?" Petty said.

"Well, I'm using these facilities based on my Harvard ties," Reed said, indicating the lab table, the rows of test tubes, the strange iron boxes stacked one on top of the other at the rear of the room. "And as of two weeks ago my Harvard ties don't exist. I got fired." He smiled the kind of smile that said getting fired by Harvard didn't particularly bother him. "If Tyler Junior College were to check me out I'd be a dead duck."

Petty's brows knitted. "Well, I don't know as I like that, myself. Best I remember you told me on the phone you *were* at Harvard. Or Yale—I get those places confused, tell you the truth. Us country doctors can't tell fancy college folks apart, 'cept Texas Aggies and S.M.U.'s. Aggies fart a lot, and S.M.U.'s all got a daddy in the oil bidness. But I got to tell you truthfully that don't set too well, you misrepresentin' yourself." He was laying it on just a bit thick and knew it; Petty secretly thought that anybody who got fired from Harvard couldn't be all bad.

"Now hold, hold on." Reed lifted a manicured hand, palm outward. "I didn't misrepresent anything. I told you I'd been doing research at Harvard, and that's the truth. I just skipped the part about being fired because, well, you might not've seen me and I can't overstress how important this is."

He was sitting at a ten-foot conference table, directly across from Petty. Both men were drinking coffee: Petty's was black and Reed had added powdered cream to his own. Visible through the window at Reed's back were tall, well-kept pines, mowed islands of Bermuda grass, and a red brick, one-story administration building with azaleas growing along the walk. Two summer school coeds were going up the sidewalk toward the ad building, their books held in the crooks of their arms, showing tanned legs in tasteful thigh-length walking shorts.

"Well, hell's bells," Petty said. "How important *what* is?"

"I did some checking on you," Reed said, "right after I saw the bit in the Boston paper about the animal attack here. You're—"

"That stuff made the paper in *Boston?*"

"—the only registered M.D. in Tombley's Walk. Yes, I think you might be surprised how much coverage the incident received. In fact, I'm a bit surprised that no one else has contacted you up to now, no other researchers. There are other guys doing this."

"Doing what?"

Reed fished in his breast pocket, produced a pack of Doublemint gum, unwrapped a piece, rolled it into a cylinder and popped it into his mouth. "I've just quit smoking, excuse me if I smack some. You ever heard of Ridley, Vermont?"

Petty chuckled. "You ever heard o' Muleshoe, Texas?"

"I see your point. Well, if you never heard of the town, maybe you've heard of the incident. A pack of dogs, supposedly pets, that attacked some children in a creekbed. Killed four kids, mangled another?"

"Jesus. Seven or eight years ago, wadn' it? I read about it in *Time* or *Newsweek*, one of the two."

"1981," Reed said.

"Goddamnedest thing. Put all the animals to sleep. I remember thinkin' at the time that somebody shoulda been up there examinin' them animals' heads. Wadn' anything natural."

"How about *super*natural," Reed said. "You believe in anything like that?"

Petty folded his arms and fixed his gaze on a row of test tubes. "No."

"Same reaction I had once," Reed said.

"That why you got fired? Goin' around talkin' about supernatural stuff?"

"In a roundabout way." Reed leaned forward, folded his hands on the table, and studied them, his jaw working on the gum. "Look, I guess I should tell you, I'm a Ph.D. in biology, and yes, I went to one of what you call 'them fancy schools.' Was in premed for a while. I don't put on any capes and prowl through the night wearing vampire teeth or anything. But you're overreacting."

His gaze unmoving, still on the test tubes, Petty said, "I don't see I'm reactin' at all."

"Well, let's just say," Reed said, "that your reaction or lack of same reminds me of the same way *I* reacted when I first got into this. You've seen some things that you can't explain, medically, and the mere mention of anything supernatural makes you draw up. You're a man of science, just like I'm a man of science, and deep down you're afraid that if you start talking unexplainable phenomena that somebody's going to start chasing you with a butterfly net. Am I right, or am I wrong?"

Petty looked back at Reed, studied the pleasant man in the Polo shirt, didn't notice any telltale twitches. "We've got folks actually changin' shape in Tombley's Walk," Petty said. "We got a forty-somethin'-year-old woman got bit and two days later she's got a body like a *Playboy* bunny."

Reed looked slowly up from the study of his folded hands. "If what's going on in your town is what I think it is, then you haven't seen the worst of it, my friend."

"Christ," Petty said. "I guess you're the guy that knows."

Reed's dark brows lifted. "I'm the *what?*"

"Guy that knows. You ever go to the horror movies?"

Reed smiled a strange smile. "No. I've never been able to stand them."

"Well, I guess I got a weakness," Petty said. "More'n one, tell you the truth. I go to scary pictures way to hell up in Dallas, so I'm not likely to run across any of my patients. I got a girlfriend that goes with me and, this ain't none of your business, but you ought to see her in action after one of them movies when she gets me into bed. But there's always a guy that knows. Like, there was this picture called *The Omen.* Had Gregory Peck, I guess he musta been hard-up for an actin' job at the time, and he goes to the hospital where his wife is givin' birth an' this spooky woman comes up an' tells him his own baby's dead, but here, take this kid, and shoves this baby at him. Naturally Peck does, an' this baby he takes home turns out to be a ghoul. The devil, I think. Anyhow there's a priest who comes runnin' into Gregory Peck's office an' starts hollerin' about how the kid is evil, and the priest is the guy that knows all about the ghoul an' where it come from. Later on the priest gets a church-spire stuck through him in a lightnin' storm. But anyhow, the priest is the guy that knows. An' I guess in this sitchyation, that's you."

Reed's expression was serious. He shifted his gum from one cheek to the other. "Well, you can make fun if you want, Dr. Petty. But let me show you some slides, for starters, and then maybe you won't think it's all so funny."

* * *

Jack Petty considered himself enough of a scientist to be skeptical about everything, and he knew how easy it was to stage pictures. But the slide he was now viewing appeared real enough, little squiggly critters in color. The bacteria was blue, the odd-shaped spores a livid pink. The spores weren't perfectly round; some appeared pinched in the center like water drops on an auto's windshield. "I'd have to look up what it is," Petty said. "But it's a bacteria. That rabies?" The light from the projector shone dazzlingly bright in the left periphery of Petty's vision. The projector's cooling fan whirred. The shades were down; seated on the other side of the projector, Reed wasn't visible. Petty felt as though he was watching the slides in the company of a ghost.

"I'm not surprised you'd say that." Reed spoke softly, his words barely audible over the whir of the fan. "Especially since bacterial rabies is what you folks seem to think you've got over there."

"Hell's bells, it's what the state guys right here in Tyler said it was," Petty said. "And I can identify rabies if I see it. It don't have to bite me on the ass."

"I'm not putting you down," Reed said. "A picture or microscope view of a rabies bacteria is just what you and the health department have been seeing. What you're looking at now is a picture of the strep bacteria. Now remember, I'm saying it's a *picture*, not that that's what it really is. But what you fellows have been seeing down here, are those droplets in the picture?"

"Them spores? Yeah, I've seen 'em. They're what we can't figure out."

"They're not really spores," Reed said, "and they're not really droplets, either, though they do have more the properties of a miniscule drop of plain water than anything else. Doctor, this slide is one of a group I made in Ridley, Vermont."

"Samples off the dogs?"

"Wrong again." Reed wasn't such a bad guy, but he did have the typical Harvard habit of making somebody feel like a jackass when the opportunity arose. "This slide is from a blood sample that I took from a lady who was, according to her birth record, seventy years old. She had the complexion of a thirty-year-old.''

''Like Dory Barnes,'' Petty said.

Reed was silent for a heartbeat, then said, ''She was chained and handcuffed. Four hours after I took the samples, she broke the chains and killed two policemen. A third policeman shot her on the spot and I'm not going to tell you the rest yet. I've got an interview with the policeman who killed her on tape, you can judge for yourself. The policeman's no longer a cop, I think he's driving a truck somewhere in Maine at the moment.''

''You know I can check these pictures out,'' Petty said.

''And I'd invite you to. They're real, believe me. Very real. The *pictures* are real. It's the bacteria that aren't real.''

''You tellin' me somebody drawed 'em in?'' Petty said.

''No, they were there when we developed the film. This took a lot of trial and error, and you can save yourself some time by accepting the assumption that the bacteria you're looking at just don't exist. The droplets are real, though. The bacteria, I'm not sure to this day about this, they could be an optical illusion. But I don't think so. I'm of the opinion that the bacteria are the droplets, some of the droplets that have assumed a different shape.''

''Jesus Christ,'' Petty said. ''No wonder you got fired.''

''I'll get to that,'' Reed said. There was a metallic click in the darkness; the picture disappeared from the screen, the projector carriage moved, another picture flashed on, more squiggly germs, these colored yellow, and the same strange pink outlines that Petty had come to know as spores. ''This is an illusion of anthrax,'' Reed said. ''Also from Ridley, it came from a dead cow. A *cow,* mind you, a gentle old bossy who suddenly trampled a mother and two children to death out in a field.''

''You know, I was innersted in that case with the dogs, the one you were talkin' about. I followed it pretty close, matter of fact, an' I never read anything about any crazy woman or wild cows up there.''

''No, you didn't,'' Reed said. His chair creaked as he got up and moved across the room, a nameless shape in the darkness. A light switch snapped; overhead fluorescents flickered and steadied. Reed stood by the door with his finger still on the switch. He went over to the window and opened the shade, revealing the tall pines outside, the islands of grass, the sidewalks leading to the administration building. Reed came back to the table and sat down. "You didn't, and you're not likely to hear a thing about them except from me. I've got more slides, more of the same. Some appear to be bacterial flu, some others the strep you saw. Even a couple that will be familiar to you. Bacterial rabies, just like what you've got down here. But none of them are real."

"Assumin' you're not crazy as a bedbug," Petty said, "how'd you figure out they're not real?"

"Strictly by accident, actually. The usual antibiotics didn't seem to be working. I decided to try something a bit different with the handcuffed woman, the one with the bacterial infection, so I pumped her full of ampicillin, waited an hour, then took another blood sample. It wasn't easy, she was really violent by then. The second sample, the one after the treatment? No bacteria. Not a sign of any, only the droplets were still there."

"I don't know if I need to roll up my britches legs or not," Petty said. "But I'd like to have a look at *that* picture."

"There were . . ." Reed scratched his head; visible through his thinning hair, his scalp reflected the overhead fluorescent. "There were a number of them. After the incident with the woman, I tried it on the cow and a couple of dogs. Same result. An hour after the injections, the germs had simply disappeared. But I can't show you the pictures."

Petty scrunched down in his chair and rested his shin against the edge of the table. " 'Bout what I figured."

Reed's jaw thrust slightly forward. "Think what you want to. I don't have the pictures because they were taken from me. Look, I was doing research up at Harvard on a grant, and it was orders from H.E.W. people in Washington that sent me up to Ridley in the first place. I simply did what I was told. Incidentally, the reason you didn't read anything about the case except the incident with the dogs is because the second I showed up in town there was a security blanket thrown over the area the likes I've never seen. All the stories about putting the dogs to sleep? Those were spoon-fed to the newspapers just to put the story to bed. The truth was that we caged those dogs and studied them for more than a month."

Petty drew in a long breath and exhaled it, watching the man across the table, the educated man still chewing gum and speaking calmly. Petty said, "What'd you find?"

"A lot," Reed said, "none of which made any sense, scientifically. When I had my data together, most of it, anyway, a couple of men in dark suits escorted me down to Washington. I showed the H.E.W. folks what I had and, well, they sent me back up to Ridley, told me to keep on with what I was doing. Which I did, only more. I started poking around among some of the locals to see if I could determine when all of that strange behavior in people and animals had begun.

"Two weeks later I got a call from Washington. They told me to fold up my tent, proceed forthwith back to Cambridge and go to work. And above all, to forget anything that had happened to me up in Ridley, Vermont."

"Sounds like one of those cover-ups," Petty said.

"That's what it was. But during the two weeks since I'd been to Washington I'd found out a few things that just wouldn't let me leave well-enough alone. Oh, I left town per their instructions, but I took along a few things. Blood samples, mostly. For the past five years I've been going ahead with my work, the grant work, but evenings I've been running a lot of tests. On lab animals."

"That have anything to do with them?" Petty extended an arm, pointing to the rear of the lab, to the strange iron boxes stacked against the wall. The boxes were gray steel, about three feet wide by eighteen inches high. There were three of them, stacked one on top of the other.

"It does," Reed said. "It certainly does. I made a big mistake, about a month ago, telling my Harvard colleague what was afoot. He won't admit it to me, the bastard, but he contacted the H.E.W. people and let them in on what

I was doing. Two weeks ago my grant was canceled (that's another way of saying I was fired) and here I am."

"What's your stake in it?" Petty said. "I mean, if I was you I'd probably say to hell with it, and go do something else."

"Oh, I'm not a crusader." Reed was smiling again, that strange half-smile that Petty didn't know quite what to make of. "I've got the best motive there is," Reed said. "Profit. Whatever it is that's got the government wanting to expend whatever it is that's necessary to hide it from the public, well, it's got to be worth a fortune to find out how to combat the thing."

"Now, there you've said a mouthful," Petty said. "And the main thing that's got me about ready to think you know what you're talkin' about is what you just said. Men that go around campaignin' without no motive are usually nutty as fruitcakes. That's been my experience."

"Amen," Reed said. "Now those metal boxes you've been glancing at while we've been talking, two of them are vented cages. The open sides of the cages are to the wall, I don't want to upset my . . . mice. The third box is inch-thick plated steel, and the only openings in it are a food slot on top and a viewing slot in the side. We'll get to it. Ready to take a look?"

There was a strange tingling in Petty's scalp. He shrugged. "Ready as I'll ever be," Jack Petty said.

JACK Petty hadn't been sure what to expect when Winthrop Reed had turned the cages around, but as Reed had strained and grunted, lifted the top metal box, placed it on the floor, and turned it so that Petty could look inside, Petty had winced and involuntarily closed his eyes for a split second before opening them and blinking, noting the look of satisfaction on Reed's face as he did. Inside the cage, behind the steel wire mesh, were mice. Plain white laboratory mice, nothing more, only . . . Christ, but they were *healthy* mice. Big and sleek, looked as though they'd been on some kind of superdiet. Petty looked at Reed and shrugged his shoulders. Reed, the strange smile now on his face as though painted there, heaved the second cage from the stack, spun it around, and stacked it on top of the other visible cage.

More mice, only these were smaller, weaker looking. It occurred to Petty that these were actually normal lab animals, but sitting atop the other cage with the big sleek mice in view they appeared sickly by comparison.

"You've already noticed the difference in the two samples, so I won't point it out," Reed said. "You're also going to notice that the bottom cage, the one with the healthier mice, has a reinforced steel mesh, while the cage with the normal mice has a plain old chicken-wire covering. That's to keep the bigger animals from biting their way out of the cage."

"Oh, bullshit, Dr. Reed. I'll give it to you that them mice on the bottom look like they might be on steroids or something, but they're not going to bite through wire."

Reed hesitated, blinked a couple of times, fished a wrapper out of his shirt pocket, took the gum from his mouth and rolled it inside the paper into a ball. "No, they can't. Not now, not in the form they're in."

"Christ, are we goin' to have a werewolf tale? I've been warning some folks in Tombley's Walk about spreadin' *that* rumor in a country town."

Reed chuckled, the first time during the meeting that the Harvard man had laughed out loud. "Werewolves require a full moon, if I remember the legend correctly. Once a month, like a menstrual cycle."

"Don't know as I ever thought of it that way," Petty said.

"You may find these beasts you're dealing with to be a whole lot worse than werewolves," Reed said. "They can change at any time, given the orders."

"You're getting pretty far out in the pasture," Petty said.

"I may be, at that. I'll just let you observe something." Reed placed a hand on either side of the top cage and hoisted it back atop the lone box that he hadn't yet moved.

"What's in there?" Petty said, indicating the closed box. "That Frankenstein?"

"You'd be surprised," Reed said. "I think you really

would. Now please hold your remarks until I'm through." He went back to the conference table, hoisted a navy blue Adidas tote bag on top, unzipped the bag, and fished inside. He came up with what looked to be a ball of cheddar cheese—it could have been American cheese, but Petty thought that the color was too dark for American—enclosed in cling-wrap. After he'd unwrapped the cheese he went back inside the bag and found raw red meat enclosed in tinfoil. As he kneaded some of the meat into the cheese, Reed said, "It's ordinary hamburger, and this is sharp cheese."

"I had it figured for cheddar," Petty said.

"Same difference. Our friends won't touch the cheese without the meat."

"Aw," Petty said.

"No, it's the truth." Reed paused, his fingertips over the ball of cheese, then reached for more hamburger. "Let me tell you something about the mice. These scrawny little guys, and I wanted to let you watch them in action for a reason, the sickly mice have all received small periodic injections of infected serum. Serum with the droplets in it, nothing more. Blood samples taken later showed illusions of the rabies bacteria, and some of the mice actually seemed to be sick for a while. But I'm pretty sure they were faking. *Convinced* that they were faking, especially since when I left them alone they got better by themselves, without any treatment."

"A mouse ain't got *that* much sense," Petty said. "It ain't like they were tryin' to stay home from school or somethin'."

"Exactly. We're talking mental telepathy here. Please close your mouth, Doctor, you're either going to make a derisive remark or laugh at me, and I can assure you I've had plenty of both over the past few years. Please. Just observe."

"Well, one question."

Reed uttered an exasperated sigh. "What is it?"

"It's about those fat critters, the ones in the other cage. They get bigger doses of the serum, that why they're healthier?"

Reed glanced at the big sleek mice, looked back to Petty, watched Petty, and walked over to the cages with the ball of cheese and hamburger in his hand. "No. No, they've had personal contact. We'll get to that." He stood outside the cage, reached for a metal rod hanging on the closed box, poked the rod inside the cage. The mice didn't scurry away, just favored Reed with disinterested gazes, their sides moving in and out. The cheese dangling loosely by his hip, Reed hooked the rod through an eyelet in the floor of the cage and opened a trapdoor that looked to be about one inch square. Petty walked over, stood on tiptoes behind Reed, watched intently as Reed poked the rod through the floor opening and slid back a door on the topside of the closed metal box. The mice in the cage began to squeak, their noses and whiskers twitching, and huddled closer to the opening. "Now you're going to see some activity," Reed said. He withdrew the rod, opened a small door that was cut into the mesh, and rolled the ball of cheese into the cage. Then he stood back, folded his arms, and looked to Petty. Reed didn't say anything.

Petty felt slightly foolish as he realized that he was still on his tiptoes. He lowered his heels to the floor and continued to peer into the cage. Slowly, deliberately, one mouse who had a black spot on the tip of its pink nose made its way over to the cheese. The ball of cheese and raw hamburger was about half the size of the mouse, and an old cartoon image floated through Doc Petty's mind. The image was from a Tom and Jerry cartoon he'd once seen, an image of Jerry swallowing a glob of cheese that old Tom had left there as a trap. Jerry had taken the ball in one gulp, and his midsection had swelled up like a basketball. The image disappeared from Petty's mind. He waited for the mouse inside the cage to bite the cheese.

The mouse went around the cheese and, using his snout, rolled the ball toward the opening in the floor of the cage. The other mice crouched in a semicircle around the opening, their noses twitching. The cheese ball bumped its way to the opening and settled there, too large to fall through into the closed steel box. The mouse who'd been rolling the ball joined the others and crouched beside them.

From behind Petty, Reed said, "They won't touch it again. Not until they've got orders."

Petty turned. The Harvard man had retreated to the conference table and was kneading more meat into a second cheese ball. "Watch them closely, Doctor. You might miss something," Reed said.

Doc Petty returned his attention to the cage. For long seconds, nothing happened. Then the cheese ball wiggled. It bounced up once, then four claws poked their way up out of the opening and encircled the cheese. Four *long* claws, each one the length of a mouse's tail. The claws retreated, dragging the cheese down through the opening. Crumbs of cheese and raw meat dropped around the perimeter of the hole. Jack Petty's throat was suddenly dry. He swallowed.

"You'll have to take my word on some of this," Reed said, walking purposefully back to the cage with a second cheese ball in his grasp, "but they'll feed it until they starve themselves to death. The big boss ate less than an hour ago, so I'm hoping he'll let them have this one." He opened the door and rolled the ball inside the cage. "Some of it, anyway."

Petty licked his lips and watched the mice in the cage repeat the process. This time, the laborer was a different mouse, a little fellow even scrawnier than the others with hind legs like bent pins. Each time the mouse shoved the cheese ball with its nose, little tendons in its legs stood out and its sides heaved. Finally, with a final mighty shove, it rolled the cheese into place over the opening and uttered a tiny squeak that Petty interpreted as a mouse's version of a grunt. It panted its way over to the other mice and squatted beside them to watch the cheese. Its whiskers were wiggling.

The waiting time seemed even longer than before. Finally, just as Petty felt a sneeze coming on and was about to stifle it, the cheese ball moved ever so slightly. Petty held his breath. A single long claw poked its way out of the opening and nudged the cheese. The cheese rolled over once and stopped about an inch away from the opening. Petty could hold it no longer. He sneezed, and inwardly cursed himself. The mice in the cage didn't seem to notice the sound; they sat with their noses twitching for a heartbeat, then attacked the cheese ball.

And did they ever attack the cheese. They squealed ravenously as they surrounded the ball, tore yellow chunks out of the side, and wolfed them down.

At Petty's side, Reed said, "It's been twenty-four hours since they've had a bite. I doubt any of them would last another day, and I think our big friend in there knows it, too. He takes them right to the limit, past the extent of their endurance, really, but never starves them to the point that any of them die. Total control. He has it. Total control."

Petty turned his attention back to the cage. The cheese ball had disappeared; the mouse with the black spot on its nose was wolfing down the last remaining crumb. "Christ," Petty said. "Like a bunch of piranhas."

"Not a bad comparison," Reed said. "Not bad at all." He went over to the conference table, pulled out a chair so that its back was at right angles to the table, sat down, folded his arms, stretched out his legs, and crossed his ankles. In addition to the knit Polo shirt, he wore stonewashed jeans and white Reebok smooth leather sneakers. He smiled like Franklin must have smiled when the lightning had finally struck the kite wire. "I'm bringing you along rather slowly, Doctor, and there's a purpose in that. I'm wanting you as an ally, and too much too fast would simply scare the hell out of you. That wouldn't do either of us any good."

"What's in the box?" Petty said, moving over and sitting down across the table from Reed. "The thing with the talons."

"Another mouse. Don't look so incredulous, Doctor, that's what it is. I'll get to it. Now, those worker mice—that's what I call them—in a project like this one you have to make up names for your subjects as you go along. Those worker mice have had small doses of the serum, all by injection. The bigger boys, the ones in the other cage, well, you'd never believe this but they used to be a sorrier lot than the ones who just ate the cheese. I was a couple of years into these experiments, had already produced the big kahuna, as a matter of fact, when I decided to see what would happen if I just put some of the test mice in the box with the big fellow. What happened is the most interesting part of the entire project. It's also the least believable, but I just don't have time to show you all the proof. You can believe what I'm about to tell you or not believe it, it's up to you, but the less that you believe the more danger your community is in. That's the truth."

"There ain't a thing I've just seen that I would've believed an hour ago, Mr. Reed," Petty said. "So now I guess I'm ready to swallow just about anything."

"That's the mood I'm hoping you're in," Reed said. He shot a glance in the direction of the closed steel box, a glance that was almost loving. "One by one, I put a hundred and seventy different mice into the, well, the lion's den. The big fellow killed all but the half dozen you're seeing now. It was pretty grisly, he mangled the poor bastards terribly. But certain ones—and the really tough part of the study was determining how he chose the survivors—certain ones he merely nipped, just enough to draw blood. But they were really wounds, I verified that, but the bites healed in a matter of, in one case at least, twenty minutes. I've studied just about every life-form there is at one time or another, but I've never seen anything to equal the healing of those wounds."

"And you're sure they were really lacerations," Petty said. He was picturing Dory Barnes, the condition she'd been in when they'd taken her to the hospital, and the way she'd looked the other day at Billy Ed Whitley's funeral.

"No question about it," Reed said. "And some of them were pretty deep gouges. My God, with the length of those claws just a slight scratch is enough to go halfway through a normal-sized mouse." He got up and went over to the lab table, picked up a small test tube, rolled it between his palms as he reassumed his position in the chair. "Another nervous habit, Doctor," Reed said. "You'd be amazed at the variety of pacifiers I've found since I gave tobacco up. Once their wounds healed, those mice had changed. Every man jack of them, bigger and stronger. Perfect physical specimens.''

''Any females?'' Petty said.

Reed threw back his head and laughed. ''Excuse me, that isn't really funny, but yes. Only I didn't bring the girls along, they're all pregnant. The big kahuna likes to copulate with the girls after he's through scarring them up a bit.'' His brows knitted. ''You ready to have a look?''

Petty swallowed and licked his lips. ''I feel like I did the first time I saw the movie *Psycho*. Goddam right, I want to see it, but I've heard so much about it I'm about half scared to.''

Reed stood and laid the test tube aside. ''Another good analogy. I promise you that you won't be prepared for this, and that it will be a shock. Come on.'' Without looking at Petty again, Reed went over to the closed steel box and opened a slot on the side that was about an inch high by three inches wide. He stepped to his right and folded his arms. ''It might jump at you, Doctor, but remember that steel is strong enough to withstand a howitzer shell. And don't let the odor throw you, it's something else we'll talk about.''

Petty took a deep breath. He'd have to give the Harvard man this much credit, Winthrop Reed knew how to build up the suspense. But, hell's bells, Jack Petty was a doctor, wasn't he? He'd been through medical school, dissected cadavers with a cool and confident stroke while other students lost their cookies in the john, and had treated some pretty grisly compound fractures in his time. What in the name of ever-loving hell was he afraid of? But scared or not, Jack Petty thought, this Harvard smug's not going to have the satisfaction of seeing my knees knockin' together.

He got up and strode quickly over to the steel box, bent from the waist and peered in through the slot.

He wasn't prepared for the brightness inside, and for just an instant the single light bulb attached to the battery-powered socket on his lower right drew his full attention. It was a small bulb, not much bigger than a camera flash. There was sudden movement to Petty's left, in the periphery of his vision, and he shifted his gaze through the slot in that direction. For just an instant, Jack Petty was sure that his heart had stopped.

The thing that he was looking at had the body of a mouse, a big fat mouse half again the size of the bigger creatures in the cages outside, but there the resemblance ceased. Its smooth fur was white and thick. Its lower limbs were thick as chair legs, and its forelegs were no longer legs at all. They were . . . arms. Arms that were bent at the elbows, like human arms, only where the hands should have been were four-toed paws with two-inch talons curving from the toes.

Petty blinked, conscious of the smell that now assaulted his nostrils. It was an acidic stink, and it was somehow familiar. Petty searched his brain, trying to remember where he'd smelled the odor before, but before the answer came to him he looked at the thing's face. All thoughts flew from his mind.

The creature's eyes were red-rimmed and filled with hate. Its snout was a good four inches long; its teeth sharp and the size of corn kernels. Petty's eyes widened. As he looked once again at its body, the thing sprang at him.

There was no warning, no sound at all. One instant the creature was sitting there, its sides moving in and out; the next second it was coming directly at the slot. Its jaws widened. Its hot breath flowed against Petty's eyelid. Its teeth clanged against metal, and Jack Petty reeled backward away from the opening.

There was a low growling on Petty's right and, instinctively, he turned in that direction. The mice in the lower cage had . . . changed. God Almighty damn, Petty thought, the bastards have *changed.* What had been big sleek mice were now smaller versions of the thing inside the box. As Petty stood with his mouth agape, the creatures hurled themselves against the steel mesh of the cage, their jaws snapping. One strand of steel bent and sagged.

Petty stepped—leaped, actually—away from the snarling things. His ankle struck a table leg. He went over backward, arms flailing at air. His shoulders struck the floor, then the back of his head landed with a sound like that of a bat hitting a ripe melon. Pain shot through his head and down his spine. A sickening feeling in the pit of his stomach, the ceiling whirling, splinters of agony shooting into his brain, the growling of the creatures in his ears—

Jack Petty passed out on the floor.

"I'LL grant you it's a nasty bump," Winthrop Reed said. "The skin is broken, but beyond that I don't think you're going to be any the worse for wear." He dabbed at the back of Petty's head with a cotton pad soaked in alcohol. Cool liquid ran through Petty's hair and touched his scalp. A sharp burning sensation followed. Petty winced. He was seated at the conference table with his head bent forward as Reed leaned over him from behind and applied the medicine.

Petty's head was throbbing, but the cobwebs had practically cleared from his brain. "I ain't gonna be hurtin' physically for long, I got hangnail patients in worse shape. But I won't be gettin' much sleep for a while. Christ."

Reed wadded the cotton pad, tossed it into a tall wastebasket, then sat beside Petty and rested his chin in his cupped hand. "I thought I'd warned you sufficiently, but I've had years to get used to all of this."

Petty glanced toward the rear of the lab, where six normal, if excessively big, white mice now sat peaceably in their cage. "How many folks have seen this, Mr. Reed?"

"You're the second. The first was my supervisor up at the college, and a week after I'd showed him all this was when my grant disappeared. Somebody in Washington pulling the strings, of course. There are government people working on the same thing, that's why I'm surprised that you haven't yet heard from anyone else. The government researchers have got pretty much of a jump on me since they've had the advantage of free access to the Ridley area. I've had to develop my own research. Ridley's disappeared, you know."

"It's what?" Jack Petty said.

"Vanished. There are no more road signs, the current map doesn't even show the damned place. I tried to go up there once, two years ago, and the National Guard had a roadblock across the highway. Whatever's still up there, nobody's going to see without maximum security clearance."

"Well, you're wrong about one thing."

"What's that?" Reed said.

"This ain't nothin' supernatural. I've seen enough myself to know that. Whatever this is, a germ's causin' it, and that's somethin' we can eventually cure. Where you figure it comes from? I guess that's in your research, too?"

"But of course. And you can think what you want about it being supernatural, but no disease known to man can cause what's happening here. But the government seems to go along with you. Of course, they would. There's nothing in the regulations to cover what we call the Unknown.

"As for where the droplets originated," Reed said, "I haven't the slightest idea and neither does anyone else. But that's not uncommon, nobody ever knows for sure where new strains develop. Maybe they drift down from the atmosphere, and in some other galaxy somewhere the ruling species is made up of people who turn into monsters when they feel like it. Frankly, Doctor, I don't consider the origination of the spores to be near so important as the cure. And that's where I don't seem to be making much headway."

Petty gingerly rubbed the back of his own head. "Christ, and without doin' any experimenting on my own I got to accept what I've seen, that the spores go around disguisin' themselves as rabies or flu or whatever bacteria. That tells me that this sickness is God Almighty *thinkin'*. That it wants us to think it's somethin' else."

"Exactly," Reed said.

Petty stroked his chin and gazed out the window, toward the administration building. A custodian in matching gray shirt and pants was sweeping the walk with a push broom. Petty said, "What do you reckon it's doin' in Tombley's Walk?"

"I don't have the slightest idea. As a matter of course we—we, hell, the government with me sneaking around behind their backs—investigate all reports that hint of anything irregular. Any animal attacks, any abnormal behavior by people. I was down here in Texas, as a matter of fact, just two years ago when the man ran berserk and opened fire on a packed Sunday church service. A small town near Houston."

"I remember it," Petty said. "Who could forget?"

"Terrible thing. But it wasn't what I was looking for. No, this outbreak of yours is the first real case I've seen, since what happened in Ridley. If something isn't done, well, your town might disappear from the face of the earth in a year or so. It sounds like fiction, but take my word for it, friend. That can happen very easily. It's already happened in Ridley, Vermont, and once my old friends up in Washington get wind of what's happening down here in Texas you can look for the National Guard to surround the town and for all practical purposes put it out of existence."

"What's that odor?" Petty said. "Christ, does it stink inside that box! I've smelled it before. On a dog that came around the church house last Sunday. Somebody shot the poor critter, it acted mad as a loon."

"In its urine?" Reed said.

"Yep."

Reed got up and strolled over to the window, popped another stick of gum in his mouth, leaned both hands on the sill, and gazed at the administration building as he said, "It's just what it smells like. Hydrochloric acid, but the urine dries into something I've never seen. An odd sticky substance."

"Like tree sap," Petty said. "Or molasses."

"That odor is the best indicator I've found, the subjects' urine has the same property regardless of what form the creature happens to be in at the time." Reed looked at Petty over his shoulder. The Harvard man was showing the beginnings of a smile as he said, "So all you have to do, Doctor, anytime you suspect someone might be infected, is have them piss."

"Those spores. How come they disguise themselves?" Petty said.

"My theory is that they thrive on antibiotics," Reed said. "Somehow they know that doctors, convinced that they're dealing with a bacteria, will use antibiotics. I've seen some evidence. Penicillin and ampicillin seem to make the disease a bit stronger. But I've tried the reverse, and I can tell you that a lack of antibiotics won't kill the disease, though it does seem to stabilize the condition to leave the patient without medicine. The big kahuna in there was on penicillin for a time, and he grew almost half again as long as I kept the doses up. Since I stopped the antibiotic he hasn't grown any."

"Well goddammit," Petty said. "If it's really a disease I don't give a rat's ass *where* it comes from. There's a way to get rid of it."

"Exactly," Reed said. "That's why I'm here. You don't think I'd come to Texas because I *like* this godforsaken part of the world."

3

As she neared home, Melody forced herself to slow down. She wasn't going to do herself or anyone else any good if she broke her neck. She hit the brakes, watched the speedometer needle wind down to a sane and sensible thirty miles an hour, braked again and made the turn off Davy Crockett Boulevard onto her own street with scarcely a whisper from the MG's tires. Sweat was making rivulets on her forehead, her heart was pounding, and her knuckles were white as she gripped the steering wheel.

Had she witnessed what she'd just seen anywhere else in the world, she'd have merely gone to the nearest phone booth and called the local law. But not here, not now. You can't call the sheriff when he's leading a parade of zombies toting mangled bodies away.

She had to call Bud. He wouldn't be at home. He'll be at the library, she thought, so that's where I'll try to call him. But that presented another problem. Helen Bragan, who'd been the librarian for over forty years, and who along with Amy Averitt, the telephone operator, eliminated the need for a local paper in Tombley's Walk, would answer the phone. What reason would Melody Parker have for calling Bud? Her brow furrowed in thought, her heartbeat slowing to a gallop, Melody bounced into her driveway, drove past the house into the garage, and turned the ignition off. She was so busy with her problems that she failed to notice Macko Breden's ancient Ford pickup.

Macko's pickup was standing in front of Melody's house, its bald right front tire straddling the curb.

MACKO Breden's head hurt and his nose was running. The back of his throat was scratchy. Little Jeannie was the cause. Getting herself sick and spreading the germs to healthy folks. Letting the little brat have one with the back of his hand that morning had improved Macko's mood, but it hadn't helped his flu bug. To make matters worse, aside from being sick and having a whale of a hangover, Macko had to fix Melody Parker's sink this morning. Melody Parker, the highest-toned rich cunt in Tombley's Walk. No way was Macko going to make it without the hair of the dog. The hair of a *bigger* dog, as a matter of fact, so on the way over to Melody's house he'd stopped by Bert Adams's, the hard-liquor bootlegger's place, and picked himself up a pint of Rock Springs Sour Mash Bourbon Whiskey. The ten dollars that Bert Adams had charged for the pint had left Macko Breden with two bucks in his pocket, a hangover throbbing in his temples, a flu bug crawling through his nasal and throat passages, and a hard-on for the world. A few belts of the whiskey had done wonders for the hangover, but the hard-on wasn't about to go away.

To make matters worse, the rich cunt hadn't been home when Macko had showed up at her door. Bitch had a lotta nerve, calling up and asking a man to do some work on her house and then not even having the by-God decency to be there when he came. Probably she was out shakin' her ass around someplace. Macko had cursed at nobody in particular, kicked the doorjamb, and had another belt of the whiskey while he thought things over. Wasn't nobody gonna by-God stand Macko Breden up.

Stumbling and cussing, he'd lugged his toolbox around to the back of the house to search for a way inside. The back screen door had been locked, and so had the first two windows that he'd tried; but the third window, the one leading into Melody's sewing room, had slid esaily upward when Macko had yanked on it. He'd hoisted the toolbox over the sill—the whiskey bottle had clanked around inside the metal box, and for a fleeting panic-stricken instant

Macko had thought he'd broken the ten-dollar bottle of rotgut—then climbed in himself, stood on the carpet and looked around. He'd been nervous at first, though the booze coupled with his flu bug had made the nervousness no more than an irritating tug at the back of his mind. What if the bitch is home, after all? he'd thought. The one thing he didn't want was Melody putting in a call to Sheriff Buck Ainson.

After yesterday, Macko Breden wanted no part of Sheriff Buck Ainson. Spooky sumbitch, him and his fuckin' deputy. All Macko and his buddy Bob Bill Stoner had been trying to do was their duty as citizens, calling in to report Rog Hornby's body laying in that cooler out there at Jasper's. Hell, Ainson and Deputy Beamer had acted as though there was something wrong with Macko and Bob Bill for being inside the place to begin with. They just didn't understand real drinkin' men, that real drinkin' men couldn't stand around and let a honky-tonk stay closed, not during business hours.

And come to think about it, Ainson hadn't acted like any normal lawman that Macko had ever seen, and neither had Ainson's deputy. Hadn't even acted *surprised* that Rog was dead, just stood around and favored Macko and Bob Bill with fishy stares and wanted to know what the two of them were doing inside Jasper's in the first place.

Ainson had finally said, his eyes unblinking, "Y'all boys wait for us outside, me an' Sonny got some talkin' over to do." Then Macko and Bob Bill had stood in the parking lot until it had dawned on Macko that standing around out here waiting on those two spooky lawmen might not be the smartest thing to do. Sober, they'd have never had the nerve, but Macko and Bob Bill were just drunk enough to say to hell with the sheriff and his deputy, get in Bob Bill's truck, and move on down the road. Ever since then Macko had had this nervous twitch.

A few more swigs of the whiskey had quieted Macko's nerves, and he'd taken a tour of Melody's house. Not much had been of interest until he'd reached her bedroom, ransacked her dresser drawers and found her underwear. There he'd spent quite a bit of his time, touching each and every filmy panty and bra.

He was downstairs in the sitting room—standing by her open glass breakfront cabinet, in fact, looking over polished silver tea services, punch bowls, and china place-settings, and wondering whether a pawnshop up in Dallas would give a shit whether the stuff was stolen or not—when Melody rounded the corner and pulled into her driveway. The MG flashed in the periphery of Macko's vision as it passed the front of the house. He stepped to the window, kept hidden behind the drapes as he peered outside, and watched Melody's dark hair flutter in the breeze in the open convertible. She was wearing sunglasses, her head held straight to the front and her lips set in a line as she drove the MG past the corner of the house in the direction of the garage.

Macko's first impulse was to run. Had he been sober, he would have gone out through the front door, made his way across the front yard to his pickup, and driven away before Melody had time to park her car and come into the house. But he *wasn't* sober, and the whiskey clouds in his brain covered up any straight thinking that Macko Breden was capable of. He was remembering the light filtering through a pair of her black lace panties, the feel of the lace as it slid between his fingers. His face wrinkling in a nasty grin, Macko gently closed the breakfront cabinet, picked up his bottle from the table and tiptoed softly upstairs into the bedroom.

MELODY hop-skipped her way out of the garage, crossed twenty feet of lawn, went up the steps, and unlocked the back door. She hustled her way through the utility room and on into the sitting room, reached the bottom of the stairs, and began to climb. Halfway to the second story she paused with her hand resting lightly on the banister.

She didn't know the freaking phone number at the library, so what was she going to do when she reached her bedside phone? She could ring up Amy Averitt and tell Amy to connect her with the library, but she was taking enough of a chance by going through Helen Bragan to talk to Bud without stirring old Amy up as well. Besides, the directory—Tombley's Walk wasn't big enough to have a phone book of its own, but the numbers were included in a two-county directory that Southwestern Bell updated every two years—was hanging from a cord underneath the wall phone in the kitchen. Her mind made up, Melody bounced downstairs, into the kitchen, picked up the directory, and thumbed through it. She found the number, cradled the receiver between her neck and shoulder, and punched the dial buttons. She folded her arms, leaned one shoulder against the wall, and studied red-and-white checkerboard linoleum, the old-fashioned sink and drainboard, and listened to the rings on the line. Finally there was a click in her ear and Helen Bragan's voice said, "Library. Help ya?"

Melody summoned up her best I'm-a-country-girl tone. "Hi, Helen, it's Melody Parker. Listen, you know that new fella in town, Bud Tanner?"

Helen's voice was cozy and buddy-buddy. "Yeah. Where you been, Melody? You don't come down to study much anymore."

"I been busy, court an' all. Come fall I'll be catchin' up on my readin'. Listen, is that Bud Tanner around there in the library?"

There was a pause, then Helen said, "Whatcha want with him?"

Melody rolled her eyes and looked at the ceiling. God might've *made* nosy old biddies like Helen Bragan, but Melody would bet that the Master was kicking himself. "He's a client, Helen, I'm working on a case for him. Would you mind checking to see if he's there?" Over in one corner of Melody's kitchen, where the cherry-patterned ceiling paper met the grapevine-patterned paper on the wall, a spider had been constructing a web.

"He's been back yonder in the stacks awhile," Helen said. "I can give him a message iffen you want."

I'll bet you could, Helen, Melody thought. She said, "Well, it's kinda confidential. Could you get him on the phone, please?"

"Hold on." There was disappointment in Helen's voice, and Melody pictured the librarian's mouth in a pouty bow as she went away to look for Bud. After Melody had stood first on one foot and then the other for a minute or so, Helen came back on the line and said, "He's gone, I guess. Ain't noplace here I can find."

"Holy . . . Did anybody see him leave? No. Never mind, Helen, I've been too much of a bother already. Thanks for checking." She hung up, picturing old Helen with her mouth open, ready to ask more nosy questions.

Now Melody *was* in a quandary. She went over to the kitchen table and sat down. She might not be safe here in her own house; the sheriff and his loony posse might, at this very moment, be on their way over. She pictured the blank stare on Doug Ellison's face as he'd come toward the MG, and the thought made her shudder. She needed to warn someone, but who? Maybe the F.B.I., up in Dallas, and she'd actually tensed herself in preparation to get up and go back to the phone when she sighed and relaxed. She'd never known anyone to get any results out of the F.B.I. for at least a month or two, and Melody didn't have that much time. Besides, calling any outside law enforcement agency could have some bad repercussions where Bud was concerned. No, she had to talk to *him.* If she just stayed right where she was, eventually Bud would either call or come by. But when? What if Buck Ainson came before Bud arrived? And Melody couldn't just leave Bud a note telling where she was for the same reason—the sheriff might find it before Bud did. She glanced toward the counter by the sink. The dregs of yesterday's coffee were still in the glass pot of the Sunbeam coffeemaker, and by now would be strong enough to give Melody just the jolt that she needed. She glanced at the microwave, and was crossing the room intent on heating some of the coffee and gulping it down, when the linoleum behind her creaked and she was conscious of someone else in the room.

She gasped and halted in her tracks, wanting to turn toward the sound but afraid to. Afraid of who was there. But it *had* to be Bud. No one else would know where she hid her extra key. She smiled in relief, expelled air from her lungs, turned around and said, "Oh, I'm so glad you—"

Macko Breden was leaning against the wall beside the phone. His thumbs were hooked into the belt loops of his jeans and he was grinning.

Melody's body sagged, and she took a quick step backward to steady herself. So it wasn't Bud after all, but at least it wasn't that god-awful Buck Ainson and his herd of zombies. "Macko," Melody said. "You scared me to death."

"Ain't nothin' to be feared of, Miss Parker," Macko said, his voice thick and slurry. "You ferget I was supposed to work on your plumbin'?" He emphasized the word *plumbin'*, and his gaze swept her head to toe. His grin was more of a cockeyed leer.

The smell of booze assaulted Melody's nostrils. She'd heard some stories about Macko Breden and his drinking, but up to now she hadn't paid the stories much mind. She'd never even paid much attention to Macko himself; the times when he'd been over to fix something around the house she'd ignored him as though he were a piece of furniture.

"I guess I'd forgotten," she said. "There's been a lot on my mind lately."

He stood away from the wall and advanced toward her. He was listing some. He wasn't wearing shoes; his socks made whispery scraping noises on the floor. "Been some things on my mind, too, Miss Parker," he said. "Pretty woman like you livin' here alone, bet you don't go out with many men."

God, she thought. Jesus H. Christ Almighty on a crutch. That the handyman would take this very moment, what with everything else that was going on, to decide to put a move on her would have been funny if it hadn't been for the gleam in Macko's eye. And Melody realized as she looked at Macko, took in the breadth of shoulder and the big sinewy forearms, that physically she wouldn't have a chance with him, drunk or sober. She did her best to speak calmly but failed in the effort as she said, "Macko, I . . . well, I don't have time for you to work over here today, so I'm afraid you'll have to be going."

Macko's lips pulled back from yellowed teeth. One of

his front teeth was chipped at a forty-five-degree angle. He raised his voice in a mimicking falsetto and said, "I don't have time for you today." Then, lowering his voice to its normal tone, "I ain't goin' to be doing no *work*, lady, leastways not the kind o' work you're talkin' about. You an' me are gonna do somethin', though." He was only about two feet from her, his whiskey breath hot on her cheeks. He reached out and clamped a hand on her shoulder.

Melody's lips parted, but for an instant she was unable to make a sound. Bud, the sheriff, even the mangled torsos she'd seen, all were now forgotten. All she could see, all she could think of, was this foul-smelling hulk of a man, this filthy-looking moron who was putting his hands on her. Melody threw her head back and screamed at the top of her lungs.

Macko recoiled a step, his craggy face making a grimace. Then the crazy grin returned to his lips. "Ain't nobody can hear you, an' I'll tell you somethin', missy. Macko likes his women to holler, just a little." He came at her again.

She broke and ran, breath rushing from her lungs, crossed the ten feet of linoleum to the kitchen counter and yanked open a drawer. Knives and meat forks clanked and slid. She reached inside and her hand closed around a wooden handle—she hoped fleetingly that she was holding the cleaver, but she didn't really know. Whatever it was, it was a weapon, and whatever it was she was going to use it on this animal.

Macko came alongside and grunted as he slammed the drawer on her wrist. Tears of pain leaped into Melody's eyes. Her fingers relaxed and dropped the handle. Macko spun her around to face him, put his arms around her and pulled her arms up behind her back. Her wrist swelling and throbbing, her arms aching as though they were going to break in two, Melody decided that she was about to die.

His chin scant inches from her nose, Macko said, "Up to you, missy, how's it goin' to be? You goin' to treat Macko nice? You won't be sorry, many a woman's glad she's been nice to me."

Her lips trembling, Melody shook her head.

Macko tensed, released one of her arms, doubled his hand into a fist and drove it into her midsection. Whatever fight had been left in Melody now flew away as air whooshed out of her lungs. God, it hurt. God, it . . .

She went limp. Cackling, staggering drunkenly, Macko threw her down on the floor. He fell on top of her, tugging frenziedly at his belt as he did.

THAT morning, Bud had decided to do something—anything—to make himself feel useful. Talking with Melody the night before had brought him a great sense of relief, but along with the relief had come a feeling of frustration. Ever since he could remember, Bud had prided himself on being a take-charge individual—an attitude to which he'd attributed his business success and which, in the long run, had probably been responsible for his actions on the steps of the L.A. federal courthouse. But during his months on the run he'd been so intent on staying ahead of the law that he hadn't had time to think about taking charge of anything. And *that* situation was something that Bud Rigler made up his mind to change.

So what better way to sink his teeth into something than to dive elbow-deep into the strange goings-on in Tombley's Walk?

So he went to the library. Since he'd been to the library—under the guise of doing research on his nonexistent novel—so often since he'd been in town, he wasn't going to draw much attention there. Only this time, instead of browsing aimlessly through the fiction shelves in search of something to take his mind off his situation, Bud went directly to the medical section. Once among the books, however, he didn't have the slightest idea where to begin. Symptoms, maybe? Hell, symptoms of what? Jack Petty hadn't had any explanation for the changes in Dory Barnes, and Petty was a doctor. So instead of doing research, and instead of doing anything to make himself feel useful, Bud spent the better part of the morning sitting at a table in the library and staring off into space, more frustrated than when he'd come.

Bud drove his Toyota pickup out of the library parking lot and cruised the block and a half to the square with his mind wandering aimlessly. Just as Sheriff Buck Ainson had done a few days earlier, Bud paused at the corner of First Avenue and Davy Crockett Boulevard to eye Matthew Tombley's statue. He'd boned up on town history as one of his first priorities after coming to Tombley's Walk, and felt a strange kindred to Matthew Tombley. Like Bud, old Matthew had been a wanderer, and there was more than a little evidence that Matthew had been a fugitive as well. He watched the sparrows hop and twitter on the statue's hat for a moment, and was just about to continue on out First Avenue to his rented house when he thought of Melody.

She'd had a client to see this morning, so she'd told him, and there wasn't much chance that she'd be in her office. Her day's itinerary, as a matter of fact, included a trip to Tyler to take her client to see a doctor. Bud wasn't sure exactly where Tyler was located, but he did remember that it was a forty-five-minute drive. No, there wasn't any real possibility of seeing Melody before nightfall, but something else she'd mentioned now flashed into his mind.

There was something wrong with the sink in Melody's kitchen, a leak of some sort. She'd mentioned having a handyman—Breder? Breden?—over, and had also mentioned that the fellow wasn't very dependable, which was his privilege in Tombley's Walk since he had practically cornered the handyman market. Well, it was an outside shot, but if the handyman had failed to keep his appointment, then maybe working on the sink was a way for Bud to spend his time. Then, at least he'd get *something* done. He checked the Toyota's rearview mirror, looked right and left on Davy Crockett Boulevard, then made a sweeping U-turn in the middle of First Avenue and drove the three blocks to Melody's house.

Her shades were drawn and there wasn't any sign of life around the place. He cruised slowly by the house, checking over the bed of azaleas, the spotless white wooden fence, the mowed and clipped lawn baking in the sun. He'd worn pale blue tennis shorts and a navy Jack Nicklaus Golden Bear golf shirt this morning, but even dressed as he was he was beginning to perspire. The Toyota's air conditioner was going full-blast, but it was still hot inside the pickup's cab. He drove to the end of the block, pulled into a driveway and turned around, and went back to Melody's to park. There was an ancient pickup—a Ford, Bud noticed as he looked at the hood ornament—standing in front of him with one of its bald tires up on the curb. Bud's forehead wrinkled. Could it be the handyman's? Likely it was, and if so the old boy could stand some parking lessons. Bud decided he'd better let well-enough alone and leave. Bud restarted the Toyota and dropped the lever into gear. Just as his truck jerked forward, he caught a flash of white to the rear of the house.

It was Melody's car. The MG's bumper was visible through the open garage door. He killed his engine, got out and took two long strides in the direction of the front door, then stopped in his tracks. He chuckled softly. Barging in on Melody with the handyman there would start local gossip. He shrugged, turned around, and was retreating to his Toyota when a high-pitched scream from within the house reached his ears.

The scream was faint and sounded far away. But it was Melody, and the scream was one of pure terror. All else forgotten, Bud whirled, vaulted over the picket fence, dashed across the lawn and up on the porch, grabbed the door handle and twisted.

The door was locked. The goddam door was locked. He cocked his head and listened for the scream to repeat itself, but heard nothing. Had he been imagining things? He had a mental image of himself, bursting into the kitchen out of breath while the handyman used a pipe wrench under the sink and Melody sat calmly at the table, drinking coffee.

He sighed. After hearing that scream he couldn't leave anything to chance. He had to get inside the house. Had to. He was hopping on one foot, ready to take off one of his Reebok sneakers and smash a window, when he remembered the key that Melody had told him about. He stood on tiptoes and felt along the ledge above the door.

His fingers came in contact with the metal key. Breathing a sigh, hoping against hope that everything was all right inside the house, he fitted the key in the door, turned it and went inside. He paused in the entryway, when a new sound came to his ears, a muffled cry, practically a sob, from back inside the kitchen. He moved toward the sound. His hands were in fists and there was tension in his neck and shoulders. Melody was flat on her back on the floor beside the sink. A man—a dirty-looking, fiftyish man with greasy, unkept hair, wearing faded jeans and a grimy T-shirt, shoeless, wearing only dirty white athletic socks—was on top of her. The man's fly was open and he was in the process of unbuttoning Melody's blouse. Her body was limp and her eyes were closed. As Bud came into the room, the man looked up. His eyes were bloodshot and his gaze bleary.

EVEN through the boozy haze in his brain, through the excitement he felt at finally getting his hands on Miss Juicy Parker, Macko Breden knew he'd messed up. Who was *this* rich-looking asshole? Probably thought he was about to be some kind of hero asshole. Well, Macko Breden had news for him. Yelling, Macko Breden charged. He hit Bud with a flying tackle, and the two of them tumbled through the kitchen door and into the dining room.

BUD grunted and flew backwards, head over heels, his attacker growling and snarling like a beast and pummeling Bud's ribs and midsection. Bud's head collided with a dining-table leg. There was a sickening thud, pain shot through his head, and for an instant the ceiling whirled. He was flat on his back. The filthy man was straddling his chest. Whiskey breath assaulted Bud's nostrils as callused dirty hands closed around his throat and thumbs dug into his windpipe.

The filthy bastard was strong as an ox. Bud grabbed the man's wrists. The grip on Bud's throat was like vibrating bands of steel. Gagging, choking, Bud kicked and rolled.

The man rolled with him. One of the dirty man's shoulders hit the floor hard and the grip around Bud's throat loosened. Bud managed to get one foot underneath himself and rose to one knee. Gasping, fighting for breath, Bud stood unsteadily and backed away.

The dirty man lay still for a couple of seconds, his eyes glazed. Then he too stood. He was listing on his feet, a puzzled expression on his face.

Bud knew one thing: hurt as he was, he wasn't going to have a better opportunity than he did now. He took a short step forward and sent a stinging left jab onto the point of the filthy man's nose.

The blow was straight and had some power behind it, and landed right on the button, with a sharp popping sound. The dirty man's head snapped backward on his neck, and he staggered drunkenly away. Blood ran suddenly from his nostril and down his upper lip to his mouth. Disbelief was in his eyes. Encouraged, Bud Rigler waded in.

He brought a solid right up underneath the man's chin. There was another satisfying crack as the punch landed solidly, and the man staggered away once again. He was weaving, unsteady on his feet. The two solid punches had fueled Bud's adrenaline, and he moved confidently in to finish the man off. Suddenly, without warning, the filthy man broke and ran.

Bud was too surprised to move. He really hadn't believed that he had a chance against the man, and was probably more shocked at what he'd done than the man was. Frozen in his tracks, his mouth agape, Bud watched the filthy man run into the living room, bump the divan hard with his hip as he went by, throw the front door open and charge out on the porch. He ran with a slight limp, and his stockinged feet made soft thumping noises on the wooden porch.

Bud went to the front window and looked outside. The man lurched his way across the yard, threw open his pickup's door, and climbed laboriously into the driver's seat. The pickup's door slammed. Its engine chugged, then roared. Its bald front tire bounced down from the curb; the pickup careened wildly down the street and out of sight around the corner.

An image of Melody silent on the kitchen floor flashed into Bud's mind. His chest heaving, he sprinted back through the dining room and back into the kitchen. Five feet inside the door he stopped in his tracks.

Melody was sitting up. Her back was leaning against the refrigerator and she was gingerly touching her stomach. Her eyelashes fluttered and she smiled weakly at him. "How'm I goin' to get my sink repaired?" she said. "After all that, I'll never get him back over here."

"It feels like I've been doing about ten thousand sit-ups," Melody said. "Ooo, be a nice color in the morning. I'll tell you one thing, this won't do. It'll show." She pulled her halter top off over her head, stood before her dresser in khaki-colored Jamaica shorts and strapless bra, opened a drawer, and selected a red T-shirt that had *I'm a Virgin (This is a Very Old Shirt)* written in white script on its front. She put the T-shirt on and smoothed its hem around her hips.

Bud was sitting on her bed with his legs crossed, leaning back, propped up on one elbow. There were black bikini panties tossed at random on the foot of the bed, another pair, this one beige, on the floor halfway between the bed and the dresser. "He really went through your things. I don't think I've ever seen a real live pervert before."

"Makes my skin crawl," Melody said.

Bud dropped his fist lightly on a pillow. "I can't believe this. The guy could have killed me, I guess, and gotten away with it because we can't even call the law. How can you be so calm about it?"

Melody was applying rouge to her lips. "Well, you can believe it's a front. Jesus Christ, ever time I think about those bodies, I . . . Bad as old Macko was, he was nothing compared with that gang of zombies."

"And you're sure your imagination wasn't running away with you?"

She gestured with her lip brush. "I saw what I saw. Two black people, or what was left of them, and the sheriff and four of our citizenry hauling the bodies away on stretchers. One thing to be thankful for, at least I didn't have the pleasure of seeing whatever it was old Dory was carrying in those garbage bags. I *would* have lost my cookies.'' She looked directly at him. Her face was still calm, but there were dark circles under her eyes. ''We've got to get away from this house. Probably the only reason they haven't been over here already is because it's daylight and somebody'd see them. Daylight didn't bother them where I ran into 'em, but a white neighborhood would be a different story.''

Bud intertwined his fingers and clasped his hands on his thigh. ''Go where?''

''That's the sixty-four-dollar question,'' Melody said. ''We can't go running to the state police, F.B.I., or anybody, not with the warrants out on you.''

Bud's gaze lowered. ''I'd turn myself in before I'd let anything happen to you.''

Her face softened for an instant. ''You know, I think you would.'' Her impish half-smile returned. ''Nah. Then I'd have to run around the country defending you. I think the first thing to do is go out to Jack Petty's office and wait for him. He's gone to Tyler. Oh, wipe that look off your face, Jack Petty was nothing but a fling for me, and you can bet I meant less than that to him.'' She dropped her wallet and car keys into a small carrying purse and snapped it closed. ''So what we've got here is a choice between the law and the ghouls. Or right now the ghoulish law. One way or the other, Budro, we'd better get our butts in gear.''

4

ROG Hornby's sister Fedora daintily blew her nose into a lace hanky. She was a well-groomed woman of fifty-two (though she didn't let on her age to anyone, including her husband Albert, who'd forgotten in twenty-nine years of marriage exactly how old his wife was) and was wearing a high-necked dress of mid-calf length and a dove-gray color, suitable for the occasion. "I ain't arguin' that Rog was a saint, Ezra," she said. "But no way would he leave any propity to *her,* not after what she put him through." She extended a bony arm and pointed at Dory Barnes, who was seated just inside the courtroom railing with her legs crossed in a saucy attitude. Dory wore a tapered, form-fitting pink blouse, cut low in front, along with designer jeans and open-toed spike-heeled pumps.

County Judge Ezra Porter rattled the papers before him, held them at arm's length, tilted his chin back, and read through the bottom portion of his bifocals. He was thin as spaghetti, with huge bags under his eyes, and his black robe was about two sizes too big. Thick hair sprouted from his head like snow-white monkey grass. As he went over the papers he said, "We ain't here to determine what Rog would do and what he wouldn' do, Fedora. Nobody knowed that but Rog, and he ain't among the livin' no more. The purpose of this here proceedin' is to determine the validity of this will bein' offered for probate." He adjusted his glasses on his nose and peered at Dory Barnes. "You represented by counsel?" he said. Overhead, antique ceiling fans turned and made soft flapping noises.

District Judge Jack Puckett, wearing a dark green suit, white shirt, and green tie, got snappily up from his chair beside Dory and folded his arms. "Here, your honor," Puckett said. He was short and baby-fat chubby, with rosy cheeks and soft pink hands. There was nothing to prevent judges from practicing law on the side, and often in Tombley County litigants would retain the district judge to represent them in county court and vice versa. The practice gave both Jack Puckett and Ezra Porter something to do when there weren't any cases pending in their respective courts, which in Tombley's Walk was most of the time.

"How 'bout you, Fedora?" Ezra Porter said. "You got a lawyer?"

Fedora put her hands on her hips and tossed her head. "You know I ain't got no lawyer, Ezra. I was goin' up to see Jack Puckett myself, but that . . . *woman,* she'd done been up there. I done called down to Melody Parker's too, but she ain't in."

"Well, maybe we can't have no hearin', then," the judge said.

"If the court please, Your Honor." Jack Puckett took two steps in the direction of the bench. "We've got a going business here. If Jasper's is to open up tonight, then we've got to have a decision."

Ezra Porter leaned back in his swivel chair and touched his clawlike fingers together. "Now, that'd be terrible, iffen them boys didn't have noplace to drink beer an' chase women." Standing off to one side of the bench, E.J. Joseph cleared his throat. Aside from his jailer's duties, E.J. also acted as bailiff in both the county and district courts. He was wearing his tan county uniform, and his look said that he didn't like the idea of Jasper's being closed for even one night. E.J. was over six feet tall with huge hands and bearlike shoulders. He had a big round stomach and sagging jowls, and ruptured vessels on his cheeks from too much drinking.

"I'm not here to moralize, Your Honor," Puckett said.

"But the tavern provides an income, and my client's entitled to that."

"No she ain't," Fedora said. "Not from my brother's propity, she ain't."

Judge Porter leaned forward, took his glasses off, and tapped an earpiece against one of his front teeth. "Well, 'pears we got a problem. Fedora, you goin' to say this here will ain't genuine?"

"I didn' see Rog sign it," Fedora said, straightening.

"We've got a witness to that," Jack Puckett said. "Our own sheriff." Still seated against the rail, Dory Barnes was regarding Fedora with an arched eyebrow.

"*Buck* seen him sign it?" the judge said.

Puckett fondled his own chin. "That's my understanding from my client, Your Honor."

Judge Porter scratched a snow-white bushy eyebrow. "Fedora," he said. "These hearin's take up a lotta time. Ain't there some way you an' Miss Dory over there can get together on this?"

"I don't see no way, Ezra," Fedora said. "Lessen that woman wants to leave my brother's propity alone."

"A moment, Your Honor." Puckett bent from the waist, put his hands on his knees and listened while Dory Barnes leaned over and whispered in his ear. Then Puckett straightened and said, "Can I have a word with Fedora? I think maybe we can eliminate the need for a hearing on this."

"Now, that's what I like to see," Ezra Porter said. "Litigants cooperatin'." He extended a hand toward Fedora, palm up. "Go ahead on."

Puckett approached Fedora, stood a couple of feet away from her and said, "Dory wants to be fair."

"She ain't never been fair in her life," Fedora said.

"Look. She's got the goods, will, everything. If it comes down to it, she controls the whole works."

Fedora sniffed. "Iffen that's true, it's true. But I ain't takin' the word o' no Caldonia lawyer. I didn' vote for you for district judge, neither."

"Let's get down to brass tacks. Isn't what you're wanting out of this an income?"

Fedora blew her nose into her hanky, then looked to her husband. Albert was seated in the spectator's section on the front row, bent foward from the waist in an attentive attitude. Fedora returned her gaze to Puckett and said, "Well, Rog *was* helpin' some. You know Albert ain't worked in a spell."

"So what're we arguing about?" Puckett said. "My client doesn't have to have everything. You let her operate Jasper's and she'll pay you fifty dollars a night. More than fair."

"How I know I'd get paid?" Fedora said. "I wouldn't trust *her.*"

"She'll pay you a month in advance," Puckett said. "Right now, as soon as we get the will accepted."

Fedora licked her lips, hesitated. "I got your word on that? I ain't takin' *her* word."

"No problem," Puckett said. "I've got the money in my pocket."

"Well, all right, then," Fedora said. "I don't suppose I'd do too good if we was to have a hearin' nohow. I ain't got no lawyer an' my tongue'd tie itself up in knots."

"I think you're doing the right thing," Jack Puckett said.

JACK Puckett hoped that he'd made it through the hearing without showing how dizzy and light-headed he felt. As he walked away from Rog Hornby's sister and approached his client Dory Barnes, Puckett resisted the temptation to rub his breastbone just below the hollow of his throat. The soreness was practically gone and in its place was a maddening itch. He went to Dory's side and whispered in her ear, "She's going to take it, but there's a problem. We're going to have to pay her now. I've told her the money's in my pocket, I don't know what came over me to say that."

Dory threw her lawyer a sideways wink, uncrossed and recrossed her legs. " 'Course she's takin' it, darlin', an' won't be long 'fore she's wantin' to give the money back to us. You done just fine, an' soon as you walk out that door you're gonna have the money give to you.'' She jerked her head toward the rear courtroom exit. ''Money ain't no problem for Raven's people.''

5

BUD drove downtown on First Avenue at a snail's pace. The most direct route to Doc Petty's office was to proceed on First a couple of blocks past the square, turn right on a little-traveled blacktop road called Johnson Drive, and proceed on to F.M. 61. There was a more out-of-the-way path to the Pine Tree Clinic, one which consisted of a series of poorly paved and gravel roads through the woods outside of town, and Bud and Melody had thought seriously of going that route. But they'd finally decided on the more direct way for two reasons: as long as they went in Bud's yellow Toyota pickup (Melody's MG would be the vehicle that the bad guys would be on the lookout for) and kept within the speed limit, no one was likely to stop them, and if someone *were* to apprehend them they'd rather have it happen in town in front of plenty of witnesses than out on some isolated country road.

Bud sat erect in the driver's seat, gripping the steering wheel firmly, while Melody had one leg curled up underneath her and one arm draped over the seatback. They both were silent during the short ride downtown. They came to a stop at the intersection of First and Davy Crockett, and as they idled for a moment before proceeding on their way Bud reached over and gave Melody's hand a reassuring squeeze. She smiled weakly at him. Bud looked to his left down Davy Crockett Boulevard. Cars and pickups were parked on both sides of the road, but there was no moving traffic coming in his direction. He swiveled his head to the right. The coast was clear in that direction as well. He took his foot off the brake and gave the Toyota a little gas. As the truck moved into the intersection, Bud applied the brakes and came to a sudden halt.

"Who's that?" Bud said.

Across the street, standing on the corner in front of Matthew Tombley's statue, a man was watching them. He was tall and thin and angular, a gaunt man of around fifty who had an enormous Adam's apple. He was wearing slacks along with a dress shirt whose sleeves were too short for him and a collar that was too tight. He wore a black tie. He was staring directly at the Toyota, long arms at his sides.

In the seat beside Bud, Melody gasped. "It's Mr. Norton. He's one of 'em. I swear to God, he's one." She put both feet on the floorboard and sat rigid as a stake.

Bud gritted his teeth. "Well, it's broad daylight," he said, his gaze sweeping the square, falling on the knot of people on the courthouse steps, on the two men who were leaving the county parking lot and crossing the street, briefcases in hand. "Mr. Norton can look all he wants to, but I doubt he's going to *do* anything right here in front of all those folks. Hang on, Miss Parker, we're moving ahead."

He drove on. The speedometer hovered near fifteen miles an hour as he passed the corner, conscious of Norton's piercing glare. Norton moved quickly to the curb as the Toyota passed and, visible in the corner of Bud's eye, a county vehicle pulled alongside Norton. It was the tan deputy's Plymouth, and Sonny Beamer was driving. As Melody uttered a sob, Bud steadied his gaze on the road in front of him and continued on down First Avenue with the speedometer's needle frozen on twenty. Whatever else they might do, he thought with a bitter laugh, they can't give me a ticket.

He watched in the rearview mirror as the county car pulled slowly from the curb and fell in behind him. The two-car caravan bumped through another intersection and left the square. A block farther on, men and women sat inside Edna's Cafe having breakfast. Across the street from Edna's the drive-in windows of the Tombley County National Bank were open for business. As Bud drove past the bank, bubble-gum flashing lights came on in the county Plymouth's grille and its siren sounded one brief hoot. On the sidewalks and curbs and inside the restaurant, heads turned and people stared.

Well, thought Bud, you can run or you can stop. If you run you'll probably get far enough so that you're out in the country when the souped-up cop car finally runs you down. And then this deputy, zombie, or whatever he is can do whatever he wants to you and there'll be no one to tell the tale. Bud looked apologetically at Melody, then shrugged, pulled over, stopped and turned the engine off.

To Melody, Bud said, "It's the only way that makes any sense."

Her eyes wide, her lips in a tight line, Melody nodded.

The county Plymouth's door opened and Deputy Beamer alighted. Visible in the Toyota's sideview mirror he approached the driver's side, thumbs hooked under his belt, his eyes hidden behind mirror sunglasses. On the sidewalk, over to Bud's right, a pudgy woman who was carrying a paper shopping bag stopped in her tracks. Her lips parted.

The deputy was now standing beside the Toyota's window. Bud shrugged, rolled down the window with his left hand, reached for his wallet with his right. The wallet contained his counterfeit driver's license and the pickup's registration papers. Blandly, forcing his expression to remain calm, Bud said to the deputy, "What's the problem?"

For a heartbeat Sonny Beamer didn't move, just stood there beside the Toyota thumbing his belt buckle, his face expressionless. Then, without warning, he took one step backward, went into a crouch and drew his revolver. He steadied the gun in both hands and aimed it dead-level between Bud's eyes. "Climb out slow," Sonny Beamer said. "Put yore hands on the roof an' spread yore legs."

Bud was vaguely conscious of Melody as she moved slightly in the passenger seat, but his attention was riveted on the pistol's barrel. On that round, nasty-looking blue-black metal barrel aimed directly at his face from about a foot away. A drop of sweat rolled down Bud's cheek. He licked his lips, then said, "You can have it your way, but hear me out. Nobody in town knows, at least Melody hasn't told them, about those bodies you people were getting rid of this morning. You can keep it that way if you want to let us go, but take my word for it that if you arrest us we're going to put the word out." A crowd had come out of Edna's and gathered at the curb across the street. Bud didn't chance turning his head to look behind him, but he heard footsteps from that direction that indicated that the woman with the shopping bag now had company as well. Bud licked his lips, then said, "Take my word for it, deputy. You can't keep us from talking to these people around here."

Sonny Beamer's lips pursed in hesitation. He swiveled his head around toward the crowd in front of Edna's; Bud fleetingly considered grabbing the pistol barrel, then thought of Melody in the car with him and decided against it. Beamer looked back at Bud. Then the deputy straightened. He had a strange smile on his face.

Raising his voice, glancing around at the gathering mob of people, Sonny Beamer said, "Now, you folks listen. This here man's a fugitive from the State of California. He's wanted for murder, so youall back away now. He might be armed." Then, as the crowds on the sidewalk shrank back as one, Sonny Beamer said to Bud, "Now git yore ass outta that car. Ain't nobody goin' to listen to you no-how."

6

Dr. Jack Petty didn't particularly like the idea of having two confrontations with eastern-college smart guys on the same day, but under the circumstances there wasn't any way out of it. Winthrop Reed, in fact, had turned out to be pretty likable, but this Dr. Benjamin Cave at the Canton Memorial Hospital was a horse of a different color. Cave looked like a milk-fed quarterback: slim, with broad shoulders tapering down to a narrow waist, and the kind of coordinated movements associated with a scratch golfer or top-notch pool hustler. Cave also spoke in a confident manner, and unlike Reed made no attempt to hide the fact that he thought Jack Petty was a hick from the sticks. All of this rubbed Petty the wrong way, and Petty's irritation was even stronger because he knew that Cave was lying through his asshole.

Cave dropped the chart he'd been holding so that it landed softly on his desk blotter. "It can't be wrong," he said. "We've got the best people reading these things."

"According to your data," Petty said, standing and leaning over Cave's desk, "you read this sample yourself."

"Well, that makes the accuracy of the reading more certain, Doctor," Cave said. "I don't make that kind of mistake."

Petty hesitated, thought about letting Cave get himself further out on a limb, then decided that he didn't have time to fart around with the guy. Petty tapped the chart with his index finger. "Oh, there ain't nothin' wrong with the report. It's just that the sample you sent ain't Sonny Beamer's blood.''

Petty would have to say this much for Cave, the city-bred doctor was a cool one. His expression didn't change at all, and there was just the barest flicker at the corners of his eyes. ''Oh?'' Cave said. He ran his fingers through his thick salt-and-pepper hair.

''Really, I got to say you're pretty unlucky,'' Petty said. ''Wadn' a chance in a thousand of anybody knocking it off, hell, you're smart enough to make the phony sample the same blood type. You just got a bad break in that the guy taking the sample over to Tyler was Sonny Beamer's family doctor. Me. I've doctored all them Beamers, even Sonny's dad 'fore he run off to Dallas with that younger woman. And even me, I never would have figured anything was wrong with the sample, but I knew there was supposed to be somethin' in Sonny's blood that wadn' there. That Dr. Reed over to Tyler, he's the one I took the samples to, he just thought I'd brought him some blood from somebody that wadn' infected. Trouble was, I knew better. Nobody ever grew as much as Sonny Beamer in less than twenty-four hours exceptin' that comic-book character that used to holler, 'Shazam!' ''

''I could get tired of this in a hurry,'' Cave said, folding his arms. ''You're being ridiculous, Doctor, why don't you just shazam yourself out of here.''

Petty sat down in a chair in front of Cave's desk and crossed his long legs. Jack Petty's mood had gone up and down like a diver on a springboard on this day, but he was now calm and collected and cool as a cucumber. Cool and confident in the knowledge that this s.o.b. now sitting across from him had, for some reason, pulled a fast one, and that Jack Petty had this city-slicker doctor by the balls. ''I 'spect you can run me off, in which case you'll have seen the last of me for about twenty-four hours,'' Petty said.

Cave raised his eyebrows. ''Come again?''

''That's about how long it's gonna take me to come back over here with a herd from the attorney general's office, with court orders. I never done this before, tell you the truth, but they tell me where you're talkin' medical endangerment of a whole community you can get the court order even faster. Maybe this afternoon, if I can get ahold of the state boys.'' Petty's gaze swept the room, took in Cave's medical licenses on the wall, the rich mahogany furniture, the two stubby combination-lock file cabinets sitting on the carpet in one corner.

Cave shifted his weight, nervous now, fiddling absently with a solid glass paperweight in the form of a sphere. There were little bubbles of air inside the glass, spaced at even intervals. ''That's a serious charge, Doctor. Endangerment of what community?'' Cave's tone had lost a lot of its authority, and he was no longer talking from up on his pedestal.

''You ain't seen what I saw this afternoon,'' Petty said. ''But believe me, you don't know what you're fuckin' with. I'm givin' you more credit than you're probably due, but I don't think you'd be falsifyin' anybody's records if you knew just what was really wrong with 'em.''

Cave set down the paperweight and picked up a pointed letter opener. The letter opener's handle was carved wood with gold thread inlays. ''Maybe I should have my lawyer sit in on this,'' Cave said.

''Goddammit, man.'' Petty suddenly pounded the desk with his fist, and for a second thought Cave was going to jump straight up from his chair. Petty said, ''I'm not after your license, though I probably ought to be. There's too much at stake here. Now, what is it, money? I ain't as dumb as I look, Doctor, and I 'spect you went up to your ass in debt to open this hospital. It'll pay itself out over the long run, but you might need some quick cash. Tell you the truth, I'm hopin' it's money. Otherwise it means you're somehow in with these ghouls, maybe even one of 'em yourself. Now, I'm goin' to give you exactly thirty seconds to tell me what's been goin' on over here, or else the next folks you're gonna talk to are gonna be them state lawyers I was talkin' about.''

Cave's gaze dropped and he studied the letter opener as though he were thinking of slashing his own wrists. Or someone else's throat. It occurred to Jack Petty that if this big-city doctor should turn out to be one of *them,* then he might at any second transform himself into a raving beast and tear Petty limb from limb. Petty's heartbeat quickened. Finally, Cave wet his lips. He said weakly, "How did you know the sample wasn't Deputy Beamer's?" Matter-of-factly, just like that.

"Nothin' to it," Jack Petty said. "Sonny come by a week ago for a booster shot. Traces of the serum shoulda been still in his blood, but they wadn'. Like I said, you played unlucky."

Cave's fingers were now trembling as he held the letter opener, and the corners of his mouth were twitching. For just an instant Petty felt sorry for the man, but the feeling went as quickly as it had come. Ol' Jack Petty had done his share of boozing and womanizing in his time, and it was true that his main attraction to the medical profession was the dollars that his practice brought in. But never, not once in his whole career, had Petty ever falsified anyone's records, not for love, not for money, not for anything. As far as Jack Petty was concerned, doctors who crossed over the line got just what they had coming to them. As though he was reading Petty's thoughts, Dr. Benjamin Cave said weakly, "I suppose it's a waste of time to try to make you go away and forget this."

Jack Petty didn't even blink. "I suppose it is," he said.

Cave smiled briefly, but his eyes were misting along with the smile. His shoulders sagged, and suddenly he didn't look near as young nor near as athletic as he had just moments ago. He gestured toward the mahogany furnishings in his office, toward the oil painting of a pirate schooner, sails unfurled, Jolly Roger whipping in the breeze, sailing through high rolling waves in a thunderstorm. "Jesus Christ," Cave said. "You wouldn't believe what this stuff costs."

"Yeah, I would," Petty said. "I've priced a few of 'em. You ain't the only one with expensive tastes, but most folks check their bank accounts before they haul off and buy."

"I guess . . ." Cave began, then cleared his throat.

Then he said, "Coming to town and setting this hospital up, I guess I thought I needed to put on a few airs."

"I been figurin' that," Petty said. "Nobody gets as rich as you look in the time you been here, 'less they got one helluva bankroll to begin with. Look, we ain't got *time* for this. Do your soul-searchin' when this is over. What kinda shit you been into?"

Cave straightened his posture. "Well, it's not as though I've been selling *drugs.*" Then he sagged once more and his gaze dropped to the surface of the desk. "Not exactly."

"Well, what *have* you been sellin'? Come on."

"Just prescriptions."

"An' that ain't sellin' drugs?" Petty said.

"I said not exactly. Prescription medicine. No Demerol or morphine or anything."

The answer came to Petty in a flash. "Lemme guess. Antibiotics. Penicillin, ampicillin, stuff like that."

Cave blinked helplessly. "How did you know that?"

" 'Cause it's what they want. It's what . . . Jesus, I just ain't got time. Whoall you been sellin' it to?"

"One thing leads to another. I had to falsify Deputy Beamer's records because if I hadn't, then the wrong people would know about the prescriptions." Cave looked at the ceiling. "It was just one loan. Just one lousy fifty-thousand-dollar loan, two months ago, just enough working capital to keep us afloat until some government money came in."

It took just a moment for what Cave was saying to sink in. A moment during which Jack Petty got all the answers. Well, maybe not *all* the answers, but plenty enough to last for a while. His mouth agape, Jack Petty took a deep breath, then said, "Fuck. Justin Barker."

"If you already know all of this," Cave said, "then why are you over here grilling me? Why didn't you just bring the state men and their warrants?"

Petty waved a hand as though he were batting at mosquitos. "I didn't know, not 'til now. Anybody around these parts that needs a shaky loan, well, Justin's their man."

"You'd be surprised," Cave said. "There were more,

but the Tombley County National Bank was the only one that didn't want a big percentage of the hospital." He rolled his eyes. "Christ, I wish I'd gone to one of the others."

"How much and what antibiotics we talkin' about?"

Cave leaned back in his swivel chair and rested one ankle on the opposite knee. "I hate to answer that."

"You're wastin' time. You're already in deep shit, what difference does it make *how* deep?"

Cave uttered a sigh of resignation. "None, I suppose. The medicines you've already named, penicillin and ampicillin. Several . . . gallons. A hundred of each, I think. Liquid."

Petty was speechless for a second, unable to speak, looking in disbelief at this big-city doctor. Finally Petty said, "I guess Barker's settin' up his own pharmaceutical company. Somethin' like that."

"He told me his wife was ill."

"Jesus Christ . . ."

Cave raised a hand. "I know, I know. But there was the loan and, well, I suppose I wasn't thinking straight at the time."

"So you gave him enough antibiotic to float a battleship—his wife. Come to think about it, Betty Barker ain't been around town in a while. The womenfolk are beginnin' to chatter about it. Justin must be figurin' on buildin' himself quite an army—if he's goin' to need that much. And where the hell did *you* get it, yore hospital don't use . . ."

Cave was silent, staring at the desktop. His eyelids flickered slightly, but otherwise he didn't move.

"You son of a bitch," Petty said evenly, then stood with his hands in fists at his waist. "You son of a *bitch.* You been givin' the patients sugar-water or somethin'. Most of 'em are gonna get well anyway, they'll never know the difference. What about your staff? They had to know this was goin' on."

"No." Cave touched his fingertips together, still staring vacantly. "No, they didn't. I became the medicine dispenser myself. I told them all it was for economy reasons, and as long as the bottles had the right labels they didn't have any reason to check them out. And I *did* keep some of the real antibiotics for extreme cases. Where they were really needed.''

''Boy, I'll tell you one thing,'' Petty said. ''You're lucky I ain't got more time. If I did, I'd beat the livin' shit outta you.''

7

FOR just a second, sitting there in the cab of his yellow Toyota pickup with Melody beside him, Bud was unable to move. The shock set in in waves, rolling first through his throat and upper chest, then shuddering its way through the rest of his body all the way down to his toes. He'd been so caught up in the present, so involved, and actually *glad* to be involved in a way, in the weird happenings in Tombley's Walk that his own past had slipped into the back of his mind. But suddenly, there it was again. *Boom,* as though Deputy Sonny Beamer had ordered Bud's past front and center, as though Beamer had decided that this outsider was getting too involved in things that were none of his business and needed putting in his place.

Beamer repeated himself. "I said for you to git yore ass outta that car." He was still in a half-crouch with his revolver held in both hands and extended in Bud's direction.

So it had finally come, just as Bud had always known it would. As he raised his hands to ear level, palms facing outward, applied pressure on the handle with his knee to open the door, and climbed slowly down to stand on the pavement, Bud was actually smiling. He turned his back on Beamer and placed his hands on the roof of the truck, moving automatically, as though he were an actor in one of the cop shows he'd seen on TV. Beamer moved in close behind him, kicked first one inside ankle and then the other. Bud spread his legs.

Beamer said, "Now raise your hands." When Bud

obeyed, the deputy clamped a handcuff around one wrist, drew both of Bud's hands behind his back, and slapped the other bracelet on. Bud sighed, relaxed, and stepped away from the car. For an instant Bud locked gazes with the woman who was carrying the shopping bag. She was still at the curb with her mouth agape, and a cluster of about a dozen men and women had joined her. Bud looked down, past his tennis shorts, past his lean calves and thighs, and concentrated on his sneakers. A dab of mud on one toe contrasted with the spotless white leather. The deputy grabbed an elbow and spun Bud around to face him.

Melody had squirmed across the seat and was now behind the wheel of the Toyota. She was turned sideways in the cab, facing Sonny Beamer, her feet resting atop the rocker panel. "What'd you say the charges were? Sonny? Sonny Beamer, I'm talkin' to you."

Beamer's eyes were hidden behind his mirrored sunglasses. He was half smiling. "Ain't none of your problem, Miss Parker, though I spect I gotta take you in, too. As a witness."

This Deputy Beamer was one of the men whom Melody had said was carrying a body away that morning, and Bud supposed that Melody was scared to death. He didn't blame her. But there was no trembling in her voice as she said, "You're goin' to hold a *witness?* Bullshit, Sonny, you don't even have this guy charged with a local crime. Witness to what?"

Beamer was suddenly uncertain. Whatever else it was that they taught in law school, intimidation was at the top of the heap. Beamer hesitantly licked his lips, then said mechanically, "I'm . . . takin' you in, Miss Parker, along with this man here." His voice was suddenly at a different pitch, as though he were silently moving his lips while a tape recorder played the words.

Sure they're taking her in, Bud thought. They had the perfect excuse to arrest Bud, the California warrants, but Melody Parker was something else again. But under the circumstances (if Bud had had any doubt whatsoever that Melody had actually seen what she thought she'd seen that morning, the doubt was now completely gone), they needed Melody off the street even more than they did Bud. And once the two of them were in custody, in the privacy inside that county building on the square, they could do what they wished with Bud and Melody.

Melody shot Bud a glance that said she was thinking exactly the same thing that he was. She stood down from the pickup and balled her hands into tiny fists at her waist. The top of her head on a level with Sonny Beamer's chin, she said, "No you're not. Not without a warrant you're not, and you don't got one. Now I'm goin' to my office, Sonny, an' don't you try an' stop me." Then, to the people at the curb, she said loudly, "You folks hear that? This deputy's tryin' to arrest me an' he don't even know what the charges are. Another example of the workin's of this sheriff's department around here."

The knot of people at the curb began to chatter among themselves. Melody turned back and faced Sonny Beamer. "That's my client you got there, Sonny. You see that nothin' happens to him, you hear?" She stalked away with her backside twitching, went past the crowd to the end of the block, and disappeared around the corner.

Deputy Beamer relaxed and watched her go, his pistol hanging loosely at his side. Melody had hit the nail on the head, there wasn't much that Beamer *could* do, not with all these witnesses around. Finally Beamer holstered his gun and took Bud by the elbow, leading his prisoner down the street in the direction of the courthouse with its third-floor jail.

ONCE she was out of sight around the corner, Melody began to sob and broke into a run. Her office was a block straight ahead and a half block to her right, and she made the short trip with her open-toed sandals splatting on pavement, breath whistling between her lips, the hem of her red T-shirt bouncing around, and tears streaming down her cheeks. Her office was a former antique store with big draped picture windows and a glass-paneled wooden door, located across the street from a park playground, and catty-corner from the rust-colored, brick, one-story Jim Bowie

Elementary School. Melody fumbled in her purse for her keys, unlocked and threw open her office door, went inside, and closed it behind her. Then she leaned her back against the wall and waited for her breathing to subside and her pulse rate to sink below a full-fledged gallop. She found a hanky in her purse, blew her nose and wiped the tears from her face. She had streaked her makeup, but right now she didn't give a damn.

The office consisted of a small reception area (with no receptionist, of course, a Tombley's Walk law practice couldn't afford such luxuries) and a ten-by-twenty inner room where her own desk sat. Air-conditioning came from a window unit wedged into the bottom slot on the door. The unit wasn't running and the air was stifling hot. She reached over and flipped a switch. The fan began to hum and the cooling coils began to whisper. As she moved to her desk, flipping on the lights as she passed through the doorway, sudden cold air played around her calves and thighs. She shivered.

Goddammit, she thought. God*dam*mit. She'd run a cold bluff on Sonny Beamer and gotten away with it (if he'd pointed his pistol at her she probably would've fainted dead away right there on the street), but what now? Having Bud in jail was enough of a problem, but at least Melody was free to do something about it. Free, that is, until they came for *her*, and her office was the first place that they would look. She quickly retraced her steps and locked the door from the inside. Great, Melody, now they can come crashing through the window. She returned to her desk, sat in her chair, and fidgeted.

Since she sure as hell wasn't going to do anyone any good by stewing around, she forced herself to think and consider the priorities. Number one: stay free. If Melody herself were to go to jail (or worse—who knew *what* those zombies had in mind for her), then she could forget about any help from anybody. Number two: do everything possible to get Bud out of the soup. Number one was a matter of staying loose and out of harm's way; number two was something else again. Since she knew (and the knowledge caused a sinking feeling in the pit of her stomach) that

Tombley County had a legitimate excuse for holding Bud, reason told her that there wasn't much she could do about setting him free. Hell, if they were holding him for extradition to California he wasn't even legally entitled to bond. There was one possibility, only one, and it was a long shot at best. The sheriff's department didn't jail anyone without notifying Rod Lindenhall, the county attorney. Melody had a pretty good working relationship with Lindenhall (who was divorced and liked to go nightclubbing up in Dallas, and who had tried to make more of the relationship but Melody had kept it arm's length), and there was a chance that she could prevail on Rod to get the district judge to set a bond. She didn't *expect* any results, but didn't know of anything else to do, so she picked up the phone and called Lindenhall. The county attorney, just like the rest of the government officials in Tombley's Walk, was strapped for funds, so when Lindenhall answered in person and said, "Rod Lindenhall," then cupped a hand over the phone and said loudly to what Melody knew to be a nonexistent secretary, "I've got it, Evelyn," Melody almost laughed in spite of the situation.

"It's Melody, Rod."

"Hi." His voice went up a fraction of a pitch and his tone showed interest that he wasn't doing a good job of hiding, if he was trying to hide it at all.

"I want to talk about settin' bond for a client of mine."

Melody pictured Lindenhall frowning at the phone, probably taking his feet off of his desk and hunching slightly forward. The county attorney, a couple of years older than Melody, was a Texas Tech law school grad who wore polished western boots, along with slacks and a sportcoat. Melody had never seen Lindenhall in a suit—even when he was in trial—and he generally wore a big round western beltbuckle over which his belly pooched out. "Oh?" Lindenhall said. "Who?" Now Lindenhall would be putting on his wire-framed glasses and looking around on his desk to see if he had a file.

"It's an extradition case. From California, I guess the warrant came from information on the N.C.I.C. computer."

"Melody, I . . ." Papers rustled, making crackling

noises over the phone. "Look, can I call you back in a minute?"

Something rattled the door to Melody's office. Her eyes widened as she looked in that direction, but there was no one there, no shape or outline visible through the thin drape covering the glass panel in the door. Probably it was the wind, but the noise reminded Melody that she had no business staying in her office any longer. She said quickly, "I must be mistaken, Rod." Then she hung up before Lindenhall could answer.

The short conversation with the county attorney had told her all that she needed to know at the moment. Fugitives from California were a rarity in Tombley's Walk, and there was no way in the world that Lindenhall should have to find a file to discuss the matter. No way, that is, unless Sonny Beamer had arrested Bud without notifying the county attorney's office, which had to be the case. And if Lindenhall didn't know anything about it, that meant . . .

Christ, Melody thought. They're not holding Bud for extradition. No *way* are they, those . . . those whatever they are's, Buck Ainson and his Band of Merry Men. Arresting Bud was just a way to get him off the street. An ice-cold shiver ran through her as it dawned on her that her problem wasn't just setting Bud free. It was keeping him alive.

And *that* realization brought home another reality: Melody didn't have another second to waste in getting the hell away from her office. She opened her desk drawer, found a nickel-plated Towner .32 automatic pistol she kept in the office for protection along with a small box of shells. She dropped the gun and the ammunition into her purse, then got up and crossed the room to turn off the lights. Someone knocked on the outside door. Melody stopped in her tracks.

It wasn't the wind this time, a man's silhouette was outlined against the drape. She went to the front door and said, her voice wavering slightly, "Who is it?"

"I almost went right by, girl," Doc Petty said from the other side of the door. "Your car ain't outside."

A sigh of relief escaped her lips and she unlocked and

opened the door. Jack Petty was leaning against the doorjamb. He was wearing pale blue slacks and a white Izod knit shirt, and there was a worried frown on his face. "An' I don't ever recall you bein' inside your office with the door locked, either."

Melody's knees felt as though they were about to buckle, and she leaned against the doorjamb for support. "Jesus God, Jack. What's goin' on in this town?"

Melody had seen Dr. Jack Petty under a lot of different circumstances in her life (including some bedroom situations where Petty's performance hadn't quite lived up to his reputation), and one thing she'd always liked about the old rogue was that his sense of humor never seemed to go completely away. That wasn't the case at the moment. Jack Petty's features were drawn, on the verge of haggard, and there wasn't a hint of a smile on his lips. "I don't got all the answers," Petty said. "But I got a lot of 'em. It ain't good. Let's go inside, Melody, we need to talk."

"We can't do it here," she said. "We've got to—"

She stopped in midsentence, her gaze beyond Doc Petty. As she watched, the county deputy's car pulled from around the corner to stop at the curb a half block down the street. Sonny Beamer was at the wheel and Doug Ellison was riding shotgun. Both front doors of the Plymouth opened at once and both men got out. They came from opposite sides of the car and approached Melody's office. Both men appeared calm, and neither seemed to be in a hurry. Jack Petty's car, a tan four-door Fleetwood, was parked in front of the sheriff's vehicle, its rear bumper about ten feet ahead of the Plymouth's nose.

"I don't have time to explain, Jack," Melody said. "But if you've ever done anything in your life, you get us out of here. Right now."

"Well, I can . . ." Petty began, then trailed off. He'd followed Melody's gaze, and had turned partway around and was now watching the two approaching men. In a near-whisper, he said quickly to Melody, "Watch yourself, girl. That ain't really Sonny Beamer you're seein', he's one of the somebodies I know somethin' about."

"You're tellin' *me*," Melody said.

Beamer and Ellison were less than ten yards away now, walking side by side like Wyatt Earp and Doc Holliday on their way to shoot it out with the Clanton boys. Both men were without expression. Beneath his mirrored shades, Sonny's lips were set in a line. Jack Petty stood away from the office entry, took a step in the approaching men's direction, and said, "Afternoon, boys."

"Hello, Doc," Sonny Beamer said, his voice mechanical. "We'll be needin' a word with Miss Parker there."

Petty reached out and took Melody's arm. She followed his lead, took a step over the threshold, and stood beside Jack Petty. Petty said to Sonny Beamer, "Well, it's gonna be a quick word. This young lady's got some medical problems, and I'm takin' her with me." He escorted Melody another step away from the building, closer to the curb where they'd be in plain sight of anyone who happened by.

For just an instant, Sonny hesitated. He shot a quick glance at Doug Ellison, who just stood relaxed with his big arms folded in front of him. Sonny licked his lips and said, "This is county business. I think it's got precedence over doctor business."

Jack Petty looked at Melody. His expression was calculating, considering. Finally he shrugged and said, practically under his breath, "What the hell." He faced Sonny Beamer once more. "Ain't no point in bullshittin', Sonny," Petty said. "If you still go by Sonny, though you an' me both know you ain't the same Sonny Beamer that growed up around here. Now, here's the sitchyation, as I see it. I done been over to that phony doctor at Canton, an' I got a pretty good idea what's goin' on around here. We ain't no physical match for you two, but I'll guarantee you one thing. We can yell awful loud. Folks in Tombley's Walk all know me, an' you know they're goin' to listen to me. I don't think you ghouls, or whatever you want to call yourselves, are ready for people to know about you as yet. Once you get 'em all on your side, well, then it won't make any difference, but right this instant there ain't enough of you to go around. Am I right?"

Sonny shuffled his booted feet and cocked his head. He didn't answer.

"That's about what I figured," Jack Petty said. "Now me an' Miss Parker are gonna get in my car an' drive away. I wouldn' be tryin' to stop us, lessen you want the whole town to know about you."

As though Petty had put in an order for them, three women came down the street. Two of them were elderly, the third a plain girl in her twenties, all wearing modest print dresses. Sonny Beamer had to step aside to let the women pass. He tipped his hat to them. Across the street on the playground, two little boys in shorts were climbing on the jungle gym and two little girls wearing sunsuits were going up and down on opposite ends of a seesaw. Seated on a park bench near the playing children, two women chatted.

"See what I'm talkin' about?" Jack Petty said. "You don't operate too good in broad daylight. We're goin' now. It's your play, Sonny, what happens here is up to you."

Petty kept his hold on Melody's arm, escorted her around Beamer and Ellison to the Fleetwood. Melody was trembling, at the same time hoping against hope. Could it be, could it be in this wild crazy world that had come into being, that these two zombies were just going to let them go? Petty's movements oozed with confidence. He opened the Cadillac's passenger door, put Melody into the seat, walked around the front of the car and got in on the driver's side. He started the engine and pulled unhurriedly from the curb. Sonny Beamer and Doug Ellison watched them go, watched in silence. For just an instant as the Cadillac drove away, Melody felt faint and stars danced before her eyes.

"You get ready to grab this steerin' wheel," Jack Petty said. "I'm tellin' you, girl, I'm liable to have a heart attack before we get outta here."

8

BUD had no way of knowing whether the jailer sitting out in the corridor was one of them or not. "E.J." was what Sonny Beamer had called the man. Well, if E.J. *was* one of them, he didn't have the look about him. The jailer was a stooped bear of a man with ruptured vessels in his cheeks, quite a bit the worse for wear, and most every one of *them* that Bud had seen was a perfect physical specimen.

All the way down the street to the county building, and up the three flights of stairs to the district court, Beamer hadn't spoken to Bud. By the time they'd arrived outside the courtroom, Bud's wrists had been aching. Sonny had deliberately secured the handcuffs so tightly that the metal dug into his flesh. Dory Barnes, in designer jeans and pink form-fitting, low-cut blouse, had been standing in the hallway outside the courtroom. Beamer had said to Dory, "Watch him. I'm goin' in after E.J." And then left Bud waiting with Dory as a guard while he went into the court to find the jailer.

Normally, left in the charge of an unarmed woman, Bud might have made a run for it. But Dory Barnes wasn't any normal unarmed woman, and it occurred to Bud as he stood docilely by that, once their identity was known to someone, *they* didn't seem to make any effort to conceal who was and wasn't one of *them.* Despite the spot he was in, Bud continued to marvel over the change—not only in appearance, but in earthy sexuality—that had come over Dory, and he wondered whether, if it had been *this* creature rather than the old Dory who'd approached him at Jasper's the other night, he'd have resisted her.

As they'd stood there waiting, Dory had showed him a saucy grin and said, "Things'll be jumpin' out to Jasper's tonight, darlin'. Shame you ain't goin' to be there, little Dory might just try you on for size."

Bud had stood there with his hands cuffed behind his back, self-conscious as passersby in the hallway had gawked at him, and studied his toes. "I suppose I'd like to be just about anywhere besides the place that I am," Bud had said. "But isn't Jasper's closed? Poor Rog Hornby bought it the other night, it's my understanding."

"That ol' fart ain't around no more," Dory had said. "You got that right, but ain't nothin' goin' to keep Jasper's closed. It's little Dory's place now, darlin', case you ain't heard. Why, I'm havin' my grand openin' party tonight. The customers are in for somethin' like they ain't never seen." She cocked her head to one side and her eyes narrowed. " 'Course I 'spect you'd figure that, much as you know about us."

The remark had stabbed through Bud like a hot poker. Sonny Beamer had seen Bud in the car with Melody and could probably put two and two together about what she'd told him, but how had Dory Barnes known? There wasn't any way she should have. And what was Bud doing standing out here in the hallway? He wasn't any legal expert, but shouldn't the deputy be taking his prisoner, a man wanted in the State of California, in front of the judge? A feeling of something wrong—no, more of something *not right* about the situation—flooded over him, and he'd just made up his mind to take his chances with Dory Barnes and make a run for it, handcuffs and all, when Sonny Beamer had come out of the courtroom with the jailer in tow.

Sonny had told E.J., "Now you keep an eye on him, this ain't no drunk-drivin' prisoner." Then Sonny and Dory had walked away side by side toward the wide staircase leading down to the street. A man had joined them, a beefy thirtyish man who looked like a weight lifter and who was wearing a muscle shirt and jeans, and the three of them had left. E.J. had told Bud, "You heard the man. Now you don't give me no trouble, friend, and I won't give you none, either." Then he'd taken Bud up one more flight of stairs to the third-floor lockup, placed him in a cell, and clanged the door closed. E.J. had removed Bud's handcuffs through the bars.

And now Bud sat on the bunk in his cell and studied the jailer. The bunk was solid metal, supported by metal legs sunk into the concrete floor. The mattress on which Bud sat was made of heavy green plastic and stuffed with a material that had the resiliency of folded rags. The cell was about five feet wide and ten feet deep, and was one of ten identical cells arranged side by side in clusters of five each. A concrete-floored corridor ten feet in width separated the two rows of cells. In the back corner of Bud's cell was a porcelain commode and sink. In the wall beside the sink was a tiny barred window, about six feet above the floor. Bud's cell was the only one that was locked; all of the other doors stood open. There was one other prisoner, a bleary-eyed man with a few days' growth of grizzled beard who was shuffling around in a filthy cloth jumpsuit and plastic sandals, sweeping the corridor with a push broom. The jailer, E.J., was sitting at a metal table at the end of the double row of cells. He was wearing a tan county deputy's uniform. His feet were propped against the edge of the table and his chair was tilted back. He was reading a newspaper. The push broom made whispering sounds and the sweeping prisoner's sandals slapped occasionally on the concrete. There was an odor of bathroom disinfectant mixed with stale tobacco.

Surprisingly, Bud was calm. All during his time on the run he'd pictured this day, pictured the time when the steel door would finally clang shut behind him, and he'd imagined that he'd be petrified. But his concern for Melody had overcome any worry about himself. He placed one foot flat on the bunk, rested his forearm on his knee and his chin on the forearm, raised his voice and said, "Jailer, I need a word with you."

E.J. swiveled his shaggy head to glance at Bud, then rattled his newspaper to straighten the pages and continued his reading. "Ain't got nothin' to say to you, boy." He lowered the paper and peered over it down the corridor. "You jus' keep on a-sweepin', Freddy, an' don't pay him no mind. Shee-it, you're missin' a bunch of spots. 'Pears we're goin' to have to pull Bob Bill Stoner in for a little stay." His voice was gruff and boozy-hoarse.

Freddy grimly shoved the broom in rapid little strokes. "Bob Bill Stoner got a lot more practice. Gets a lot drunker, too."

E.J. grinned, showing yellowed teeth. One of his front molars was missing. "Drunk don't play no part in it. Drunk or sober he knows how to do a floor. Damn sure does."

Freddy paused for a moment and looked over his shoulder. "You goin' to bring a six-pack in? I could do with somethin' cold."

"Iffen I do," E.J. said, "you ain't gettin' none. Not no better than you're sweepin' that floor." He closed the newspaper, folded it, and laid it on the table, then said to Bud, "How 'bout you, boy, you a sweeper?"

Bud wasn't believing the conversation he was hearing, but said, "It's been years."

"Don't make no nevermind about the hallway, I can't let you out to do no sweepin' 'cause Sonny says you got to stay locked up. But in a spell I'll be passin' that broom through the bars to you."

"Any chance of me making a phone call?" Bud said.

E.J. took his feet down from the table, hunched forward, and pointed a finger. "Ain't no chance of you doin' shit. Now, I'll tell you all I'm goin' to. Yore ass is sittin' right smack in the middle o' the Tombley County Jail, an' I aim to see that yore ass keeps a-sittin' there. You get supper at five, that's about an hour and a half from now, an' tonight we're cookin' a mess o' red beans an' cornbread. You look like a fella used to eatin' steak an' all that fancy shit, but you won't get it here. If you don't like yore supper we won't take no offense, fact is me an' Freddy hope you don't 'cause then we can eat yorn. Now, you might think you see ole E.J. drinkin' a beer or two after sundown, but yore mind'll be playin' tricks on you. Now, 'til Sonny Beamer says different, that's all the information you're gettin'." He picked up the paper, opened it, raised his legs, and crossed his feet on the corner of the table.

Bud tried another question: "How long will it be before the California authorities come for me?"

"I don't know nothin' about no California," E.J. said.

The answer caused a little cloud to drift in Bud's mind. Of course he doesn't know, Bud thought. He doesn't know and nobody besides that Deputy Beamer and Dory Barnes and whoever else is part of their group even knows why I'm in here. Whatever else these . . . whatever else *they* have in mind, they don't have any intention of calling anybody from California or anywhere else. Outsiders are something that *they* don't want in Tombley's Walk. "Well, when can I see a lawyer?" Bud said.

"I don't know nothin' about that, neither," E.J. said. "But tell you what, you quit runnin' yore mouth an' let us have some peace around here an' I'll see what I can do about that in the mornin'."

"In the *morning?* Don't I have a right to see a lawyer?"

"What you got a right to do is to quit jawin', boy," E.J. said. "Now like I said before, I got nothin' more to say to you."

Bud lay back on the hard bunk and stared at the ceiling. He swallowed and closed his eyes. He had a long and sleepless night before him.

9

It was gathering dusk when the sparrow prepared to take flight. It had been wallowing in the fountain on the corner of First Avenue and Davy Crockett Boulevard, just as it did every day at sundown, and it hopped up on the stone bank even as the final swish of its tail feathers sent droplets flying and ripples scooting over the surface of the water. Once out of the fountain the sparrow was still, its sides moving in and out with its panting, its coal-black eyes wide and alert. The sun had already disappeared behind the building roofs across Davy Crockett Boulevard, and the lengthening shadow of the Woolworth's had become one with the lengthening shadow of the Rialto Theatre. Soon all shadows would combine into nightshade, broken only by the deeper shadows cast by the moon.

The sparrow wasn't capable of real thought, but was a creature of habit, steered by instinct. In daylight hours it fed, hopping about on forest pine branches searching for beetles and wood mites, and occasionally diving to spear an earthworm, ravenously consuming several times its bodyweight in a single day. At sunset it bathed in convenient water. Its surroundings—the stone cherub spewing water through its trumpet, the towering statue of Matthew Tombley—meant nothing to the sparrow, only existing for the bird as places to perch and hop and dive. After dark the sparrow roosted in one of the tall elms on the square—on the exact same branch of the exact same tree each and every night, as a matter of fact, at a point where on this particular night it could've looked down on Bud Rigler through his cell window—and tucked its head underneath its wing to sleep.

The sparrow did have a sort of memory, vague mental images of things past that were stored somewhere in its tiny brain, and it was the sparrow's memory that generally caused it to act. At daybreak it pictured beetles and wood mites as it flew into the forest; approaching sunset would focus the water of the fountain in its mind. At nightfall the sparrow should have been picturing the selfsame branch in the selfsame tree as it prepared to retire. But the tree branch wasn't the picture in its mind at the moment, and the change in its mental habit was strangely frightening to the bird.

The image wasn't clear. Images were *never* completely clear in the sparrow's mind; rather they were blurred pictures of water and beetles and wood mites as though taken with a camera that was slightly out of focus, but these habit images all had one thing in common in that the sparrow understood what they were. But the mental picture that the bird now had was something unfamiliar. In fact, what the sparrow was now experiencing wasn't really a picture at all, it was more like a swirl of crazy-quilt colors, a mixture of red and green and blue and purple and violet that flowed and mixed and separated like gay beads in a spinning kaleidoscope. The bird ruffled its feathers, twitched its tail, took a short hop to one side and swiveled its head to stare directly behind itself at the water in the fountain. The image of the shifting colors wouldn't go away.

The sparrow's brothers and sisters were having the same experience. One by one they had hopped out of the fountain, and the circular cement bank was now so thick with confused, twitching birds that the bank itself was virtually invisible. Behind and above the fountain, hundreds more huddled on Matthew Tombley's hat and covered his shoulders and arms and hands. The nearby evergreen trees were alive with the birds.

For all of its short life the sparrow had been devoid of any emotion save fear. It hunted for food because all birds since time immemorial had done the same; it flew and bathed and twittered and slept for all the like reasons: it was a sparrow and therefore it behaved like one. It could sense the presence of a nearby cat or possum or squirrel, and the nearness of one of its natural enemies would make its heart beat faster and teach it to be afraid. But though the sparrow had no way of understanding this, the swirling colors in its brain were emotion themselves, and the emotion was . . .

Anger? Some of that, yes, but what the sparrow was now experiencing was more a feeling of hate. Hate for . . . ? It didn't know. The sparrow hated it knew not what, but it was full of hate and the hate had completely blocked its habit images. With no memory left to cause the sparrow to act, its instinct took over. It flew.

A scream of anger and frustration erupting from its throat, the bird launched itself skyward. Its brothers and sisters followed suit; from the bank around the fountain, from Matthew Tombley's hat and shoulders and arms and hands, from the nearby evergreens that quivered with the weight of the birds, they rose as one into the rapidly darkening sky. Like a cloud of coursers, the flock rose and dipped and rose again over the courthouse and the square, the screeches and cries of the birds becoming an ever-increasing din and rising to a crescendo.

THE sparrows' screams brought Bud Rigler to attention. He'd been lying prone on the rock-hard mattress, staring at nothing, thinking of nothing as well. His mind was too tired for thought. With the first cries from the flying birds, his head snapped toward the barred cell window. He got up, barefoot now, crossed over and stood on tiptoes. There was a towering elm tree out there, its branches outlined against the darkening sky like twisted fingers. Aside from the tree he saw nothing. The concrete floor was cool on the balls of his feet.

Behind him in the corridor, E.J. Joseph dropped an empty Lone Star can on the floor. The can rattled and rolled its way over to bump against the metal bars of the cell. The grizzled prisoner, Freddy, was seated across the table from E.J., and the two of them were playing checkers. Freddy sipped his beer as he studied his next move. E.J. reached down, twisted a fresh can of beer out of the cluster held together by molded plastic, popped the ring-tab with a quick tiny hiss of air.

His speech slurred, E.J. said, "Somethin' spookin' them fuckin' birds." Then, raising his voice, "Hey. Hey you, city fella. You jus' as well go back to bed, them sparrows ain't goin' to help you none."

THE flock of shrieking birds headed to the northwest, in the direction of the old deserted dumping ground, and the sparrows' cries over his hovel shook Macko Breden into head-splitting wakefulness. Goddam that whiskey and goddam this flu-bug and goddam that high-toned bitch Melody Parker and her faggot boyfriend, and goddam them fuckin' birds.

The filthy sheets were soaked. Summer nights in Macko's house were stifling as it was—he'd once thought about making a deal for an old-fashioned G.E. window air-conditioning unit, but the fuel pump on the ancient pickup had gone out about then and so much for the cooling plans—and the fever coursing through Macko's body had made it even worse. Lying on her side next to Macko, Mae's breathing was ragged. A single bulb glowed over the kitchen sink and the light spilling into the bedroom showed her lean body clad only in nylon panties whose elastic was giving out, her small breasts sagging toward the mattress, the fist-sized red marks on her stomach that were turning purple, the scabbing-over gash on her right cheek underneath her eye. The incident at Melody Parker's house had left Macko in a still-drunk and nasty mood, and Mae Breden was showing the signs of it.

Macko rolled out of bed and stood on shaky legs. He was clad in jockey underwear. Phlegm rose in his throat and he hacked and coughed the thick stuff up into his mouth as he stumbled over to the bathroom, went in, and closed the door. He yanked on the string to turn on the overhead light, half staggered over to the filthy porcelain toilet and spit the wad of phlegm into the bowl. Then he went over and leaned on the sink to stare at himself in the cracked mirror.

What he saw wasn't pretty. His eyes were red-rimmed and bloodshot and his skin had a pasty fevered look about it. His two-day beard was mottled with gray and there were angry red scratches from Mae's fingernails on his cheek (Heifer's been givin' me a lotta shit lately, he thought, might haveta trade her ass in) and beads of sweat were on his forehead. Macko didn't have a thermometer, and wouldn't have known how to read one if he had, but he didn't need anyone to tell him that he was burning up with fever and his joints ached like fire. His head throbbed from the whiskey and his nose was running. He pulled a wad of toilet paper from the roll, blew his nose and wiped his upper lip, then dropped the paper in the commode. He didn't bother to flush.

Macko Breden had been healthy as a horse for all of his fifty-three (naw, that ain't it, he thought, *forty-six* is what I been tellin' all them young gals out to Jasper's) years, and if he'd caught the Revenge then somebody had done give it to him. And that somebody was damn sure goin' to pay for it, and Macko knew just who that somebody was. Jeannie, the little cunt, her going around in her underwear with her nose running half the time, using her nakedness to lure old Macko off into her bedroom and give him her sickness. And while he was thinking about it, where was that little bitch anyhow?

Jeannie had been spending a lot of time off in the woods lately. Just two mornings ago Macko had come home at dawn after boozing all night with Bob Bill Stoner, and he'd caught the little girl creeping across the backyard toward the stoop. He'd have to say this for the little bugger, she had some guts about her. Not even after a good working over with Macko's fists out beside the outhouse would she tell him where she'd been, and Macko had gotten so turned on during the whipping that he'd just taken her inside and given her another humping from a by-God real man to remember him by. The little cunt had made him so horny that he'd forgotten at the time what he'd been trying to find out from her in the first place. But right now, standing in front of his bathroom mirror with the fever surging through his bones, he remembered it again.

He was pretty sure that Mae didn't know where Jeannie was running off to. If she *had* known, she damn sure would have owned up to it during the ass-whipping Macko had given Mae just a few (Fuck, what time is it? he thought) hours ago. Her pleading denials, uttered through bleeding lips, had finally convinced Macko that she really didn't know her daughter's whereabouts, so Macko had finally taken second choice and dragged his old lady into the bedroom and fucked her brains out before rolling over and passing out himself. He'd sobered up now (at least, he was as sober as Macko Breden ever was during his waking hours), and he wasn't horny any longer (like all alcoholics, Macko pictured himself as a real stud when he was drinking; the truth was that he generally passed out before he could give any sort of real sexual performance), but he was still determined to teach the little cunt Jeannie a lesson for putting the fever in him.

He left the bathroom and half stumbled over the hardwood floor to Jeannie's room. The little girl's room was more of a closet, *had* been a closet at one time as a matter of fact, a four-by-six cubbyhole occupied by a single army cot and a pile of broken toys and dolls in one corner. The door had a clasp and a padlock on the outside, installed by Macko to help keep the little girl in line, and the padlock rattled and bumped against the wood as he opened the door. There was no one in there. The dirty sheets on the cot were always rumpled, so it was impossible for Macko to tell whether anyone had slept in the room. He mumbled under his breath as he went back into his bedroom. There he pulled on a pair of denim overalls and crammed his feet into tennis shoes that were gray and streaked with mud. He went out on the back stoop and squinted to peer into the darkness of the yard. Moonlight bathed the old gray outhouse, the rocks and empty beer cans strewn about on the ground, the forest treetops as they moved gently in the breeze from the south.

The screaming of the birds was now far in the distance, and Macko listened with his head cocked to one side. It wasn't the right time of year for the sparrows to be kicking up a racket such as they were; the shrieks were sounds heard in late fall and early spring but never, to Macko's recollection anyway, in the middle of July. Fuck it, he thought, I ain't no birdwatcher. He went down the steps into the yard, his tennis shoes soundless, the bottom wooden step groaning slightly under his weight. His packed and throbbing sinuses upset his balance, and as he moved across the yard he stumbled and righted himself. Ten feet beyond the outhouse he stopped and looked upward at the moving, rustling treetops, and swallowed bile as a coldness shuddered through him.

Like everybody else in the world, Macko Breden had a secret. Though he'd never in a million years admit it to anyone (and wouldn't even admit it to himself in broad daylight), darkness scared Macko shitless. *Terrified* him. Made his spit dry up. Nine nights out of ten (or more like ninety-nine out of a hundred) Macko was too drunk by sundown for his fear to overtake him. Besides, if he *should* feel the jitters coming on, a couple of belts of good whiskey would generally chase them away. But his occasional sober evenings were a different story—absolute horrors, as a matter of fact—and more than one night had passed with Macko huddled under the covers with his head buried in the pillow until sunup. Mae had noticed it once, but when she'd asked him about it the following morning she'd gotten the back of his hand for her concern. But now, standing in his own backyard under the moon with fifty-foot elms overhead rustling in the breeze, Macko was about as afraid as he'd ever been in his life.

A flock of leaves blew by yards away on his left. Macko jumped. In the forest, an owl hooted. He recoiled a step. Wherever she was and whatever she was doing, Jeannie Breden was at the moment safe from her stepfather. No fucking way was Macko going to set foot in them spooky woods. He cupped his hands over his mouth and in a shaky voice said loudly, "Jeannie. Jeannie, you out there? You come on here iffen you are."

There was no answer, no sound other than the wind in the trees. Macko giggled in terror; more phlegm rose into his mouth and he spit it out on the ground. Fuck it, he told himself, let the little cunt spend the night out there, it ain't nothin' to me. He turned to retreat toward the house, took one long stride in the direction of the porch. Something moved on the other side of the outhouse, something standing erect, its shadow cast on the ground in the moonlight.

Rooted in his tracks, his lips pulled back in terror, Macko stared bug-eyed at the shadow. Its shape was distorted; it could have been man or animal, Macko couldn't tell. There was a fallen tree branch to his right, a good-sized piece about five feet long and the thickness of a Louisville Slugger, and Macko stooped to pick the branch up and grip it in both hands. He raised his voice against the noise of the wind. "You motherfucker back there, I got me a club. You go on now, lessen you want me to beat the shit outta you." The effort of picking up the branch made his sinuses throb even more.

The shadow swayed slightly, but whoever was behind the outhouse didn't come forward.

"I ain't foolin' you none, you get the fuck outta here," Macko said.

The shadow stayed put, blending with other shapes now, becoming one with the shadow cast by the outhouse.

Macko decided that his mind was playing tricks on him. Had to be. Couldn't be nobody stumbling around out here, 'ceptin' the little girl Jeannie maybe, and that shadow was way too big to be hers. Macko let the tree branch dangle by his hip and stepped forward.

Sheriff Buck Ainson came around the corner of the outhouse and stood facing Macko from about five feet away. The sheriff's pistol was drawn. Its barrel was aimed directly at Macko's breastbone.

Recognition didn't come to Macko immediately. He'd known Buck Ainson for most of his life—for his *whole* life, in fact, at least the part of it that Macko could remember—but the sight of someone that he knew stepping from behind his outhouse in the middle of the night was something that Macko wasn't ready for. At first, all he could see was the gun. That barrel seemed to Macko to be about six feet long, the hole in the end of the barrel the size of an archery bull's-eye. Goddam, was somebody here to rob him? Somebody prowling up in the darkness after the fourteen dollars Macko had to his name after his drinking bout? His gaze traveled up the pistol barrel, past the pudgy hand and thick bare arm, past the short-sleeve uniform shirt with the emblem on the sleeve, and came to rest on Ainson's face. Relief flooded through Macko. His fingers loosened and the tree branch thudded softly to the earth. He said, "Goddam, Sheriff Buck, you scared the shit outta me."

Ainson's eyes and nose were in the shadow cast by his hat brim; his mouth, round chin, and lower lip reflected pale moonlight. Standing rigid as a statue, only his mouth moving, the sheriff said, "You turn around and march, boy." The sound was that of Buck Ainson's voice, but then again it *wasn't* Ainson's voice. The tone was metallic and raspy, as though Macko were hearing a tape of Buck Ainson recorded in an echo chamber.

Macko Breden was slow-witted to begin with, and the shock of seeing Ainson, plus the heavy throbbing in his sinuses was confusing Macko's senses even more. March, the sheriff had said. March the fuck where? Macko swiveled his head and looked behind him. The first line of forest pines was less than fifty feet away; fingers of moonlight probed among the trees, revealing pine needles and cones on the ground, an occasional patch of bare dark earth.

Ainson prodded Macko's shoulder with the pistol. "I done told you to march, boy," Ainson said. "Now, you get a move on, I ain't sayin' it again."

A dull light was beginning to flicker in Macko's consciousness. He turned back to Ainson. His tone an octave higher, his speech faster, Macko said, "Now, hold on, Buck. You ain't heard the truth, not iffen you been talkin' to that Parker woman. I was mindin' my own business, just tryin' to do my work, she come up to me wigglin' around an' puttin' her hands on me. Wadn' none o' my doin'."

Ainson stepped closer, grabbed with his free hand, took a grip on Macko's upper arm and shoved.

The strength of the pudgy sheriff was a shock to Macko. Shit, he thought, this ain't that same fat little man I been seein' for all these years. Ainson's grip was like a steel cable and the shove sent Macko stumbling, his arms flailing at air, landing on his side in a heap. Macko's breath whooshed out of his lungs and there was numbing pain in his ribs. His bicep was on fire where Ainson had grabbed him. Snot was running down Macko's face and his head felt as though it were about to split wide open.

Still lying on his side, Macko looked up at the sheriff and said, "You gotta listen to me, Buck. That girl's evil, goin' around tryin' to tempt men. You're a god-fearin' man, you know I ain't shittin'."

His face expressionless, Ainson stepped closer. He kept his pistol trained on Macko, leaned over and hauled Macko to his feet. Then he shoved once more, and this time Macko didn't fall. He lurched and stumbled toward the woods, staggering, keeping his feet beneath him through teeth-gritting effort. Fear was a cold knot in Macko's belly, and when he heard the unmistakable click of the pistol's hammer airing back he came within a whisker of fainting on the spot. "I'm goin', Sheriff. Leave me be, I'm goin'." His hand spread out on either side, Macko hesitantly entered the woods. Whatever waited in the dark forest, no way could it be as bad as the crazy man who was following.

Macko stumbled through the trees with the sheriff's ragged breathing scant feet to his rear. Macko's foot banged against a root; he stumbled and sprawled headlong. Pain razored through his ankle as it twisted with his fall. He screamed. The sheriff said tonelessly, "I said 'git.' " Then he hauled Macko up on his feet again and prodded with the pistol. Maybe fifty feet away in the darkness, something grunted then growled softly. Macko squinched his eyes tightly closed and limped ahead, dragging his wounded ankle, his feet moving through the carpet of needles with a soft brushing sound.

When they stopped they were in a clearing. About ten

feet in front of Macko stood a tree stump. The stump was about four feet high and just as thick as it was tall. Its top was angled where the saw had cut the tree down years ago. Ainson took the lead now, grabbing Macko by the wrist and leading him over to the stump. God Almighty, Macko thought, the bastard's really gone crazy. He ain't takin' me to no jail, he's goin' to execute me right here on the spot. Goin' to whack off my head like a Thanksgivin' turkey, is what this crazy bastard's goin' to do. Macko planted his one good foot and stopped. Ainson hardly noticed, only glanced over his shoulder and gave another tug. Macko lurched the final steps to collide against the stump. He grunted in pain.

There was something made of hard metal attached to the angled surface on top, and Macko groped the cold metal with his fingers. Someone had screwed an eyebolt the size of a bird's egg into the dead wood. Macko's brow furrowed in numbed surprise as he grabbed the bolt's ring and tugged. It didn't budge; it was firmly anchored into the stump. Suddenly there was a clanking rasping sound, and before Macko could move Buck Ainson had clasped one bracelet of a pair of handcuffs around Macko's wrist and locked the other bracelet through the eyebolt. The sheriff backed away, his pistol held level.

Completely terrified now, his ankle throbbing along with his sinuses, Macko began to bawl. Through wracking sobs, Macko said, "Now goddam, Buck, you ain't goin' to *shoot* me. Please, Buck, I'm goin' to change I swear to God I am. Please don't." The handcuff chain dragged across the stump with a tinny clink.

Ainson holstered his pistol, snapped the cover over the gun's butt, turned his back on Macko and strode purposefully away. He began to climb the nearest grassy mound.

Macko's fear of getting shot now changed to a fear of being left alone in the darkness. The same grunting growl that he had heard in the woods now sounded again, from behind him, maybe fifty feet away. The wind moaned through the treetops. A stench now assailed Macko's nostrils, the same acidic stink he'd smelled in his backyard the past Sunday. Macko looked pleadingly toward Buck

Ainson's retreating backside. "Don't leave me, Buck," Macko said. "Don't *leave* me here, I ain't . . . I'm goin' to be a good man, Buck. A god-fearin' man, I swear on my departed mother's grave."

Ainson didn't falter in his stride. His rounded shoulders rigid, his chubby arms slightly akimbo in the moonlight, he reached the crest of the mound and disappeared down the opposite bank.

The growl sounded again, splitting the air to Macko's rear, closer this time.

MACKO spent the next quarter hour between saying his prayers for the first time in his life, cussing Buck Ainson, Mrs. Ainson, and whatever little Ainsons there were, and hugging the stump in a deathlock. The guttural, snarling growl repeated itself three times, and each time it did Macko scrabbled, sobbed, and cringed against the dead wood. The bestial sound didn't seem to be getting any closer, but it was moving. Each time the thing in the darkness growled it was still behind Macko, still back there where he couldn't see it, but once it was on his left, once directly to the rear, another time off to Macko's right.

It's stalkin' me, Macko thought. The fuckin' thing's *stalkin'* me, slinkin' around back there and takin' its time about it. It's gonna come. It's gonna come chargin' any second, gonna jump on poor ol' Macko an' tear his guts out. Oh, Jesus, it's gonna come, I can feel it in my bones. Feel it in my . . .

Swirling haze of color. Goin' to feel it in that shifting, changing mass of color swirling around in my brain. The same flowing colors that the sparrow had seen earlier, *hate* that had caused the bird to take wing. Only, in Macko's mind the feeing was different. In Macko's mind the colors were the thing back there in the darkness hating *him.* Hating pool ol' Macko Breden, who'd never done nothing to it. Who'd never done nothing to nobody that Macko could recall. Who'd never . . .

Ahead of him a light began to glow. A soft, muted light up there over the crest of the mound where the sheriff had gone, a light coming Macko's way, growing stronger.

Somebody comin' along to help ol' Macko, somebody goin' to get Macko the fuck outta here. Somebody that was going to . . .

The light was coming from a lantern, a yellow lantern dancing like a firefly as it came over the crest and started down the slope in Macko's direction. Little Jeannie was carrying the lantern, Macko's selfsame lovin' stepdaughter, comin' to set him free.

"I been lookin' for you, Jeannie," Macko said. "I's worried to death about you out here all alone, child, you come on down here an' let Daddy see you. Come on now, you hurry, there's a critter back yonder we got to get away from." Relief flooded through Macko's veins for an instant, but the swirl of hate-colors wouldn't clear out of his mind.

The lantern's glow turned Jeannie's skin a ghostly yellow shade, and flickering shadows danced across her cheeks and nose. There was a strange little I've-got-a-secret smile on her face. She approached to within ten feet of the stump, carefully set the lantern on the ground and sat down beside it. She hugged her little knees to her chest. Her stringy, unkept hair hung onto her shoulders in matted tangles. Dark smoke came out of the lamp and swept upward, and the stench in Macko's nostrils now mixed with the odor of burning kerosene.

"Jeannie," Macko said. "We got no time to play around now. You get me a-loose from here an' we'll go home."

Still hugging her knees, still smiling, Jeannie crossed her ankles. "My father's coming," she said. "He told me I could watch." Her tiny voice was barely audible over the moaning wind in the treetops.

Macko's gaze was suddenly riveted on the child's chest, just beside the shoulder strap of the halter she was wearing. There was a laceration there, one he didn't remember seeing before. Jeannie's cuts and bruises were familiar to Macko since he'd put most of them on her body himself, but this was a new one. It looked to be a pretty deep gouge (the flickering shadows cast by the lamp probably made the wound appear deeper than it was), but strangely enough it wasn't bleeding. As Macko watched, the cut seemed to grow smaller, as though it were healing before his eyes. He blinked. It was them movin' shadows from the lamp, it had to be.

Macko raised his voice: "I ain't playin' with you, girl, now you move yore ass over here an' get me a-loose."

She didn't answer, didn't move, just sat beside the flickering lantern and continued to smile. Her eyes were dancing, excited.

Scant feet behind Macko, something scraped the ground. It wasn't a *scrape,* really, it was more of a scratching noise, like a giant clawed foot pawing the earth in anticipation.

Eyes wide in terror, spittle drying and caking in his mottled beard, Macko swiveled his head around. Fear clogged his throat, stifling his scream into a wounded moan.

The big creature was standing erect in the lamplight. It was hairless. Its massive shoulders were like a man's, but its huge arms were bent into the praying position like a mantis's forelegs. Its hands were hairless forefeet with claws the size of railroad spikes extending from the toes. Its flesh-colored snout, yellow in the lantern's glow, was nearly a foot in length. Huge drops of foam dripped from its teeth and plopped heavily into sparse grass. Wrinkles of hate lined its muzzle. Over narrowed eyes, its brow was furrowed in a scowl. The beast's belly and abdomen moved in and out with its ragged breathing. An enormous semi-erect penis dangled between its legs and swayed from side to side. Unable to look any further, Macko turned away and buried his face in his bent free arm. The air was thick with the stench of the thing.

Big claws encircled Macko's waist, lifted him as though he weighed nothing, and dropped him on his belly on top of the stump. Macko's breath whooshed out of his lungs and pain seared his ankle. His bug-eyed gaze met Jeannie's. She was still smiling.

There was suddenly a thought in Macko's brain, a thought that, like the swirling mass of hate-color, he hadn't put there himself. He was vaguely aware that the thought was the beast's, a mental presence inside him every bit as strong as the physical being to his rear.

You won't die, the thought told him.

There was pressure on the fabric of his overalls, hard pressure for an instant, then a ripping noise as the thick denim tore like paper. The fabric parted, and Macko was suddenly naked to the backs of his knees. The remnants of the overalls were bunched around his waist in front. The warm night wind blew across his buttocks and the backs of his thighs.

The thought came again, stronger than before. *You won't die, but your life will be worse than death.*

The frozen scream now tore itself loose form Macko's constricted windpipe. His terrified yell split the silence. Ten feet ahead of him, Jeannie blinked but otherwise didn't move. Her smile widened.

Grunting, growling softly, the beast hunched over him from behind. Its rough hands parted his buttocks. Big claws dug painful gouges into the flesh of his hips.

Macko's eyes opened even wider. God Amighty, the thing was going to . . . it was goin' to *bugger* him. Right out here in this fuckin' dump site, it was going to—

The monster slammed into his rectum. His sphincter denied it passage for a heartbeat, but, thrusting, the creature entered him. It grunted with effort, straining, moving up and down, its huge teeth sinking into his shoulder and sending huge spouts of blood coursing down his spine.

Macko Breden's screams filled the hot night air. Seated beside the flickering lantern, Jeannie covered her mouth with her hands and giggled deliriously.

10

SAM Devine waited until dark before he broke into the house. There wasn't any real reason to wait. He'd crouched in the bushes at sunset and watched the target, driving his black Cadillac Fleetwood, go down the circular drive and head for the center of Tombley's Walk; since his notes told Devine that the target's wife was strangely missing, departure of the target would leave the big house empty. So he could have gone on in, but he didn't. There wasn't any departmental regulation to cover what he was doing, but experience had taught Devine that warrantless searches were better conducted under cover of night.

It had been twelve years since Sam Devine's first break-in, and approximately a decade since he'd had any twinges of conscience over commission of a burglary. Burglaries were what they really were—nothing but out-and-out violations of the local law and the Fifth (or was it Sixth? Devine sometimes got the numbers confused) Amendment, but if the higher-ups in the Bureau wanted to call them "warrantless searches in the furtherance of national security," then that was okay with Devine. Right up there with unauthorized wiretaps, warrantless searches were just part of the job. Part of the grind toward age-fifty retirement and a cushy security job with an oil or computer company to supplement the three grand a month pension that his high-five year average, GS-13 salary was going to yield for the rest of his life. Three more years to the promised land.

Sam Devine's first burglary had been in San Francisco,

at a psychologist's office, and he'd had the jitters so badly that it had taken a sharp slap in the face from his supervisor to calm him down. Then, shortly after his transfer to an outpost office near Zanesville, Ohio, Devine had read the name of Daniel Elsberg in the newspapers, he hadn't even known that Elsberg and the target psychologist in Frisco were one and the same. And if he *had* known, it wouldn't have mattered to him because, by the time he read of Elsberg, Devine had already done four more burglaries and the Elsberg break-in was old news to him.

Under cover of darkness he now stood erect in his hiding place among the crepe myrtle bushes along the eastern edge of Justin Barker's property. He extended his arms to stretch stiff muscles and joints, a man of medium height, neither tall nor short, fat nor skinny, but unremarkable and unmemorable, wearing a drab brown suit and skintight, kid leather gloves. His hair was moderate length and barbered in a moderate style. His pale blue eyes held a permanent expression of boredom. The gloves probably weren't a necessity even though his fingerprints were on record. The F.B.I. computer was programmed, on receipt of any inquiry regarding Devine's prints, to spit out a reply of "Unidentified" and shoot the information on to his superiors in the Bureau. Nonetheless, Devine wore gloves. Experience had taught him that if he and the Bureau were to part company under less than amicable circumstances, his previously unidentified fingerprints might suddenly become the basis for his own prosecution. In this day and time, Devine thought, a man can't be too careful. The Heckler & Koch Squeeze-Cocker P7K3 .380 automatic holstered in light blue nylon under his armpit was likewise untraceable.

His current assignment with the President's Task Force on White Collar Crime was a soft one, and that was just the way Sam Devine, nearing retirement, liked it. Though directed primarily at bankers and Savings & Loan people, the white-collar task force would, basically, go after anyone who wouldn't shoot back at them. While guard dogs and Uzi-toting Hispanics were likely to be protecting the dope dealers, bankers were pushovers. Devine stifled a yawn, then went around to the back fence and climbed over it to stand in the yard.

After admiring the crystal-clear water as it shimmered in the moonlight, he skirted the pool to climb the two redwood steps onto the back deck as he fished in his pocket for a single brass key. He'd made a wax impression of the doorlock two nights earlier, then driven up to Dallas and had a pleasant expense-account lunch at a West End pasta house while the boys in the office forged a duplicate for him. He inserted the key. The lock resisted, then turned with a click. With a final glance around the yard, Devine opened the door and went inside.

He stood in the entryway, fumbled for the small flashlight he carried in his breast pocket and turned it on. The probing beam revealed a long and plush leather sofa, matching leather recliners, a rear-projection Mitsubishi TV with a 50-inch screen. A compact VCR sat on top of the Mitsubishi. Also in the den was a white-brick fireplace with matching Mr. & Mrs. oil paintings hanging over the mantel. Justin Barker was wearing slacks and a golf shirt in his picture; Mrs. Barker was curled into one corner of a couch—the same leather sofa, in fact, that decorated the room in which Devine now stood—and was wearing a black lounging outfit. She was a hazel-eyed blond, and Devine wondered briefly whether Justin Barker had done her in. She'd been missing for three months, and while the Bureau had taken note of the fact because it wanted Mrs. Barker as a witness against her husband if she was willing to testify, not much was being done to track her down. Murder wasn't a federal crime, and there wasn't anything in the file to indicate that anyone had kidnapped her. A wife-killing was a local problem, and if the local boys expected any federal help they were whistling in the wind.

Devine wasn't sure what he was looking for, but he was pretty certain where to begin. The information wouldn't be anywhere in this room. A highbrow room like this, Sam thought, is where crooked rich guys throw football-watching parties and serve up bloody marys to a bunch of other rich guys who are just as crooked as they are. But for all the big show, bankers were pretty dumb when it came to hiding evidence. They all kept records, and they all kept them in the bedroom. Some of them had a safe; others left the checkbook in plain sight where the old lady could read the balance and decide she'd better come across with an extra blowjob or two. Devine didn't waste any more time in the living room. He followed his flashlight's beam out into a long hallway and began to climb the stairs to the second floor.

The staircase was carpeted in heavy shag with three-quarter-inch padding underneath. The padding gave softly under his feet as he ascended. There was a six-foot grandfather clock at the head of the stairs, its pendulum swinging with a monotonous *tick-tock, tick-tock,* and Devine's eyebrows lifted as he looked the clock over. It was a Meyerson, just like the one Devine's ex-wife had always wanted, and he briefly wondered whether the stereo salesman she was now married to had ever scraped up the money to buy her one. It was a cinch that Devine could never have done it. The padding beneath the second-floor carpet wasn't as thick as that on the stairs. A board creaked slightly as he moved down the landing. There was a polished banister on his left; a mahogany rolling server supporting a sterling silver tea service sat majestically on his right. When he reached the end of the landing he stopped and frowned.

There were two adjacent doors down there. One has to lead to the target's bedroom, Devine thought, the other to a guest room. He had plenty of time, he was certain, so it didn't matter which room he tried first. He went to the door on the right and gripped the knob. It turned easily in his grasp and the door opened a foot or so on silent oiled hinges. Devine froze, his free hand traveling instinctively to transfer the flashlight to the fingers wrapped around the knob, then moving inside his lapel to touch the butt of the .380.

There was a strange odor coming from within the room, a goddam *stink,* like rotten eggs. An acid smell. And another scent as well, a—Devine sniffed the air as he tightened his grip on the pistol—hospital odor. The carpet ended at the doorway; the room inside was tiled. Devine cocked his head and listened. Aside from the ticking of the grandfather clock on the landing he heard nothing.

Devine wasn't afraid, only slightly nervous. No one was in the house, he was sure of that, and even if someone had been at home they weren't likely to be carrying a gun. Nevertheless, he held the .380 ready and aired the hammer back as he reached around the doorjamb, found the light switch, and clicked it on. Brightness flooded the room. Devine turned off his flash, put it away, and stepped inside. He uttered a gasp of surprise, then softly disengaged the hammer on his pistol and reholstered the gun below his armpit. He leaned his back against the wall and folded his arms.

His first thought was that the target was in the abortion business. Must be aborting elephants, though. A wry smile touched Devine's lips as he looked over the two king-sized beds that were pushed together, and that occupied most of the room. The headboards of the beds were pushed against the far wall, and there was about six feet of floor space around the sides and foot of the beds in which to move around. An inch-thick slab of wood had been laid across the two sets of box springs with the mattresses on top of the wood so that whoever—or whatever—was sleeping in the twin king-sized beds could lie directly in the center without falling down between the mattresses. The sheets and blankets were in piled and rumpled disarray, and near the headboard of one of the beds (here Devine's bored eyes widened slightly), something had gouged its way through the fabric into the stuffing. *Four* somethings, as a matter of fact, four sharp somethings that had made parallel rips in the mattress. Mounds of cotton were poking out through the tears. Devine fished in his side coat pocket for his small Canon camera as he gave the rest of the room a quick once-over with his gaze.

On the side of the beds to Devine's right were four side-by-side metal hospital scaffolds from which four hanging bottles of clear liquid were suspended upside down. Intravenous feeding bottles. The scaffolds were adjusted so that the bottles hung at staggered heights, the lowest-hanging bottle toward the head of the bed and the highest toward the foot. All four bottles were connected by Plexiglas tubes, so that the liquid would flow from the highest-hanging bottle to the lower ones as the lowest bottle emptied. The feeding tube was connected to the lowest bottle. The tube's valve was closed, and the end of the tube was on the hanger at the bottle's neck with the needle sticking upward. Quite a setup, Devine thought, you just have the elephant lie down in the bed and shoot the juice to him.

Against the wall beside the scaffolds stood two fifty-five-gallon stainless steel drums. The drums and the scaffolds were on rubber wheels, which explained the tiled floor. As he quickly snapped pictures, Devine made a mental note to find some kind of container in the house—a shot glass, perhaps, from the bar he'd noticed in the den behind the leather couch—in which to carry a sample of the liquid up to Dallas to the lab boys. If the liquid turned out to be plain old glucose instead of speed or Demerol, Sam Devine was going to be disappointed.

After he'd photographed the room from all angles, Devine turned off the light and went back out onto the landing. He still hadn't found what he'd come for (though what he *had* found was enough to knock one's eyes out), and he still needed to search the target's bedroom. He moved to the adjacent door, had turned the knob, and was preparing to enter, when movement on the other side of the door stopped him in his tracks.

There wasn't any mistake about the movement; someone had brushed against the wood on the other side. Devine still wasn't afraid, but the thought of someone seeing him made him worry. If this were a drug investigation he wouldn't have any qualms about shooting whoever was in there, but a white-collar search was a horse of a different color. And whoever was on the other side of the door already knew that Devine was in the house, he didn't have any doubt about that. He turned on his flashlight and swept its beam along the crack underneath the door, at the same time placing his ear against the wood. He heard ragged breathing. No point in taking any chances; he decided to get the hell out of there. He'd taken one long stride in the direction of the staircase when there was a whoosh of air as the door opened.

Instinctively, Devine turned toward the noise, aiming his flashlight, digging inside his coat. The flashlight's beam reflected from a huge hairless paw that came at him from within the room. Big sharp claws spread themselves in the light. There was sudden pain in Devine's hand, and the flashlight thudded to the carpet. The claws raked the side of Devine's face, hung in the flesh, ripped something away. Dazed, Sam Devine went down on the landing.

The left side of his face was numb; warm, sticky wetness oozed from his ragged wound. His flashlight lay about a foot from his nose. Something white and round was spotlighted in the beam, something the size of a small plum with sticky traces of red on its surface. Devine's jaw dropped in disbelief as it dawned on him that the plum-shaped thing was his own left eyeball. As terror flooded over him, razor-sharp claws tore the rest of Devine's face away.

11

MARGARET Ainson paused for a moment just before going up the front steps to the Tombley's Walk Church of Christ. A shudder ran through her as her gaze lingered for a moment on the spot where the poor dumb brute of a dog had fallen the previous Sunday morning. It was dusk. The gathering darkness made seeing difficult, but the outlines of the bloodstains on the walk were still there. Or were they? Were they outlines of the stains, or were they merely shadows? As Margaret squinted for a better look, a loud screeching noise filled the air. She started, wringing her hands as she turned toward the sound.

It was only birds. The startling loud noise came from a flock of sparrows over on the courthouse square, a block away. Like many of the good folk in Tombley's Walk, Margaret Ainson kept feeders in her yard, and she knew the cry of panicked sparrows as well as she knew her husband's voice. The sound increased in volume and she pictured the birds as they rose, wings flapping, over the courthouse roof. That's where they would be, all right, the sparrows would have been bathing in the fountain by Matthew Tombley's statue this time of day, and something had frightened them. It was the wrong time of day for the flock to take wing; the cry that Margaret was now hearing shouldn't be heard until after daybreak. More weird goings-on in Tombley's Walk. She hurried up the steps and entered the church. Once she was inside the House of Lord, the peace that passeth understanding came over her.

Or did it? The peace that passeth understanding *should* have come over her in the House of the Lord, but the secure feeling she had once the door closed behind her and the racket from those screeching birds was no longer pounding her eardrums quickly went away. The same strange uneasiness she'd had all day flooded over her. Margaret nervously smoothed her print cotton go-to-meetin' dress and hurried down the aisle to her pew. *Her* pew, nine rows from the front on the right-hand side, the same pew she and Ernie had occupied (or that *Margaret* had occupied, with Ernie faithfully at her side when the Demon wasn't coursing through his veins) each and every Sunday morning, Sunday night, and Wednesday midweek prayer-meetin' for lo these many years. Brett and Ruthie Guthrie were already seated in *their* pew, one row in front of Margaret by the center aisle. Ruthie, a big hunk of a woman who was two years older than Margaret, and whose go-to-meetin' dress was navy blue with a high white starched collar, looked over her shoulder and favored the sheriff's wife with a smug nod. Been many a day, thought Margaret, since Ruthie Guthrie has taken her place in the House of the Lord before Margaret Ainson, and Margaret made a silent vow not to let it happen ever again. Being the first of the flock to gather at the river was a habit ingrained in Margaret Ainson's soul.

Though it was still a half hour before the service was to begin (summertime prayer-meetin' was at nine in order to give the menfolk a chance to come in from the fields during daylight savings time), it was a late arrival time for Margaret Ainson. Margaret had a good reason for being late, of course; she'd sat fidgeting at the breakfast table for nearly an hour before deciding that Ernie wasn't coming home in time to go. She'd finally told herself that law enforcement business was keeping her husband (she refused to consider that the Demon Whiskey had taken command; Ernie had only been born-again for a short while on this occasion), then had held her head high and gone to the House of the Lord alone. A sheriff's Christian wife had no business wringing her hands off to one side.

Something was coming over Ernie Ainson, something

different from his drinking problem, and something different from his womanizing with the harlot Tulip Patterson. Margaret had learned over the years to put up with the drinking; Ernie was really as good as gold, and let him who could've been the football star that Ernie had been in his youth and come through it without some sort of mark of Satan, let *that* brother be the one to cast the first stone. And one thing led to another. The hero-worship showered on him in his youth was responsible for Ernie's drinking, and it had been the drinking led to his whoring with Tulip Patterson. Margaret had known about Tulip and the sheriff for years, though she'd never let on to the townfolk that she knew. Margaret suspected that the Tombley's Walk citizenry took it for granted that the sheriff had the wool pulled over her eyes, and she never would have set them straight in a million years. The way it was, the town felt sorry for her; if they were to learn that she knew about Ernie's affair, the townspeople would think that Margaret Ainson was an ignoramus for putting up with the situation.

The quiet solitude of the church's interior—rows of silent pews, the fragrance of cedar, the sprays of palm leaves in hanging pots beneath the tall stained-glass windows lining both sides of the auditorium—normally gave peace to Margaret's soul, but that wasn't the case on this particular evening. The feeling of something *not right*, the sense of evil in the air, had begun that afternoon when Brother Leroy Abbey had called.

Abbey was only the fourth preacher to serve the Tombey's Walk Church in all of Margaret's fifty years, and she didn't like him. No, that wasn't right, Christian charity wouldn't let Margaret *dislike* anyone, least of all a parson, but . . . Well, suffice it to say that she didn't *love* Brother Abbey with the same fervor as she had Brother Malcolm Kinely, the preacher before Abbey, nor Brother Jacob Inman, who had proceeded Brother Kinely in the pulpit, and especially Brother Dimmitt Stanley, who had been over seventy years old when he'd immersed her in baptism when she was a girl, and for whom Margaret Ainson would have gladly laid down her life. The other Tombley's Walk ministers had been conservative family men and devoted to the Word. Abbey, on the other hand, was a strutting peacock, a smallish man who swaggered in place in the pulpit, whose starched collars were higher and whose white cuffs were longer than they needed to be, and who preened around in paid-for-in-Dallas blown and razored hairstyles. A man so taken with his own appearance simply couldn't, Margaret felt in her heart, have the best interests of the flock on his mind. And the fact that Abbey had begun to grumble openly to the elders over the fact that the congregation hadn't built him a house as yet was further proof, to Margaret's way of thinking, that Brother Abbey was more materialistic than spirtual.

And the phone call had been an insult. After all, Brother Abbey *had* been the preacher for more than a year. Margaret could have excused the call had Abbey been on the job less than a week, but Abbey had been around long enough that he certainly should have known that anyone as faithful as Margaret Ainson didn't need to be reminded to come to midweek prayer-meetin'.

"I'm deliverin' a special message tonight, Sister Margaret," Abbey had said. Margaret had been stiffly silent for a moment, then thanked the preacher for calling and hung up. She'd spent most of the afternoon with her ear to the grapevine, checking with the other sisters in Tombley's Walk, and the fact that Abbey had made the identical call to each and everyone of them did take away some of the sting. But not near all of it. As though Brother Stuffed-Shirt thought that the faithful sisters of Tombley's Walk might *not* come to prayer-meetin' unless he reminded them. The nerve.

As the flock assembled in twos and fours—and came, some of them, in even bigger groups, the Wascomb family, who lived south of town and farmed cotton along the interstate access road, brought all six of their children into the worship, from the tall strong boy of nineteen who was back at home after failing at Texas Tech University down to the nineteen-month-old squalling little girl who continually upset the service, who couldn't walk as yet and had to be toted—Margaret Ainson said her separate prayers. She said the prayers each and every day, but she'd never believed that the Master heard the ones she said at home over the roar of the washing machine or the whispery hum of the dryer, even though she spoke the prayers as loud as she dared without upsetting her neighbors. But the prayers spoken in the quiet of the meeting house were sure to reach the Master's ears. She said one for Ernie and asked the Lord to help him wrestle with his problems; another was for Eleanor Beamer, her best friend and one of the most faithful of the flock, and whose tribulations with her son would end soon if Margaret's prayer was heeded by the Lord. At the close of Margaret's prayer for Sonny Beamer's soul, she raised her eyes as Eleanor herself arrived to take her place directly in front of Margaret. She had sat behind Eleanor in church for so many years that Margaret doubted whether the worship would have much meaning for her at all without Eleanor's tall gaunt form between her and the preacher, and without Eleanor's strong (if somewhat off-key) soprano to booster the congregational singing. Eleanor was wearing a high-necked gray dress and a touch of rouge. She reached over the back of her pew and affectionately patted Margaret's arm. The two women nodded to each other. Pure warmth flooded through Margaret's soul; Eleanor knew that her friend had been discussing Sonny's tribulations with the Lord. Praise be, praise be.

The auditorium was now full; the silence of the church was broken by the rustling of summer dresses, an occasional muffled cough, a whispered conversation here and there. Irritated as she was over the phone call from Brother Abbey, Margaret had to admit that the preacher's strategy seemed to be working. Midweek prayer-meetin' normally brought out only the most fervent of the flock, but one and all seemed to have gathered together for Brother Abbey's special message. She checked her watch. It was nine on the nose, time for the worship to begin. She reached for a hymnbook and opened it on her lap; strictly by chance the hymn on the exposed page was one of Margaret's favorites, Number 121, "Rock of Ages." As Margaret hummed the opening bars softly under her breath, the rear door of the auditorium opened and Brother Leroy Abbey came in.

Barged in was more like it. The door swung inward with a force behind it and banged against the inside wall. Three hundred heads turned as one; surprised murmurs and a few startled gasps filtered through the air. Margaret half rose from her seat, craning her neck over the heads of the seated congregation for a better view, and as she gazed on Brother Abbey the feeling of something *not right* flooded over her once more, flooded over her and engulfed her very soul and being.

Instead of his usual natty suit, Brother Abbey was dressed in casual clothes. Much less than casual, actually, his pale blue denim work shirt was frayed and the jeans he wore were grimy around the pockets. His coal-black hair was in wild disarray. There was a piercing gleam in his dark eyes and he hadn't bothered to shave. As he stood with hands on hips and glared around at the faithful, two men came in to stand behind him. One of the men was Doug Ellison—whose presence in church was a first for him to Margaret's recollection—wearing tight jeans and a black muscle shirt. Margaret blinked in alarm as she realized that the second man was Sonny Beamer. Behind her, Eleanor uttered a choking sob and said softly, "My boy."

Sonny wasn't in uniform. He wore a T-shirt with a large hole in the fabric that exposed his hairy navel. The T-shirt's sleeves were cut off at the shoulders; in place of his former scrawniness Sonny showed big biceps with blood-swollen veins running the length of the muscles under his skin. He walked stiffly over and closed the door, dug in his jean pocket for a key, locked the entryway. They've closed us in, Margaret thought. Oh, sweet Master, they've *closed us in.* She clutched the hymnbook to her breast and begun to pray silently.

Brother Abbey left Ellison and Sonny at the rear of the auditorium and approached the pulpit and purposeful strides. All of the strut was gone from his walk. He passed abreast of Margaret's pew with his gaze firmly straight ahead. He ascended the two steps to the rostrum and turned on his heel to face the congregation. Without a word, without so much as a reassuring nod to the flock, Brother Leroy Abbey began to take off his clothes.

Sweet Master, he's *doing it,* Margaret thought. I've been right about that man, no one so . . . so *materialistic* should be doing the Work, now he's become a raving lunatic. Standing up there desecrating the pulpit, he's—

Abbey savagely tore the lapels of his shirt apart. Buttons popped off and flew out on both sides of him. He yanked off the shirt and cast it aside, standing naked to the waist, dark hair sprouting from the center of his chest, his muscled belly moving rapidly in and out. He stood rigid for an instant, nostrils flaring, then hooked his thumbs under his waistband and tore open his fly as viciously as he'd shredded the lapels of his shirt. Margaret was too stunned to move a muscle. All about her, women gasped. Margaret averted her face from the sight and covered her eyes with her hand.

Not in God's house, she thought. Not anywhere, Sweet Master, would she look on the nakedness of any man other than her husband unless she was forced to do so, but in God's house she'd die before she'd look. Some women might stare, but not Margaret Ainson. And not Eleanor Beamer, her sister in the Lord. Margaret peeped between her fingers to confirm that Eleanor shared her moral chastity.

Eleanor stood rigid, openmouthed, staring at the stripping preacher as though hypnotized. Keeping her hand over her eyes, still peeping between her fingers, Margaret reached forward and tugged the fabric below the point of Eleanor's shoulder. "You stop it, Sister Beamer," Margaret hissed. "You stop looking at that spectacle this instant."

Eleanor continued to stare at the pulpit. Margaret dropped her hand and followed Eleanor's gaze as, behind her, a woman screamed.

Where Brother Leroy Abbey had stood seconds ago there was a panting, naked beast. A *beast,* a hairless, snarling creature that surely must have risen from the depths of hell. Its snout was long and hideous, its teeth razor-sharp and glinting in the light. Above its narrowed evil eyes its thick black hair was in tangles. Its hands were pink, four-toed paws with long, wicked-looking, curved nails. Its enormous penis (Sweet Master, Margaret thought, once again covering her eyes, then peeping between her fingers to make sure her vision hadn't deceived her) swung limp between its legs. On Margaret's left and behind her, a woman screamed. From somewhere in the crowd a man shouted, "My God!" As Margaret decided that Judgment Day had finally arrived, and set about to prepare her soul to meet the Master in person, the creature lifted its snout toward the ceiling and howled.

It wasn't quite the howl of a wolf, but somewhere in between a wolf cry and the screech of a wounded owl. A startled hush fell over the congregation as the wall reached a crescendo and trailed off, echoing from the church rafters and reverberating from the walls. Before the echoes had died away, answering howls came from the back of the room.

Margaret turned. The entire assembly was on its feet, good folk in go-to-meetin' suits and summer-weight dresses, most of the clothes a drab gray or navy with a few gayer prints in view—like the dress Margaret herself was wearing—all with horrified looks on their faces, a few heads now turning at the eerie cries now coming from the rear of the auditorium. The standing crowd blocked Margaret's view; she moved to the end of the pew and bent from her ample waist to look directly up the aisle toward the exit. Two more naked, snarling beasts were back there, blocking the door with their bodies, howling, snapping at air with fearsome jaws, two demons from hell among the faithful. As Margaret uttered a prayer (her mind too numbed for an original prayer, she settled for the opening line "Now I lay me down to sleep . . ."), a terrified cry came from near the podium. Margaret's head snapped back around.

The demon at the front had a man in his grasp. It was a chubby man in his thirties, a man with a round happy face now drawn with terror, a man—Sweet Master, Margaret thought, that man only received his salvation a fortnight ago—named Homer Wright who'd moved to Tombley's Walk from Daingerfield the previous winter. Wright was yelling at the top of his lungs, kicking, wriggling, his feet and arms flailing at air while the monster's talons encircled his thighs and held him aloft. As Margaret gaped, the beast turned Homer Wright sideways, closed huge jaws around Wright's fat neck and bit the man's head off.

There was a crunch like a nutcracker chomping down on a walnut. Homer Wright's head, still with the expression of horror on its face, thudded to the floor and rolled over. Blood spurted from the gaping wound in the torso, hit the creature's face, cascaded down the creature's chest and shoulders. The beast cast the still-squirming body aside, stepped forward and seized another man, this man a white-haired gent wearing a brown suit. Margaret turned her face away as terrified yells and moans came from the rear of the auditorium. Back there, a teenage girl made a break for it, reached the exit door and tried to pull it open. One of the two monsters at the rear grabbed her around the waist and, twisting and biting, fell to the floor with her, out of Margaret's view.

Margaret Ainson was suddenly calm. The hymnbook was still firmly in her grasp, still open to the same page. Finally, just as it always did in the House of the Lord, the peace that passeth understanding came over her. With her free hand she touched Eleanor Beamer's shoulder, and Eleanor turned to Margaret with a smile of understanding on her gaunt face. Margaret was gratified; her sister in the Lord was feeling the peace as well. Margaret offered to share her songbook; Eleanor grasped one cover and Margaret held the other as the two lifelong friends bent their heads over the page and made a joyful noise unto the Lord for the last time on this earth. With smiles of charity on their faces they raised their soprano voices in perfect off-key harmony: "Rock of Ages, cleft for me, let me *hiiiiide* myself in thee."

12

TERRY Hackney got drunk about once every two years and got mad less often than that. But tonight as he pulled his ten-year-old Volkswagen Hatchback off the Interstate access road and bounced into the parking lot of Jasper's, he was in the process of getting drunk *and* mad. Though he'd never unholstered his .357 Magnum Python in the line of duty in his whole seven years as a Tombley County Deputy Sheriff (and had never used his .357 Ruger Security Six revolver, either, except to shoot one dog in the head and Sonny Beamer in the ass the previous Saturday), he had the Magnum ready for action, its cylinder loaded, lying beside him on the seat. If he found his Junie inside Jasper's with another man, he was going to kill somebody—either Junie or the man or both—and then turn the gun on himself and blow his brains out.

Getting fired from the sheriff's department had left Terry distraught and morose—so much, in fact, that those who knew him best doubted that he'd ever recover. It wasn't that he was in love with being a lawman, not at all. In fact, he hated it. He was so tenderhearted that the thought of arresting anyone other than rapists and murderers put a lump in his throat. And if the fugitive *was* someone dangerous, Terry would get so scared that his knees would actually quiver during the arrest, he wouldn't be able to keep anything on his stomach for days thereafter, and he'd toss and turn and walk the floor for nights on end.

But though he hated the job, being a deputy gave him some respect that he'd never had in his life. When he'd been growing up in Tombley's Walk he'd been myopic and overweight, the butt of all jokes. He was the boy in school who never had a date unless a girl, in last-minute desperation, needed someone harmless to take her to the prom. Even then, once at the dance, Terry was likely to spend the evening in misery, stuffing marshmallows into his mouth in some dim-lit corner while his date rubbed bellies with every other boy in the gym.

He credited his status as a lawman with winning his Junie. He'd been madly in love with her since the third grade and more than once had suffered a cut lip or fractured nose from one of the men around town who'd bragged too loudly about what a good blowjob Junie had given him, protecting her honor even though he couldn't recall her ever favoring him with so much as a friendly nod. But his badge and uniform had changed all that. The fact that his first face-to-face encounter with his lady fair had come about over a baggie of Colombian gold that had fallen out of her purse had completely slipped his mind. The lid of grass was forgotten, in fact, about fifteen seconds after Junie had dropped it on the sidewalk, then slipped her hand into his and told him what a big ol' handsome policeman he was.

And now he feared (was *convinced,* in fact) that the loss of his job was going to mean the loss of his Junie as well. And the thought of losing her made him drink and the drinking made him mad. He found a parking space between a GMC Supercab and a Ford Bronco, killed the engine and cut the lights, stared dumbly for a moment at the trash barrels overflowing with Lone Star and Pearl longnecks, at peanut and pork-rind wrappers blowing across the asphalt. He took the pint of Roaring Springs Kentucky Bourbon (for which Bert Adams had charged him fifteen dollars) from under the seat, unscrewed the cap, had a good-sized belt of the awful-tasting stuff, recapped the bottle, and put it away. Then he checked the cylinder on his Magnum, jammed the gun into his waistband, got out, and walked unsteadily toward the entrance, a short chubby young man in size forty Levi's and a dark blue denim shirt with fat pouches sticking out over the back of his belt against the fabric. His brain was foggy and tears were beginning to flow down his cheeks.

When he'd first shot Sonny Beamer and, truthfully, given Sheriff Ainson the details of what had happened, the sheriff had told him not to worry. Had told him, in fact, that if anyone was going to lose his job over the incident it would be Deputy Beamer. But less than forty-eight hours later, Ainson had done a complete reversal. Hadn't even had the guts to fire Terry Hackney in person, had left his final pay and termination papers in Terry's message slot, waiting for Terry when the pudgy boy had reported for duty. That had been Monday, and so far Terry hadn't even been able to talk to the sheriff about it.

He'd needed a few drinks then, to get up the nerve to tell Junie. He'd told her when he was sitting in his rocking chair with a pint of Roaring Springs propped against his knees (a different pint from the one now underneath his front seat; he'd bought four pints from Bert Adams in the past two days, and Bert was now wondering whether Terry's firing had been a fake and the law had nothing better to do than set the local bootlegger up), and Junie, clad in push-up bra and black bikini panties, was sitting up in bed eating a box of Whitman Sampler chocolates that he'd bought for her out of his final county paycheck. The baby had been asleep in its crib. Terry had stammered around a bit, then, with a swallow of whiskey flowing down his gullet, had blurted out the news.

Junie hadn't even blinked. She'd uncrossed her legs, rolled over to face him, and popped a chocolate-covered cream into her mouth. "Well, you better get your ass to huntin' a job," she'd said, chewing. "I ain't goin' on no welfare, darlin'."

Later on that afternoon, Junie had dressed and gone out. The haughty twitch of her fanny as she'd gone through the door was the last that Terry had seen of her up to now. Terry had stayed in a stupor the past day and a half, doing his best in his drunken state to feed and change the baby, and finally tonight he'd given in and tried to run Junie down. He'd called Junie's mother (who hadn't seen Junie in two years though she lived right there in Tombley's

Walk, and who told Terry on the phone that she'd just as soon not see her hussy of a daughter no more), her sister, every acquaintance of Junie's that he could think of, and finally dialed the number out to Jasper's. Dory Barnes had answered the phone and told him, "Why, she's right here, darlin', helpin' me with my grand openin'. 'Course, she can't talk right now, she's entertainin' some of my customers. If you know what I mean."

Shortly thereafter, Terry had gotten dressed. He'd loaded his Magnum, given Terry Jr. a bottle, and staggered drunkenly out to his Volkswagen. And now here he was, stepping up on the front porch of the honky-tonk, stopping for a moment to gaze unsteadily at the headlights going by on the interstate, yanking the door open, and stepping over the threshold. A gust of hot summer wind blew against his cheek as the door swung closed behind him.

There was something wrong inside Jasper's, and had Terry been sober the something would have dawned on him in an instant. There were people in there, sitting in twos, threes, and fours at tables and strung out along the bar, and even two cowhands shooting pool, all of the faces ghostly in the blue fluorescent light. Most of the people were drinking beer, and that was as it should have been. Terry took an unsteady step forward, rested a hand on the butt of the Magnum, and cocked his head to one side.

There wasn't any music. Terry Hackney had never been a honky-tonk man. In fact, other than checking out someone's missing husband or restoring order after an ass-kicking or two, he'd never been inside Jasper's in his life. But every time he *had* been in the joint, the blasting jukebox had been enough to knock somebody over. But now it wasn't playing; the hard-core guzzlers were sitting around and holding muted conversations or just staring off into space. Even the pool-shooters were quiet, only the rumble-and-click of the cue ball to indicate there was a game going on. Terry took a moment for his eyes to get used to the dimness, then, his brains still foggy from the whiskey, went past the tables and up to the bar. His hip bumped a table at the edge of the dance floor. No one was dancing.

Instead of Dory Barnes, Bob Bill Stoner was tending bar. He was wearing a black western hat pulled low over his eyes and his belly overhung his belt buckle. He came over and leaned on the beer box, tilted his hat back on his head and raised his eyebrows. He didn't say anything. There was a nasty-looking scar on his neck, a wound that was just beginning to heal. As Terry Hackney watched, the wound seemed to grow smaller. Terry closed his eyes and shook his head. Had to be the whiskey. Had to be.

Terry touched the handle of his pistol. "Ain't wantin' no trouble, Bob Bill," he said, his voice slurred. "Ain't wantin' nothin' but my wife, don't make me cause no shit in here."

Bob Bill showed no surprise, no expression at all. He jerked his thumb in the direction of the door behind the bar. "Back yonder." His voice was mechanical. "Back yonder in the office." Then he picked up a towel and methodically wiped the beer boxes. He showed a slowly spreading smile, then said to Terry, "Havin' 'em a gang bang back there, you better get a move on."

The words filtered through Terry's whiskey-dulled senses like flowing honey. Gang bang. *Gang bang.* A gang bang was something done out in an open filed back when Terry had been in high school, a circle-humping of some old whore from over to Caldonia or somewhere. It damn sure wasn't anything his Junie would do. She might be back there in that office, might even be talking to another man, but a *gang bang?* Couldn't happen, no way. Reeling, listing from one side to the other, Terry Hackney went around the bar and through the door to the office. It used to be Rog Hornby's office, but ol' Rog wasn't around no more. As Terry stumbled down the ten-foot hallway and began to pound his fist on Rog's door, he was sobbing.

A voice, muffled by the door, said, "I'm waitin', darlin', come on in." It was Junie's voice, Junie's soft little voice. Sobbing, his chest heaving, Terry hefted the Magnum in his right hand and pushed the door open with his left.

There was an old couch against the far wall, an old cloth divan with cotton poling out here and there. By one end of the sofa was a small table. A lamp was on the table, an unshaded lamp with a single bulb glowing. Junie, Terry's darlin' Junie, lay on the couch. Her head was propped against the armrest, her shiny black hair spread out on both sides of her pretty face. She was naked, her bare arms outstretched toward whoever happened to come in.

With a cry like a wounded animal, Terry stepped inside the office and raised the pistol.

Something hit his arm from the side, with enough force to numb him to the shoulder. The Magnum hit the floor and went off with a *boom* that shook the room and blasted against his eardrums. The bullet knocked a hole in the ceiling. As Terry turned, something closed the door behind him. The light went out, plunging the office into instant blackness.

The first tearing swipe from the claws sent pain searing through his windpipe. When the talons ripped into his throat a second time, he couldn't feel anything at all.

13

AT one o'clock in the morning, two cars entered the county parking lot across from the courthouse and office building. They converged from opposite ends of the lot and parked side by side. The air was still and hot, Matthew Tombley's statue a dim outline against the blackened sky. The tall elms on the square had their branches upraised like leaved skeleton arms. One car was Justin Barker's black Cadillac Fleetwood; the other the sheriff's county Plymouth. Barker got out, wearing golf slacks and a knit shirt along with white Reebok leather sneakers, and sat on his front bumper. His gaze was on the upper floors of the courthouse building. Sonny Beamer, now in uniform, got out of the county car and stood in the parking lot beside Barker. Doug Ellison came around the Plymouth from the passenger side, folded his arms and lowered his head.

Beamer spoke first. "You got anything on Miss Melody?"

"She ain't far away," Barker said. "I ain't got her pinpointed, but she ain't left the county, her waves are too strong. Little lady's got a mind on her. Easy to pick up on."

Beamer indicated the third floor of the courthouse building across the street. "That mean we should wait?"

"Ain't no reason to," Barker said. "Him first, and then her, it don't make no difference. They're the only ones in Tombley's Walk know for sure about our people."

Beamer nodded, sighed, touched Doug Ellison on the

arm. The two left Barker sitting on his fender and crossed the street, taking their time about it, leisurely climbing the courthouse steps, looking neither right nor left. Just before they entered the courthouse, Sonny Beamer took his mirrored sunglasses off.

PART III

Epidemic

"And the Lord hath said unto us that we will be few, but that the evil shall be a host, a multitude. It will be hard, brethren, and the evil will vent their wrath on us and try to put their evil mark upon us all."
—Brother Leroy Abbey at Tombley's Walk Church of Christ, early summer, 1986

1

MELODY never felt really comfortable with Jack Petty, even when they'd been the hottest and heaviest—mainly because of the difference in their ages and the fact that she had known everybody in Tombley's Walk was talking behind her back—and since they'd quit seeing each other she'd felt really out of place around him. So when Melody and Petty arrived at the clinic to find Rachel Matthews already there and waiting, Melody breathed an inward sigh of relief.

"I didn't know you were with anybody," Rachel said. She was wearing cutoff jeans and a beige T-shirt which read *Q102-Rockin' Texas* across its front, and she was perched on one corner of Petty's desk with her legs crossed. Melody gave the skimpy outfit the once-over and decided that if the good sisters were here right now, Rachel's days in the ladies' chorus would probably be numbered.

"Well, she's one somebody," Petty said, indicating Melody, "and there's another somebody on their way. We got big problems, girl, gettin' bigger every minute. Now I got to visit with Miss Parker here, so why don't you wait out in the lobby."

Rachel's mouth formed a pouty little bow as she got up and went out. She paused long enough to pick up the current issue of *Field & Stream* that lay on a table near the exit, then passed through the entryway and closed the door behind her. Petty sat down behind his desk and leaned back. "There's not a hell of a lot of time, so you ask and

I'll answer what I can. If I take off doin' the talkin' I'm liable to tell you a lot of stuff you already know."

Melody had a seat in the armchair directly across from him. "Rod Lindenhall didn't know anything about them arresting Bud," she said. "That tells me they don't really have any inquiry on Bud, so how'd they know he was wanted in California?"

Petty folded his hands behind his head. "They've probably known all along. They got some kind of telepathy between them, and I 'spect they know what we're thinkin', too. Bud musta found out about 'em, an' that gave 'em the chance to use what they knew about him to lock him up. He tell you what he knows?"

She shook her head. "The other way around. I was down in the black section of town this mornin' and ran across Sheriff Ainson and four others totin' some bodies away on stretchers. The bodies were all in pieces." She shuddered as the image of the torso falling from the stretcher flashed in her mind.

Petty lifted his eyebrows. "I knew as early as Sunday that somethin' was wrong with Buck Ainson, but Christ, I didn't have no idea. Who was with him?"

Melody told him.

"Sonny an' Dory figured to be there," Petty said. "An' now we got Doug Ellison an' the preacher. No tellin' how many others there are, an' their numbers will be growin'. By leaps and bounds."

"What's goin' on, Jack?"

Petty blinked, expressionless, one trimmed eyebrow arched. "You ain't seen one of 'em change, then."

"They're *all* changed. Every one of 'em's got his faults, but up 'til now I'd never have thought they'd—"

"That's not the kind of change I'm talkin' about. I'm talkin' about a physical change. Men turnin' into monsters."

In spite of the situation, Melody nearly laughed out loud. "Are you goin' to tell me *you've* seen somebody change?"

"Not some*body,*" Jack Petty said. "Not a man. But I *have* seen changes, and if a man's goin' to change the same way, then I don't want to be there when it happens."

* * *

MELODY had to admit that Winthrop Reed didn't *look* like a lunatic. He looked more like Joe Average Guy, maybe a bit of a sport and on his way to the golf course or the racetrack. The story Reed had just told, sitting calmly in Jack Petty's swivel chair, certainly had *sounded* like the ravings of a lunatic, and if hadn't been for the fact that he had Doc Petty convinced, Melody would have been thinking about calling for the butterfly nets. But there were too many odd goings-on in Tombley's Walk for Melody to laugh off anything, no matter how crazy it sounded.

"One thing that it means," Petty said, "is that Bud don't have a chance 'less we can get him out o' that jail."

"But he's not . . ." Melody wrung her hands in her lap. "He sure doesn't know anything about what Dr. Reed was talking about. He only knows that those guys were hauling mangled corpses away this mornin'."

Reed sat forward and folded his hands. "We're dealing with practically a hundred-percent unknown factors. I know my laboratory animals communicate telepathically, but I don't have the slightest idea how much of my own thoughts they can or cannot read. They may know exactly how much your friend, Bud, knows, and they may only have a vague idea. Either way, they've got no reason to leave him alive. They'll be very stealthy in their actions until there are more of them than there are of us. Then they won't care what we see. They made a big mistake up in Ridley, Vermont, by letting themselves be known while they were still vulnerable. We're talking about a near-microscopic society here, but one with intelligence and a long memory. They can exist only by controlling the host, by changing the host's physical makeup when the right time comes. These animals—dogs, squirrels and whatnot that they've controlled while disguising themselves as rabies bacteria—well, they're not really satisfactory hosts because they don't have the status that humans have. Once the droplets—spores, you call them, Dr. Petty—take over a few homo sapiens I don't think you'll see any more mad dogs around."

"Now that you mention it," Petty said, "the dog bit Sonny Beamer is the last case I've heard of."

"So now we're seeing a pattern. They'll kill whatever humans they don't, for whatever reason, see as good hosts, use them for food, and preserve the others to manipulate. Anything they see as a threat they'll eliminate. Such as your friend Bud. And you too, Miss Parker, I'd be lying if I said I thought you were safe." Reed rubbed his scalp through his thinning hair.

Melody felt her shoulders hunch closer together as the others in the room looked at her in silence. Reed continued to rub his scalp. Jack Petty, seated on the corner of his desk, brushed his pant leg. One of his feet was swinging back and forth. Rachel Matthews, still in her skimpy jean cutoffs and T-shirt, was slowly chewing gum.

Melody slid her hand inside her purse and touched the butt of her Towner .32 automatic pistol. "Well, I can't think about what they might do to *me,*" she said. "For right now we got to think about goin' down to the courthouse tonight. I doubt Bud will be alive in the mornin' if we don't."

It had taken some talking on Jack Petty's part to convince Melody that they had to wait until after midnight to try and free Bud. Her first impulse had been to go in at the first cover of darkness, get the drop on E.J. Joseph, and simply walk out of the front door of the courthouse with Bud in tow. But now, as she stood on the small loading dock at the rear of the clinic and watched Winthrop Reed back his old Dodge Econoline van up to the landing, she had to admit that Petty had been right all along.

With Bud securely locked inside the jail, the sheriff and his monstrous friends could take their time about dealing with him. All they had to do was wait until the wee hours of the morning and it was a lead-pipe cinch that no one would be up and about around the square to see them working at whatever evil they'd dreamed up.

E.J. Joseph would be the main consideration, both for Bud's rescuers and the enemy. Sober, E.J. was a pretty good watchdog and guarded the jail as though it were his last chance for survival (which, in fact, his job as a jailer was). But it was common knowledge that E.J. couldn't sit up all night without tipping a few, and anyone entering the jail at, say, two in the morning, was sure to find the jailer in a drunken stupor if he hadn't already passed out. So though she didn't cherish the idea of leaving Bud locked up one minuted longer than necessary, Melody knew that their chances would be better after twelve.

So she tried to put Bud out of her mind and concentrate on "it." Both Winthrop Reed and Jack Petty had made several references to "it" during the brief meeting in Petty's office, and had finally agreed that the best way to bring "it" into the building was across the loading dock through the swinging double doors. As Reed backed the van toward the dock with Jack Petty off to one side windmilling with his arm and shouting directions, Melody leaned on a metal tow-wheeler and watched. A raised platform rolling dolly was about ten feet away from where Melody stood, and Rachel Matthews was seated on the dolly. Rachel was still chewing gum, and looking over Rachel's strong good legs, firm breasts, and vacant expression, Melody decided that Jack Petty had finally found the girl of his dreams. The van's rear end bumped softly against the wooden dock. Jack Petty climbed up on the dock and opened the van's double doors. Melody stepped forward for a closer look at "it."

"It" turned out to be a steel cage on wheels. The cage was about four feet high by four feet wide, and around six feet long. It was mounted on spoked wheels, and it was just dawning on Melody where she'd seen a similar contraption before when Winthrop Reed climbed onto the dock and met Melody's gaze with his own.

"You're right," Reed said with just a hint of pride in his voice. "I bought it from a circus. From an auction, really, a forced sale on some circus equipment belonging to one of many shows that couldn't compete with Gunther Goebel-Williams. Its intended use was for transportation of the big cats. I've . . . well, reinforced it. Those bares are hardened steel, twice the thickness of the ones that were originally in place, and the roof is a full three inches thick. The remodeling made the thing weigh a ton, and the axles took some redoing to support the load. But there she is, I don't believe there's anything that's going to get out of there.'' He walked inside the van, moved toward the nose, braced himself against the back of the seats and got ready to push the contraption onto the loading dock. He paused.

''At least, not anything that we've seen before,'' said Reed. ''Our friends haven't given it their best shot as yet.''

''Now, I'm not sayin' it's a bad idea,'' Jack Petty said, bending from the waist, his palms on his thighs, his chest heaving rapidly. ''Christ, what a job. Hell, no, it ain't a bad idea, it's a *good* idea. It's just that . . . well, what you goin' to do? Say, 'Here, Mr. Monster, just step right in'?'' The big steel cage-on-wheels stood in the center of the conference room of the clinic with the table and chairs pushed over in a cluster to one side. Winthrop Reed was in one of the chairs, his rump pushed forward, his legs outstretched, his elbows on the armrests and his chest heaving as well. Rachel Matthews stood in the doorway with her hand on her stuck-out hip. Melody sat in a chair close to Reed with her legs primly crossed and hoped that neither man had a heart attack.

''I've thought it over from every angle,'' Reed said, puffing. ''And I can't say I've got the answer to that. But I do know we've got to have a subject to study. There's got to be a way.''

Melody stroked her own chin. ''They do sleep, don't they? At least the hosts have to. Maybe you can catch one of 'em then.''

''Aside from the men we know about, Sonny Beamer and them, we don't know whoall is actin' as hosts,'' Petty said. ''How would we even know where to go about lookin' for one of 'em?''

Reed inclined his head against the chairback and continued to huff and puff, not saying anything.

Rachel Matthews said from the doorway, ''Well, I know where *I'd* look. Out to Mae Breden's place.''

Melody, Petty, and Reed turned their heads to look at Rachel, as though she'd just appeared out of thin air.

Finally Petty said, "Why's that?"

" 'Cause Mae told me there's been some howlin' out in the woods. Strange noises in the middle of the night." Rachel spoke in hushed tones, like someone who had heard a lot of camp fire ghost stores. Melody suspected that Rachel *had* heard a few.

"Well, it's an idea," Reed said. "But I wouldn't put a great deal of stock in country-dwellers' tales. Most of them are legend or gossip. Or both." At Reed's use of the term *country-dwellers' tales,* Melody and Petty both had shot razored glances in the back-East professor's direction. Rachel continued to beam as though she hadn't heard.

Petty raised a hand and straightened. His breathing was subsiding. "Now hold, hold on," he said. "Less hear her out. You an' Mae Breden used to go around a lot, didn' you, Snooks?" His use of the pet name brought him a sharp glance from Melody. Petty noticed, and his cheeks reddened slightly.

"She 'as like my *sister,"* Rachel said. " 'Course that's 'fore I found you, Jack. I ain't seen much o' Mae since you an' me started goin' around. An' she married that Macko." She wrinkled her nose.

"A little-traveled area of forest would serve as a meeting place," Reed said, sitting upright.

"Gives me the creeps," Melody said. "Her baby's livin' out there with her, idn' that right?"

"The little girl's out there right enough," Rachel said. "Only she ain't none o' Macko's." She blinked. "She's that rich fella Justin Barker's."

Melody's jaw dropped. "Mae Breden's daughter is *Justin Barker's* child?"

"Nobody else's," Rachel said. She put both hands on her hips for emphasis.

"Don't you be spreadin' things like that," Petty said, taking a stride in Rachel's direction. He glanced at the ceiling. "Lessen you're sure."

"Well, I s'pose I *ought* to be sure," Rachel said. "It was me that innerduced 'em."

Rachel paused, a not-overly-beautiful girl with a well-formed body, out of her league in the intellect department and well aware of it, clearly enjoying the feeling of having the Ph.D., M.D., and L.L.B. giving her their undivided attention. Melody continued to watch Rachel. Winthrop Reed rubbed his eyes with a thumb and forefinger and blinked in interest. Dr. Jack Petty went over and leaned against the converted circus cage. Visible beyond him on the wall was a large framed black-and-white photo, a picture of the lobby of the clinic with Petty himself in the foreground before the reception desk, glad-handing the U.S. congressman from the district and the then-mayor of Tombley's Walk. In the picture, Petty was wearing a conservative dark suit and tie. Melody wondered fleetingly—and nearly giggled out loud at the thought—why Petty hadn't been wearing a golf outfit, the way he *usually* slouched around in his office.

Rachel took a step toward the center of the room and stood practically at attention, like a fourth-grader about to recite the Pledge of Allegiance. "It was after my husband died, me an' Mae started bein' friends. We was both so broke then, but couldn't nobody say we was lackin' for men around. 'Specially Mae. You'd never know it now the way that Macko's changed her, but ain't never been a prettier girl around Tombley's Walk that I ever seen. We used to go out dancin' together, sometimes out to Jasper's but mainly over to Tyler 'cause the men over there had more money to spend. That was 'fore you got me that settlement, Miss Melody."

Both men now glanced at Melody, who said in a soft voice, "It wasn't any more than you had comin', the way you lost your man." She was hoping that the subject of Mae's settlement wasn't going to go any further; the fact was that melody had settled the case for quite a bit more than it had been worth and then spent the next few weeks dodging let-me-buy-you-a-drink phone calls from the Traveler's Insurance Company adjuster. The lawyer's portion of the settlement had gone a long way toward setting up Melody's office. Rachel self-consciously licked her lips and went on.

"Anyway, one night over to Tyler me an' Mae was dancin' up a storm at the County Line Club—well, you know it ain't really in Tyler, exactly, but more like in between Tyler an' Kilgore. But there we were, I remember the band that night was Jerry Max Lane from Foat Wuth, and all of a sudden in walks Justin Barker. He was slummin', 'course, way over to the County Line club so's his wife wouldn't get no reports of where he was at. He didn' even know me an' Mae, but first thing you know he come ast me to dance and I did a few times. Then he wanted me to go off with him, but I says, I told him, 'Listen, ain't you a married man?'

"That kinda shook him up, I guess," Rachel said. "An' then I told him I knew who he was an' that really set him to sweatin', an' I says, 'Don't worry none about me gossipin', I don't care what you do but I don't date no married men.' An' he goes, 'Well, what about your friend over there?' Well, Mae was younger than me an' hadn' had the experience with married men an' all, so I jus' kinda shrugged an' told him that was between him an' Mae. Next thing I knowed he was hittin' on her really hard, and then she was leavin' with him in that big yella caddylack o' his, I think that man drives a differnt color ever year. They went on for four or five months after that, slippin' off over to Tyler when nobody was lookin', an' I think I was the only somebody in Tombley's Walk knowed all about it.

"Finally Mae she come up pregnant an' Justin Barker told her he'd fix an abortion up, but she didn't want none o' that. She raised that child up on her own best she could without no help from no daddy, an' the daddy livin' up in that house on the hill an' pretendin' he don't know his own child. But she never told on him an' up to now I ain't told nobody either. I spect it's time to, though. I never will understand after all she went through to keep that child, why Mae went off an' married that sorry Macko."

There was silence for a moment, broken only by the sound of Winthrop Reed clearing his throat and shifting in the chair. Finally, Jack Petty said, "Well, you can't say ol' Justin ain't been buildin' the community up."

* * *

WINTHROP Reed leaned back in Jack Petty's swivel chair and said to Melody Parker, "It's hard to say how much resistance you're going to encounter. There's a pack leader, in my laboratory community I call it the big kahuna, but one of the hosts has control over the others. They won't do anything to you, or do anything else for that matter, without some kind of mental communication from the leader. If somehow the leader has its attention elsewhere, is distracted somehow, maybe you won't be detected at all. It's a pleasant thought, but I certainly wouldn't count on it."

Melody's lips set in a grim narrow line. She fished the Towner .32 out of her purse and showed it to Reed. "I've got this," she said.

From his position leaning against the file cabinet, Jack Petty snorted. "Christ, Melody, that's a popgun. If anybody shot me with that and I found out about it, I'd tell their mother on them. I don't know what you'd do with that against a normal man, but one of these . . ." He shrugged his shoulders and made a give-up gesture with upturned palms.

"It's all I got." Melody lowered her gaze, the feeling of helplessness sinking in. "It's better than nothin'."

"*Much* better than nothing," Winthrop Reed said. "I don't care how small the firearm is, a well-placed shot can kill. We're not dealing with invulnerable beings here, they do die. Poisons, bullets, all of these have the same effect on them as they do on us." He paused and scratched his chin. "On the hosts, anyway. If only that were the case with the droplets. We've just got to have a subject to study, if we're going to get anywhere."

"That's the first thing on the calendar in the mornin'," Petty said. "For tonight we got to think about the fella up in the jailhouse."

"It's natural you would say that," Reed said. "But I've got to look at the big picture. It would be so much simpler if I knew who the big kahuna in the Tombley's Walk group is."

Petty stepped away from the file cabinet and put his

hands on his hips. "What Rachel told us got me to thinkin'. Could be it's Justin Barker."

Melody's head snapped around to look at Petty. "She only said he was runnin' around on his wife. That's not any news to anybody's lived here more than a week."

"Yeah, but ol' Justin's been actin' funny. There's his wife, for one thing. Ain't nobody seen her an' nobody seems to know where she is. An' you know Justin's got his finger in everthing around here, can't nobody have a spellin' bee without him gettin' up an' makin' a speech. But not lately. Lately he's been hard to spot. Plus, well . . . Rachel talkin' about how that little girl's his child, that brings somethin' else to mind. If that ruckus out by Macko Breden's place *is* connected to the whatever-they-are's, then maybe the little girl . . ." He looked around the room like a man grasping at straws. "Well, it's as good an idea as anybody else has got. Plus, I ain't told you this, but that asshole of a doctor over to Canton's been sellin' Justin drugs. Penicillin an' ampicillin, a hundred gallons of the stuff."

Reed sat bolt upright. "Christ, man. Why *haven't* you told us?"

"I just found out this afternoon, an' since then I been helpin' women get away from deputy sheriffs an' helpin' other men lug god-awful contraptions into my buildin'. But them drugs make it a cinch that Justin's in on somethin' even if he ain't the leader himself."

"I'd say so," Reed said. "Indeed I would. I think we need to look around out at Breden's, first thing tomorrow. If we find nothing there, then it's on to Mr. Barker's. We might be bearding the lion right in his den, it'll be very dangerous."

Melody stood, her arms folded, her chin held high. "Not any more dangerous than what we've already been through. An' what we're goin' through tonight, tryin' to get Bud out o' jail."

JUST at twilight, Melody went for a short walk with Jack Petty. It had been her idea; she'd taken him off to one side in the clinic lab and told him that they needed to have a private talk. His chin had lifted in surprise, but then he'd nodded.

They were ambling along in the sparse grove of trees fifty yards behind the clinic, crunching pine cones beneath their feet and kicking little piles of needles aside. Dusk was settling fast and the lights inside the building were casting window-shaped patterns on the clinic lawn. The air was still and heavy. Daytime heat was cooling to summer-night warmth.

"I wanted to get some things out in the open," Melody said. "After all, you an' I got more at stake here than most people."

"I don't know as I got *that* much at stake," Jack Petty said. "As long as I got my license I can doctor anyplace."

"Come on. The investment in this clinic? Plus your goin' practice? I know you don't like to admit it, but it's not the easiest thing in the world for a man your age to go off and start over where nobody knows him."

"What's wrong with my age?" Petty said irritably, then softened the pitch of his voice and said, "Don't answer that. Hell, I *know* what's wrong with my age. An' don't think I ain't been worryin' about the long run, if all this should take our little town off the map. But, well, an' I ain't sayin' this to get you uptight, girl, but it looks to me that you're takin' a lot of risk for a man that ain't got no stock in this town at all. Your friend down there in the jail ain't part of Tombley's Walk, an' I doubt that he's too worried about this wide place in the road."

Melody leaned against the trunk of a pine. The rough bark rubbed against her upper arm. She wet her lips. "I love him, Jack," she said.

"Well, that's . . ." Petty trailed off, then said, "Hell, Melody. I'm not one that ought to be givin' any kind of advice about somethin' I don't know nothin' about. But don't get love mixed up with a case o' the hot-pants."

She chuckled softly. "I hadn' had a case o' the hot-pants since I quit seein' you. I told Bud all about what went on between you an' me. He's the only one I've ever told about that."

Petty put his hands in his pockets, looked at his feet,

raised his gaze to meet hers. "Well, you're crazy for it. But I guess I'll be goin' downtown with you tonight."

"Thanks for the offer," Melody said. "But I can't see that'll help anything. I got a gun. E.J. Joseph won't be in any shape to give me any trouble, really, and if one person can't get Bud out then two won't do much better. Besides, there's no point in chancin' losin' both me *an'* you."

"Well," he said, "less just say I'm insistin' on it. I don't care if I can't do nothin' but holler for help, I ain't lettin' one little girl go down there on her own."

A wave of gratitude went through Melody, and as she stood away from the tree there was the tiniest lump in her throat. She cleared the lump and started to say something, but as she opened her mouth to speak the sound of screeching birds filled the air.

The flock was a dark shape against the dark of the twilight sky, weaving, separating, coming together again. The twittering cry reached a crescendo, then faded as the flock went overhead and headed into the distance.

THEY went downtown in Jack Petty's four-door Fleetwood, the only new Cadillac in Tombley's Walk besides Justin Barker's. Petty stuck to the back streets, even stopping once and killing the lights while an ancient pickup bumped and rattled its way through an intersection in front of them, and approached the courthouse from the rear. He entered the square from the northeast corner, turning right off Davy Crockett Boulevard onto Second Avenue and parking parallel to the curb in front of the courthouse's back entry. They didn't speak on the fifteen-minute ride; Melody sat upright in the Fleetwood's plush leather passenger seat, cradling her small purse between her bare thighs. Her Jamaica shorts and T-shirt were sticking slightly to her skin. Occasionally she'd squeeze the soft imitation leather of her purse to be certain that the Towner pistol was still inside.

There were no lights visible, either in the courthouse itself or any of the low buildings across the street. Had they been on the other side of the building, near Matthew

Tombley's statue, the lights in the third-floor jail windows would have been in view, but from where they were parked downtown, Tombley's Walk looked like a ghost town. The moon was hidden behind the bulk of the courthouse and the dome was a vague overhead shape against the darkened sky.

Jack Petty stirred beside Melody, leaned back in the driver's seat and rested his arm on the seatback. "In half a century of livin' around here I don't ever recall goin' in the back door."

"I don't either," Melody said. "I don't know as *anybody* has since John Ed Dearborn's trial in what, seventy-one? Buck Ainson kept ol' John Ed in the jail over in Canton, used to go over an' shackle the prisoner and lead him through that back door an' up the steps into the courtroom. Claimed he was doin' it for security reasons, but even then I thought it was funny there was always a lot o' newspaper people waitin' on Buck an' John Ed to snap their pictures."

"Well, if nobody's usin' the back way," Petty said, "then how do you know it ain't sealed?"

Melody's lips upturned in a small grin. "I only said I've never been through the door. That dudn' mean I don't have a key to it."

His outline barely visible in the dimness, Jack Petty lifted his chin.

"Rod Lindenhall gave it to me," Melody said. "Couple of years ago, we were in trial. He slipped me the key in the courtroom and said why didn't I meet him in his office that night to lay the groundwork for some plea negotiations. Well, ol' Rod didn't have any intention of layin' any *groundwork,* so I never took him up on it. But I did take the key, I thought someday I might need it."

Cautiously, glancing left and right, they crossed the twenty feet of sidewalk and climbed the five steps to stand before the back entrance to the courthouse. Melody's sandals made little scraping noises on the concrete while Petty's sneakers were noiseless. Melody fished inside her purse, moved the Towner automatic aside, found the small brass key. With a deep intake of breath she inserted the key in the lock and turned it. The latch clicked open, the door moved inward with a protesting squeak. Melody whispered, "We can't afford to turn on any lights so we're liable to do some stumbling around."

Petty extended a hand, palm up. "Well, after you, then. If anybody falls down it's not goin' to be me. My age, remember?"

Melody took three cautious steps inside, narrowing her eyes, straining to see. She saw only darkness and sensed rather than saw Jack Petty behind her. She groped with her hand and found the polished banister, then reached her other hand behind her and firmly grasped Jack Petty's arm. Her purse dangled from the wrist on the hand which touched the bannister. Slowly, with Melody leading the way a hesitant step at a time, they began to climb the stairs.

They made the turn at the second-floor landing and continued upward. There was a steel door on the third-floor landing, and Melody paused outside and placed a silencing finger on Petty's lips. An eight-inch-square window was in the door with small solid bars covering the opening. She stood on tiptoes, pressed an eye against the barred window, and felt her own sharp intake of breath as she looked directly at Bud.

His cell was directly across the narrow corridor, and he wasn't asleep. He lay on a hard bunk with his hands clasped behind his head, one knee bent, the other ankle resting atop the bent knee. He was staring at the ceiling, and a shadow of beard was beginning to show beneath his sideburns and on his upper lip. Melody had actually drawn in a breath to call out to him when, heard on her left and out of her line of vision, a chair scraped on the floor and something hit a table surface with a sharp bang.

E.J. Joseph's voice called out, loudly and drunkenly, "Triple jump? 'At's a *triple fuckin' jump?* Goddammit, Freddy, I oughtta lock yore ass up for the night. Ain't givin' you no more beer, neither."

Another man's voice, higher-pitched, only slightly less slurry than E.J.'s: "I caint help it, E.J., yo're one a the sorriest fuckin' checker-players I ever run across. I don't like this fuckin' Lone Star no way, next time you bring Pearl, you hear?''

''Got me a pris'ner wantin' to call the brand o' beer,'' E.J. said. ''Listen, Sonny, I'm runnin' this fuckin' jail.''

In the darkened hallway, Melody leaned close to Jack Petty and said, ''Get a good hold, we're goin'.'' Then she slipped the key into the lock and turned it. There was a soft double click and the knob turned in her hand. Melody reached inside her purse, steadied the pistol in her hand, and pushed the door inward. As it swung silently open a foot, a loud jangling noise filled the innards of the jail. Melody froze with her hand still on the knob.

THE ear-splitting sound of the bell shocked Bud into a sitting position on his bunk. The voices of the drunken jailer and prisoner had subsided in Bud's consciousness to a background drone, and he'd even been able to doze off for a few minutes a half hour earlier. He'd been lying there staring at the ceiling, his mind many miles away—on a Southern California beach scene, in fact, with Beth wading thigh-deep in choppy ocean water and Jenny shoveling sand into a pail with a toy shovel held in chubby babyhands—when the jangling noise jarred through his system. As he sat bolt-upright, the jangling ceased, then sounded again in two short blasts.

Outside Bud's cell in the corridor, the prisoner Freddy sat frozen with a red checker held inches off the board, in the midst of making a move. In his other hand Freddy held a can of Lone Star Beer inches from his gaping mouth. He said, ''The fuck's that?''

E.J. lurched forward. The front legs of his chair banged the floor. His bearlike shoulders hunched, E.J. said, ''Somebody ringin' the entry bell, from outside. Nearly one in the mornin', who in hell's comin' up here this time a night? Likely ol' Buck, maybe he brung more beer with him.''

Bud watched the hulking deputy rise and, listing badly, go over to the doorway through which he'd ushered Bud into his cell hours earlier. Something moved in the corner of Bud's eye, drawing his attention directly across the corridor from his cell. There was another door over there, a steel door with a tiny barred window near the top, and earlier Bud had wondered about is purpose. It was now cracked open, and Melody Parker had her head and one shoulder inside the jail. She grinned and squinched one side of her face into a broad cute wink. Bud's heart practically jumped into his gullet.

On Bud's right and down the corridor, E.J. stood looking through a peephole into the outer hallway. He closed the peephole, turned, and gestured wildly at Freddy. "Lawman outside," E.J. hissed. "Get yore ass in that cell."

An irritated expression crossed Freddy's face. He got slowly up, retreated toward his cell, stopped, looked at the can of beer in his hand. He guzzled more beer, returned to put the can on the table, then went inside his cell and closed the door behind him. The key was in the lock, with more keys dangling from a ring below it. Freddy reached through the bars, locked his own door, tossed the keys across the corridor onto the table. Then he lay facedown on his bunk and buried his face in his arms.

E.J. staggered to the table, retrieved his keys, went up and opened the entrance. As he stood aside he said, "Trifle late, Brother Beamer. How come you bringin' civilians in here?"

Sonny Beamer came in, followed by a stocky man with a weight lifter's build who was wearing a muscle shirt. Bud couldn't recall ever seeing Sonny's companion before. Beamer's mirrored sunglasses hung outside his shirt pocket, suspended by an earpiece that was in the pocket. His hat was tilted back and his eyes expressionless. The stocky man's jaw worked slowly from side to side.

Beamer's lips moved but his features remained set as he said, "Doug Ellison here's been deputized. Sheriff done it hisself."

"Well, *I* ain't heard nothin' about it," E.J. said. "An' 'pears to me Buck'd tell me 'fore he'd tell anybody. Lord knows me an' Buck Ainson was a team, playin' for the 'Roos."

Beamer looked at Ellison, who continued to stand motionless with his thumbs hooked through his belt loops. Beamer said to E.J., "Well, Doug's takin' Terry Hackney's place. Sheriff sent us up here to take charge of a prisoner."

Bud was leaning against the inside of his cell door, and his hands now tightened convulsively around the bars.

"Take . . ." E.J. weaved unsteadily, and confusion crept into his glazed expression. "Sheriff Buck done told you to take that city-boy over yonder someplace?"

"To transport him," Beamer said mechanically. "Got an out-o'-state warrant on him."

"So the boy told me," E.J. said.

Bud was grasping at straws, but raised his voice and said, "Don't listen to them, jailer."

"You heshup," E.J. said. Then, to Sonny Beamer, "You goin' to take responsibility, aintcha?"

Beamer and Ellison nodded as one.

"Well, it beats all I ever seen," E.J. said. "But I s'pose there ain't nothin' wrong with it." He came, staggering slightly, to Bud's cell and unlocked it. He stood aside. "He's all yorn. I'll be checkin' with Buck, Sonny, you better not be bullshittin' ol' E.J."

Bud was wide awake now, the adrenaline flowing, and strangely enough he wasn't afraid. His survival instinct was taking over. He backed one long stride away from the cell entry and balled his hands into fists at his sides. "Are you out of your mind?" he said. "I'm not going anywhere with these people, not until I talk to my attorney."

The prisoner's reaction was clearly not what Beamer and Ellison expected. For an instant, both men looked unsure, trading glances, their heads cocked to one side as though waiting instructions from somewhere. Finally Sonny Beamer's expression cleared and he said, "Guess we'll have to truss him up."

E.J. still appeared drunk, but seemed to be sobering some. He took off his hat and, holding its brim between his thumb and forefinger, scratched his head with his remaining fingers. "Ain't sure about this, Sonny. Man's entitled to talk to his lawyer's what they always told me. There ain't no lawyer been up here to see this fella, an' far as I know he ain't got one. An' ain't nobody goin' to get trussed up in *my* jail 'less I'm the one doin' the trussin'." He replaced his hat on his head and squared it, then faced Bud. "Don't get the idea I'm cottonin' to you, city-boy. But I don't allow no firearms up in my jail an' don't allow no prisoners gettin' mistreated." Then, to Sonny Beamer, he said, "I don't s'pose you mind iffen I give ol' Buck a call over to his house."

There was the same blank expression for an instant, the same look that Bud recalled Sonny Beamer having during the short walk to the jail after the arrest. As though Beamer were hearing something that no one else in the room could. Beamer said, "Buck ain't at his house."

E.J. hunched his rounded shoulders together and folded his arms. He still was swaying in place, though not as much as he had a few moments ago. "Well then, I reckon it's goin' to be mornin' 'fore any prisoners get moved outta here."

From just inside the steel door across the corridor, Melody Parker said, "Everbody stand where they are." There was a small pistol in her hand, pointed in the general direction of Beamer and Ellison. Her feet were planted firmly and her chin set in a determined attitude. Bud's hands relaxed and unclenched as Doc Petty came in behind Melody and stood at her side. The top of Melody's head was on a level just below the point of Petty's shoulder.

Now E.J. was *really* confused. He took off his hat and scratched his head again. "You his lawyer, Miss Parker? Doc, we ain't got no lame up here." Across the corridor from Bud's cell, Freddy rolled over on his bunk and raised his head. He blinked dully.

To Bud, Melody said, "You come on out an' get behind me." Then, to E.J., "I know you don't know what's goin' on, but we're takin' him with us. Those two there, E.J., they're not normal. You'd better be watchin' yourself."

Relief flooded over Bud as he took three big strides across the corridor, gently touching Melody's shoulder as he passed. He nodded to Petty, who showed him a wry smile. Bud wasn't sure whether they were going to make it out in one piece or not, but if he ever got Melody alone again he was going kiss her to near the suffocation point. As he turned to face the lawmen across the corridor, something uttered a vicious growl.

The sound caused the hair on Bud's neck to stand on end. It was like the sound he'd heard at the zoo when he'd stepped too near the tiger's cage, a warning growl that ended in a low snarl.

Across the corridor, Sonny Beamer and E.J. stood motionless, but Doug Ellison had changed. His face was a beast-face, a long hideous snout and a gaping beast-mouth with huge pointed teeth. His shirt was in shreds around his massive chest and his hands were hairless paws. Bud opened his mouth to yell, but before he could make a sound the creature growled again and charged.

The snarl of the beast was mixed with Melody Parker's scream. She stood directly in the path of the creature, the creature now traveling, swift as night, on all fours. Bud took a stride, ready to throw himself in front of Melody. As he did, the pistol in Melody's hand made a noise like that of a mallet striking a block of wood.

A small round hole appeared in the creature's snout, beside the cheekbone. The beast hesitated, stumbled, clutched at its own throat. It growled again, a snarl of pain and shock, staggered, pitched over on its side on the floor. Clawing at its windpipe, it thrashed its legs. Its body stiffened, then went instantly limp. Its head rolled to one side, its eyes staring directly at Bud. A trickle of blood ran down its snout and curled into one of its nostrils. Its final breath came in a long sigh, then there was silence.

On Bud's left, Petty said softly, "Jesus Christ."

Melody began to cry hysterically, her shoulders heaving. The gun hung loosely at her side.

Things had happened too fast for Bud to feel any shock; that would come later. For now all he could see was Melody, all he could hear was her sobs. He stepped forward and put his arm around her, and she buried her head in his chest.

Dr. Jack Petty moved quickly. He stepped around Bud, grabbed the pistol from Melody's hand and leveled it at Sonny Beamer's chest. E.J. stood beside Sonny with his mouth agape, all of the dullness gone from his eyes. Over inside the cell, the prisoner Freddy uttered a yelp, rolled onto his belly, and hid his face.

Petty said, ''Sonny, if that's still what they call you, don't move unless I tell you. Youall can die, can't you?''

Beamer tensed, started to come forward, then relaxed and stood still. E.J. backed away from Sonny like a man trapped with a wild bull.

Bud's gaze dropped to the fallen beast on the floor. It was a beast no longer; where the creature had lain, Doug Ellison now reclined, his dead eyes staring at nothing. The now-familiar rotten-egg stench filled Bud's nostrils. He put a hand on Melody's cheek and turned her face away from the sight.

Jack Petty held the gun at arm's length and approached Sonny Beamer. Beamer's eyes moved in his head as he watched Petty, but otherwise Beamer was still as a stone. Petty placed the barrel of the gun against Sonny's cheek. ''Bud,'' Petty said, his gaze on Beamer. ''You take her through that door and down the stairs. I'll be followin' with this one.''

Bud didn't understand, and his eyes widened. Petty said, ''Go on now. I'll explain later, but we got to take him with us. Stand back, E.J., we're leavin'.''

E.J. didn't need any more encouragement. He retreated into Bud's empty cell and sat down hard on the bunk. Bud turned Melody around and steered her past the open steel door. He was on a landing over some stairs; the steps descended into unseen blackness. He looked back over his shoulder, still cradling Melody's head against his chest. She was whimpering softly.

Jack Petty and Sonny Beamer were just on the other side of the doorway. Petty still held the gun against

Beamer's cheek. Petty said, "It's three flights down and through a door into the street. My car's straight in front of the door. You'll have to feel your way along the banister, I'm goin' to be too busy with this one to be givin' any directions."

WHEN they reached the side of Doc Petty's Fleetwood with Bud still holding on to Melody and cradling her head against his chest, she insisted that she could drive. Bud backed away from her and, after studying the little tear-streaks on her face and the determined tilt of her chin, decided that he'd better chance it. She did seem to be getting ahold of herself, and the fact of the matter was that Bud didn't have the slightest idea where they were going. He held the door for her while the Caddy's warning buzzer sounded (the rasping noise made Bud jump slightly, then he leaned over and saw Petty's keys dangling from the ignition lock) and she slid behind the wheel. She smiled bravely at him, touched a switch on the door panel, and her seat hummed forward. Bud closed the door with a solid thunk, then went around and got in the passenger seat. Padded leather gave comfortably beneath his buttocks and the backs of his thighs.

Jack Petty came out of the darkened courthouse exit with Sonny Beamer in tow, Beamer moving like a wooden man, stiffly erect, while Petty followed a half step to Beamer's rear with the pistol against the deputy's cheek. Petty allowed Beamer to slide across the backseat, then climbed in beside him and placed the barrel of the pistol firmly on Beamer's temple. His gaze steadily on his captive, Petty reached out behind him and slammed the door. His nose and cheekbones, highlighted in the glow from the Fleetwood's interior light, disappeared instantly in sudden darkness. There was an odor of plush leather and, as Melody started the engine, the air conditioner whispered and a faint cold breeze flowed from the vents.

Jack Petty said, "I'm goin' to tell you one time, Sonny. We're goin' for a drive. Now I'd suggest you don't do any talkin' on this trip, 'cause you might accidentally tell a lie. An' I'm tellin' you, if I see your nose growin' so much as a fraction of an inch I'm goin' to blow your head off." He chuckled at his own joke, then said, "I think we can go on now, girl. Don't have a wreck if this pistol goes off, it'll just mean ol' Sonny was doin' a little changin' on us."

2

IT was pretty much of a cinch, Bud thought, that Sonny Beamer wasn't going to tell anybody anything. Beamer sat inside the converted circus cage in the clinic conference room, his legs drawn up Indian style, his forearms resting on his shins. His muscled bare shoulders were hunched forward and his uniform shirt was in torn strips hanging loosely at his waist. His trousers were also in shreds from his big thighs to his ankles. The second Doc Petty had prodded him inside the cage with Melody's pistol and then closed and padlocked the door, Sonny had transformed himself instantly and had raged and torn and bitten against the bars. One bar was now slightly buckled in the center, and as Bud remembered that the bar was made of reinforced steel a shudder ran through him.

Seated on the edge of the conference table, Winthrop Reed said, "Christ, what a specimen. You don't know how far and wide I've been searching for you, my friend." He wore cloth unironed slacks and gray suede loafers; one foot dangled from his ankle and rocked slightly back and forth in rhythm with his speech. From within the cage, Sonny Beamer favored Reed with a glare that would melt ice, then returned his vacant gaze to his lap.

Melody, still in Jamaica shorts and her *I'm a Virgin* T-shirt, sat near the table in an armchair. She glanced at Beamer inside the cage and tightly hugged her arms about her waist. Bud reached over from his own chair and squeezed her arm. She smiled briefly at him, then lowered her eyes.

Reed got up, put his hands in his pockets, bent from the waist for a better look at the captive. In addition to his slacks he wore a Harvard T-shirt. His thinning hair was uncombed and a few strands waved about his head like bug tendrils. "Somewhere in you there's the answer," Reed said. "I've just got to find it."

"Long-range answer," Dr. Jack Petty said, coming into the room from the back of the building. "I got a short-term answer right here." In one arm Petty cradled a Remington 12-gauge pump-action shotgun with a long shiny barrel; his other hand was wrapped around the butts of two pistols. One pistol Bud recognized, a standard military .45. The other was an old hogleg of a revolver, a Wild West–looking gun that was likely an antique. Petty laid the pistols on the table, then climbed up beside them to sit and cradle the shotgun across his lap. "We need a little more firepower than the popgun o' Melody's."

"There's not going to be a shoot-out, is there?" Bud said. "That's a bit much, with everything else."

"Not a chance, if I'm guessing right," Petty said. "They're not coming for us while we're armed, not 'til they've got enough on their side so they can waste a person or two. I brought these arms in, mainly, so ol' Sonny there would see 'em." He bent closer to the cage and spoke directly to Beamer. "An' you're seein' 'em, aintcha Sonny-boy? Right now you're tellin' 'em all about it. That's good, now they won't chance comin' over here to save you right now, an' we got us a little breathin' room 'til we can check out ol' Macko's place tomorrow." Beamer continued to stare into space, and Bud had the eerie feeling that Sonny's brain waves, right at that instant, were shooting off toward the outskirts of Tombley's Walk.

Melody looked at Bud then said softly, "I'm goin' out there. Youall carry the guns, 'cause if I see Macko I might just haul off an' shoot him. Ever time I think of what he did to me and of that little girl livin' out there with that bastard I turn to Jell-O."

"I guess it's us three," Petty said. "Dr. Reed there, with this shotgun for company, will be baby-sittin' ol' Sonny here." Petty grabbed a chair, pulled it over in front of the cage and sat so that he and Beamer were face-to-face. Petty said, slowly and carefully, "Now, you tell your people, or whatever they are, that we're packin' a lot of firepower. Buck Ainson's got guns, sure we know that, an' so does just about every man in Tombley's Walk. But you'll wait won't you, Sonny. If you can get enough bodies under control, then all you'll have to do is surround us so we can't go anywhere and starve us out. Well, you just send *this* little thought off to your bossman. This is where we live, Tombley's Walk, and no bunch of freaks is going to run us off. So why don't you and Justin Barker and the pack of nasty little germs you're carryin' go someplace else?"

There was a moment of silence while the man inside the cage stared at the man in the chair, only feet away, thicknesses of reinforced steel bar separating the two. The tension in the air literally hummed. Bud got us, intending to go over and place a reassuring hand on Petty's shoulder, when some unseen force assaulted his mind.

Inside the cage, Sonny Beamer had transformed. He was the raging beast, and the beast sprang forward to clutch the bars with taloned paws and gnash at the metal with teeth like gears. The bent bar strained and creaked, and for an instant Bud was sure that it was going to give way. He grabbed Melody's arm, hauled her to her feet and held her protectively close.

The attack was a sensation such as Bud never felt before, as if a squid had affixed itself to the top of his head and stabbed its tentacles into his brain. There was a bolt of agony and more, a swirling crazy quilt of color and a feeling of . . . *hate*. It *was* hate, someone or some *thing* not in the room, but still sending out . . .

Bud reeled backward a step. Jack Petty suddenly clutched his head in both hands and groaned. Melody gasped, and then sobbed. Winthrop Reed stood up from his seat on the corner of the table, shut his eyes tightly and touched the fingers of both hands to his temples.

The invading force was going as suddenly as it had come. Bud staggered forward, as though a pressure that had been pushing him back was released and his resistance was met with instant nothing. He felt light-headed as if on pure oxygen.

Then the beast was Sonny Beamer once again, sitting back on his haunches and folding his arms, glaring hate at his captors through the bars of the cage.

Jack Petty was on his feet, gingerly rubbing his head just above his ear. "Jesus," he said, and then again, "Jesus." He turned to face Winthrop Reed. "Well," Petty said, "there's your subject, Mr. Back-East College Professor. Now. How you goin' to study the bastard?"

3

THE following morning when Petty, Bud, and Melody left the clinic, there was something almost comical in the way that Winthrop Reed stood guard over Sonny Beamer. He was seated at attention on the edge of the conference table with the butt of the shotgun on the table between his legs and the barrel pointed upward at the ceiling, and looked for all the world like a scholarly Minuteman. As his three companions said their good-byes, Reed favored them with the forced smile of a man about to hang.

As Bud held the door open while Melody slid across the seat to the center, and Petty climbed into the driver's seat of the Cadillac, Petty said, "Hope there idn' any trouble, old Reed might shoot himself. Might outrun the bullet even if he did, though."

They had spent the night on hospital beds, Reed and Petty sharing one double room while Melody and Bud slept in the other. Rachel Matthews had gone home. She hadn't wanted to, but Petty had told her that there must be someone left to go for help should anything happen to those at the clinic. Melody had told Bud in private that Petty's speech was a put-on; the fact was, according to Melody, that Jack Petty was the type, if he couldn't sleep with a woman, he'd just as soon not have her around.

They'd stood watch in four-hour shifts, and once when Bud had come to awaken Melody for her turn she'd slipped her arms around his neck and kissed him, warm lips moving against his and her tongue darting into his mouth.

"It'll have to do for now," she'd said, "but don't think you'll get off this easy once I get you alone."

Bathing had been a problem—not for the men, only for Melody. All four men had showered at the clinic and put back on the clothes they'd been wearing, but when it had come Melody's turn she'd put her foot down. "No way," she'd said. "Like it or not, we're stopping by my house."

Bud and Petty had exchanged glances, then Bud had said, "It's chancy. They know where you live and might be waiting for us."

She'd put her hands on her hips and squared her shoulders. "Don't care. Don't care if they cook me for supper, these goddam clothes are sticking to me and if I'm goin' to die I'm goin' to go freshened up."

Petty and Bud had exchanged more looks, then simultaneously shrugged their shoulders and given in. But now, climbing into Petty's Cadillac for the short trip to near the center of Tombley's Walk, Bud had second thoughts. "What about me?" he said. "I'm still a fugitive and you two helped me escape from jail. If the wrong person happens to see us in town it will all be over."

Jack Petty paused, his fingers grasping the ignition key in the lock, his foot on the accelerator, and looked thoughtfully at Bud, then at Melody. Finally he shook his head and started the engine. "We're in no more danger in the middle of town than we are right here," he said. "They know exactly where we are, know what we're thinking. Maybe not all, but most of it. We got to gamble that as long as we're armed and there's less of them than there are normal people, well, they're not goin' to do anything as long as we're out in the open. Gives a man thought, though. Long as we're at Melody's we better damn sure keep our fingers on the trigger."

They drove into town at a leisurely pace, the Caddy's speedometer needle well within the speed limit—"I'm not givin' 'em any excuse to stop us," Petty said—until they came abreast of Edna's Diner, across the street from the spot where Sonny Beamer had taken Bud into custody. There Petty stopped for a moment and watched a group of people who were standing near the curb. The people—

a man and woman in their forties or fifties with the woman holding a female toddler in her arms, a big muscular teenage boy, and two younger children—stood docilely in a cluster and returned Petty's gaze. The man was dressed in overalls and work clothes, the woman in a plain cotton dress. The teenage boy had sinewy arms and a thick football lineman's neck. Finally Petty eased the Cadillac onward. The people turned their heads as they followed the car with their collective gazes.

"Uh, oh," Petty said, slowing to turn right and drive to Melody's house, "their numbers are growin'."

Bud had his arm across the seatback and was looking out the back window. As the car rounded the corner the group of people disappeared from view behind the Edna's Cafe. "Who are they?" Bud said.

"Them's the Wascombs," Petty said. "Pretty good folk, they're farmers. Or they were. That boy's home this summer after flunkin' out of college, and his mama had him by the clinic last week for some shots. Flu or somethin', I don't remember. That kid's nearly doubled in size, you see the neck on him? An' old man Wascomb looks twenty years younger than he did two days ago. My eyes aren't that good, but you see the scar on the old man's neck?"

Melody hugged herself and scooted down in the seat. "I didn' need to see all that. Just the way they were lookin' at us was enough for me."

Petty doubled his hand into a fist and lightly pounded the steering wheel. "Christ. We got no way of knowin' who's one of 'em an' who idn't. I don't think we got much time left to do anything about what's goin' on. At least that's the way it looks to me."

THOUGH Melody's house seemed deserted, Bud left Petty downstairs with her while he checked the upstairs out. He couldn't say that he was in *love* with Melody, the image of Beth was still too fresh on Bud's mind for him to make that commitment, but he wasn't about to let harm come to her if he could help it. Over her feisty protests he climbed the stairs, her small pistol in his hand, and entered her bedroom. Her dresser and bed were undisturbed; the spread was still slightly rumpled where Bud himself had sat the day before, watching her dress after he'd chased Macko Breden away. As he entered her bathroom he caught movement on his right, whirled, and came within a hair of shooting his own image in the mirror. He looked dumbly at himself for a moment, noting the gauntness around his eyes and the troubled set to his mouth, then went back downstairs.

While Melody showered and changed, Bud watched the front of the house through the living room drapes. Petty stayed in the kitchen for a time, peering through the window over the sink, then came into the living room and sat on the sofa. Bud turned his head, holding the drapes parted, and watched Petty. "I'd forgotten food," Petty said. "Suddenly I'm about to starve."

"I could see a bite myself," Bud said.

"Well, I'll do some rummagin' around," Petty said, getting up and retreating toward the kitchen. "She used to keep a leftover casserole or two around. Girl's one helluva cook."

Petty got halfway through the dining room, then froze in his tracks and turned slowly around. Bud hadn't moved, one edge of the right-hand drape held between his thumb and forefinger, his face turned in Petty's direction. The two locked gazes.

Finally, Petty shrugged and grinned weakly. "Been a long time ago," he said. "Not much in Tombley's . . . well, not much around here for a young girl to do."

Bud did his best to hide his irritation, but let some of it show through anyway as he strode past the doctor into the kitchen. "*You* watch the window," Bud said. "If there's anything to eat in here, *I'll* be the one to find it."

When Melody, her face shiny clean, fresh makeup applied, wearing junior-size jeans and a red-and-white checkerboard shirt with the tail flowing around her hips, came into the kitchen, the two men were sharing a roast beef sandwich, each with a neatly severed half resting on a small plate in front of him. Bud had taken only a couple of small bites; Petty was chewing, his mouth crammed full, washing the food down with red cranapple juice.

"Well, I'm ready," Melody said cheerfully. "At least the Maker will find me clean, if I happen to meet him today."

As the Fleetwood turned off the asphalt and began to move slowly up the dirt road leading to Macko Breden's place, an eerie nervousness came over Bud. He sat with his weight against the passenger door, looking out the window at sparse Johnson grass, small scattered bleached rocks, cracked dry black dirt, three lonely pine trees in the distance, the run-down frame house that grew steadily larger over the Cadillac's nose, forest treetops visible over the house's sagging roof. There was a tickling in his innards as though a hundred butterflies' wings were beating in there, and the feeling had a strange familiarity. It was the same sensation he'd had on the night—only days ago? It seemed like months—when he'd gone into the woods behind Jasper's and stumbled across Billy Ed Whitley's arm. Bud hugged Melody gently around the shoulders, more to steady his own nerves than to calm hers. She showed him a tiny smile and scooted over to sit closer to him.

"I been here once," Jack Petty was saying. "You have to go in through the back, old Macko had the front door boarded up some time ago. 'Bout a year ago, the welfare folks had me come out here to check Mae over, said they had information she'd taken a pretty good beatin'."

"All those complaints and nobody's ever done a damn thing about 'em," Melody said.

"Wadn't any way to," Petty said. "Damnedest thing I ever saw. Mac wouldn't let me lay a hand on her. Not the little girl, either, I saw what looked to be some pretty good bruises on the child's arms and asked about 'em. Mae told me that all of 'em were just peachy an' to leave 'em the hell alone. Old Macko, he was about half drunk walkin' around swiggin' a can o' beer, an' he just kept grinnin' at me. I couldn' *make* the woman let me look at her, so I gave up an' went on back to the clinic. Should have called the law an' had all three of 'em taken into custody I guess."

"And gone through a lot of red tape," Melody said.

"I've been through it. The only time the bureaucrats will do anything is after somebody's dead. Then it's too late, o' course, but it makes good newspaper stories."

Petty steered to the left, off the road and across a blanket of scrubby weeds, and parked at the side of the house. The planks that formed the house's wall were rotting, a stained dingy gray in color, with splotches of chipped paint as reminders that the house had once been painted a pale yellow. The screens on the windows were ripped in places, showing rusty wire sticking out in tangled masses. Jack Petty got out and led the way around to the back. Bud opened the door for Melody, then brought up the rear behind her. He was still wearing the tennis outfit he'd put on the previous morning; the hems of his shorts showed grime in spots, collected on the filthy jailhouse bunk where he'd spent most of the night. His sneakers made little scraping noises on the hard-packed dirt. The air was hot and still, and from the nearby forest came the *chirrup* of feeding locusts.

There was a sagging old outhouse behind the main building and the ragged yard was strewn with cans and empty beer bottles. Petty went up on the back stoop of the house with Melody and Bud close behind. A board creaked under Bud's feet and for an instant he thought the porch was going to give way beneath him. He stumbled slightly and righted himself. Petty stood just outside the back door, scratching his chin.

"It's open," Petty said, then indicated the yawning doorway. Bud leaned forward and looked inside, at a filthy kitchen sink, at bowls and saucers piled high over the surface of gray dishwater, at dried food clinging to the surface of the bowls. The faded and cracked linoleum on the floor had once been a cheerful Little Boy Blue pattern; caked-in grime now covered the little boy's golden horn. "It's open," Petty said again, then raised his voice and said loudly, "Anybody home?" The three stood on the porch and listened to the answering silence for a moment, then went inside. As Bud entered the kitchen a lone drop of water fell from the tip of the faucet onto one of the bowls in the sink with a dull plop.

"Why're we trespassing?" Bud said. "I thought that what we're looking for, if it's here at all, would be out back in the woods."

Petty shook his head, his face grim. "Just 'cause nobody answers dudn't mean nobody's here. Macko might be in here sleepin' it off, an' if the crazy bastard hears us prowlin' around his place he's likely to start shootin' at us. We need to check out the house to make sure. Believe me we do."

Bud shrugged and nodded. After a few seconds of silence, Petty nervously cleared his throat and said, "Well, who's goin' first?" Melody giggled.

Bud glanced at her, then said, "I suppose I'm elected. I'm already a fugitive, what's a little breaking and entering?" He moved on through the kitchen. As he passed the sink the odor of spoiled food assaulted his nostrils. He wrinkled his nose and blocked his nasal passages.

The door from the kitchen opened onto a short hallway, covered in rotting carpet, which led to another open door through which the corner of an iron bed was visible. Bud moved quickly, swallowed the lump on panic building in his throat, took three long strides down the hallway and entered the bedroom. Two feet inside the door he reeled backward and collided with the wall.

At first he thought the girl in the bed was asleep, but then his gaze fell on her open, unseeing eyes. She had been a thin girl, with narrow hips and stringy unkept hair, and the bruises on her bare stomach were turning from purple to black. He breathed a long sigh and relaxed, and as he did his nasal passages opened and the stink of early decay filled his nose. He put his hand over his mouth and gagged silently, then raised his voice and said, "Here, Doc. Back here, there's . . ." As Bud stared at the corpse, heavy footfalls sounded in the hallway and Jack Petty came in.

Petty walked over beside the bed, looked down at the still form, his saddened face showing no surprise. "Christ," he said, then shook his head slowly and repeated, "Christ," Then he said, "No point feelin' for a pulse."

From the doorway, Melody said in a faint little-girl voice, "The poor thing." Bud looked. Melody was leaning on the doorjamb, and her eyes were misting.

"This is one we can't chalk up to the savages," Petty said. "At least, not the savages we been worryin' about. Christ. From the looks o' those bruises I'd say her spleen's likely ruptured. She took one thrashin' too many from him. Christ."

"She was pretty once," Melody said. "She was. God, Mae, what got into you marryin' that man?"

Bud stood away from the wall. "Isn't there supposed to be a child?"

"God," Melody said, then went quickly to a door on the other side of the room and opened it. As she looked inside she said in a monotone, "Empty. Empty cot, empty. I'd heard rumors the son of a bitch made the child sleep in a closet. Good God, he really does." She leaned her forehead against the closet doorjamb.

Bud crossed over to her, averting his eyes from the corpse on the bed, and gently massaged her neck. "You've been doing fine up until now. Don't let this make us all crazy," he said.

She turned. "I'm not. I've been scared to death, but not even close to losing my mind. This . . . *thing* that's been going on out here, that sorry wad doing this to his family, has made me just fuckin' *mad* enough that I'm not afraid of any Frankensteins. And if I lay eyes on Macko Breden again I just might kill him."

"Well, we can't help her," Jack Petty said, backing away from the bed. He reached into the picket of his pleated tan slacks, withdrew Melody's Towner .32 pistol, handed it to Bud, then took his own revolver out of his other pocket and checked the cylinder. He shook his head sadly and said, more to the dead girl on the bed than anyone else. "If I'd done what I should have a year ago, she might be alive." He turned, walked to the doorway, stopped, and turned. "Come on, what we're lookin' for idn't here. Bud was right, we never should have come in this house to begin with."

* * *

As Bud followed Melody's slim figure and the tall, slightly stooped outline of Jack Petty through the forest, he was subdued inside. Other than at funerals he'd never in his life seen a dead body—unless Beth and Jenny's killer had died instantly on the L.A. federal courthouse steps; Bud liked to think that the evil-looking Hispanic had suffered some before expiring—before last night, and now he'd seen two in the past eighteen hours. The shooting of the man-beast up in the jail had brought him a sense of relief, but the sight of the abused and battered girl's body had sent a deep gloom over him. The shadows cast by the trees seemed darker than they out to have, and the occasional ray of sunlight slanting into the woods seemed to him to carry no real brightness. In spite of the stifling heat he was cold inside.

They were approaching a clearing, a large area of sunlight visible through the tree trunks. Petty stopped, one hand upraised, looked at Bud and Melody over his shoulder and placed a silencing finger to his lips. The doctor was wearing a yellow golf shirt damp with perspiration and sticking to his back. His warning given, Petty took two more strides, his feet making swishing noises in the blanket of pine needles, crouched behind a tree trunk, and peered out into the clearing. Melody followed suit, squatting on her haunches beside Petty and craning her neck to look around the other side of the tree. Bud walked up behind her, bent from the waist and rested his palms on his knees, and watched the clearing over the top of Melody's head. On Bud's left, Petty murmured, "Jesus Christ."

About fifty yards of flat ground stretched out away from the tree where they were hiding, fifty yards of bumpy earth covered in wild grass and weeds with an occasional pine cone scattered about. Beyond the flat surface was a series of mounds, like a miniature mountain range. The tallest of the mounds was about fifteen feet in height, the smallest the level of a man's shoulders. Perhaps twenty yards from where Bud stood squinting into the clearing was a big flat tree stump, like a legless solid table. The naked body of a man lay facedown across the surface of the stump, a broad-shouldered muscular man with deeply tanned arms and neck. The shoulders and torso had been fish-belly white, but now, baked by the sun, the exposed flesh had turned the color of cooked lobster. There was a gaping wound in the man's right shoulder and a dried river of blood curving downward onto the small of his back. Bud heard Melody's sharp intake of breath and placed a hand reassuringly on her shoulder. Bud had made up his mind to take a closer look, and had even taken a step around Melody and out into the clearing, when the man on the tree stump groaned loudly and moved. Bud froze in his tracks.

The man got painfully to his feet and stood beside the tree stump, and Bud could now see that the man's wrist was handcuffed to something metal embedded in the stump's wood. Torn remnants of what had been clothing were bunched around the man's calves and ankles. His graying hair was long and unkept. He used his free hand to gingerly touch the wound on his shoulder, then turned around and sat down on the tree stump. He was now looking directly at Bud, and his and Bud's jaws simultaneously dropped in shock.

Bud was looking at the twisted, unshaved features of Macko Breden, and for an instant everything else in view—the clearing, the mounds, the bright sunlight—seemed to disappear. All Bud could see was that evil face, and in his mind he was picturing Macko hunched over Melody's still form in her kitchen. Bud had shoved the Towner pistol into the pocket of his shorts, and he now mechanically wrapped his fingers around the gun's handle. As he did, Macko gave a terrified yelp and ducked around behind the tree stump.

Bud was conscious of Melody and Jack Petty now standing beside him. The pistol was in his hand, held loosely by his hip. Macko's shackled wrist still lay on top of the stump, and the thought entered Bud's mind to go ahead and shoot Macko in the arm. Suddenly Macko's head rose above the level of the stump and he began to babble in terror.

"Oh thank the Lord," Macko said. "Praise God you

good folks have come.'' Spittle was running from the corners of his mouth and down his stubbled chin. ''There's terrible monsters out here, there's beasts in this forest you never seen before. Oh I'm a sick, sick man, an' what the beast done to me. Oh God, what he done to me.'' He covered his face with his free hand and began to sob.

Bud looked down at Melody. She was standing with hand on hips, one hip held higher than the other, and her head was cocked to one side. All of the fear, all of the sadness was gone from her expression, and she was regarding Macko through angrily narrowed eyes.

''Well, tough shit,'' Melody said.

As he listened to Macko Breden tell his story in halting, terrified tones, Bud felt a touch of amusement. He and Petty and Melody stood in a semicircle around the tree stump while Macko sat on the stump and fingered the wound on his shoulder. When Macko said, his eyes wide, ''An' he done it. I swear to God, sir, right there with my own little girl lookin' on he done it to me,'' Bud actually felt like laughing in the man's face. Looking on Macko and remembering what the wretch had done, Bud was unable to feel any sorrow for what had happened to the man, and as Macko finished his story Bud glanced at Melody. It was obvious that she was enjoying the story also. Even Jack Petty's lips were twitching.

''An' he's comin' back,'' Macko said, whining. ''He done told me so, not in words, but that critter can *think* things into a man's mind. You got to get me outta here.''

For a moment there was silence, broken only by the distant whir of locusts and Macko's snuffling sobs. Then Jack Petty stepped forward, folded his arms, and bent his head. ''You won't get any sympathy from this group o' folks, Macko. Not with your wife layin' back there dead from one o' your beatin's.''

Macko choked off a sob and raised his blank gaze. ''Mae?''

Petty balled his free hand into a fist. ''Don't be lookin'

innocent at me, not when I got this gun.'' He gestured with the big revolver, and for an instant Bud thought Petty was going to fire. Then Petty relaxed and said, ''But we can't leave your worthless rump just sittin' out here.''

''*Why* can't we?'' Melody said.

Petty glanced down at her, then returned his gaze to Macko. '' 'Cause we just can't. Come on, Melody, we'll leave Bud standin' guard over this sorry . . . I got a tire hammer an' a flat-end tire tool in my trunk that ought to bust the handcuffs loose. Watch him, Bud. If some kinda monster shows up, well, see if you can shoot ol' Macko before it gets to him again.'' He took Melody's arm and steered her back toward the woods, in the direction of Macko's cabin. At the edge of the forest he paused, turned, and beckoned. Pistol hanging loosely at his side, Bud crossed the twenty feet of clearing, stood by Petty and cocked an ear.

''You understand why I'm doin' this, dontcha?'' Petty said.

''I really don't,'' Bud said. ''Can't leave a man to die, I suppose, not even that worthless lump.''

'' 'S got nothin' to do with it. Not savin' Macko's hide, if it wadn' for some other things I'd shoot the bastard right where he sits. Don't think for a minute I wouldn'. But didn' you notice anything?''

Bud looked to Melody, who shrugged, then looked back at Petty and raised his eyebrows.

Petty went on. ''We're all to het up to think straight, but Macko's been attacked by one o' the whatever-you-call-'em's. The head one, Justin Barker, 'less I'm missin' my guess a long way. You see that laceration? Jesus. But it's not healin'. It's a big ol' festerin' wound, wide open, an' Macko's still the same horse's-ass he was before the thing got ahold of 'im.''

Bud looked back at Macko, still huddled on the stump, then returned Petty's gaze. Bud's lips parted.

''You got it,'' Petty said. ''For some reason Macko's immune to the spores. Like it or not, we got to haul his worthless behind back to the clinic were Winthrop Reed can study him.''

* * *

BUD held the tapered end of the tire iron against the handcuff chain with the chain stretched between Macko's wrist and the eyebolt, across the flat surface of the stump. Jack Petty steadied the upper end of the tire iron, gripped the handle of the steel hammer about a foot from the hammer's head, and swung the hammer in a two-foot upward-then-downward arc. There was a dull metallic *bonk* as Macko winced and looked away. The target link in the chain was dented, but still in one piece. Petty took a fresh grip on the hammer and brought it crashing down a second time. *Bonk.* The chain parted. Macko staggered backward on his haunches, steadied himself with a hand on the ground, then began to rub his wrist where the bracelet was still attached. Squatting naked in the clearing with his unkept hair and stubble of beard, his eyes darting left and right in his head, Macko resembled a scene from *Clan of the Cave Bear.*

Petty picked up a pair of light blue, thickly padded coveralls that lay in a heap on the ground and tossed them at Macko. The garment landed heavily across Macko's arm and thighs. Petty said, "I keep 'em in my trunk for cold weather. You might do a little sweatin' in all this heat, but at least they'll cover your nakedness up. Put 'em on."

Macko scrambled into the coveralls, glancing nervously in Melody's direction as he hopped first on one foot, then the other to jam his own legs into the legs of the pants. He stood, shrugged into the upper portion of the garment, and zipped up the front. Now Macko resembled a polar expedition. As he grimaced and touched the cloth over his wounded shoulder, Petty said, "Don't you be bleedin' all over my huntin' clothes." Then as Macko adjusted the coveralls around his body, the distant sound of a racing engine penetrated the clearing.

Bud started and came to his feet, the Towner pistol held ready, while Petty yanked his own revolver out from underneath his belt and looked around. The engine noise reached a peak, died to an idle, then raced again into a second crescendo. Petty touched Bud's arm and pointed. "It's comin' from up there," Petty said. "Over that hill."

He was pointing toward the top of the tallest of the grass-covered mounds.

Stealthily, moving low to the ground, Petty and Bud climbed the mound, lay side by side on their stomachs, and peered over the top. Jack Petty's breathing was fast and ragged. Bud raised up on his elbows for a better look.

Fifteen feet below where they lay, and across another fifty yards of clearing, a GMC supercab pickup was backing directly toward them. A potbellied, shirtless man, wearing jeans and boots, was standing behind the truck and waving directions that the driver could see in the side-view mirror. Buck Ainson, still in his tan sheriff's uniform, stood off to one side with a shotgun, barrel pointed down, cradled in the crook of his arm.

The bed of the truck was piled high with black, zippered, heavy plastic bags. Each bag was about six feet long, and Bud made a quick mental estimate of thirty or forty of the bags jammed into the back end of the truck. The supercab bumped to a halt and the engine died. As the potbellied man lowered the tailgate, Brother Leroy Abbey got out of the cab and came around to the rear. One at a time, Beamer and Abbey began to hoist the bags out of the truck and drop them heavily on the ground.

"Christ," Petty murmured softly. "Christ, they're *body bags*. Between the law an' the funeral homes there's *not* that many body bags in Tombley County. They had to import 'em an' store 'em somewhere." He lowered his head to rest on his forearm. "It's startin'. Christ, it's startin'. Likely they're hidin' the bodies for now, but once they've added enough to their number they won't be worried about any coverin' up. Then it's likely they'll—"

Bud clutched Petty's arm. Petty lifted his head in surprise, but Bud wasn't looking at the doctor. Bud's gaze was far below on the pickup and the men unloading the bed, and his expression was tight. Petty turned his head and followed Bud's gaze.

Buck Ainson was staring directly at them. The pudgy sheriff hadn't moved from his spot, the shotgun was still cradled in the crook of his arm, but his face was upturned to the top of the mound. Bud steadied his pistol in Ainson's direction and squinted down the barrel. Petty reached out and forced Bud's hand downward.

"No use in it," Petty said. "Save it for later. Don'tcha see? They're not goin' to fool with us right now, 'cause they got no orders to. No mental instruction. Christ, they're like a bunch of battery-operated toys. Best thing for us to do right now is get Macko back to the clinic an' hope that Harvard smart-ass can figure out why he idn't changin' like the others. That an' do a lot of prayin.' I guess I'm out of practice doin' that."

4

DR. Jack Petty held the final suture taut between tiny forceps and gave the thread a tug that was quite a bit harder than necessary. Macko Breden yelped, winced, and twisted his body where he lay facedown on the padded examining table. With a surge of satisfaction, Petty snipped the thread and lay his pointed scissors aside. "Sixty-nine," Petty said. "Not quite a record but damn near it. I took eighty-three stitches in Joe Dabney's leg a few years ago, the time he fell off his tractor and got balled up in the mower blades. Sorry 'bout the lack of anesthetic, Macko, but we can't afford to shoot you up with anything until we've finished our study." He adjusted his knee-length white doctor's coat, which he wore over jeans and a yellow golf shirt, walked over to the small desk against one wall of the examining room and sat down. The reason he'd given Macko for not using anesthesia while stitching the wound was a lie; the fact was that Winthrop Reed had drawn enough of a blood sample prior to the stitching to test Macko for everything known to man. Petty noted Macko's pained expression and smiled inwardly.

Macko sat up gingerly on the table. As he adjusted his hospital gown around his body he said in a barely audible mumble, "Whatcha studyin' me for?"

"Oh . . ." Petty hesitated, tilted back in his chair, and interlocked his fingers behind his head. "Oh, this and that. Your temperature's a hundred and one, 'spect you had a few chills out in the woods last night in spite of the heat. You're going to live, which won't be good news to certain folks. I'm going to tell you a few things that you may or may not listen to."

Macko hunched forward, his big wrists and hands poking out through the armholes in the gown. Now freed from his shackles and with a bowl of hot chicken noodle soup in his belly, Macko's insolent leer had returned and his voice had lost its whiny tone. "What you wantin' to say?" he said.

"You're a sick man, not anything too serious, and that shoulder has taken a pretty rough tearin' up. As long as you're under the weather we're goin' to treat you like any other patient around here. Better than any other patients, as a matter of fact, 'cause you're the only one we got right now. I've shut down the clinic for a few days because of the study we're doin'."

Macko shifted on the table and let his bare feet dangle off the side. He sniffled and wiped his nose with the back of his hand. Petty yanked several Kleenex from a box on the desk and handed them over to Macko.

"You'll get good food and plenty of rest," Petty said, "and as long as you don't give us any trouble you'll get none from us. But that dudn' mean anybody's going to forget what you done. We can't turn you over to our local law enforcement folks for several reasons, but there's a dead young girl out in your cabin and if there's not enough to hang you for that, there's the assault on Miss Parker that Melody's chompin' at the bit to tell somebody about. I'm not tellin' you anything you don't know, but you can look forward to spendin' some jail time when you're up to it. I don't have any idea how much. But in case you got some idea that you can sneak off from this clinic while we're not lookin', you just remember that thing that got ahold of you out in the woods. It's still out there somewhere and likely it's still got a hankerin' for you. And if you *should* duck the monster you'll have me to reckon with, and I'd shoot you without battin' an eye. You need to keep that in mind in case you're thinkin' about runnin' off."

Macko continued to sniffle, holding the Kleenex to his nose and not saying anything.

Petty rose to his feet. "That's all the speech I'm givin'. You got a nice bed down the hall and you know the way to it. You get some rest now, Macko." He left Macko sitting on the examining table and went down the hallway into his own office. Winthrop Reed was seated behind Petty's desk with Melody and Bud in chairs across from him. All three were tight-lipped. Petty went out to the reception area, dragged a third chair back into his office and sat down beside Bud. "Macko's goin' to pull through, dammit. What'd you find?"

Reed took off his glasses and rubbed his eyes. "All of my education's going for naught, I suppose. How can I be so stupid?"

Petty glanced at Bud and Melody, who said nothing, then said to Reed, "That's a good question, assumin' you *are* stupid."

A microscope with a slide underneath the lens sat on the desk along with four more glass slides off to one side. Reed picked up one of the slides and held it gingerly between a thumb and forefinger. "It's something that should have been one of our first experiments. In my own defense I should say that it's never occurred to the government researchers either, at least not to my knowledge. We've all been looking at the forest and forgetting about the trees."

Petty studied the ex-Harvard man, studied the slight droop to Reed's chin, and for the first time felt a little bit sorry for the scientist. He said, "Well, you're not the first one."

"No," Reed said. "And unfortunately for the world, not the last. They'll find a cure for AIDS one of these days and, in spite of the uniform opinion against the idea, they'll find a way to stop cancer too. When they do, some researcher's going to become a big celebrity and the public at large will never know that the cure, this great discovery, is something that any scientist worth his salt should have come up with years ago if he'd only been using his head."

"Trial and error," Petty said. "One helluva lot more error than trial."

"No question," Reed said. He got up from the desk, walked over to the window, thrust his hands into his pockets and looked outside. Visible beyond Reed's slightly rounded shoulders was a lawn of mowed grass, one corner of the parking lot, and the tall pines of the woods to the rear of the clinic. "Back, back when I first began these experiments it was easy to see that the droplets—or spores, depending on whether you want to use Dr. Petty's descriptive term or my own—were disguising themselves. Since antibiotics seemed to make the droplets thrive somewhat, we made a natural assumption. Not a scientific determination, mind you, but an *assumption.* And like most assumptions that aren't based on research, the assumption was eventually accepted as fact. Miss Parker. Bud. I'm sorry, but I've got to ramble somewhat to get my thoughts in order."

Melody laughed, a silvery chuckle, crossed her legs, and folded her hands on her denim-covered thigh. "I have a hundred and thirty-five undergrad hours, Doctor, plus whatever hours it took to muddle through law school. Professors that ramble aren't exclusive to Harvard." Her speech was suddenly clipped and precise, punctuated with only the slightest hint of her native East Texas twang.

"I suppose they're not," Reed said, "it seems to be a common malady." He turned to face the room, his hands still deep in his pockets and thrusting outward against the fabric of his pants. "To be brief, the assumption was that the appetite for antibiotics was the droplet's only motive for disguising itself. Wrong." He shook his head slowly. "Wrong, wrong, Christ Almighty wrong. Your friend in there—Mack?"

"Mack-*o,*" Melody said. "An' he's not anybody's friend that I know of around here."

"I was being facetious, of course. I've taken a generous blood sample from him, plus some rectal smears. He wasn't lying, incidentally. He's really been, well, sexually assaulted."

Bud, Petty, and Melody all exchanged glances. "Good," Melody said.

Reed went on as though he hadn't heard. "The samples were all negative with respect to the droplets. But our friend's got bacterial influenza. Common strain, nothing unusual about it."

"How you know," Petty said, "it's not the spores, goin' into one of their disguises?"

Reed shrugged his shoulders. "Tests, I'm not making any assumptions at this time. I tested with ampicillin, which the droplets would have absorbed. No, this was really a flu bug. The . . . semen in the rectal smears . . ."

He glanced nervously at Melody, who giggled and said, "I'm a grown woman, Doctor."

Then Reed said, "It's my upbringing, I suppose, I've always been a bit embarrassed to discuss delicate matters in a class of female students. I'm sorry. The semen was loaded with droplets, but with a drastic change. The droplets in the semen were shriveling up. Most of them, in fact, had already ceased to be functional. And the bacteria had invaded the semen as well."

"Christ," Petty said. "You mean you've never—"

"Remember what I said." Reed held up a silencing hand. "Assumptions, and I'm not the only researcher that's been guilty of that. Since the droplets seemed to thrive on antibiotics, there was never any reason to suspect they needed the drugs for protection as well."

"Well, you'd damn well better be sure this time." Petty said. "There's too much at stake."

"Oh, I am," Reed said. "As sure as one series of tests can make me. I also did some testing on Deputy Beamer's blood. Miss Parker was kind enough to hold the pistol on him while I drew a sample."

"He never moved a muscle," Melody said. "You know, I was almost hoping he would."

Petty glanced at Melody, noted a firmness to her chin that said that she wasn't kidding. She would have loved to have shot Sonny Beamer. Petty looked back to Winthrop Reed. "And?" he asked.

"Same results," said Reed. "The bacteria dominate the droplets and eliminates them. Any antibiotics that Deputy

Beamer has been taking, and I suspect that's quite a bit, have worked their way out of his system during the time he's been our guest. If we were to inject Deputy Beamer with a good-sized dose of flu serum right now it would likely cure him—of the droplets. I don't have any way of knowing whether or not the deputy himself would die."

Petty rose to his feet. "Christ. It can't be that simple. It just can't be."

"I'm afraid it is," Reed said.

"So all we got to do is shoot 'em up with a little flu bug and this craziness will go away?"

"That's an oversimplification," Reed said. "The subjects might all die."

"Well, they might," Petty said. "But they'd be better off than in the shape they're in."

"I can't disagree with that," Reed said. "And keep in mind, Doctor, that we're just talking about *one test*. To be certain, we'd have to experiment thousands of times, under all conditions and with all manner of variables."

"We don't have time for that," Petty said.

Reed lowered his head. "I know. If our—my—research hadn't been so faulty up to now we *might've* had time. But we don't. We're going to have to chance that we're right."

Bud had been sitting quietly, has gaze shifting back and forth from doctor to professor. He cleared his throat. "Not to butt in between men of science," Bud said, "but it appears there's a pretty good-sized problem even if you *are* right. These people, at least from what I've seen, these people aren't going to just make an appointment and come out here to the clinic for a vaccination. We're talking about some pretty savage . . . well, you understand what I'm getting at."

"Sure do," Petty said, his gaze on Reed.

Reed sat back down behind Petty's desk, absently opened a drawer, lifted his brows in surprise, and brought out a crumpled half-pack of Pall Mall cigarettes. "I didn't know you smoked, Dr. Petty."

"Those belong to a patient," Petty said. "A guy that dropped 'em on my desk and said he'd never smoke another one."

Reed chuckled. "The selfsame vow I made. God, they smell wonderful." He put the cigarettes away and made a steeple with his fingertips. "You're making a good point, Bud. But it's not as difficult as it may seem. Remember, these subjects act only on specific mental orders, from their deity. In the case of my laboratory animals the orders all come from the creature I've come to know as the big kahuna. But when he sleeps, the rest are all docile. Hell, I can pick them up in my hands. If the big kahuna were eliminated . . ."

"It'd be like takin' candy from a baby," Petty said. "So all we got to do is go up there to that house on the hill and shoot ol' Justin Barker. 'Course, I don't think Justin's gonna just stand around and let us take dead aim."

Reed scratched his chin. "I think you're wrong."

Petty sank back down into his chair. "You mean you've got something that'll make ol' Justin stand around while we shoot him?"

"Not about that," Reed said. "I think it's the wrong assumption to make that Mr. Barker, though he's the one that seems on the surface to be directing them, that Mr. Barker is in fact the deity."

Reed paused, looked around the room, seemed to draw some satisfaction from the fact that he now had everyone's undivided attention. He cleared his throat and went on.

"I've got the benefit of my experience with the laboratory animals. Their deity is the creature I call the big kahuna. I tried one series of tests, in a steel-reinforced environment, of course, where I imprisoned the big kahuna and all of his subjects in the same area. I was taking the chance that he'd kill some of them, but there wasn't really any danger of that. Once the subjects come under his influence they're not in any physical danger from him. He's the biggest and strongest, of course, but when they were all in there with him he refused to lift a finger. Or in this instance, a claw." He smiled at his own little joke, saw that the others were still grim-faced, then went smoothly on like Johnny Carson when one of his one-liners happens to fail. "All of the food, all of the waste disposal—they're quite fastidious, incidentally, and when there's no opening in the cage for disposal the big kahuna has the subject eat their own waste, *and* his—all of the things that required any physical exertion, well, he simply refused to perform. Sat back on his haunches and let the subjects do the work. Almost as though the mental effort required to keep them under control was all he was willing to put forth. Which, in fact, I suspect is exactly the case."

"That's not the way Justin operates," Petty said. "He's right out there with the troops, on the front line. Was him in person that did the job on Macko. Had to be."

"My point exactly," Reed said. "I'm not at all sure that the subjects know, or even care for that matter, exactly from whence their mental orders come. If they do think about it, they probably assume Mr. Barker is directing them, but I think they're wrong. No, there's another entity somewhere that's controlling Barker as well as the others. Probably physically located nearby, possibly at Barker's house. My understanding is that it's quite a big place and that Mr. Barker lives alone."

"Except for his wife," Petty said. "Only nobody's seen her in months. There's been a lot of chitchat around Tombley's Walk about where she is. Some think ol' Justin might have done her in, but I don't think so. Doris Barker is probably the one thing in this world that Justin's afraid of, particularly that she might catch him in some of his screwin' around."

"I might can shed some light on that," Melody said. She scooted her chair slightly forward as all heads in the room turned to face in her direction. "Last night," she said. "Last night while we were sittin' around here waiting for dark to go in after Bud, I had a long talk with Rachel Matthews. Or she had one with me, I didn' have a chance to say much. Mostly she wanted to talk about her chances of getting Jack to marry her.'' Melody shot an accusing glance in Petty's direction, and Tombley's Walk's only practicing physician reddened slightly under the wilting gaze of Tombley's Walk's only practicing lady lawyer. ''Of course,'' Melody said, ''I didn' offer any opinion on that, I didn' want to hurt the girl's feelin's. But she did get off on the subject of Mae Breden's affair with Justin, and she told me some things that she didn' bring up when she told all of us about it. Like that Justin, whenever he was doin' a lot of running around, would just send his wife off on a trip. To Europe or someplace.''

Petty grabbed the ball, glad for the chance to talk about something other than his intentions where Rachel Matthews was concerned. ''Done that for years,'' Petty said. ''One thing about Justin, he's never minded spendin' his money.''

Melody laughed a dry laugh. ''So long as it's gettin' spent on something that *Justin* wants. If it's for somebody else, well, that's a different story.''

Petty said, ''Funny thing about that boy. Lived here all his life, but he's one that nobody knows very well. And his wife . . . I don't know anybody that knows much about her either.''

''Sure you do, Jack,'' Melody said. ''Justin did his best to *keep* people from knowin' anything, but tryin' to do that in Tombley's Walk is just askin' for everybody to start nosin' around. All the women in town can quote Doris Barker's history, word for word. Helen Bragan down at the library dug up the dirt on her years ago.''

''I never heard anything about her,'' Petty said.

Melody showed Petty a sour face, then said, ''You're not supposed to, 'cause you're a man. Doris Baker was—*is*—a snow bunny that Justin met up in Colorado one winter at Aspen. Got to admit she has some looks about her, and they say she's hell on wheels when it comes to skiin' or ice-skating or any of that stuff. Tennis whiz too, though they say the best way to beat her is to get her worryin' about whether her fanny looks cute in the particular tennis outfit she happens to be wearin' that day.''

''Christ.'' Petty was suddenly on his feet, a tenseness between his shoulder blades as he looked to Reed, then back at Melody. ''Christ,'' he said, ''I've talked to her about that. All these women come in for checkups and talk a mile a minute and I don't pay much attention to what she's sayin.' That girl grew up on skis and ice skates.'' He expelled a long sigh. ''She's from Vermont, Dr. Reed. Looks like your research idn' the only thing that hasn't been on the ball.''

Reed's eyebrows lifted. ''From Ridley.''

''Montpelier,'' Melody said. ''Or else Helen Bragan didn' do her homework right.''

''No difference,'' Reed said. ''Fifteen, twenty miles. And up to Ridley is where one goes from Montpelier to go skiing.''

''And she was up there last winter,'' Melody said. ''Rachel Matthews knew that, she told me Justin's wife goes to Vermont *every* winter. That's where she was a lot of the time Justin was playing around with Mae Breden.''

There was silence for a moment. Then Winthrop Reed said, chuckling, ''I suppose we have our answer. Amazing how simple the whole thing is when everyone puts their heads together.''

EVERYONE agreed that it was going to be necessary to go to Justin Barker's house and, so to speak, beard the lion in its den. But when Petty and Reed began to plan the route they were going to take, Bud said suddenly, ''No. No, *I'll* go. Alone.''

There was heavy silence in the room as three heads turned as one to stare at him. Finally Jack Petty said, ''Why you? Melody and me grew up in this town and Brother Winthrop Reed here's got a load of time tied up in this thing. Not to mention the money Mr. Reed feels he's goin' to make if we're right. But you got no stake in Tombley's Walk.''

Bud locked his gaze with Melody's, watched her eyes

mist and her expression soften as she heard him say, "That's not quite true."

She lowered her lashes.

Petty looked back and forth from Melody to Bud. "Don't guess it is," he said. "But that dudn't change the fact that one man alone's got no business goin' up there."

"I don't agree," Bud said, rising to his feet, pacing back and forth in the small office, feeling his old management instincts return for the first time since he'd been on the run. "And let's don't get personalities into this, I'm not trying to be a martyr. But I'm the most expendable, mainly because, as you say, I'm not really a part of this town. Dr. Reed's the one with all the knowledge about this phenomena that's happening, and it doesn't take a genius to see that the town doctor's going to be needed. Plus, there's the physical factor. Let's face it, I'm quite a bit younger than either of you, and I suspect that the confrontation we're talking about is going to require some physical exertion."

Melody had wriggled into one corner of her chair, curled one leg underneath, and was sitting on her ankle. One arm was thrown over the chair back and there was an amused expression on her face. "Well spoke, Captain," she said.

Bud relaxed, expelled air from his lungs, felt sort of foolish over his own take-charge attitude as Petty said from the other side of the office, from near the window, "He *is* makin' sense, though."

Winthrop Reed had taken off his glasses and was sucking thoughtfully on an earpiece that was dangling from one corner of his mouth. "I think," he said, then paused. "One man, armed, will probably do as well as all of us. I doubt there's going to be any element of surprise. I believe they know what we're planning to do."

Bud cocked his head to one side. "How can you be sure of that?"

"Well, really I can't," Reed said. "But I think it's better to *assume* that they know than it is to go off half-cocked. Regardless of whether they're sure an attack is coming or not, they will have the deity's lair well guarded. You can expect a great deal of opposition on your way in."

"I'll have a gun," Bud said.

"Two," Petty said. "You take both pistols. We can make do here with that old blunderbuss shotgun of mine."

Bud placed his hands on his hips, a lithe young man in tennis clothes, looking much more on his was to the country club than to his real destination. "When?" Bud said.

"The sooner the better," Reed said. "The longer they're allowed to go their own way, the bigger stronghold they're going to build."

"Tonight," Petty said. "You up to it?"

Bud thought about it, then said, "Tonight's better. If we wait until tomorrow and I have to sleep on it, I might just back out."

"Wouldn' blame you," Petty said, crossing the room to the hallway door, pausing, turning to face Bud. "Take me a few minutes to get ready. Come on down to the examining room in, say, a quarter of an hour."

Bud's forehead creased. "Why?"

"Why we got to give you a dose of the flu," Petty said. "Damnedest thing I ever saw, makin' a man sick so he can get his job done."

"Does it hurt?" she said.

"Yes. Well, not that much, it's sore is all." Bud gingerly touched his left triceps where the doctor had plunged the needle in. He winced. His sinuses were beginning to clog and the area between his shoulder blades was beginning to throb and ache. His throat was dry and scratchy. He changed the subject. "The air in Texas doesn't even cool at sunset."

They were seated side by side on a big fallen log just inside the perimeter of the forest. Across fifty yards of mowed clearing, the clinic's lengthening shadow was touching the edge of the road. The upper half of the sun's flame-orange ball was visible on the western horizon. A squirrel, bushy tail rippling, sniffed here and there among pine needles about twenty feet from the log. It spotted Melody's shoe, rose in alarm on its haunches to look her in the eye, then darted to safety up the trunk of a nearby pine.

"They're a lot more skitterish out in the woods," she said. "In town, the ones right around the square, they'll steal the food right off your plate if you happen to be picnicking." She leaned closer to him and placed her forehead against the point of his shoulder. "I wish you weren't goin'."

He flattened his palms on the log next to his hips, stretched out his legs and crossed his ankles. "It's the only way that makes sense." The scent of her perfume drifted into his nostrils, growing fainter as sinus drainage steadily worked it way into his nasal passages.

"I know that. It's just that I got a right to be a little selfish."

"I'll be okay. You just make sure these doctors have plenty of medicine ready to get rid of this flu they've injected me with." He shifted slightly, letting the warmth from the sun beat on his aching arm. "When this . . . when this is over I'm going to have a choice to make."

She laughed softly. "I hope I'm it."

He reached over and smoothed her hair. "That's not the choice I'm talking about. Assuming we're successful in what we're trying to do tonight—and I refuse to consider that we won't be—assuming we're successful, a lot of people will be coming here. Investigators and so forth. It's foolish to think that someone's not going to find out who I am. So I can either move on or I can surrender and take my punishment, whatever it's going to be. I don't know what I'll do, to tell you the truth."

She breathed a sigh. "I've thought about that."

"I know you have," he said.

"I've thought about it and thought about it, tried to put it out of my mind, and then thought about it some more. I've make a lot of 'This Land Is Our Land' statements to Jack Petty, but to tell you the truth I don't like the idea of being in Tombley's Walk if you're not going to be around here. Law practice or no.'' She gave him a glance that was defensive and almost fearful. ''I'm laying myself open, and I'm not used to doin' that. Please don't step on me.''

''Melody,'' he said, then cleared his throat and rubbed his cheek. ''Boy, that shot takes effect in a hurry. Melody, I'm not sure just what to say. I don't know if I could make a commitment, not this soon after . . .''

''I know,'' she said. ''No, hell, I *don't* know. I haven't been through what you have. Goddammit, why can't we have more time to know?''

''We could run a test. Maybe I've been exposed to these scientists too much, but we could experiment on our own.''

She raised her face to his and lifted her eyebrows. He leaned closer and kissed her lightly on the lips. Just the act of shifting his weight caused the heaviness in his sinuses to throb, and he was suddenly light-headed.

He said, ''What I'm saying is, and I know it's a lot to ask, but what I'm saying is that you could go with me when I leave town. On a trial basis, with both of us knowing up front that that's what it is. If it doesn't work out, well, you could always come back to Tombley's Walk.''

''That's pretty easy to say. But no, I couldn't. I might go to Dallas or someplace and take up law, either with the government or one of the big firms, but once I left town here I don't think I could come back. There'd be too much gossip goin' around.''

''You'd know more about that than I would,'' he said, his gaze now on his own toes. ''I don't suppose you could chance blowing you whole career.''

''Now, I didn' say I *wouldn't.* Just that it wouldn't be that easy.''

He studied her for a moment, studied the short, springy black hair and the small dimples at the corners of her mouth. Beth would certainly like this girl. Yes, she would, he thought. He turned his attention to the west and narrowed his eyes to the glow of the setting sun. ''Let's think on it,'' he said. ''After tonight, let's both do some serious thinking.''

5

BUD had a problem with the interior climate control in Dr. Jack Petty's Cadillac. If he spun the thermostat dial below seventy-five degrees and the air-conditioning began to blow, Bud began to shiver with a feverish chill. But with the dial moved above seventy-five and warm air blowing from the vents, he would sweat profusely. Finally, just as he left the pavement and began to ascend the winding gravel road leading to Justin Barker's house, he moved the lever to the OFF position and used the buttons on the door to lower all four windows. That seemed to help some. Hot night air blew against his cheeks and gravel popped and flew from beneath the Fleetwood's big radial tires. The headlights illuminated the gravel road before him, scrubby underbrush, and an occasional twisted fallen branch from a tree. Above him, visible in glimpses as he rounded curves in the road, the Barker home was a bulky shape against the star-filled sky. The moon shone down like a ghostly yellow, filtered spotlight.

He'd known that the flu serum injection was going to make him ill, but he hadn't expected this. His throat was dry and sore, his head like an aching lump resting on his shoulders, and it was all he could do to keep from pulling over to the side of the road and curling up on the front seat in the fetal position. Both pistols, Melody's Towner .32 and Jack Petty's big revolver, lay next to his hip on the seat cushion. He touched their handles, closed his eyes and shook his head, put both hands on the steering wheel, and grimly steered the Caddy onward and upward. He flipped on the radio and forced himself to concentrate on David Allan Coe's twangy guitar and tenor country voice.

He was nearing the crest of the hill, was just about to pass under the wooden arch that marked the entry to Barker's property, when the hate-thoughts invaded his mind. He'd expected it—Winthrop Reed had given him quite a lecture on what to look out for—but he hadn't been ready for the intensity. The one time he'd felt the alien thoughts before, back in the clinic's conference room, the sensation had been as though a squid had attached itself to his head and jabbed its tentacles into his brain. The experience had been frightening enough in itself, but was nothing compared to what he felt now. What now poured into his mind was like a series of blows from a thousand hammers.

The swirling colors were brighter than they had been before, brilliant reds and violets and purples that seemed to blend into one spinning mass and then blast into glowing fragments, only to swirl and revolve and become the shifting colors once more. And the thoughts themselves were not like mental images at all, rather it was as though some being were sitting beside him and shrieking an eardrum-rending series of words. *Hate you, you fucker. Going to KILL you, you fucker, you're going to die up here. Going to tear your heart out and eat it, you bastard, oh, hate you, HATE you, HATE YOUR FUCKING GUTS, YOU—*

"Concentrate," Winthrop Reed had told him, "on anything. It doesn't matter what, anything to keep its thoughts under control. It will destroy you with its mind if you let it."

Bud forced a mental image on himself, an image of . . .

It was as clear as on the day it had happened. The ascending stone steps of the federal courthouse, the two marshals turning slowly as he approached, the (*HATE YOU, YOU FUCKER, HATE, HATE*) bewildered looks on their faces. The scarred face of the slender Hispanic, the know look, the resignation as (*GOING TO BEAT YOU TO DEATH WHILE I FUCK YOU, YOU FILTHY*) Bud raised the pistol and pulled the trigger. The dream-pistol jumped in his hand as it fired, then the image disappeared as the hate-thoughts suddenly receded from his mind. He jammed on the brakes, brought the Caddy to a screeching halt just inches before it plowed nose-on into the flower bed at the end of Justin Barker's driveway. He drew in a tortured breath and peered wide-eyed through the windshield.

Jack Petty had laboriously drawn him a map of Justin Barker's grounds, and the map now lay folded on the seat beside the pistols. Bud had the map committed to memory, and its image jumped into his consciousness as he surveyed the two-story brick Colonial, the wide front porch, the stockade fence along the eastern side that surrounded the backyard and pool. There was a steel-barred gate across the wide front door just as Petty has said there would be; the only access to the house would be over the fence, around the pool, and across a brick patio to the back entryway. Bud groped in the glove compartment for the black plastic flashlight, thumbed the switch, blinked wide-eyed in the flashlight's beam. He jammed the Towner .32 into the waistband of his shorts and, holding the flashlight in his left hand and Petty's revolver in his right, climbed out of the Cadillac and closed the door with a thrust of his hip. As he did, Sheriff Buck Ainson stepped from behind one of the white pillars on the front porch, extended his gun and fired.

It was the glint of a stray moonbeam from the barrel of the sheriff's pistol that saved Bud's life, just the barest flash in the corner of his eye that caused him to jump sideways. The firecracker report of the gun came just an eyelash-flick before something thudded into the car door, rocking the Cadillac on its springs. Bud was on his knees in the gravel driveway, tiny rocks biting into his flesh and the fever raging in his sinuses as he steadied the big revolver at arm's length and squeezed the trigger. The gun blasted and jumped in his hand, its recoil slamming him backward into the side of the Fleetwood.

Buck Ainson flew across the porch as though a horse had kicked him, went down in deep shadow. The sheriff's moan of pain drifted into Bud's ears; Bud started to go onto the porch, hesitated, let the pistol hang at his side. There was no time. Still holding the flashlight, he sprinted in a half-crouch toward the stockade fence. As he did, the hate-thoughts filled his mind once more.

You've killed him, you dirty fucker, I'm going to get you for that, going to tear your guts out you filthy—

BACK at the clinic, at the very instant when Bud jammed on the Fleetwood's brakes just prior to plowing into Justin Barker's flower bed, and the hate-thoughts released their hold on Bud's mind, the thought-tentacles gently slithered their way into the dull consciousness that was Macko Breden's. Awakened as though by a gentle nudge, Macko sat up on the edge of his hospital bed and blinked his eyes in the darkness. The bedsheets were a faint whiteness in contrast to the sooty outlines of the nearby chairs. Macko's fever had subsided during the night; the stitches in his wounded shoulder stung when he moved, the sting accompanied by a maddening itch.

A single thought came to Macko, clear as radio music: *I told you you wouldn't die. But I'm coming for you.*

A sliver of ice jammed into Macko's stomach as he recoiled in fear and said loudly, "Where the fuck you at?" He raised a protective arm and shielded his face.

Nothing moved in the room; Macko heard only the sound of his own ragged breathing. Must be the goddam fever, he thought. He lowered his arm and sat up straight.

I SAID I'M COMING FOR YOU, YOU FUCKER.

Macko scrambled into a fetal position, covered his face and sobbed. "Not no more o' that. Please. Don't do nothin' more to a poor man's tryin' to get by."

Softer, more gently: *Do you want to be free?*

"Free?" Macko weakly raised his head. "Oh free, yes, sir, free, ain't nothin' I wouldn' do."

The thoughts directing his movements, the tentacles probing here and there into his brain, Macko got up and padded barefoot to the door. He opened it silently and peered out into the hallway. Twenty feet away from where he stood, light streamed from Doc Petty's office and made an oblong pattern on the darkened hallway tiles. Muted voices came from within the office, Doc Petty's ragged tenor and—Macko cocked his head to one side—the Parker bitch. It was her, all right, the same cunt who'd tempted Macko and got him into this mess in the first place. Macko hesitated, listened to the thoughts in his head, nodded, crept down the hallway past Doc Petty's partly open door. He caught a glimpse of Melody, clad in jeans and a red bandanna-patterned shirt, as she leaned intently over Petty's desk. Petty was out of Macko's line of vision. Limping slightly, the tentacles still probing the recesses of his mind, Macko proceeded silently down the hallway to the conference room. Its door was likewise ajar, and Macko flattened against the wall in the corridor and peeked inside.

Sonny Beamer, nude, sat inside a big steel cage. His ankles were crossed Indian style and he was staring blankly ahead. There was a man in a chair by the side of the cage with his back to the door, and Macko grimaced and touched his shoulder as he recognized the man as the one who'd drawn the blood from Macko's arm. Another smart fucker, probably rich as well. The thought-tentacles issued their instructions. Macko Breden, a grin of hate on his face, stepped into the room, picked up a metal chair from against the wall, and brought it crashing down across the back of Winthrop Reed's head and shoulders.

BUD ran low to the ground, his sinuses throbbing with every jarring step, the hate-thoughts shrieking curses in his brain. He forced himself to concentrate on the treated redwood planks as, gasping for breath, he approached the fence. The flu serum injected in his veins was taking its toll, and for just an instant Bud thought he was going to pass out. Then his head cleared; he jammed the flashlight into his waistband alongside the Towner .32, put one foot on top of the fence, and vaulted over into the backyard. As he stood panting and looked around, the hate-thoughts suddenly vanished.

The subsurface lights in the pool sent blue-green moving shadows along the surface of the fence. Water lapped rapidly against the concrete bank. Bud stood for a moment and caught his breath, yanking the flashlight from under his waistband, his gaze traveling across the surface of the pool, lingering on the chaise longue, the table with the umbrella unfurled over its top, past the furniture and across twenty feet of clipped lawn to the patio. The patio was brick, the back door a vague outline in the dark shadow cast by the house. Slowly, carefully, his head revolving warily from side to side, Bud skirted the pool, went across the lawn. He coughed phlegm into his mouth and spat it into the yard, then stepped up onto the patio.

The brick was hard under the surface of his Reebok sneakers, the mortared spaces between the bricks making little ridges across his shoe soles. The porch was half in flickering aqua light from the pool, half in the shadow of the overhanging roof. He moved slowly, crossing over the lighted section of the patio and into the shadow. There was quick movement on his left in the darkness, a small sigh, an intake of breath. His heart leaping into his gullet, Bud whirled and leveled the revolver in the direction of the sound.

The flashlight's beam illuminated a child. Nothing more, a little girl with long stringy hair, ragged denim cutoffs exposing grimy knees, and faded blue Kermit the Frog tennis shoes with the toes cut out. Her eyes round as saucers, she held out her tiny arms. "Help me, mister?" she said.

Bud let the pistol dangle at his side and stepped forward, keeping the flash trained on the small form in front of him. Though the girl's hands, arms, and legs were dirty and unkept, her face was scrubbed clean and her cheeks seemed to glow in the artificial light. Her arms still held out to him, she smiled.

"What are you doing here?" he asked, and stepped forward as a guttural snarl sounded just inches behind him and something struck him between the shoulder blades with the force of a battering ram. He pitched forward on the bricks, conscious of the child stepping quickly out of his way, landing on the point of his shoulder and feeling pain shoot upwards into his neck. The revolved clattered across the porch toward the door; the flashlight flew in the opposite direction. Then giant teeth ripped into the flesh of his upper arm and he was aware of nothing but the tearing of muscle and tendon and the terrible snarling in his ears.

As Winthrop Reed toppled out of his chair and hit the floor in a lifeless heap, the shotgun he'd been holding across his lap rolled over and thumped softly against the wall. Macko barely noticed the gun. He set the chair aside, watched intently for the scientist to move. Reed lay still. "Key," Macko said. "Key." As he dropped to one knee and dug into Reed's pants pockets, Macko spoke in a near-gibberish to Sonny Beamer, who continued to sit stone-faced inside the cage.

"Come to hepya," Macko said. "Come to letcha out, I'm yore friend. You tell 'em, Sonny, Deputy Beamer, sir, you tell 'em Macko's no enemy. See? See here, I got it." He triumphantly held the brass key up, then stepped forward and jammed it into the lock on the cage door. Tumblers clicked and the bolt slid. Macko swung the barred door open wide, stepped backward, and regarded Sonny Beamer as though Beamer were Macko's personal god.

Sonny Beamer's eyebrows lowered in a scowl. He raised his eyes to look at Macko. His lips curled away from his teeth. There was a sound as though fabric were stretching as Beamer's face elongated itself into an ugly snout. His shoulders hunched closer together; his arms bent upward like mantis forelegs as his hands and fingers twisted and molded into hairless paws. His fingernails narrowed and thrust outward, curving into wicked talons. A low growl escaped from deep within Sonny's throat. He sprang forward, grabbed Macko by both shoulders and sank his teeth into the side of Macko's neck. Macko screamed once. His head twisted with a sound like snapping twigs. His face pointed sideways parallel to his shoulders, blood streaming from the gash on his neck, Macko went instantly limp.

The thing that had been Sonny Beamer cast Macko Breden's body aside like a rag doll and stood for a moment over Winthrop Reed's still form. Then, grunting and growling softly, the beast walked upright out of the conference room and down the corridor toward Jack Petty's office.

As Bud went down on the patio, the hate-thoughts assaulted his brain. *I told you, you fucker. HATE YOU, HATE, HATE, HATE YOUR GUTS.* As the hate-thoughts battered his mind, the beast ground its teeth into his upper arm and dug its claws into his ribs.

Bud acted on pure instinct. His revolver and flashlight gone, the beast raging at him with superhuman strength, he groped at his waistband, found the handle of the Towner .32, yanked the pistol free. His eyes shut tightly against the pain in his arm and side, Bud pointed the barrel of the Towner behind him, at a spot just above his bleeding arm, and pulled the trigger. The gun went off with a loud popping sound. The bullet slammed into something, some part of the monster's face; the monster grunted in surprise. Its teeth loosened their hold, its talons released their hold and receded from Bud's ribs. The beast relaxed, its dead weight pinning him underneath it. A final rush of warm breath blew against Bud's cheek, then the monster lay still on top of him.

Bud scrambled from underneath the body, groped across the brick toward the house until he found the flashlight. He rose painfully to his feet, flipped the light on, directed the beam toward the fallen body of the monster. The flash illuminated the nude, quiet form of Dory Barnes. Her red hair lay softly against the nape of her neck, her cheek rested on her forearm. Her eyes were wide and unseeing. There was a small round hole in her face, just beside her nostril. Blood was oozing from the back of her head and wetting her hair.

A soft whimper came from the shadows to Bud's left, and he pointed the flashlight in that direction. The child was huddled against the wall of the house, hugging her knees to her chest and crying. He ignored the pain in his arm and the throbbing in his sinuses and went over to her. He bent and picked her up. She struggled weakly, kicked at him, turned her face away. He held her tightly against his chest with his good arm, let the Towner .32 and the flashlight dangle from his hand. He went over and turned the doorknob, winced as he pushed against the door with his injured shoulder. The door moved inward. Still carrying the struggling child, Bud entered the house.

He was in a lighted, carpeted den. A white-brick fireplace was built into one wall with he-and-she oil portraits hanging over the mantel. They were a good-looking couple; the man was trim with just the slightest hint of a belly, wearing a dark green golf shirt and pale green slacks. The woman, a honey blond with dancing hazel eyes, was wearing black lounging pajamas and was curled languidly into one corner of a plush leather sofa. Bud's gaze left the pictures and swept the rest of the room. It was a huge den, perhaps forty feet long, with a dark wood handcarved bar and a Mitsubishi TV set that had a 50-inch rear-projection screen. In the center of the room, facing the TV, was a long leather sofa flanked by matching brown leather recliners. The same man whose portrait hung over the mantel was seated in one of the recliners. He was wearing bathing trunks and a white fishnet shirt with a high collar. He stood, turned to Bud, and smiled.

"That's a nasty-looking shoulder, pardner," the man said in a heavy East Texas drawl. "Better sit a spell an' let's have a look." He stepped forward, his arms hanging loosely at his sides. His mouth continued to smile, but his eyes were dead lumps of coal.

Possibly from loss of blood, possibly from the flu injection, possibly from a combination of both, Bud was getting dizzy. The room seemed to revolve and he staggered back a step, nearly dropping the child. He strengthened his grip around her waist and said to the man, "Don't come any closer." His tongue felt thick and his own words reached his ears as though from far away. He raised his free arm and pointed the Towner pistol unsteadily at the man.

"Now hold," the man said, stopping and raising his hands, palms outward. "Justin Barker's the name, it's my house you're standin' in. No need for that." He continued slowly toward Bud, his eyes sending a message to the child. The child kicked outward, knocking Bud's arm aside and pointing the pistol away from Barker. At that instant,

Barker charged. His face elongated into a snout and he uttered a low warning growl.

With the last ounce of strength left in him, Bud cast the little girl aside and hit the carpet rolling. The impact to his wounded arm sent fire shooting through his limbs. The beast that had been Justin Barker, its clothes now in tatters about its rapidly changing body, overshot its mark and tripped, sprawling headlong, regaining its footing in an instant and turning to charge again.

From where he lay on the carpet, Bud shot the creature through the heart, then raised the pistol and shot it again, this time in the eye. The creature howled, pitched over on its face, transformed at once back into Justin Barker, and died. Barker's mouth was agape; a trickle of saliva ran from one corner of his mouth down his cheek and dripped on the carpet. Where his eye had been was a red oozing tunnel into his brain.

Bud regained his feet, wanting to rest, wanting to sleep away the fever and the pain in his upper arm. As he looked groggily around the room, the child scrambled from the place where he'd dropped her, near the couch, and bolted for the front of the house.

Bud went after her, feeling as though his feet were sloughing through quicksand. He caught her in the foyer, near the big front door, just as she started to climb the stairs. He held her underneath his one good arm as she whimpered and struggled and sank her teeth into his hand. He nearly dropped her, then regained his hold. There was a partially open door in the foyer, leading into a small closet. Inside the closet were galoshes and winter coats on hangers. Bud stepped quickly over, thrust the squirming child into the closet, and slammed the door. He grabbed a dining table chair from against a nearby wall and propped it firmly against the door's handle. As tiny fists banged on wood from within the closet, Bud stepped back and let his ragged breathing subside. The pain in his shoulder had receded to a dull ache. His sinuses were throbbing like bass drums. He peered up the darkened stairway and listened intently.

Somewhere up on the second floor landing, a clock

ticked. The hate-thoughts were still there, but they were somehow weaker. He ignored them, gathered what was left of his strength, and began to climb the stairs.

MELODY was carrying two empty cups out of Jack Petty's office, intending to go for coffee refills, when she saw the beast coming. For an instant she was frozen in the doorway, unable to move. The creature was coming toward her at a half-limp, walking erect, the claws on its feet making little clicking sounds on the hallway tile. Its taloned hands were raised, and its lips were pulled back from its teeth in an insane grin.

Melody dropped both cups to shatter on the floor and jumped backward. She slammed the door, placed her shoulder against it while she slid the dead bolt into place, and ducked to one side. Jack Petty sat behind his desk with his mouth agape.

Petty said, "What the hell are you—?"

Something smashed against the door from outside. The upper half of the door splintered into kindling as a big hairless, taloned paw thrust itself into the room. Jack Petty paled, his features slack, and sank down behind his desk like a man going underwater.

BUD reached the head of the staircase with his head swimming, stopped, and stared at though hypnotized at the illuminated face of the grandfather clock directly in front of him, listened in fascination to the rhythmic *tick-tock* as the pendulum rocked slowly back and forth. The clock chimed the half-hour; the single reverberating note shook Bud into action. He made the turn at the head of the stairs and proceeded down the landing. He was gripping the flashlight in his left hand, the Towner .32 in his right, and he now clicked the flashlight on. Its beam glinted on a sterling silver tea service atop a rolling server. He skirted around the server with the beam directed on the carpet, pausing for a moment to examine three round spots that could have been blood. He touched one of the spots. It was damp. He continued on down the landing and paused outside two closed doors that stood side by side.

Light streamed from underneath the right-hand door. Bud rubbed his forehead with the back of his hand that held the flash, then tucked the flash into his waistband. Whatever he was looking for was inside that lighted room. He could sense its presence, feel its nearness in his aching sinuses. He touched his injured arm and winced. He was ready. All fear and apprehension left him as a strange coldness came over him. He held the pistol ready, reached out and firmly gripped the handle, turned it, opened the door, and entered the room.

There were two king-sized beds shoved together occupying most of the floor, and the thing that lay in the center of the beds was looking at him. It was on its back, and its width was the full width of one of the beds. It was female; its hairy sex gaped at him from between its enormous legs. Its breasts were the size of pillows and sagged to either side of its chest. Its eyes were red-rimmed and bloodshot, its snout the length of a man's forearm. On Bud's right, alongside the bed, were three hospital scaffolds supporting hanging plasma bottles; a tube extending from one of the bottles led to a needle that was inserted into the creature's neck. As it continued to stare at Bud, the hate-thoughts in his brain raised in volume to a scream.

The thing rose to a sitting position, started to come forward, the needle popping from its neck to dangle and swing freely from the end of the tube. Thick blond hair sprouted from the creature's head. It grunted, raised a taloned paw, and prepared to deliver a murderous swipe.

Perfectly calm, his nerves steady, cold hate for the beast blotting out all fear, Bud raised the pistol and shot the creature between the eyes.

As the beast ripped Jack Petty's office door into shreds and, roaring in hate, came across the floor toward Petty's desk, Melody ran across the monster's path and dove headlong over the desk top. Her arm scraped painfully over wood. Then she was down, landing with a thud on Petty's back, scrambling, huddling down against Petty and closing her eyes. Talons scraped on wood as the beast climbed over the desk after her. Its breathing was loud, ragged, and interspersed with guttural snarls. Melody shielded her eyes with her forearms.

The scrambling, clawing noise ceased. There was a heartbeat of silence, then the sound began again. Only the noise was softer, the scratching sounds not so intense. Melody raised her head. The thing was crawling backward, away from her and Petty. It disappeared from sight over the edge of the desk.

Melody locked gazes with Jack Petty. Petty's eyes were round as saucers, his mouth slack. As one, they looked at the spot where the creature had disappeared. Slowly, still holding on to one another, they stood upright.

Sonny Beamer, nude, was backed into one corner of the office and sitting on his haunches. There was a vacant look on his face. He was breathing slowly, his bare chest rising and falling.

Jack Petty said, "Sonny?"

Beamer swiveled his head slowly in the direction of the sound. "Help me?" Beamer said. "Jesus, help me, I done wrong." He buried his face in his folded arms and began to sob.

Bud walked slowly, the acrid stench of rotten eggs in his nostrils, back down the landing, past the grandfather clock with its monotonous swinging pendulum, and, head bowed, descended the stairs. The Towner pistol hung loosely at his side.

He'd watched the monster pitch backward onto the bed, watched its bladder empty in death, watched its talons begin to recede and its snout shrink back into the beginnings of a human face. He hadn't wanted to see any more, was loathe to look on the human form of the thing he'd killed. He wanted to remember it as it had been when he'd pulled the trigger. So he'd simply turned and walked away.

He felt drained, spent. He wanted only to be gone from this place, wanted only to make his feverish way back to the clinic and take some medicine. Take anything to remove the throbbing in his sinuses and the pounding in his skull. And to touch Melody.

At the foot of the staircase he paused. Tiny, pitiful sobs

were coming from within the closet where he'd imprisoned the child. He removed the chair lodged against the handle, and opened the door. The little girl was huddled in a corner of the closet, underneath a hanging overcoat. He stuck the pistol in his waistband next to the flashlight and picked her up. She cried louder, hugged him tightly, and buried her face in his neck. He carried her through the front door, averting his gaze from Sheriff Buck Ainson's still form, went down the gravel drive to Jack Petty's Cadillac. He put the child in the front seat and, as she continued to sob, climbed in behind the wheel. He placed the pistol on the seat beside him and started the engine. He touched his wounded shoulder, winced, put the lever in reverse and backed slowly down the drive. He wanted the gun beside him. If his wounded shoulder suddenly began to heal, Bud was going to shoot himself.

6

DR. Jack Petty carefully measured his words as he spoke to the three government men seated in his office. "Hundred and twenty-seven. All in unmarked graves, out yonder at the old dumpin' ground. Took us two and a half days to dig 'em all. We had a mass funeral service. Those of 'em that had folks in town, their families attended. We picked the burial site because, well, that's where nearly all of 'em were anyhow, stored in body bags."

The man from H.E.W., a pudgy, pink-cheeked man in his mid-thirties who was wearing a dove-gray suit, white shirt, and gray tie, glanced at the man from the Environmental Protection Agency, then said to Petty, "And you knew, you knew this was a top-priority, top-secret matter where we were concerned, and you went ahead and buried them without consulting anyone?"

Jack Petty shrugged and didn't answer.

The man from E.P.A., tall and thin with thick brown hair that was obviously a hairpiece, shifted in his chair and crossed his bony legs. "That's serious, Doctor. Might even have some criminal implications. Of course, that's Edward's bailiwick." He gestured toward the man from the F.B.I., who was sitting behind him against the wall.

Edward, the F.B.I. man up from Dallas, who was wide-shouldered and blocky and wearing a black suit and matching tie, said, "I'm strictly here as an observer, Joe, I've made that clear. I came at your people's request, there've been no charges filed. As to whether there's been a possible violation, I can't comment on that. It'd be up to the U.S. Attorney." He narrowed his eyes under shaggy brows and looked to Petty. "I'll ask you, Doctor," Edward said, "and let's make it clear that no one is under arrest or entitled to any Fifth Amendment protections, but I'll ask you. Did anyone use the phone to set up any arrangements? Possibly mail a check to, well, someone who helped with the burial?"

Petty shifted his gaze from one government man to the other, first looking at the two seated directly across from him and finally at the F.B.I. man seated alone behind them. All from different federal agencies, but Petty wondered briefly if there was some central training place where government people went to study how to be a pain in the ass. Petty chuckled. "Hell, I've seen enough TV to know not to answer that one. We've got sixty-five—no, check that, sixty-four. One died. Heart attack, didn' have anything to do with the spores or what's happened here. But one died. We've got sixty-four people under treatment. Dr. Winthrop Reed's out makin' the round right now while we're talkin', matter of fact. We've got everybody accounted for, both the folks who were in church and the ones out at the honky-tonk. The others are ones that had the sickness before. Some of the ones that were doin' the meanness, we're treatin' 'em all alike."

The man from H.E.W. turned to the man from E.P.A. and said, "One thing's good, Joe. A private burial service, well, there's nothing official about that. I'm assuming no death certificates were issued, no graves officially designated. I don't see any difference between that and, say, a grave where a murderer has buried his victim."

"No," Joe said, brightening, playing with his striped tie with one hand while the other hand fondled his hairpiece, "I don't either. Which means that we don't need any sort of court orders in order to exhume the bodies. For further study purposes."

Petty had expected that. He stood, turned his back to the government men, thrust his hands into his pockets and looked out his window across the fifty-yard mowed clearing toward the piney woods. The mid-July sun was directly overhead. A fat, tan, shorthaired dog with its tongue hanging docilely out was sitting at the edge of the forest in the shade of a tree. "You fellas aren't goin' to be digging up any corpses," Petty said. "Not around here."

There was a pregnant pause during which Petty envisioned the federal men exchanging glances behind his back. The E.P.A. Joe said, animosity creeping into his tone, "I don't think you fully understand what's going on here, Doctor. We *fellas* will dig up what ever we wish to dig up, and that includes the very foundations of the town hall if necessary. We're talking serious government business here."

Petty turned back to face the room, sat in his chair, simultaneously swiveled to his right and tilted back, folded his arms, and gazed at the ceiling. "Us country folk are smart enough to figure out we can't stop you, if that's what you're a mind to do. But if you *do* decide to take our little town apart, there's nothin' you can do to keep it out of the newspapers, what you're up to."

The pink-cheeked H.E.W. man favored Petty with a tight-lipped smile. "If anyone can *talk* to the press. To put it bluntly, Doctor."

"Way ahead of you," Petty said. "We thought about that. A female resident of Tombley's Walk had done flown the coop. She's got documents, figures, slides, everything she needs to let somebody know just what's goin' on up here. And boys, that includes the shit you folks pulled in that little town up in Vermont. Ain't nobody doin' to Tombley's Walk what's been done to Ridley. This town's been here, and all the folks that live here like it that way. Once this is cleared up, we intend to go on livin' life just the way we have been."

"What—? Just a minute." Joe dug into his breast pocket and produced a small writing pad and a black, government-issue, retractable ballpoint pen. He clicked the silver button on the end of the pen and prepared to write. "What's this lady's name? And we'll need to talk to her, to verify—"

"Bullshit you'll talk to her," Petty said. "Her name's easy, you can find that out by findin' out who's missin' around here and who idn' buried out at the dump. Melody

Parker. First forty-eight hours she dudn' hear from me, and she starts talkin' to folks. Oh, and she's a lawyer, in case you might think she dudn' know what she can do and what she can't."

Edward of the F.B.I. stood behind the two other men. "Doctor, and I'm still just observing this, but there are provisions for holding you. For security reasons if nothing else."

"Holdin' me?" Petty laughed. "You can do that. Or I can tell you where Melody is an' then you'll surround the town with your National Guards and hold all of us like we were prisoners. I'd rather take my chances not tellin' you where she is."

"I think," the H.E.W. man said, rising to his feet, "that we'd better terminate this meeting for now. I don't have the authority to discuss this matter, with the new wrinkle in the situation." He nodded to Joe, who rose also. "We'll get back to you, Doctor."

"Get back to me all you want," Petty said. "But what I'm sayin' idn' going to change. You leave us alone up here, we'll keep our mouths shut about what you folks been up to."

"Have it you way," Joe said, then took one long stride in the direction of the exit. He stopped and turned. "By the way, Doctor, what *is* this treatment you're giving these victims?"

"I'm in private practice," Petty said, "and Winthrop Reed just got his ass fired by you lovely folks. I've checked on it, there idn' any requirement for either of us to tell you anything. I'm these people's doctor, prescribing a cure the best I know how, and Dr. Reed's assistin' me. Sometime before long we might let you in on it."

The H.E.W. man's pale eyebrows lifted. "For a price?"

Petty grinned. "It's occurred to us."

The H.E.W. man and the E.P.A. man exchanged glances, then shrugged in unison. "Good day, Doctor," Joe said. The three government men started to leave.

"Just a minute," Petty said, standing. "I got something to talk over with the F.B.I. In private."

The three men halted. Edward said, "I'm just an observer."

"Well, observe this," Petty said. " 'S got nothin' to do with what we've been talkin' about here. Nothin' to do with these folks." He nodded toward H.E.W. and E.P.A.

"I'll listen," Edward said. "But if this *does* concern these other agencies I'm going to bring them back in. You gentlemen wait outside." The last part was a command, and it occurred to Petty that Edward was giving a lot of orders for an observer. H.E.W. and E.P.A. left. Edward sat down across from Petty.

Petty produced a brown wallet from his top drawer and tossed it over in front of the F.B.I. man. Petty said, "We're holdin' a corpse up here that we didn't bury. The I.D. in there says he's one of yours."

Edward fumbled with the wallet, held a small clear plastic I.D. case between his thumb and forefinger and read it. "Devine. Yes. What happened to him?"

"I got no way of knowin'," Petty said. "But I think he was breakin' in someplace where he didn' know what he was getting into. Anyhow, your folks should give Rod Lindenhall a holler. He's our county attorney, and he'll release the body. We've already embalmed what's left of him, we didn' want him to stink up the premises too much."

Edward looked slightly amused. "Appreciate your concern. We'll take care of it." He got up and turned once more to leave.

"There's somethin' else," Petty said.

Edward sat back down, crossed his beefy legs, and looked expectant.

"There's another body we *did* bury up there you fellas are goin' to have an interest in. Fella name of Rigler."

"Oh?"

Petty reached into his desk once again, this time coming up with a universal fingerprint card form bearing the seal of the Tombley County Sheriff's Department. "Buck Ainson, rest his soul, had this fella in custody for a while. Seems the record shows him to be a federal fugitive. From out of California, I think."

"I wouldn't know anything about a California warrant," Edward said.

"I didn't expect you would," Petty said, walking around his desk and handing over the fingerprint card. "But I do imagine you can get the record straight as to what's happened to him."

"That I can do," Edward said, pocketing the card. "Anything else?"

"Not now. If there is I'll call you."

Edward nodded, the two men shook hands, and Edward left.

Jack Petty went over to sit behind his desk, fingering the skinned place on the back of his right hand. He'd injured the hand while he and Bud had been digging the final grave, after all the mourners had gone, the grave that was going to contain the empty pine box.

"Wouldn' you know I'd hurt myself," Petty had said, "diggin' a hole for a man that ain't even goin' to use it."

7

MARIANNE Throckmorton, the economy class hostess on Delta Flight 347 from Dallas-Ft. Worth to Fort Lauderdale, thought that she could spot a really happy couple when she saw one. She ought to be able to, she'd split up enough happy couples in her life.

The computer software executive with whom she'd spend the previous night at Loew's Anatole Hotel on Stemmons Freeway in Dallas (Marianne considered herself to be pretty slick; she didn't do any fooling around at the airport lodgings where the crews normally spent the night, for fear that word would get back to the Delta pilot who was Marianne's steady bang in her home base of Atlanta) was a good example. She'd met him on a Denver-to-DFW when he'd been traveling with his wife and three children, and all it had taken was a gentle bump with her hip while he'd been on his way to the lavatory to get his hormones cooking on the front burner. Last night he'd told her that he'd stashed away a good portion of his savings in a secret account, had transferred the title to his Buick Park Avenue into his company name, and was ready at last to break the news to his spouse of fourteen years. He'd told Marianne all of this with his head nestled between her thighs, and she hoped that her grip on his ears as she'd guided his face into her crotch had been firm enough so that he didn't have any inkling of what was about to come. Her mission accomplished, just as it had been with the Denver insurance man, the Miami banker, and the New Orleans boiled shrimp magnate, Marianne was preparing to dump on the guy. It was the way that she got her kicks, and she figured that it was nobody's business but her own.

She had, in fact, already picked out the computer man's replacement. The replacement was seated on the aisle, three spaces in front of the two-row smoking section. He was a good-looking bastard, full-cut mop of center-parted hair and soulful brown eyes with just a hint of sadness around the edges. If little Marianne was going to play, she might as well play with a real hunk. Made it all more fun.

The guy was injured, which to Marianne was sort of a turn-on. He was wearing a knit Polo shirt and his left arm was in a white cotton sling. The outline of bandages on his upper arm were visible through the snug-fitting fabric of his shirt. He had broad shoulders and good pecs, a flat belly, and the kind of pelvis, Marianne thought, just made for an extra-strong thrust or two.

The fact that her target's female companion was a pretty cute trick in her own right just made it more of a challenge. The companion was an itty-bitty thing with short dark hair and a slim figure snugged into white cotton slacks and a navy knit pullover. Marianne had noticed the two of them the moment they'd boarded the plane, and had even done a little eavesdropping in preparation for making her move. The little brunette spoke in a soft Texas twang; the hunk in an accentless tenor that had to be rooted in Southern California. California beach man making it with Cowgirl Corinne. That was okay with Marianne; she figured she could show the beach man a thing or two in the saddle herself. As she backed down the aisle with the other economy class hostess pushing the food cart and Marianne asking the passengers whether they preferred the chicken or the beef stroganoff, she shot occasional glances over her shoulder in the direction of the target. He was pretending to ignore her. Marianne, a leggy dishwater blond with a tiny waist, who wore a size thirty-six with a D cup, figured that he couldn't ignore her for long.

Marianne paused in the aisle beside the couple. The floor vibrated beneath her low-heeled shoes and the 707's engine noise was a distant muted hum. The vents blew air with a soft hiss. The California hunk was reading a magazine, *Texas Highways,* holding it in one hand while the hand extending from his sling dangled loosely in his lap. Cowgirl Corinne had one leg drawn up underneath her on the seat and was sitting on her ankle.

Marianne bent slightly forward, giving the hunk a sure-to-catch-the-eye profile body shot, and showed her capped white teeth in her most dazzling, knock-'em-dead smile. "The chicken, sir?" She batted her eyes. "Or the . . . beef?"

The hunk didn't even look up from his magazine. "Nothing for me, just a Coke." Then, to Cowgirl Corinne, "You going to eat, Melody?"

Cowgirl Corinne favored the hunk with a gee-but-I-love-you look that practically turned Marianne's stomach. "Not if you're not," Cowgirl Corinne said. Then, to Marianne, "I'm havin' Diet Pepsi, if you've got it."

Quickly, almost haughtily, Marianne dumped ice into two clear plastic cups and served the drinks. Then she backed down the aisle, smelling the tobacco from the smoking section and doing a slow burn. The *bastard.* Well, he wasn't going to ignore her for long.

MARIANNE got her chance about ten minutes after she'd finished serving. She was in the rear galley, putting trays, covered food dishes, and used plastic cups away, when the California hunk got up from his seat and joined the line of passengers waiting to get into the two lavatories. He stood in line behind a chubby man in a gray suit, and in front of a woman in her fifties with blued white hair and a pair of tinted glasses dangling from a silver chain around her neck. The hunk was reaching underneath his shirt and scratching his wounded upper arm. There was a puzzled, worried look on his face. Visible beyond him through the row of windows, the bank of clouds underneath the belly of the 707 resembled billowing whipped cream.

As the hunk came abreast of the galley, Marianne said to him, "We're actually ahead of schedule, can you believe it? A whole lot better than my regular route." Perfect entry. Now the hunk was going to ask her, Oh? What's your regular route? Followed by, Where are you based? And, shortly thereafter, she'd have him panting.

He turned his brown eyes on her, continuing his worried look, still clawing at his upper arm underneath his shirt. God, she thought, he's not even *seeing* me. The hunk said, vacantly, "Oh? Oh, that's nice." And continued down the aisle toward the john.

Now Marianne was *really* pissed. She clanged two trays into the galley slots with an extra-hard shove, then found herself locking gazes with the woman with the blued hair who was behind the California hunk in line. The woman was sucking on one earpiece of her tinted glasses.

Marianne favored the woman with a frozen I'm-a-Delta-hostess smile and went back to putting away the dishes.

MARIANNE stared daggers at the California hunk's broad back as he returned to his seat. Never know what you missed, buster, she thought. As Marianne started to go back to the jump seat and resume her reading of *Rock Star*, by Jackie Collins, a hand tugged at her arm. Marianne turned. It was the blue-haired woman, the one who'd gone into the lavatory when the hunk had come out.

"Miss," the woman said in a harsh whisper. "Miss, I chose Delta for this flight, though I usually go on American. I'll not make *that* mistake again." Her lips were set in a pencil-thin line.

Oh, *God*, Marianne thought. Oh, God, God, God, another Fucking Frequent Flyer. She summoned up her Delta training and forced herself to look concerned. "Oh, I'm sorry," she said. "What seems to be the trouble?"

The woman leaned closer, still whispering. "Well, miss, you need to get somebody to work in the lavatory with some Lysol disienfectant. It *stinks* back there. It smells like rotten eggs or something."

CROSLAND BROWN lives in Forth Worth, Texas, with a wife who disappears for months at a time and six children who have very large teeth. He also has a dog and a cat who play well together, and who soak his carpets with strange-smelling urine.